FROM ROSWELL TO AREA 51

EARTH'S SECRET ALLIANCE

TONY B. RICHARD &
LYDIA PAYGE

This is a work of historical fiction. All names, characters, businesses, places, events, locales, and incidents are either the products of the author's imagination or used in a fictitious manner.

Disclaimer: This story is set in 1947 where, unfortunately, period-typical racism, sexism, and ableism occurred. The intensity has been deliberately reduced for the audience of this novel, but keep in mind it will still be mentioned. In no way do the racist comments made by some of the characters reflect the real-life views of the author.

Second Edition, February 2026

Cover Design | germancreative
Editor | Carolin Petersen
Interior Design | Carolin Petersen
Typeset in Arno Pro & Kallisto
This book makes use of AI for editing purposes.

ISBN 978-1-0698372-5-7 (paperback)
ISBN 978-1-7781914-9-7 (ebook)

visit *www.tonybrichard.com*

EARTH'S SECRET ALLIANCE

This book is dedicated to all those who have been bullied.
Those who have been subject to blackmail, racism, peer pressure,
religious, or sexual assault/orientation persecution.
We hope you find your "General Jones".

TABLE OF CONTENTS

FOREWORD

Before you read this book, there is one truth you must accept: life exists on other planets. Aliens are real. How do I know this? Well, I've met them. It all started in 1947, when I, at twelve years old, stumbled upon the truth. I was there when the UFO crashed in New Mexico. I was there in the aftermath as they covered it up.

The US government wanted to keep it secret, but I've always been an investigative journalist—even then. I knew too much, so they offered me a job. What choice did they have? Hire me, or... well, what could they do to a young girl in a wheelchair? In this role, I was tasked with compiling reports and interviewing the humans and otherworldly visitors alike. Geogram was a great help. The Zalmen transcripts filled in many of the details, and helped the others remember even more.

I've kept it secret all these years, but finally the truth will be revealed to the public. Now, seventy-five years later, the United States government lifted the censorship. All information regarding the event has been made public, but what is the truth?

I'm here to help you sort through the rumors. Some conversations I witnessed firsthand; others I've reconstructed from documents, recordings, and interviews with those who were there. Where I've had to piece things together, I've noted it. The truth is too important for anything less than complete honesty. Here's what really happened all those years ago.

Charlotte "Charlie" Baker

PRINCIPAL CHARACTERS / DRAMATIS PERSONAE

A guide to help readers keep track of the key figures in the Earth–Zalma alliance.

THE MILITARY:

Malcolm Dow, a private
Adam Rabinowitz, a private
Francis "Frank" Jones, a 4-star general
Bryson "Bryce" Lawless, a corporal
Ryan Wilcox, an ambassador
Donna Warren, an assistant
Jack Scornson, a 4-star general
Greg Newman, a 2-star general
Charles "Chuck" Cameron, a specialist
Bruno Abbott, a warrior
Colin McKenzie, a pilot

THE ZALMEN:

Geogram (Jee–OG–rum), an ambassador
Ronderra (Ron–Der–RAH), a leader
Agugua (A–GOO–gwa), a captain
Joanua (Joe–ANN–wa), an engineer
Edugra (Ed–OOO–gra), an expert
Sarara (Sa–RARE–ah), a teacher
Kanara (Kan–AR–ah), an instructor
Takar (Ta–KAR), a boy
Janara (Jan–AR–ah), a girl

THE CIVILIANS:

Charlotte "Charlie" Baker, a reporter
Mary Goss, a genius
Brian Howard, an engineer
Lance Harper, an engineer
Randy Quinn, an engineer

MORE PRONUNCIATIONS:

Zalma (ZALL–mah)
Zalmen (ZALL–men)
Ymit (YEM–it)
Moad (Moe–ADD)
Moadites (Moe–ADD–ytes)

Emotions are red,
Good is blue,
Green me thinks,
Looks good on you

PART 1: MALCOLM AND ADAM'S FIRST CONTACT

CHAPTER ONE

GEOGRAM FIGHTS FOR EARTH

Geogram
THE PLANET ZALMA
February 1947

Charlie's note: [When Geogram first shared the council's translated transcripts with me years later, I could barely believe what I was reading. The fate of two worlds decided in a single meeting, and it all hinged on human compassion. Looking back, I wonder if we deserved it.]

The sky itself was on fire, and Geogram watched with snow-white skin of fear. Though the planetary deflectors held, he knew that it was only a matter of time before his precious planet burned too. The Moadites had increased the frequency and strength of their attacks over the last hundred years.

Geogram's neutral color was light purple, but he and many of the others in the council chambers were now pure white, or in emotional flux between red, green, and blue. None of their prior attempts at peace had worked, and they were surely doomed.

He fidgeted with his silver robes and turned his attention to First Minister Ronderra, who stood at the head of the council. With a wave of his hand, the first minister dismissed the viewing screen and addressed the room. "I once again ask our council for suggestions of peace. Do any wish to speak?"

The minister of research raised his hand. "I nominate Geogram to speak. He has been studying the planet Earth and has come to me with an idea."

Geogram swallowed. He ran through his proposal in his mind once more. After studying human languages, his native tongue felt strange in his mouth. "Earth's nations are fractured, but they have recently succeeded in ending a great conflict through diplomacy."

A great murmur filled the room. It was broken by the minister of resources. "Why have they experienced conflict in the first place?"

"Well, this is their second world conflict, which they call *war*," Geogram explained, using the human term. "Their technology is primitive, but it mirrors the Moadites—meaning they might actually understand our enemy."

"You wish us to ally with aggressive beings?" cried the yellow-skinned minister of medicine.

Geogram rallied his nerve. "I understand your concern, Minister, but this is why I believe they will be invaluable to us. They *were* aggressive with one another, I admit, but the inhabitants of Earth are also capable of great compassion and forgiveness."

"How can you assure us that their peace is reliable?" the minister of resources spoke again. "A second world conflict only proves that they are a changeable species. How would we be able to trust their resolve to help us?"

"My research shows that the inhabitants of Earth—*humans*—do not have a single planetary government. They are composed of multiple nations and have multiple leaders. The closest they have to a planetary-wide governing body is what they call their *United Nations,* in which they aim to work in harmony," Geogram explained.

"How does that help us?" asked the minister of education. Her skin rippled green.

"One such nation, the *Americans,* did not initiate their world conflict, but were instrumental in ending it. I am sure that if we contact the *Americans* first, they will help us end our own conflict without the need of *weapons.*"

The minister of education stared back at him blankly. "What is a *weapon*?"

"I apologize for my slip of language." Geogram looked around to see that the ministers were all waiting for an explanation. "A weapon is a tool used for inflicting harm or injury upon another. That which the Moadites use against us can be considered as such." As if to emphasize his point, a distant assault on their deflectors caused the council chambers to rumble. Everyone in the room ducked and eyed the ceiling.

The minister rippled green again, thinking, and said, "I see, but even if they are capable of bringing peace, why would the people of Earth help us?"

"*Computer, if we should not petition the humans for their help, what is the most likely course to follow?*" Geogram called out.

A voice answered him, ringing throughout the room. "*If you do not petition the humans for their help, there is a ninety-seven percent certainty that the Moadites shall capture Zalma within the next decade. There is a seventy-three percent certainty that Earth will be their next target.*"

Another murmur filled the council chamber, but it was the minister of medicine who spoke up once again. "Be that as it may, we should not consider dealing with a species that inflicts injury upon one another. First Minister Ronderra, please put a stop to this."

Ronderra addressed the council. "I share your concerns, Minister. I too do not wish to broker an alliance with this violent species, but Geogram speaks the truth. These *Americans* were not the aggressors, and yet they have found a way to end their world's conflict. That is what we need."

Geogram inclined his head. "Thank you, First Minister."

"All you know is what they choose to transmit," Geogram heard the minister of education grumble as her green skin took on a more yellowish hue.

"My daughter and I have cross-referenced transmissions from different governments to verify the information," he said, loud enough for her and others to hear.

"So, what are you proposing?" she asked, clearly still not convinced.

Geogram's mind raced, his daughter's translations of Earth's peace talks sparking a daring plan to seek their aid. "I propose we send a ship. I will go to negotiate with them, taking on the role of *ambassador*, a human term for those who represent their people. Since my daughter has also learned their languages well, I believe she will be useful for communication."

The minister of transportation leaned forward. "Are you both planning to go alone?"

"The journey will take many moons, far longer than any of us have traveled among the stars before. No. If my daughter and I are to go, we will require a team to fly and attend to the ship—a captain, an engineer, a scientist, and perhaps others," Geogram replied.

"And what would you do when you arrive there?" asked the minister of habitation. She seemed worried, her skin fluttering back and forth between white and its usual pinkish hue.

Geogram was glad to have an answer for her. "We plan to observe and determine those who are safe to contact. I will then petition them for aid."

The minister of medicine turned up his nose. "What kind of aid do you expect from them?"

"We require a peacemaker, do we not?" Geogram asked. "I shall ask them for one. And, should our negotiations with the Moadites fail, I will ask for their help to defend our planet."

The council's skin flickered in a rainbow of doubt, but Geogram pressed on.

The minister of education spoke, "You will bring their peacemakers here?"

"I will, and, if necessary, those trained to deter conflict." These words brought forth an outcry.

The minister of medicine was the first to rise from his seat. "You plan to bring *aggressors*? *Here*?"

"What if they bring harm to *us*?" exclaimed the minister of resources.

"It is the only way for us to be properly prepared. They will not be a threat to us. We all know that the Land will protect us from a few humans, but there is only so much our guardian can do against the aggressors of Moad," Geogram replied, keeping his voice calm.

"There is no way for you to be certain," the minister of education accused.

"Our nanite technology will not bring harm. If they use it to build their *weapons*, then their *weapons* will not work against us," Geogram assured her.

First Minister Ronderra, who had stayed out of the discussion thus far, gave an approving nod. "And you will ensure this *how*? They have already proven quite capable of destruction with their own *weapons*."

Geogram paused. *How* will *we ensure this?* "They will see the advantage of our technology. In return for their help, we will share with them our fabricators and our teachings. Any *weapon* or tool they create using the fabricators shall contain nanites, and therefore will be unable to cause harm to us. We shall be safe, and we shall resolve this peacefully."

The council members murmured again, but one by one, they nodded in agreement.

"I am certain of our success," Geogram continued with confidence. "The Land has protected our home and people thus far, but our deflectors are failing, and the Moadites' attacks of fire are getting bigger and causing more damage. This is our only hope to stop them."

"My concern now is for the Moadites. Will the humans bring harm to them?" the minister of medicine asked.

Geogram hesitated. "If necessary...," he began quietly, and the room filled with a buzz of dissent, but Geogram spoke over them. "If necessary, they will use their weapons, not to bring harm, but as a deterrent against further harm. We shall not accept harm inflicted upon our aggressors, and I will make this clear to the humans. With the Land's guidance, we shall prevail without injury."

As soon as he was done, voices filled the room louder than ever before.

Ronderra raised his hands, and the voices died down. "Are there any other options?" The room was silent. "Then, we will now vote. Who wishes to move forward with the suggestion that Geogram has put forth?"

Most of the council members begrudgingly raised a hand. Geogram's skin flickered blue and red as his hope and fear twisted together. Zalma's fate was now in his hands.

"The vote is in favor. Is there anything else we wish the council to address?"

No one spoke.

"Very well. Geogram, you may proceed. We send you and your chosen team to Earth to recruit help against our aggressors. May the Land protect and guide you. Meeting adjourned."

[Geogram's mission began out of desperation, but it would end in hope. Sometimes the most important decisions are made not by leaders, but by ordinary people willing to take extraordinary risks.]

CHAPTER TWO

THE CRASH

Captain Agugua

HIGH ABOVE NEW MEXICO

[The following "crash" would change everything—for me, and for the world. The flight recorder captured every terrifying moment. When I finally heard this recording, I understood why the crash site looked the way it did.]

"Status report," the blue-skinned captain said in the Zalma language.

"Approaching the Earth's atmosphere now, Captain," the much younger female engineer said in English. She and the rest of the crew had been practicing their English for about six months.

The captain listened to the translation through his earpiece and nodded, turning his eyes back to the screen. He slid his long blue fingers forward across the floating panel in front of him, then looked over at the engineer. "Keep it steady," he ordered. "I am bringing it down."

The engineer nodded and swiveled her chair to the far side of her desk. Her fingers moved with ease across the touchscreen. A small light glitched on a monitor to the left, unnoticed. "Ready, Captain."

The captain nodded again, and the spacecraft dipped, barely nudging the invisible ozone layer around the vibrant blue and green planet below. Everything was proceeding as planned—until it didn't.

Suddenly, alarms wailed. Red lights flashed. The captain's skin turned bluish-green and his body seized. "Computer, give me virtual controls." He held his palms out flat, and his sleeves extended over his hands like gloves. Bringing his hands up, the captain began maneuvering the ship with precise twitches of his fingers. The turbulence rumbled through him. Glasses appeared over his eyes, and he pulled up the ship's status. Numbers flew across his vision. He gasped, and his skin flashed white like the depths of a dying star.

"The ship is losing power!" the engineer called from her desk. "The engine is down!" She touched the illuminated metal. "Thrusters...deflectors...everything is failing!"

"And the hull?" the captain asked.

"The hull is holding, sir," she replied. "Should we deploy the parachute?"

"Not yet." The captain kept his hands steady. He waited for his moment. The limited thrusters stuttered and choked on their last few breaths of life, sending the ship shaking and trembling, but he held firm. "Not yet...."

The spacecraft blazed as it plummeted. Flames licked up around the sides, and clouds of smoke formed at its tail.

"Now?"

"Not yet!"

Geogram's trembling fingers gripped the edges of his seat. He gulped. "Captain, I think it would be wise to deploy the parachute now."

"The ship is still blazing. The parachute will fail. It will crash."

"It will crash anyway," the engineer pointed out. She shook her head. "Deploying parachute in three, two...."

The captain brought his hands back sharply and spread his fingers. "Now!" he cried.

The parachute deployed with a snap and the ship lurched. Its speed cut in half, the fires died slightly, and it drifted down. They let out sighs of relief.

"Is it safe?" With the gloves and glasses gone, the captain inspected the monitor in front of him. Every readout glowed green. All except one. "What is wrong with this?" he asked, pointing to the screen. There was a shriek as the parachute tore apart. The spacecraft dropped like a stone, and the Earth rushed up to meet it.

CHAPTER THREE

JUST ANOTHER DAY

Private Malcolm Dow
ROSWELL, NEW MEXICO
July 8, 1947

[Malcolm never liked to talk about what happened, but years later, his journals would help fill in the gaps no one else could.]

Private Malcolm Dow had his feet wide apart, trying to stabilize himself as the truck bounced down the road. Seven other soldiers sat around him, talking and trading jokes. In the opposite corner from him, a young private named Adam Rabinowitz mumbled, "Oy vey." Dow noted that he was a little green.

"Is there a problem, little man?" the soldier sitting next to him asked snidely. On the next bump on the road, he slammed his shoulder into Rabinowitz.

"Ow," Rabinowitz said.

Dow chuckled to himself. *He's such a wimp, taking it without a fight.*

A second private took advantage of the next bump, and Dow felt his own muscles tense as both men leaned into Rabinowitz, pushing him hard into the wall.

"Ow!"

Toughening him up is one thing, but that's a little excessive.

Across from Dow, Corporal Lawless laughed. He rocked side to side with the other two soldiers. "Everyone together now, one, two, thr...."

The anger built up quickly. Something inside Dow snapped, and before he could stop himself, he yelled, "Knock it off!"

They stopped and turned to Dow.

Why did I do thaaat?

"What's your problem? You want some of this too?" Lawless held up his fist.

Dow shook his head, amused. *I could take you with one hand tied behind my back. You ain't no threat.* Lawless was just a jealous thug.

The other two soldiers looked at Dow like lions preparing to pounce. The privates beside Dow broke eye contact, careful not to look directly at anyone. Rabinowitz nodded his thanks.

"I'm talkin' to you, Dow! Are you listenin' to me?" Lawless waited for a reply, but Dow ignored him. "The only reason you made it into our squad is because of your stepdad. What happened to your real dad, anyway?"

A chill slithered down Dow's spine. His muscles tensed, but he firmly and confidently met Lawless's eyes. "He died a hero."

"Oh, is that it? You wanna be a hero? Do you think you can beat the three of us?" Lawless taunted.

It had no effect; Dow had fought bigger groups of bullies. "If the three of you end up with more cuts and bruises than me, what're you gonna tell the medic? That a black man's stronger than you?"

The three bullies looked at each other and shrugged. Just then, the truck stopped, and the engine turned off. They had arrived.

Pvt. Dow, being closest to the back, jumped out first. He systematically scanned the landscape. In the distance he saw a ranch-style house, a barn, and a herd of cows among tumbleweeds and broken fences—presumably broken from last night's heavy winds. Other than that, nothing, as far as the eye could see.

Where is the crash?

"This way, men!" Sergeant Highton called from the far side of one of the other large green trucks.

Dow turned and saw Rabinowitz standing close. They headed in Highton's direction, and Rabinowitz followed. The others were all staring at something off in the distance. Dow followed their eyes. Then he saw it. He estimated the massive disk-shaped silver object to be about fifty feet across. With the bump on top, it reminded him of an upside-down plate or a teacup saucer. The sand had partially covered it from the morning winds, but the exterior seemed to be made of ripped tinfoil, and foil fragments were all over the ground.

Lieutenant Monroe came around from the transport cab, and Highton yelled, "Ten-hut!" Everyone stood up straight.

The lieutenant had his hands on his hips as he scanned the soldiers with cold brown eyes that could cut glass. "At ease. This may look unusual, but I'm told it's hollow, some kind of parachute. Make sure you get every bit of this foil, even way up by the hills. Dismissed!"

He and Highton then walked to where the ranch owner, his son, and the local sheriff were standing. They kept looking over their shoulders fearfully at the large object, shaking their heads and increasing their speed, like they were running away from a bomb and trying not to look like it.

The troops approached the object cautiously. Looking in through the rips, Dow could see the hollow interior. The parachute had metal supports and seemed more like an umbrella than a regular military chute. At its center lay a bell-shaped object.

"Who's goin' in there to see what that thang is?" Lawless challenged. Clearly, he wasn't going to do it himself.

Everyone silently shrugged. A few mumbles broke out, and eyes shifted back and forth. Dow glanced over at the sergeant and lieutenant, who were in a deep discussion with the sheriff.

"Dow!" Lawless pointed at him. "Take point!" A wave of agreement rose from the others, and they all backed away to give him room to lead.

Dow raised his eyebrows in confusion. *On one hand, it is an unlikely honor. On the other, he is putting me in potential danger. But I'm really curious what's under there. I've never seen anything like it before. Could it be from outer space?*

Dow took a deep breath and ducked through a larger hole in the outer foil frame. Half the other soldiers followed at a respectable distance, hands on their sidearms, while Lawless and the other half spread out and looked through the different holes of the parachute.

Dow peered at the object from a distance, looking for any hazard warnings or identifying marks. Out of the corner of his eye, he saw Rabinowitz close behind him.

Dow tilted his head. "You're not worried it's going to explode?"

"I figure my chances are better with you than with them."

Dow ignored him, figuring he had a point.

It must've been scorched in the landing. Still, he saw some kind of pattern under all of it, flags of US allied countries. Rubbing off soot, Dow saw pictures of Roosevelt, Churchill, and Stalin, the leaders at the end of the war. There was also an image of President Whitmore, who narrowly beat Truman in the recent election.

"The allied leaders," Dow said.

"Whoever sent this must want to be allies," Rabinowitz guessed.

At those words, Dow felt a tingling sensation rise on the back of his neck, and he knew Rabinowitz was correct. *Interesting.*

If they want to be allies, they must *be friendly,* so he was no longer worried it would explode. He walked to the other side of the object. Inlaid in the metal was a door with a window and a big American Flag. He leaned closer, squinting through the window. It was dark, but he could still make out the faint outline of arms and legs.

He immediately jerked away, inhaling sharply. *What?*

"I think there's someone in there!" he shouted to the others, who were still watching him with guns at the ready. "And they're not moving!" Dow's heart rate quickened. The others might have been speaking, but Dow couldn't hear them over the sound of his own blood rushing through his ears. "They might be out of air!"

No one moved.

Dow grabbed the recessed door handle and yanked hard, but it didn't budge. "Help me!"

As he desperately pulled the door, he looked up at the other soldiers. Wide-eyed and fidgeting, they made no move to help.

Out of the corner of his eye, he saw Rabinowitz scanning around, likely for something to use as a lever. Just then, one of the parachute support beams detached on one end and swung down. Rabinowitz's mouth dropped open in shock, but he quickly grabbed it and pulled, detaching the other side with unexpected ease.

It took a second for the young private to regain his composure, which annoyed Dow. This was life or death! No time to stop and wonder. Luckily, it was only a second before Rabinowitz rushed back over and handed the metal support to Dow, who wedged the edge of it under the door handle, and the two of them pushed hard on the make-shift lever.

A moment later the door shifted, and there was a hissing noise, like air leaking out of a tire. Sand flew from the ground toward the door, and Dow realized the air was being sucked in, not blown out. Then the pressure released, and the door swung open. Dow and Rabinowitz fell.

Dow looked up, but sand and dust filled his vision, sending him into a coughing fit. After the dust cleared, he and Rabinowitz cautiously stepped toward the vessel and peered inside. Three small people were strapped into the seats, wearing rags.

Are those...children? Dow wondered, as his stomach churned at the thought. *Who would smuggle children?*

Dow stared for several seconds at the center body, and it was then that he began to really notice how odd it looked. Its bald head wasn't just swollen, it was far bigger than it should be, its body tiny in comparison. It was an odd shade of gray.

Dow examined the body beside it and saw that its eyes were very big and slanted. A lump formed in his throat. *They're not human!*

A jolt of adrenaline made his heart leap, and he jumped back, eyes darting to Rabinowitz. By the look on his face, he had seen them too. Dow dropped the beam, slammed the door shut and yelled, "Lieutenant!" Rabinowitz echoed the call.

It took a minute for the lieutenant to appear outside, looking in through one of the larger rips in the parachute. "What? What's wrong?" He slowly worked his way past the frame.

Rabinowitz shook all over and was trying to talk, but the words wouldn't form. Finally, Dow said, "Aliens!"

The lieutenant sneered, disbelieving. "Yeah, right!" He opened the door of the ship. "If this is some kind of joke, Dow, you're in for a world of trouble." He turned, looked, then slammed the door shut. His face had turned the color of sour milk, and his mouth moved just slightly, letting loose a string of curses.

Outside, the others hovered with curious eyes on Dow and the lieutenant. Several men near him whispered to each other. Dow believed that they had either seen inside or had heard what he had told the lieutenant.

Lt. Monroe blinked, collected himself, then turned around and yelled at them, "What are you all standing around for? I told you to clean up!" He pointed sharply at the vessel. "This container is off-limits! No one touch it, no one open it, no one even look at it! Do you hear me? No one!" With that, he rushed to the transport truck to use the radio.

Dow's heart raced a mile a minute. He felt dizzy, and a chill ran up and down his spine even though he was sweating. As he turned, he saw Rabinowitz's hands trembling. The other soldiers had pale faces and raised eyebrows. They whispered to each other as they got back to work, sending curious, frightened glances in the vessel's direction.

"Well, at least they are not looking at us," Rabinowitz said. "… what a horrific way to die."

Dow didn't hear him. Wanting to be alone, he saw some foil fragments in the distance, so he picked up a collection bag and headed in that direction, out of sight of the others.

CHAPTER FOUR

TOP SECRET

General Frank Jones

ROSWELL ARMY AIRFIELD

[General Jones was already dealing with the fallout from **nuclear testing** when aliens literally crashed into his world. The timing couldn't have been worse—or perhaps it was exactly what we needed.]

"Please help me fix this. The people around here are hard workers; they deserve better," General Frank Jones said quietly as he looked at multiple reports of the first nuclear tests and the effects of the radiation. Horrific photos marked TOP SECRET. Several depicted cattle suffering from birth defects. The rest of the papers contained purchase invoices for those cattle.

He glanced at a memo he had received that morning about an incident at Ashcroft Ranch. A team had been sent out to investigate. He felt tingles, and the hairs on the back of his neck raised as he heard a knock at the door.

"Enter," he called.

Lieutenant Hansley opened the door. He stood at attention and saluted.

After decades, Jones was tired of the constant salutes, but it was protocol. So, halfheartedly and dismissively, he raised his hand to his forehead, then dropped it. "What happened at the ranch?"

"How did you know, sir?"

Jones raised a single eyebrow but didn't answer.

"I have a message from Lieutenant Monroe. He requests your presence at the ranch with the crashed object. He also requested that you put the base on alert," Hansley said.

"Did he say what they found?"

"No, sir; he did not want to say it over the radio."

"Probably a good thing, but we don't know what we are dealing with, and I don't want to cause a panic." Jones thought for a moment. "Let's run an Alpha alert drill and let him know we will be right there. Also inform Trinity; this might be a distraction to steal our nuclear technology."

CHAPTER FIVE

STRANGER FROM ANOTHER WORLD

Private Malcolm Dow

ASHCROFT RANCH, ROSWELL

Pvt. Dow wandered around the desert near the hills, picking up debris and putting the pieces into his burlap sack. As he resettled the bag, footsteps crunched behind him. He held back a groan. It had to be Rabinowitz. Not wanting to show weakness, he kept his back to the other private.

The image of the alien children haunted him. He could feel tears welling up and didn't know exactly why. *Toughen up,* he told himself. *Men aren't supposed to cry!* He needed to stay strong.

After about an hour, Dow felt drained and the emotions wore off. He spoke without turning around. "You don't have to follow me. Lawless and his goons are back at the crash."

Rabinowitz then walked parallel to Dow. "Are we going to talk about what we saw?"

"No."

"But you saw it, right? Big heads, small bodies."

"Are you talking about yourself?" Dow raised his eyebrows.

"Are you serious?" Rabinowitz exclaimed.

That outburst made Dow finally stop and look at him. The other private looked equal parts scared, excited, and angry. Dow sighed. "OK, fine. I saw the same as you. Are you happy now? Can we get back to work?"

"Why don't you want to talk about it?"

Dow shrugged. "What's there to talk about? They're aliens, they're dead, end of story."

"You aren't curious where they came from? Why they're here? Do you think it's some kind of space lifeboat? Were they running from someone, being hunted?"

Dow didn't say anything, but a whole range of thoughts and emotions cycled through his mind. He stuffed them down like he had been trained to. Being a military man, he wasn't going to let his emotions get to him, yet he felt sorry for the alien children rather than scared of them.

Rabinowitz shook his head in disbelief. "What if it's the start of an invasion? What if they're friendly?"

Dow and Rabinowitz continued for several more paces, picking up foil in silence.

"They're dead. What does it matter? If more come and attack, I'll fight. If they're friendly, I'll shake their hands."

Rabinowitz spluttered like he couldn't believe what Malcolm had just said. "Is that it? You're going to wait to see if they attack or not? What if it's too late? What if they drop an atom bomb from the sky and kill us all?"

"Is there anything you can do to stop it?"

"No, but..."

"Exactly, so why are you getting all worked up about it? Besides, the only *Adam* bomb around here is you."

Rabinowitz deflated. "You're not a nice guy."

"Never said I was."

"So, what's with you? Are you just a soldier following orders?"

"Yep."

"What were you saying about not wanting to report to the medic that you beat them up?"

Dow stopped, grinned, and laughed. "That's a trick I learned from my dad. You see, the white guys like Lawless, they and their friends think that they're stronger and smarter than black folk. Ever since I've been asking that question, no one wants to find out. The best way to win a fight is not to have one."

"Huh?"

Dow nodded. "That's something my other dad told me…." He trailed off, suddenly overcome with pain. His smile faded and he looked down.

"Other dad?"

Dow growled under his breath as the unwanted pain of his childhood came rushing back. "My dad died saving the life of Lieutenant Gerry Smith. To repay him, Gerry and his family took care of my mom, my sister, and me. He's somewhat of a stepdad, so that's what I call him." He had no idea why he was even talking to Rabinowitz. Maybe it was because the other private was the only half-way decent guy in their squad.

"I'm so sorry."

Dow sighed. "For what? It ain't your fault. You weren't even around. He's gone, and there's nothin' you or I can do about it."

Rabinowitz went silent for a moment. "By the way, thanks for stopping them from crushing me. Why did you do it?" He fiddled with something in his hands; Dow saw that it was a piece of the foil.

"I don't know, man; what's with all the questions?"

Then he froze. The stubble of hairs along the nape of his neck stood on end—someone was watching them. He just had a hunch, but like all his hunches, he knew he could trust it.

He felt it in school when he got stuck with a seat near the front. Most times he felt it, and turned, he met the eyes of the class bully. On the rare occasion, he'd turn to meet the eyes of a girl, who would blush and look away.

Dow held out his hand to stop Rabinowitz, and systematically scanned the area. The only tracks in the sand were theirs.

Rabinowitz was suddenly at his side. "What is it?" he whispered, shoulders tensing.

"Shh. . . ." Could someone be watching with binoculars? Was it a sniper? Dow shook his head. He only had this feeling when it was someone close.

His mind shot back to the alien vessel. *I wonder if some aliens survived the crash. They could be watching us. But why?*

When he was ten years old, Dow heard a radio drama about aliens who attacked the world. *Is this an act of aggression?* Probably not, but the thought wouldn't leave him alone.

His heart pounded, and his skin felt clammy. Then, his soldier instincts kicked in, and he dropped into a fighting stance. He leaned forward with fists raised, knees bent, and muscles tensed. Squinting his eyes against the sun, he turned in a full circle, scanning the desert for hostiles. His wrists rotated slowly. Still nothing but sand and tumbleweeds. "Someone's watching us."

"How do you know?"

"I just do. You've never had the feeling you're being watched?" Dow felt tingles again and an unusual calm, like being wrapped in a warm blanket. He relaxed and straightened. "It's OK, they're friendly."

Rabinowitz, dumbfounded, shook his head and stepped back. "How do you know?"

"It's a hunch."

"Are your hunches reliable?"

"I've had hunches like this before. They never make sense, but when I follow them, good things usually happen." Dow resumed picking up debris.

"What are you doing?" Rabinowitz asked.

"Picking up debris, like we were told to do. We're soldiers, remember? We follow orders."

"But...what about your hunches, the people watching us?"

Dow shrugged. "What about them? I told you, they're friendly. They're not a threat. Get back to work."

As Dow worked, Rabinowitz stood still, shaking his head. He seemed to be thinking hard about something—but what it was, Dow couldn't guess.

All at once, Rabinowitz turned and called out, "Hello!"

"Shh!" Dow hissed, frustrated.

Rabinowitz ignored him. "We know you're here!"

"What you doing, man?" Dow's eyes were wide. He had spent the latter part of his life lying low, keeping to himself, not involving himself in other people's problems.

Rabinowitz persisted. "Show yourself!"

Dow noticed, out of the corner of his eye, about twenty feet away, something like a wheelless delivery van. Dow stumbled back. *Where did that come from?* It was smooth and silver, with a single window wrapped around the vehicle. A pocket door was open along the side. In the doorway was a bald, middle-aged being with light purple skin.

Dow took a deep breath but found it hard to exhale. The *man's* clothing looked like a monk's robe, made from the foil Dow had just been collecting.

The *man* couldn't be human, but he wasn't gray like the children's bodies. *Why is he like the others but somehow different? Is he a different kind of alien?*

The alien broke the silence. He spoke with an air of hesitation. "How did you know I was here?"

Dow shook himself and rubbed his eyes, stared at the alien, then shrugged. "I just had a hunch." He surprised himself at how quickly and naturally he answered.

"You are not scared? Like the others?"

Dow tensed, then looked away as he thought about Lawless and his buddies. "Most of them fear anything different." He detected Rabinowitz stiffen beside him and sent the private a reassuring smile. "Well, a few of them are OK. Who are you?"

"We noticed you two are not afraid. I am Ambassador Geogram from the planet Zalma. And you are?"

"I'm Private Malcolm Dow..."

Rabinowitz lifted his hand like in school. "...Private Adam Rabinowitz..."

Dow tilted his head with an amused smile. "...from the planet Earth. You don't look like the other aliens we saw."

Geogram laughed good-naturedly. "No, indeed not. Those are just dummies, modified clones grown in a lab, like plants. They were never alive. We made them to see how your people would react to beings not of your world. We remote-controlled the spacecraft to land at the nuclear test site, but there were unexpected winds and it crashed."

Rabinowitz chuckled. "You speak pretty good English."

Geogram stood tall and proud. "I have been monitoring your world's radio and television transmissions since they commenced."

"Oy." Rabinowitz cocked his head. "Why *are* you here?"

"I have come to ask for your help."

Dow's heart plummeted. *Bad enough that I stuck my neck out to help Rabinowitz, and now aliens are asking me for help.* "Not interested."

Rabinowitz's face turned slightly red as he glared at Dow. "Why do you have to be so rude? You're talking to a visitor from another planet!" he snapped. Turning to Geogram, his face and voice softened. "Welcome to Earth. Please excuse my friend."

Dow huffed.

Rabinowitz continued, "What can we do for you?"

Geogram hesitated and looked down. "We need the help of your planet, and your responses were better than the others."

Rabinowitz crinkled his forehead. “What kind of help? If you can travel through space, you must be far more advanced than us.”

Geogram’s purple skin turned pale and chalky, the color completely draining out of it. “Yes, we are. But my people are pacifists. We do not understand violence. Another planet, Moad, has sent ships to attack us.”

“That’s horrible!” Rabinowitz shouted.

Geogram nodded forlornly. He raised his hand to the side of the space vehicle, where a color motion picture appeared. Ships shaped like rockets, with a Ferris wheel in the middle, were attacking a planet.

Dow stared at the pictures, amazed by the technology but horrified by the imagery.

“Whoa! And there’s nothing you can do to stop it? Wow! How did you do that?” Rabinowitz flinched as a sudden explosion of light enveloped the image.

Geogram did not answer but proceeded, “We do not know why they have chosen to do this, and we are trying to resolve things peacefully, but our deflectors will not hold for much longer.”

Dow’s heart clenched. He noticed Rabinowitz make an aborted movement, like he’d wanted to lay a hand on the alien’s shoulder. Dow’s own hands were in fists at his sides.

Geogram’s gaze returned to the ground. “I fear if we cannot achieve peace, we will be destroyed and the Moad will gain our technology. We have no weapons to fight.”

Dow’s jaw dropped. He stepped forward, interrupting whatever Rabinowitz was about to say. “So, you want *us* to fight *your* war for you?”

“No!” Geogram said, wide-eyed. His skin became a flurry of colors, different combinations of red and green with undertones of blue.

Dow stared openly at the colorful display.

Geogram continued, "Preferably not.... We simply...wish for your negotiation skills. We saw in your broadcasts that you recently negotiated peace, and we would like you to do the same for us. We do not have much time."

"What would happen if they stole your technology?" Rabinowitz asked. Dow looked over to see that the other private's face had taken on a glossy sheen of sweat. "Would they use it against Earth?"

"I've already run projections—our systems calculated a seventy-three percent chance that the Moad would attack Earth next," Geogram said.

Dow shook his head, defeated. "Yes, typically violent people are never satisfied. Once they win one battle, they feel unstoppable and move on to the next target. How far away are they?"

Geogram's eyes moved back and forth rapidly. "With their current technology, it would take them seven of your years to travel from their planet to yours. However, if they capture our planet, it would only take them four years. In addition, if they gain our technology, it would only take them five months."

Dow's eyes popped. "What! Are you saying that we could have hostile aliens here in less than a year?"

Geogram shrugged again. "Possibly, why?"

Dow looked at the motion picture on the side of the space vehicle. "What kind of weapons are those?"

"We do not know anything about weapons, but they release more energy than the explosions we detected here on Earth two years ago."

"Atomic bombs?" Rabinowitz's face turned red. He examined the images again. "They are dropping A-bombs on your planet? They have dropped several in the last few minutes. How is your planet not already destroyed?"

"The deflectors we built to protect us from meteors have been protecting us from the Moad."

"But we don't have any such deflectors! They could destroy Earth and we wouldn't even know what hit us." Rabinowitz paced back and forth. "If we were to help you, would you give us these deflectors?"

Geogram nodded. "Of course. We are willing to give you anything you need to achieve peace."

Rabinowitz smiled. "Well! That changes everything, doesn't it, Dow? Why don't you two wait here and I'll get one of the officers?"

Geogram's skin turned chalky again. "I do not believe that would be wise. They did not react well to the clones."

"What? I thought you wanted us to contact our government," Dow replied. "That's how we do it, through our chain of command." He shook his head, at a loss for what to do. "If we can't go to any of them.... There's no way they'd let us talk to anyone higher up."

Geogram looked thoughtful. "Perhaps our information is incorrect. Do you trust them?"

"No," Dow admitted, feeling anger rise in him again. "But that doesn't matter, that's the way we do things around here. I ain't risking a court martial."

Rabinowitz smiled at Geogram. "Don't worry, we'll think of something."

"We will continue our observation for now, and then let you know. Call us tomorrow with your communicators."

"What communicators?" Rabinowitz asked.

Geogram tilted his head. "They are already in your hand."

Dow turned to see that Rabinowitz, indeed, had two polished metal rectangles in his hands where the foil had been. They were each about the size of a playing card but three times as thick, though still thin enough to fit in a wallet. They had no buttons, no switches, no markings. They looked nothing like the clunky walkie-talkies or huge radio systems the lieutenant had.

"These are communicators? How do they work?" Rabinowitz asked.

Dow and Rabinowitz turned back to where Geogram had been, but he and his ship were gone. They glanced in every direction, including up. "Where'd he go?"

Dow grunted. "Well, that's weird!"

Rabinowitz tried to hand Dow a communicator, but he refused to take it.

"That's a communicator?" Dow frowned. "Don't be so gullible."

"Why are you so insensitive? Have you figured out why you stopped those guys in the truck earlier?"

Dow gave a blank stare.

"You weren't just saving me, you know. You were stopping the bullies, bullies like the Moad."

He walked away, hating that Rabinowitz was correct.

CHAPTER SIX

JONES AT THE RANCH

General Frank Jones
ASHCROFT RANCH, ROSWELL

After sending Lieutenant Hansley off with his orders, Jones invited Colonel George Liam with him to the crash site. "What do you think we will find?" he asked, getting straight to business.

"If they called you out, I would expect a Soviet spy plane," Liam replied.

As they arrived at the ranch, Jones saw hundreds of foil fragments. The driver parked the limousine beside the military trucks, and Jones saw what looked like a shredded fifty-foot foil umbrella. He stepped out of the car.

Sweat dripped down Lt. Monroe's pasty white face as he approached and saluted. "Sir, you're going to want to see this."

Holding back his annoyance, Jones returned the salute. "Yes, what is it, Lieutenant?"

"Aliens, sir."

"Aliens?" Jones raised an eyebrow. "Are they alive?"

"No, sir."

"Shame." He motioned Monroe to lead the way. The lieutenant's feet were fast and nervous, but Jones and Liam easily kept up. The way to the crash site had already been cleared of foil, so no one was around to overhear their conversation.

As he walked, Monroe turned his upper body to address the general. His eyebrows were scrunched. "Shame, sir?"

"Yes. It's going to be hard to find out why they're here if we can't talk to them."

Monroe's face reddened. "Does it matter, sir? They are foreigners on US soil," he protested.

"What would be your course of action?"

Monroe huffed. "For Pete's sake, General! Prepare for an invasion, of course! Mount a counteroffensive. If any more of these freaks show up, we should be blasting them out of the sky."

"Settle down, Lieutenant!" Liam warned.

Jones, however, was eager for Monroe to continue. "Attack? Who? Where?" he asked.

Monroe's face was redder than ever, but he didn't say anything, so Jones turned to Liam. "Do you agree with this assessment?"

Before Liam had a chance to answer, they reached the umbrella-like structure and ducked inside. The sight seemed to steal Liam's words as his mouth dropped open. Jones drew closer to the upside-down cone-like container. He hummed. It was covered in depictions of the allied flags. The door on the other side had a large American Flag printed on it.

"It has an American Flag front and center on the door, and you want to mount a counteroffensive?" Jones asked pointedly. He shook his head in disgust, then opened the door, exposing three small gray bodies with big heads and slanted, swollen eyes. "Who has seen this?"

"Just Privates Dow and Rabinowitz, and myself," Lt. Monroe replied. "The others might've caught a glimpse from a distance."

"Where are the privates now?"

Monroe pointed toward the hills. "They were last seen heading out that way to collect foil."

"Did you find any weapons?" Jones asked.

"No sir. Not yet. But I'm sure we will."

"Tell me, Lieutenant, does the aliens' clothing look more like a military uniform, a farmer's, or a monk's?"

Monroe spluttered. "A-a monk, sir...?"

"Yes, a monk. You know, those religious people who lead a simple life and dedicate their lives to serving God?"

Monroe stared back blankly.

Liam scrutinized the aliens with calculated interest. "He may have a point. Sir."

"How so?"

Liam's face was also blank.

"You're all ready to go to war, but you can't provide me with a reason to do so?" Jones looked at their blank faces again then shook his head. "I want to keep this under wraps. I don't see anything to suggest the invasion you say we should prepare for," he said. "I'm certain they've been following the results of the war and the peace treaty. This seems more like refugees in a rowboat scenario, and I don't want to cause a panic."

He alternated looking the two officers in the eye. "I am classifying this Top Secret. We will investigate, and I will report the preliminary findings directly to the president tomorrow. You are not to discuss this with anyone other than myself. Is that understood?"

The two officers straightened. "Yes, sir."

"Good. Now I want you to put these into body bags, and take them to..." Jones scanned the area. He pointed. "That barn. Ask the farmer to remove his animals and call the local veterinarian to do a house call."

"Sorry, sir. You don't want the base doctor, sir?" Monroe asked, his face red again.

"A human doctor is only familiar with humans. I want someone who has experience with other biologics as well."

Monroe bit his lip. "Yes, sir."

"I've also acquired a safe house, a local abandoned warehouse, for just such emergencies. Liam, take everything to this address. Only use senior personnel *whom you trust.*" Jones handed the colonel a piece of paper and looked him in the eye, stressing his last words. "And escalate to Bravo alerts at the base and at Trinity. Understood?"

Liam gave a slight nod. "Yes, sir!"

"Dismissed."

CHAPTER SEVEN

JOHNNY'S RANCH

Charlotte "Charlie" Baker

ASHCROFT RANCH, ROSWELL

Here is where I come into the story: twelve years old and hot on the trail of a new scoop. My father owned the local newspaper, and I wanted to be just like him, though he never gave me the chance. I didn't know it back then, but he was just being overprotective. I was determined to prove him wrong.

That, of course, brought me to Ashcroft Ranch where my friend Johnny lived. Rumors had been circulating all over town that morning about some sort of crash, so of course I had to check it out. Sandy (my golden retriever) and I went together. Every turn of my wheels toward that ranch was an act of defiance. My father saw a girl in a wheelchair; I saw a reporter on the cusp of the biggest story of the century. As soon as we got there, I saw tin foil everywhere. It littered the ground, hung draped over the fence and clothesline, and a few pieces even drifted in the wind. One piece flew up and into my face, so I had to stop and pull it off.

I was about to throw it away, but it felt much softer than it looked. Sandy sniffed at it, ears perked. It wasn't like anything I'd ever seen before, so I folded the foil. Once it was a rectangle about the size of a pack of Dentyne gum, I couldn't fold it anymore. I tried again, and it wouldn't budge. It had become a solid piece! Fascinated, I put it in my pocket.

"Charlie!"

I looked up and saw Johnny running toward me, waving. I rolled in his direction.

"What'cha doing here?" he asked.

I grinned at him. "I heard about the crash. Why else?"

His cheeks went as red as his hair, but he looked as excited as I felt. "Can you believe it?"

He pointed to what appeared to be a huge silver umbrella in the distance. *So that's where the foil came from.* The umbrella was torn apart like one of Sandy's well-loved chew toys. More than a dozen soldiers were walking around, picking up the scattered bits of foil. I guessed that they'd come in the green army trucks, but the car was what drew my eye. It was a long green army limousine; someone important had come too.

"What is it?" I asked Johnny as I picked up the camera from my lap and snapped some pictures.

"I dunno. It just looks like a big umbrella to me, but I heard the soldiers say it's a parachute or somethin'."

"A parachute? Do you know what's in it?"

"No. Pa wouldn't let me go near it. He thinks it's a bomb, or spies, or aliens from outer space."

I looked at him. Everyone knew Johnny's pa believed in that kind of stuff, but Johnny and I were used to it. "Only one way to find out! Do you think they would let me look?"

"Nah," he said. "That top army guy there told the soldiers not to go near it, so you ain't got a chance." Johnny pointed to where one man was standing around yelling at all the others.

[He was probably right, but back then I saw rules more like suggestions.]

Sandy raised her head to sniff the air. She whined and barked in the direction of the barn. *What's that about? Does she sense something?*

Before I could investigate, Johnny turned to me, eyes wide. "You came all the way out here? That's seven miles! You must be hungry. Let's go see my ma."

I could never say no to food, so we went. I'd just have to take a look at the parachute later.

Johnny's house didn't have a ramp for my wheelchair, but he easily pulled me up the steps as he'd done many times before. On the porch, Johnny took my thermos and Sandy's dog bowl from the pack on the back of my chair and filled them with water from the spigot. He set the bowl down in the shade and gave Sandy a pat as she drank. He then put the thermos back, turned my wheelchair around and backed it into the house.

"Hi, Ma!" he called out. "Charlie came all the way from town to see the crash."

She came out of the kitchen, drying her hands on her flower-printed apron. "Charlotte, dear, you must be exhausted. Come in here and have some milk and cookies. Oh, your lovely hair's all a mess!"

[She always fussed like that, as if neat hair could make a good impression on the army.]

I pushed my glasses up my nose and tried to straighten my blonde hair. "I'm a reporter now, Mrs. Ashcroft. Please call me Charlie." Technically, I shouldn't accept food on the job, but Mrs. Ashcroft's cookies were amazing.

Johnny shoved one of the chairs away from the table to make room for me, and his ma brought us the treats on a tray.

I'd downed two cookies and a big gulp of milk before remembering to act professional. "Thank you, Mrs. Ashcroft," I said quickly. "So, when did you first notice the crash?"

"We was looking out the window at the storm last night, wonderin' when it were gonna end," Johnny said. "Then there were this orange light. We thought it were a bright star, but it grew bigger and brighter. It were headin' straight for us, and we thought we were goners!"

"Wow! What happened next?"

"Right when we thought it would hit us, it opened like an umbrella and shot sideways. It flew right over the house. I swear it was so loud it rattled my teeth! Ma and Pa was too scared to watch, but I couldn't help myself. I watched the whole thing. It crashed right where you saw it, but there were somethin' under it, like a big bell."

"Did you check it out?" I asked.

"Nah, I told ya that Pa wouldn't let me. Besides, it were too windy, too dangerous. Sand were blowing all over th' place."

I slumped in disappointment and took another cookie. "Oh, right. What about in the morning? After the storm was over?"

"Sun came up and we went out and saw the crash. Looked just like you saw—big umbrella—but Pa weren't lettin' me get no closer. All I know is we ain't never seen nothin' like it, so Pa called the sheriff right quick."

"Then what happened?"

"Sheriff shown up, an' he called the army. They shown up soon after that."

"That's it?"

"'fraid so. Sorry, Charlie...." Johnny peered out the window. "Hey, there's the animal doctor. What's he doing here? Did one of the cows get hurt?"

Mrs. Ashcroft joined him at the window, looking worried. "Not that I know of, but I'm sure your pa would've told us if they had."

We all watched as the veterinarian drove to the barn. A tall, slim man got out of his truck and walked in with his bag. Sandy's ears perked again and she barked in the man's direction. Her paws danced like they did when she was restless. Something told me that the vet's visit wasn't normal....

"Could they have put something from the crash in the barn when you weren't looking?" I asked Johnny.

"I suppose. I weren't lookin' since I saw you."

A knock came from the door, and Mrs. Ashcroft went to answer it. She returned with the sheriff in tow and Sandy wagging her tail at his side. [The sheriff always gave her treats back then.] He tipped his hat to us. "Howdy, young'uns. I saw little Miss Charlotte's pooch outside, and it's gettin' late. I should take 'em back home before it's their supper time and her father sends me out looking for her."

We all laughed.

CHAPTER EIGHT

AUTOPSY

General Frank Jones
ASHCROFT RANCH, ROSWELL

Lt. Monroe and Col. Liam were already observing the veterinarian's procedure when Gen. Jones entered. "What can you tell me, doctor?"

The vet, Dr. Fisher, shook his head, looking lost. "I suppose you're the one I have to thank for this?"

"Yes, well.... What did you find?"

"They're definitely not like anything I've seen before."

Jones was expecting as much. He could see that Dr. Fisher was disappointed in his own assessment, but there was also a glint of interest in his eyes that brought Jones comfort. "Anything else?"

"Well, if I didn't know better, I would say that they were never born."

"What makes you say that?"

The doctor moved back toward the makeshift worktable and pointed to the bodies. "The skin is soft and pliable like a newborn baby, and the lungs and bones are not fully developed, like a stillborn calf."

"Could that be part of their species?"

"I don't see how."

Jones walked around the bodies. "Any idea what killed them? The physical trauma of the crash? Possibly a lack of oxygen?"

"As I said before, I'm not sure that they were alive in the first place. But if they were, my best guess would be suffocation."

"Thank you, Doctor," Jones replied. "You can go now, but remember not to tell *anyone* about this." He leveled the man with a serious look, recognizing the ambition in his eyes. Fisher was reluctant to go. Even if he didn't know much, the aliens clearly intrigued him far more than they spooked him.

The doctor shook his head with a haggard laugh. "Who would believe me?"

After he left, Jones turned to the officers. "Assessment?" Both of them were silent, so Jones asked, "Do you believe that they are a threat?"

Liam spoke first. "These ones, no sir. But where did they come from, and are there more of them, sir?"

"And are the other ones a threat?" Monroe added.

"Recommendations?" Jones asked.

"Gee willickers. As I said before, prepare for an invasion," Monroe answered. "Mount a counteroffensive. The flags may be trying to lull us into a false sense of security, sir."

Jones was starting to get annoyed with Monroe's paranoia. He stared hard at his inferior officer. "Based on what? How are we going to prepare? Where are we going to attack?"

Monroe paused, thrown by the question, and Jones thought that was the end of it, but then Monroe said, "In space, sir."

Jones couldn't help but smile. "In space? And how are we going to get there? We don't have any vehicle capable of going to space. And what if they are friendly, as the pictures and flags suggest? Do you want to start a war with a technologically advanced species? How do you plan on winning a war when we can't even leave our planet?"

Monroe opened his mouth, but he said nothing. After a moment, he closed his mouth again. His Adam's apple bobbed as he swallowed hard.

Jones nodded. *Just as I thought.* "Lieutenant, you are dismissed." After he left, Jones turned to Col. Liam. "Take these bodies to the warehouse. I'll return to the base and book a personal appointment with the president."

Liam blinked. "A personal appointment, sir?"

"Yes, I want to brief the president in private. He can decide what to do from there."

"What about the Secretary of War and the Joint Chiefs?"

"As of right now, this is not an act of war, and therefore not their jurisdiction. And if we do bring it to them, we know what their response will be. Like Monroe, they will want to shoot first and ask questions later. Do you have a problem with an elected president deciding if we want to start an interplanetary war?"

Liam looked straight ahead, trying not to move, but Jones could see very subtle twitches. *He's going to be trouble. He masks it well, but I've seen that twitch before—on officers wrestling with their conscience, caught between duty and what they believe deep down.* "I'll tell you what. You can write your recommendation and I'll see to it that the president gets it."

Liam tilted his head. "Sir?" Then he regained his composure and stood at attention. "Thank you, sir!"

"Dismissed."

[Jones always said that "History will remember who fired the first shot. I'll make sure it isn't us." He kept that promise.]

CHAPTER NINE

UFO NEWS ARTICLE

Charlotte "Charlie" Baker

ROSWELL, NEW MEXICO

The sheriff dropped me and Sandy off at my house. He lingered by the door, wanting to come inside, but I convinced him that Dad wouldn't be home from the office yet. He left shortly after, and I was relieved; I really didn't want him talking to my parents.

When I got inside, my mom was waiting for me in the kitchen. "Where have you been, and why did the sheriff drive you home? I was about to call your dad to look for you. What trouble did you get into now?"

I couldn't help but laugh. The sheriff had said the same thing. With total confidence, I replied, "I didn't get into any trouble. I went out to Johnny's family's ranch. They had a crash out there, so I went to get the story. I got some pictures!"

"Yes, I know. Mrs. Ashcroft called me when you left. She didn't want me worrying—which *clearly* wasn't a concern of *yours*! Do you realize how far it is to go all by yourself? I suppose Sandy followed you. Did you think to give her some water?"

I winced at her tone. Once Mom got started, there was very little anyone could do to calm her down. "Yeah, Mom, I gave Sandy water along the way," I assured her. "And Johnny gave her more when we got there."

Mom didn't look convinced, but I had to try. "There is a real story there! A bunch of soldiers were picking up pieces of foil from this big parachute, then they put something from the crash in Johnny's barn and called the animal doctor. You can't tell me that's nothing." I purposefully left out the fact that I'd taken some of the foil from the ranch. She'd only make me give it back, and I really wanted to know how it had changed from flimsy foil into a solid metal bar.

She opened her mouth to continue scolding me, but at that moment, Dad walked into the room. I'd never been happier to see him. Under his arm he held a rolled-up newspaper. He handed it to me and I inhaled the scent and smiled. It was hot off the press. Then I saw the headline and my jaw dropped. 'Flying Saucer Crashes at Ashcroft Ranch'. I read it aloud. He wrote something about it already? Without even going out there to investigate?

He sat in one of the kitchen chairs and grunted. "Mr. Ashcroft called and he didn't say anything about the barn or the veterinarian. Dr. Fisher was probably just checking on the cattle; the sound of the crash was bound to scare them."

So he had heard me talking to Mom. A cold wave washed over me. "But you don't have any pictures! This is barely more than hearsay!"

"If I did, the army would just confiscate them. I almost regret giving you my old camera. If I were you, I'd get rid of that film before the army finds out and comes knocking on our door."

"They can't do that, can they? The pictures are mine!" Sandy came and licked me relentlessly. She often did this when I raised my voice. It's like she was saying, "Don't be upset, I don't want you to be upset."

Dad's eyes opened wide and his face turned red like I'd never seen before. "They can and they will. Ever since the nuclear tests, everything they do is pretty hush-hush. More than once they threatened to close me down and take everything away."

Dad looked away, and quietly grumbled. "You just don't

understand the military. This is why we should leave journalism to the men."

I stared at him. "I don't have to understand them; I have a different point of view, and that's a good thing. If we don't question our military, who will? Nobody is above the law."

"Those are the men that make the laws, Charlotte! They can do what they well please."

"The good ones wouldn't take advantage of that."

Dad huffed.

Mom's face was white as she looked back and forth between us. Then her color came back as she smiled weakly. "It's our differences that make us stronger. Charlie's doing good work. Just...be careful, honey." She nodded, putting an end to that conversation. "Dinner is almost ready. Charlie, why don't you feed Sandy and give her some fresh water? Then, get cleaned up. You're covered in dust."

[At the time, I didn't know how much that argument with my father would shape the rest of my life.]

CHAPTER TEN

MALCOLM'S MORALS

Private Malcolm Dow
ROSWELL ARMY AIRFIELD

That night, Dow couldn't help but think of Geogram's request. He lay on his bunk in the barracks, tossing and turning on the cot. *Technology from aliens?* He'd had fantasies of it since he'd seen his first *Flash Gordon* comic book. How could aliens and outer space adventures be real?

He rolled over again. *What if we* do *help them? Which humans would get their technology? What would they do with it?* Anybody would want the opportunity. He sighed, staring out into the darkness. A glint of metal caught his eye, and he flinched as an unwanted memory arose.

It was his first year of middle school. He'd been the only black boy, and with all the bullies around, he knew he had to defend himself, so he'd snuck a pair of brass knuckles into his schoolbag. The first time the bullies cornered him, he'd busted a few lips and gotten away. He felt so powerful, and brought them again the next day, but the bullies knew he had them and were expecting them. They got the brass knuckles off him, and the very thing Dow had used to protect himself was then used to hurt him.

Could the same thing happen with the aliens'—*Zalma's*—technology? It might be next to impossible to keep it out of the wrong hands. What then? The Second World War had just ended, not because the other guys had bigger weapons, but because the right people had been able to negotiate peace. Up until that point, things had only gotten worse, in Dow's opinion. Every new development in technology had made the battles bigger, more violent, more destructive. Then again…technology wasn't all bad, especially technology from pacifists. They'd be defensive. Shields and the like. And what about better medicine and transportation? It was so tempting.

He played every scenario over and over in his head until he was sure his brain was mush, but still nothing came to mind. Nothing could stop the *bad* guys from getting it too. And if that happened, the world would just be in another shootout of mass proportions. *Maybe humanity isn't ready to handle that kind of power.*

Dow cringed and rolled onto his other side. In the next bed, Rabinowitz slept soundly. Dow envied him. How could he always roll with the punches? How could he just fall asleep after everything that had happened? After their meeting with the alien, the other private had been constantly checking the pocket where he'd stuffed the communicator, but as soon as he lay down to sleep, he was out.

Dow tried to push it all from his mind—but the brass knuckles memory wouldn't go away. Neither would the fear in Geogram's eyes.

He wasn't sure which bothered him more.

[Malcolm always buried his emotions under layers of sarcasm and duty. But that night, staring at the ceiling, he was wrestling with the biggest decision of his life—and he didn't even know it yet.]

CHAPTER ELEVEN

DRILLS

Private Adam Rabinowitz

ROSWELL ARMY AIRFIELD

Rabinowitz watched Dow slide down the paratrooper zip line and practice his parachute landing fall. He knew Dow was one of the best recruits—better than him, anyway—which was why he always watched him. Today he was watching for another reason: he wanted to gauge how Dow was handling what had happened.

Before he could think too much about it, his turn came. He sprang into action. The drill sergeant, a large man with a scar down the left side of his face, glared at him with hawk-like eyes. Surprisingly, Rabinowitz caught up to Dow as he came up out of his landing roll and began crawling under the rows of barbed wire on his elbows and knees.

"Dow! Hurry up!" the drill sergeant bellowed. "What's the matter with you today, soldier?"

Rabinowitz wondered the same thing; Dow was usually at the front of the pack. "I've never been able to keep up with you before," he said quietly. "You OK?"

Dow skittered forward. "Couldn't sleep."

The response was curt, and he kept pausing to rub his eyes. Rabinowitz watched as Dow propped his rifle higher to keep it out of the dirt. There was a light scraping sound as Dow's helmet scratched against the barbed wire.

Rabinowitz kept close behind him. Given how Dow's run was going, it would be easy to pass him, but concern for his friend kept him back. He shuffled forward a few more feet, and an unfamiliar weight in his pocket shifted. It pressed against his leg, dragging on the ground as he moved. He froze.

The communicator. I swear it's moving. Is it buzzing? Can anyone hear it? He looked around, but from what little he could see, no one was paying him any mind. His body, wrought with tension, scrambled forward. He couldn't check it, but if he cleared the course, maybe he could get it to stop. He kept going with renewed vigor.

The buzz came again, making him jump. He winced as his knee struck a rock that stuck up from the dirt.

"Dow! Pick up the pace!" the drill sergeant shouted. "You're dropping behind!"

They crawled out from under the barbed wire. "Sorry, Sarge," Dow said. The man just sent them both to the next exercise with a huff.

Rabinowitz nodded respectfully to the sergeant and followed Dow. Was it just him, or was the sergeant's gaze lingering on him? He wasn't, so Rabinowitz slyly glanced around to see if anyone else was looking. Seeing no one, he felt safe to slip one hand from his rifle and into his pocket. His fingers wrapped around the cool, smooth metal. It was motionless. Maybe it hadn't buzzed at all. He didn't know what scared him more–that it had moved...or that it hadn't. Geogram had said his people were peaceful, but then, why did it feel like he was smuggling a weapon? Determined to check it again after training, he sped up to join Dow at the shooting range.

Lawless was already there, firing away with his rifle. He wasn't at all affected by the kickback or the noise, but none of his shots were very good. *Looks like being a military brat didn't help him there,* Rabinowitz thought. The outer edge of his target was riddled with holes. Call him petty, but it made Rabinowitz smile a little, especially as Dow took his own lane and began firing. After three bullseyes in a row, Dow got up and left.

Lawless glared after him. When he saw Rabinowitz looking over, his scowl deepened. "What're *you* lookin' at, knucklehead?"

"Nothing," Rabinowitz said quickly. "Nothing at all."

CHAPTER TWELVE

OLD FRIENDS

General Frank Jones

WASHINGTON, D.C.

[This is the part most people never hear about—not the crash, not the aliens, but what happened behind the doors of the most powerful office on Earth. I only pieced it together years later, from early interviews of the two men involved.]

Jones entered the Oval Office. The smell of pine oil filled his nostrils, which was nicer than the cigar smoke of the previous occupant.

"Frank." President Whitmore rose from behind the desk.

"Mr. President." Jones saluted. He had known Whitmore since the start of their military careers. It was hard being formal and calling each other by titles rather than first names, but their jobs required professionalism.

"I thought this was a personal visit," said Whitmore.

"I'm sorry to deceive you, sir. It's urgent."

The president's brow furrowed. "That bad?"

"Worse."

Whitmore begrudgingly returned the salute. "Then let's sit." He pointed to the two white leather sofas and took a seat.

Jones settled on the velvety white sofa across from him. He drew a breath. "Yesterday, a team from my base was called to investigate the crash of an unidentified flying object. Inside were three non-human bodies with unusually big heads and eyes."

Whitmore gaped. "What? Are you talking *aliens*? And you brought this to me? Without the Joint Chiefs?"

Jones handed him a folder marked *Top Secret* and a sealed envelope. "I promised Colonel Liam that I would deliver his concerns to you."

Whitmore grunted as he opened the envelope. His eyes ran over the paper as a few words escaped his lips. "General Jones…reckless…horrible mistake…Secretary of War and the Joint Chiefs…prepare for invasion, counteroffensive…impeachment…. You obviously disagree with his assessment."

Jones chuckled. "Yes, sir. Are you or the warmongers going to confirm the existence of aliens?"

"Of course not. After that radio drama ten years ago, there would be panic in the streets."

"So, no impeachment, no investigation."

The president nodded. "Ah…I see…. OK, I get your point. Give me the facts."

Jones had expected this and had already prepared his answers. "A small ship crash landed in Roswell, New Mexico, about a hundred miles from the Trinity nuclear test site, and the debris indicates it came from that direction."

Jones paused to let the information sink in. Then, he continued. "They're no threat, Mr. President; they were unarmed. The thing that crashed was a lifeboat, not a warship."

"How can you be certain?"

"If it were a military probe, they'd have been in uniform, carrying weapons, maybe even injured, to test our response. Instead, the bodies were small, like children, and were dressed like monks. The entire hull was covered in Allied flags and images of the Allied leaders. They've been watching us and are trying to communicate. That's not an invasion. That's a plea."

The president nodded slowly. "I see, but what do they want?"

"With everything I've learned so far, it's clear that they're interested in our weapons, but they don't want to just take them and leave. They need us too. They want our help."

Whitmore balked at Jones. "Help? They can travel between planets, and they want our help? What could they possibly want from us?"

"Their lifeboat indicates they are escaping a war, a war that they are losing. I'm sure they've created a refugee situation to see who is sympathetic to them, and who is not." Jones paused. "But they're not trying to settle here. By trying to land at the Trinity nuclear test site, unarmed, I believe they are asking for our help fighting that war."

"You always astound me with your deductions. What do we do from here?"

"The war is clearly one-sided. If they were the aggressors, they'd have just stolen what they needed from us and left already. If they're coming here, that means they can't fight for themselves, or their enemy is just as advanced as them and they're losing ground too fast. The fact that they're here means that whoever is attacking them can get here too. If our visitors lose their war, I'm certain that we'll be next. We should first make contact. Ally with the aliens that are here, merge their technology with ours, and—"

"*Ally* with them?" Whitmore shot forward on the sofa, his eyes wide and incredulous.

"Yes, Mr. President. If I'm right, their technology is the only way to defend Earth."

Whitmore stood up. "Are you serious? First, you talk about the aliens not being invaders, and now you're convinced that there *are* invaders on the way? And the only way we can stop them is by helping these guys who opened the floodgates to begin with?"

"Sir," Jones said, voice so calm and collected that it eased some of the president's nerves. "We must always be prepared, but we must not panic. The future will always be full of scary things, but it's how we react to it that makes all the difference."

"I know that, but this?"

"Nothing is certain. I very well may be wrong, but what chance would we have against their advanced technology anyway? That would be like us fighting with swords against a B-29 Superfortress." Jones leaned forward, gesturing for the president to sit down again.

With a softer voice, Jones said, "If they wanted to attack us, they would have. We have no way to defend against the speed of an interplanetary spacecraft. We need to focus on what we know, and what *I* know is that we haven't found the slightest sign of anything military. With everything else: the flags, the images, the clear refugee scenario…."

"Hmm…I see your point," Whitmore said, dabbing at his sweating brow with a handkerchief. "But…ally with an alien race we know nothing about, and fight a war we know nothing about?"

"Not entirely true, sir," Jones said. "We know *these* aliens didn't attack or steal from us, sir. They are reaching out to us with images that we understand."

"True." The president nodded, then paused, then suddenly shook his head. "But you must be crazy. Allying with aliens? No, *definitely* not!"

Jones hummed. *Why is he resisting? What could worry him so much? Is he worried about what the public will think of him? I can't deny that it's a reasonable concern. Heck, half the people already can't stand the other half. What would they think of aliens?* He stared, hard, at the president. *How can I counter this fear?*

Jones spoke softly, "Would you rather deal with their technologically advanced, aggressive enemy?"

"Well…." The president looked down. His eyes moved rapidly. "Are you willing to lead this battle? In space? With an enemy that you know nothing about?"

Jones sat up tall. *Now we're getting somewhere.* "I would be honored, sir! I don't see that we have much of a choice. Defending others and defending the United States—*that's* what I signed up for when I joined the army. And I have to defend Earth to do that."

"You're certain? You're putting a lot of faith in this guess of yours, Frank."

Frustration clawed at Jones. He'd thought he explained it clearly. "Not a guess, sir," he said firmly. "I made my decision with facts and that gut instinct of mine that you've always trusted."

"A hunch!" The president shook his head. "You are willing to put the future of this country, this *planet,* on a *hunch*?"

"There were lots of facts. My hunch just backs them up. Do you think that I'm wrong, sir?"

Whitmore paused, then rose and walked over to his desk. He faced away from Jones for a moment, fingers dancing across the wood. He picked up the brass name plate then set it back down. Finally, he turned back to Jones.

"Unfortunately, I do not. As usual, your reasoning is sound, and like you said, I've always trusted your gut."

Jones nodded sharply. "Thank you, sir."

"OK, you find these aliens and form an alliance with them. If you're right, you'll be going into space—who knows where or for how long. If you are wrong, well…let's not think about that."

"Yes, sir. Thank you, sir." Jones's chest swelled with pride for his friend. They were making the right decision.

The president scowled, looking pained. "Don't thank me. You do realize what you're up against, don't you?"

"Yes, sir."

"And not a word of this to anyone until you find these aliens. You don't know who is going to lose it or turn around and tell the press," the president insisted.

"Will do, sir. Shall we codename them the *out-of-town guests* then?"

"Sounds good. What do I tell the Joint Chiefs?"

"They've probably heard about the bodies and the wreckage already, so we should stick as close to the truth as we can. Perhaps a monkey-smuggling operation, but they were using a hydrogen weather balloon, which burned up in the crash."

"You think that would work?"

"Yes, smugglers are rarely concerned with safety. It'll appease them."

"So be it," the president said. "If you're wrong about the aliens...."

"If I'm wrong, history will judge me," Jones said, "but if I'm right, Earth may just survive, and that's all I care about."

The president turned to the window. "Let's just hope they're really the good guys."

CHAPTER THIRTEEN

TELEVISION

Private Adam Rabinowitz

ROSWELL ARMY AIRFIELD

That evening, Rabinowitz found a quiet place at the edge of the base behind a tree, away from everyone so he could talk in private. He took out the metal communicator, wondering how it worked. He looked for a button or something to turn it on. Not finding one, he tapped it.

"Hello? Ambassador?" Nothing happened. After a few seconds, he opened his mouth again when, to his surprise, Geogram's image appeared on the metal.

"Hello, Private Rabinowitz," he greeted with a polite nod, "or do you prefer Adam?"

Rabinowitz dropped the communicator and jumped back with a yelp. Slowly, he picked it up again. "Well, I'll be! What is this? A television?" He frowned. "But it's way too small to be a television, and it's in color!"

Rabinowitz flipped it over, trying to figure out how it worked, and noticed that Geogram's image switched sides whenever he flipped it. *Sweet!* He held the communicator up in the air to look at the bottom, and Geogram's image still appeared. It seemed to be tracking his face. Then he noticed that Geogram was staring at him, waiting patiently.

"Oh, hi!" Rabinowitz regained his composure. "Yes, umm. Are you asking me personally or in a military role?"

"That depends. Are you still willing to help us contact your government?"

Rabinowitz had been turning their previous conversation over in his head all day, and though he could still feel a tight knot twisting in his stomach, he'd reached a decision. He couldn't see any reason for Geogram to lie to him, but that didn't change the fact that he still knew next to nothing about him or his people. He had to ask. "How do I know that I can trust you?"

Geogram replied, "Have we given you any reason not to?"

Rabinowitz paused for a moment. He felt Geogram's sincerity and remembered how Dow "felt" he could trust the aliens, even before he met them. "Then I guess you should stick to Private Rabinowitz."

"Excellent. Where is Private Dow?"

"I don't think you can expect much help from him. He doesn't like getting involved." Rabinowitz wondered what had happened to make him that way.

Geogram's face drooped in disappointment. "That is unfortunate."

"Is there anyone else you think can help us?" Rabinowitz asked. There was a deep urge in his gut to help the aliens, but what could he do all on his own? If only Dow was here.

"Yes, we've scanned any and all potential allies. There are a few others whom we've deemed trustworthy. Your communicator should have our list; all you have to do is ask for it."

"Ask for it? Like, *show me the list*?" Immediately, a list displayed in place of Geogram's image. It included very few people he knew.

"Hey, wait a minute. Where did you get this list?" When he said this, Geogram's image reappeared.

"We scanned the reactions of the people inspecting the wreckage and bodies."

"But how did you get their names?"

"The same way we are talking to you. We left communicators in the debris."

Rabinowitz's body tensed. "So, you're spying on me?"

"No!" Geogram's eyes widened, and the color drained from his light purple skin again. "This communicator is *yours*. It has been programmed to respond only to your touch and voice. We cannot access it, nor can anyone else."

"*We?*" Rabinowitz repeated. "How many of you are here?"

"Including myself, there are six of us here on Earth."

"When do I meet the other five?"

Geogram turned to look at something—or some*one*—offscreen, then nodded. In seconds, the screen split and five other colorful, smiling faces appeared. Only one other had purple skin like Geogram, three were different shades of green, and the last was a vivid blue.

"Shalom. Welcome." Rabinowitz gasped, a little overwhelmed. "OK, so if I talk to these people, what do I tell them?"

The screen went back to showing just Geogram. His color had returned to light purple. "The truth?" He seemed perplexed by the question.

"*Oy vey,* that I met some aliens who want to talk to them? They're not going to believe me." Rabinowitz's heart raced. He realized he had raised his voice and quickly turned his head to check his surroundings, but he could see no one.

"I'll figure something out. How do I hang up?" As Rabinowitz said it, the screen went blank. *What now?* Maybe he would try Dow once more.

*

At breakfast, Rabinowitz slid the communicator over to Dow, keeping it covered with one hand. Dow eyed him suspiciously, but he reached forward, covering the communicator with his own hand and pulling it closer. He peeked under his hand and his eyes popped. The list was prominently displayed on the smooth metal, staring up at him. Dow shoved it back across the table to Rabinowitz.

"Are you crazy?" Dow hissed. "Bringing that thing in here."

"You know the army better than me. Who do I talk to? Do I go straight to General Jones?"

Dow huffed and whispered, "You ain't never going to get in to see the general. He has guards at his office."

"Who else then? If I contact the wrong person, this whole thing could fall apart. And the more people I try to contact, the more it's likely to go wrong."

"You're going to get yourself court-martialed. Leave me out of it." With that, Dow stood up, leaving Rabinowitz sitting alone at the table.

CHAPTER FOURTEEN

THE OLD WAREHOUSE

Charlotte "Charlie" Baker

ROSWELL, NEW MEXICO

Despite what Dad told me, I was determined to keep investigating. The next morning, before the sun got too high, Sandy and I headed back down the road to the ranch. We never made it, though. On our way there, we found a clue.

Sandy was the one who first spotted the tire tracks. They led down a side road that was supposed to be abandoned. No one had used it in years, and I would've ignored it if not for Sandy's barking. She was wagging her tail wildly, sniffing around at the mess of tracks. I suspected right away that it had to do with the crash, so we followed it to an old warehouse.

Sandy's behavior changed the moment we got close to it. She stopped her usual happy trotting and moved into what I called her "hunting mode"—low, deliberate steps with her nose working overtime. Every few yards, she'd pause and test the air.

We found a hiding spot behind a boulder, but I was puzzled when Sandy didn't lie down. Instead, she sat at perfect attention, dividing her focus between the guards and something else I couldn't see. Her tail gave the tiniest wag when she looked toward the building—not fear, but recognition.

"You know something's in there, don't you, girl?" I whispered.

Sandy's amber eyes met mine briefly, then returned to her watch. She knew we were onto something big.

I gave Sandy a treat and some water as we watched the building. We waited for about an hour, but the guards didn't move the whole time, and the sun was just getting hotter. I wouldn't learn anything if I didn't act.

I told Sandy to stay and wheeled up to the guards. They held their rifles across their chests and their cold stares gave me chills despite the heat. I held back a shudder.

My heart was racing, but I sat tall and tried to look as confident as I could. "I'm here to talk to the man in charge."

They exchanged a look.

"Do you have an appointment?" one of the guards asked. I wasn't sure if he was just humoring me or following his routine.

Without missing a beat, I replied, "Yes, I'm Charlie Baker from the *Roswell News*."

The guard sighed and made a show of pulling out a clipboard. He took his time, eyes scanning the page, then looked over it at me. "You're not on the list, kid. Go play somewhere else."

As I turned to leave, I noticed the long green limousine parked along the side of the building. It looked like the same one I saw at Johnny's ranch.

"Sandy," I whispered as I got back to her, "I wonder who that car belongs to. It must be the man in charge! Only important people have limousines, after all. I'll have to keep my eye out for it."

Sandy tilted her head, then licked my cheek. I giggled, pushing her away.

"I bet they've already finished moving everything here from the ranch, so there's no point going back to Johnny's for now. Maybe we should head into town." I rubbed Sandy's ears. "Let's go talk to Dr. Fisher, I'm sure he was there for the aliens. Mom and Dad don't believe me, but I know in my gut I'm right. What'cha think, girl?"

Sandy barked and gave me a doggy smile. I couldn't have asked for a better partner.

CHAPTER FIFTEEN

RABINOWITZ'S PLAN

Private Adam Rabinowitz
ROSWELL ARMY AIRFIELD

The only way Rabinowitz could get to the general was by going through the chain of command. On paper, it was easy, but as he stood at attention before Lieutenant Hansley's desk, Rabinowitz felt anxiety pooling in his gut. He cast a glance at the soldier who guarded the door to the general's office.

Even though Hansley was sitting, he was an intimidating figure. All of Rabinowitz's previous interactions with the man left him feeling childish and wrong-footed. Still, he had to try.

"Sir, I'd like to see General Jones," Rabinowitz said. "It's an urgent matter."

Hansley didn't even look up from his paperwork. "The general is not in. You can fill out your complaint and put it on the pile." He handed Rabinowitz a blank form and then pointed to a large stack of papers.

"It's not a complaint, sir. And I must see him right away. It's urgent."

Hansley ignored him.

Rabinowitz trembled with nerves. He clenched his fists into the sides of his fatigues to stop them from trembling. "How—how long would it take if I filled out a form?"

"If the general wishes to see you, he'll summon you when he's good and ready. *If* he wishes to see you."

"It really can't wait, sir."

Hansley shrugged.

Rabinowitz's shoulders sagged, but he folded the complaint form and put it in his pocket anyway. *What do I do now?* He wasn't sure. It wasn't like he could put what he knew about the aliens into a complaint form. Anyone could read it in the meantime, and General Jones might not even believe him. He slipped out the back door and found a quiet corner where no one could see him. There, he pulled out his communicator and whispered, "Ambassador Geogram."

After a slight delay, Geogram appeared. "Private Rabinowitz, what can I do for you?"

"I'm trying to reach General Jones, but he's not in his office."

"Indeed, he is not. He is currently in the large building where they have taken the decoy wreckage."

"Really? Can you take me to him?"

"The communicator will give you directions. You need only ask."

"Great, thanks. Um...I'm ready to hang up."

Geogram disappeared.

Rabinowitz put the communicator back in his pocket and walked around to the front of the building where he saw a row of jeeps. While he hadn't been to the old warehouse yet, he guessed it was too far to walk, especially in the mid-afternoon heat. He'd have to take one of the vehicles. *Could I?* If he got to Jones, surely the general would understand. And it would be far too suspicious to any guards if he were to show up on foot.

The base was mostly for training, so there were no guards. Rabinowitz looked from side to side as he calmly but stiffly walked up to a jeep, got in, and pushed the start button. He took out his communicator. "Give me directions to General Jones." Nothing happened. "Please," he added as an afterthought.

A map appeared, and Rabinowitz put the communicator on the dashboard. With one last nervous glance around, he drove through the gate.

Fifteen minutes later, the warehouse was just around the bend. He could see it in the distance, surrounded by temporary chain link fencing. Two guards were stationed out front, holding rifles. The communicator would raise questions if either of the guards saw it, so Rabinowitz snatched it from the dashboard and tucked it into his fatigues' breast pocket.

As he drew closer, he slowed down, feeling his heart thundering in his chest. *They'll know I'm not supposed to be here!* Not wanting to look suspicious, he stepped on the gas again, resuming a decent speed until he reached the gate. One of the guards approached.

"I have a delivery for General Jones from Lieutenant Hansley," he said with a level of confidence he didn't feel.

"Your name?"

"Private Adam Rabinowitz."

The guard glanced at his companion, who held a clipboard. When he shook his head, the guard turned back to Rabinowitz with a sneer. "You're not on the list." He noticed Rabinowitz's trembling and readjusted his rifle.

Rabinowitz's heart raced and he scrabbled for an excuse. Outwardly calm, he said, "When was that list updated? Lieutenant Hansley gave me these orders just before I left." He pulled out the folded blank complaint form, held it up, and put it back in his pocket.

The guard held out his hand. "Can I see those papers?"

Rabinowitz couldn't even remember deciding his next action. In a jolt of panic, his foot slammed down on the gas pedal.

"Hey, what are you—"

The guard was cut off as the jeep lurched forward. Rabinowitz's heart hammered, and for a moment he thought he'd got past them, but then a hand caught his uniform. The guard's muscled arm dragged Rabinowitz out onto the dusty road.

[The army Jeeps didn't have doors or seatbelts in those days.]

CHAPTER SIXTEEN

THE VET & THE GENERAL

Charlotte "Charlie" Baker

ROSWELL, NEW MEXICO

My next order of business was to interview the vet about why he was on the farm, so Sandy and I headed back into town. On the way to Dr. Fisher's office, I saw his son Robbie taking his terrier Marvin for a walk. Sandy ran over, so I made my way over to them, and the two dogs began sniffing each other in greeting. Robbie looked up.

"Hey, Charlotte!"

"Hi, Robbie," I said, but I didn't have much time for pleasantries. "Did you hear about the crash on Johnny's ranch?"

"Yeah, real wacky, huh? They're keeping it all hush-hush, but I heard Pa talking to Ma about it. The army wanted him to look at some bodies. He expected cows, but what they showed him was totally strange—tiny aliens! Would you believe it? They were dead, and the army folk were asking how."

Aliens! So I was right! "What did he find out?" I asked.

"Nothing much. He said they looked healthy. He guessed they suffocated since they were found in a tin can."

"How many were there? What did they look like?"

Robbie's eyes were wide in delight. I knew he was just as eager to share as I was to learn. "They gave Pa a right scare. Big heads and massive eyes like baseballs, though they were only this tall." He floated his hand in midair, about four feet high.

"And what happened to them?"

Robbie sighed. "He doesn't know. They asked him to leave when he was done."

"OK. Thanks, Robbie." It was something at least, but I doubted Robbie's dad would be able to tell me more. I'd just have to get the rest from elsewhere. Just then, I saw a long green limousine pull up to the diner across the street. It was the same car I'd seen at Johnny's ranch and the warehouse! An important-looking man in a crisp uniform got out and went inside the restaurant.

"Excuse me," I said to Robbie. I whistled for Sandy to follow me as I wheeled into the diner.

The man sat alone at a booth, reading the paper, maybe Dad's story about the crash. I stared hard at the front page, hoping to decipher which edition it was.

He lowered the paper, looking straight at me. "Can I help you, little lady?"

I was startled. How did he know? After I recovered, I thought that now was as good a time as any to introduce myself.

I pushed myself over to him and sat up straight. Sandy sniffed the gentleman, wagged her tail and then sat, which told me he must be a good man. "Yes, hello," I said calmly and confidently. "Are you the man in charge of the old warehouse?"

The man raised a single eyebrow as he looked at me and my press hat, and I could tell he was hiding a smile. It made me swell with the desire to prove myself. Did he think I was just a silly girl asking questions?

"And what do you know about that?"

I had to make a statement. "I know that the alien bodies and ship were taken there," I claimed, just to see his reaction.

The man smiled then, but instead of mocking, it was a warm, gentle smile. Not what I expected at all. "You seem to be well-informed, little lady. What's your name, and how did you come by this information?"

"I'm Charlie Baker from the *Roswell News.*" I held out my hand for him to shake. "And you are?"

"General Jones." He leaned over to grasp my hand firmly, letting go as the waitress delivered a plate of steak and potatoes. "You are going to make an excellent reporter someday, Miss Baker. But for now, I would like to eat my meal while it is still hot." From his tone, I knew he would not say anything more.

When I returned outside, Robbie wasn't there. Sandy trotted along beside me. "You hear that, Sandy? He said I'll be a great reporter!" I smiled, then I suddenly stopped and felt flushed. I turned to Sandy, who tilted her head at me and panted. "Did he admit that I was right?"

CHAPTER SEVENTEEN

KANSAS

Private Malcolm Dow

ROSWELL ARMY AIRFIELD

Dow jogged laps around the base, as he usually did in the evenings. He enjoyed the peace and quiet of the solitary activity, especially since Rabinowitz wasn't dogging at his heels, yapping about aliens. When he'd stepped outside, he'd briefly wondered where the other private was, but had dismissed the worry. Robin would show up later. He always did.

As Dow reached the furthest point from the buildings, the landscape around him wobbled. He slowed, dizzy and wondering if he'd pushed himself too hard, but as his vision cleared, he found himself in a room. It was brightly lit, which was jarring after the dimmed evening light, and Dow nearly bumped into a wall as he stopped short.

Two rows of what appeared to be silver desks and chairs filled the space. A multi-colored alien stood at each, staring at him intently.

Dow stared back. "I don't think I'm in Kansas anymore," he muttered. Geogram was closest to him, so Dow turned to him and asked, "Where am I?"

Instead of answering, Geogram looked at the other aliens. Dow followed his gaze. The blue man at the seat closest to the windshield bowed to him. "I welcome you to the bridge of the *Ymit*. Ymit, in your language, means Hope," he said in rehearsed English.

Dow nodded to acknowledge the blue man, then peered out the windshield. Right outside was his jogging path. "So," he said, "this is your spaceship? How did I get here?"

Geogram pointed. "You came through the door."

"Are you pulling my leg right now?" Dow asked, incredulous. There was no way that he'd just 'walked through the door'.

Geogram's eyes widened, and he glanced down at Dow's legs. "I assure you there is no leg pulling."

The two ladies—one blueish-pink and the other bluish-green—snickered.

"You might feel a little dizzy after walking through the phase variance," Geogram continued. "Perhaps you should sit down."

"The…what?" Dow looked at the doorway again. The desert was still there, but now he could see that there was a strange film stretching from corner to corner, like the skin of a soap bubble. He considered touching it, but held back.

"Joanua will explain," Geogram said, nodding to the blueish-green lady.

"Our ship is slightly out of phase. That is why you feel disoriented when you pass through the door."

"Oh." Dow blinked and tilted his head. "What does that mean, exactly?"

"Our ship exists in another…. What do you call it in your language…?"

"Universe? Dimension? Reality?" Geogram suggested.

Joanua continued, "…anyway, we no longer exist in your world, so we can't be seen or detected. Light, sound, and radar pass right through us."

Dow thought for a second. "If you don't exist, then how did I get here? I mean—how did I just walk in?"

"As I understand it, Joanua left the doorway partially in your reality." Geogram gestured to the engineer, who nodded.

Dow didn't understand and shook his head. "Were you here the whole time?"

Geogram nodded toward the blue man. "No. Captain Agugua set us down just a few seconds before you boarded."

"How? I didn't see or hear anything."

Geogram smiled. "All of our technology is built for defensive purposes. Being invisible is one of the ways we stay safe."

Dow had just about enough of this. "Right.... Well, I'll be leaving now." He headed for the door.

Geogram walked to intercept him and urgently said, "Private Rabinowitz has been captured."

Dow stopped, rubbed his eyes, looked up at the ceiling, then paced back and forth. He was still warm from the jog, but now his heart was racing for a whole new reason. What had that guy gotten himself into this time?

"I am sorry, we do not know anyone else whom we could contact."

Dow carried on his pacing. "How did it happen?"

"He went to see General Jones at the warehouse where they are keeping the decoy debris, but the guards captured him."

Geogram waved his hand toward the windshield, which turned into a screen and showed an aerial view of Rabinowitz driving up to the warehouse then stopping at the two guards. They began speaking, then the guards approached the truck. Dow shook his head as Rabinowitz tried to drive past them, only for the guards to yank him from the jeep. He turned away from the screen and continued pacing.

"Gosh darn it! What did you do that for?" one of the guards growled in the video.

"He must know something about the aliens. Tie him up, and I'll notify General Scornson."

"Scornson?" Dow stopped and his heart raced as he stared at the screen. The video had stopped when he spoke. "Not Jones?" He turned to Geogram, who nodded.

"Yes, our surveillance has revealed that General Jones is new to this base. Most of those who are frightened by our decoys are loyal to General Scornson and are sharing more information with him."

Dow stared at Geogram, alarmed. "They should be court-martialed!"

"What is court-martialed?"

Rabinowitz has been captured, and you want me to be a dictionary? "A military trial."

"What will happen to Private Rabinowitz?" Geogram asked.

Dow continued pacing. "Well, if they're not obeying their current commanding officer, they're not going to be nice. They'll most likely beat him until he tells them something. Then they might kill him and probably blame his death on you to generate more fear and hate."

All the Zalmen gasped and turned white.

"What can we do?"

"Not much. Not unless you want to get captured right along with him." Dow threw his head back with a sigh. "He got himself into this mess; he'll have to get himself out."

"But he is your friend," Geogram pleaded.

"He's not. He's just someone I saved from being beaten up once."

"So, why do you not wish to save him this time?"

"This time he got himself into his own mess. I told him not to go, but I didn't expect this." Dow avoided eye contact as he dashed for the door. "This ain't my problem. I ain't risking a court-martial."

Dow resumed his jogging pace as he circled the base, making sure not to go near the spaceship. The activity usually helped to clear his head but this time he couldn't get away from the voices that haunted him.

He must know something about the aliens. Tie him up.

Dow increased his speed so that sweat was soaking into his shirt, but he couldn't outrun the concern.

They'll most likely beat him until he tells them something. Then they might kill him….

Dow couldn't imagine bright-eyed Rabinowitz getting beaten, let alone killed in cold blood. Dow tried to convince himself he didn't care, but the image of Rabinowitz's trusting face wouldn't leave him alone. He wasn't the strongest soldier or the smartest guy, but something about him resonated with Dow. He'd seen the other private training. He always gave everything his all. It was endearing.

He'll have to get himself out.

But he is your friend.

Was he Dow's friend?

Why do you have to be so rude?…

…Please excuse my friend.

He might've wanted to be friends, but Dow never gave him that chance. He'd always rebuffed any attempt Rabinowitz made, treating him like a bother rather than a buddy. He really wasn't much better than the others. Dow increased his speed to a full-out sprint, trying to run from his thoughts.

He's just someone I saved from being beaten up once.

But that wasn't true. It was more than that between him and Rabinowitz. He'd just been too blind to see it. He remembered what Rabinowitz had said about him stopping the other soldiers from hitting him in the truck. At the time, he'd convinced himself that he'd been fighting back against the guys because he didn't like them, but deep down, he knew it was because they were bullies. Bullies picking on someone Dow was starting to care about.

He also couldn't stop thinking about the aliens. They were being bullied too, in a way. He remembered the video of the Moad ships attacking Zalma, displayed on the side of the spaceship. What would happen if they attacked Earth? Ignoring the problem would just lead to their destruction, and now that Rabinowitz had been captured, Dow was the only person who had any chance of making a difference.

Rabinowitz's face flashed in his mind - not scared, not begging, just disappointed. Like he'd expected better. The kid had looked at him like he was worth something—like he was the kind of person who did the right thing. Maybe it was time to prove him right. Dow slowed down, muttering curses. Swiftly, he spun around and walked the most direct route to where the ship had been. He was braced for the dizziness this time, but it was still jarring to suddenly be in another place. The aliens all turned to him and smiled.

"Private Dow, you are back," Geogram said cheerfully.

Dow kept his head down. "Yeah.... I'm probably going to be court-martialed, but I don't like bullies."

"Bullies?"

Dow shook his head and waved his hand. "We don't have time for that. If we're going to rescue Robin...Private Rabinowitz, we have lots of work to do."

"Excellent. Let me introduce you to the crew first. This is Captain Agugua." Geogram pointed to the blue man, who repeated his practiced greeting in broken English, starting with the formal bow.

"I welcome you to the Ymit..."

Dow interrupted, "Thank you."

"Our communications officer, Edugra, is on the captain's right." Geogram's smile was brighter as he pointed at her. "And you've already met Joanua, our engineer."

"Ladies," Dow greeted with a hand over his heart and a slight bow.

Edugra's skin flushed pink as she waved at him, and Joanua nodded respectfully.

"The last two are Kanara and Sarara. They have come to teach our technology to your people."

The couple bowed, which Dow returned.

Geogram turned back to Dow. "What would you like to see?"

Dow's military training kicked in. "I want to see everything that has happened at the warehouse since Robin's capture. Then I want to see everything since the crash. I'm looking for patterns, like when people come and go. Who the good guys are, who's bad, that kind of stuff."

"Of course. Why don't you have a seat." Geogram summoned a chair for him, which grew directly out of the wall. "Edugra will play the recordings you requested...."

Just then, a pocket door opened at the back of the bridge. Two children stepped in, clearly not seeing Dow, and went up to Kanara and Sarara. The taller one—a boy with greenish-blue skin—held a sheet of silver metal about the size of a notebook. "We have questions about our homework...."

Dow rose, causing the two kids to look over. The boy and the pink girl both froze and turned white; their mouths fell open.

"Whoa!" the boy said.

"Hello," Dow said in the voice he reserved for kids, "I'm Private Dow, but you can call me Malcolm."

The children both scurried into their parents' laps, but they were no longer white with fear.

"Takar, Janara," Kanara admonished the kids. "I thought I told you to stay in your rooms."

The girl gulped. "But you said that the Earthling left."

"Yes, well now he's back," Sarara said.

"Is he really back?" the boy, Takar, asked, eyeing Dow skeptically. "Is he going to help us?"

"I miss my friends back home," whispered the girl, so quietly that Dow almost didn't hear her. He felt a sharp tug in his chest. Yes, helping these people was the right choice. It's what his dad would have done.

Kanara stepped forward and put a hand on each of the children's shoulders. "Off you go. We will talk later."

The two kids nodded, then dashed out through the door with one last glance at Dow. He watched them go, then sighed as he turned back to the screen, which displayed the video of Rabinowitz's capture. He was in for a long night....

CHAPTER EIGHTEEN

DEBUNKED

Charlotte "Charlie" Baker

BAKER HOME

I set to work the moment Sandy and I got back home after our conversations with Robbie and General Jones. I wrote all about my discovery of the aliens crashing, their bodies being recovered, and all of this being hidden in the old, abandoned warehouse. When it was done, I had Dad's typesetter print copies for all my friends. I would have liked to add my pictures too, but I knew my Dad wouldn't develop them, and it would take too long to send the film out of town.

The next day, I saw the latest edition of Dad's newspaper. 'High-Altitude Balloon Crash-Lands in Roswell'. The newspaper was heavy in my hands, a lie printed in black and white, a truth he was silencing. It felt like a betrayal. "How could you print this?" I demanded, shaking the paper at him. *How could he do this?* Sandy whined and nudged me, but not even she could make me feel better.

Dad sat at the table, eating his breakfast. "That's what the army told me to print, and when they *tell* you to print something, you print it," he said matter-of-factly. He didn't seem uncomfortable in any way. He didn't even look up from his eggs. The fork scraped the plate like nails on a chalkboard. "You'll understand when you're older." *That* was the worst part—he sounded bored. Like my dreams were just a phase.

"But it's not *true*!"

At that, he looked embarrassed. "I know I've told you to report the truth, but sometimes it's more important to be a good citizen. And if you know what's good for you, you'll round up that story you printed and destroy it."

Tears began streaming down my cheeks. "Why should I?" My voice cracked, and I took a deep breath. "They'll never believe what a *girl* wrote." With that, I wheeled out of the kitchen as fast as I could to my bedroom and slammed the door.

I pulled the metal bar from my pocket. "I still believe in you, and I still know the truth."

CHAPTER NINETEEN

RESCUE

Private Malcolm Dow

THE YMIT, NEW MEXICO

The next morning, Dow stood, stretched, and yawned. Through the spaceship's windows, he could see the sun peeking over the horizon. "It's been a while since I pulled an all-nighter. So, you think this will work?"

Geogram nodded. "The computer estimates a seventy-six-point-three percent chance of success."

"That low? Never mind, I can work with that. How much time do we have?"

Edugra checked her console. "Private Rabinowitz, Robin, is scheduled to be picked up in twenty-seven minutes."

"That's not a lot of time," Dow said. "We'll have to move now. Are you ready?"

The Zalmen nodded.

"OK, let's do this."

Dow peered out from behind a tree down the warehouse driveway. "Hey guys, I need your help over here."

The guards sprinted toward Dow, so he ducked back into the invisible space van. It impressed him how quickly the landscape zipped by. A second later, they were in front of the warehouse door. Stepping out of the space van, he carefully opened, entered, then closed it. The hallway was empty, and none of the doors were labeled, but he knew exactly where to go; they'd planned it all out. He walked to the second door on the left and put his communicator over the padlock keyhole, and it unlocked. Dow took the lock and went inside.

Rabinowitz's hands and feet were tied up, and he had tape across his mouth. Dow winced. That would hurt coming off, but he had no choice. He held his finger to his mouth to tell Robin to be quiet, then yanked the tape off in one swift movement.

"Ow!" he yelped, then laughed. "What took you so long?"

Dow grinned back and bent down to untie him, shushing him again. They didn't have much time. Once Rabinowitz was free, Dow peeked out of the closet. Just then, one of the guards came into the hall and saw them. Dow ducked back in and whispered to his communicator. *"Activate sound cannons."* Then the racket began. It sounded like machine gun fire outside pelting the doors, and the guard took cover. Dust blew under the doorways.

Dow and Rabinowitz ran down the hall away from where the guard was aiming at the door. When Dow turned around, they were already at the end of the hallway. He followed much more cautiously, staying low to the ground as the machine gun sounds persisted.

Dow was unconcerned about being hit, knowing that it was just noise, and Rabinowitz seemed to trust him enough to follow his lead. Dow slammed open the doors at the end of the hall and stepped out into the middle of the warehouse, which was full of crates of the decoy's debris. On the far side was a closed door, which he knew led to Jones's office.

About half a dozen scientists were huddled under their desks. One still held a piece of the debris he'd been examining. Another screamed as a fresh wave of dust blew under the warehouse's exterior doors. They didn't even notice as Dow and Rabinowitz slipped behind them. The privates dropped to the floor just to be sure. It stirred up some of the dust, and Rabinowitz had to hold back a sneeze. They were halfway to the office when the sounds of machine gun fire ceased.

"Your ride must be here," Dow observed.

"My ride?" Rabinowitz asked. He was slow, wincing minutely with every forward shuffle.

"They were going to take you to General Scornson, a former commander of our base."

"What about General Jones?"

"He should be in this office."

They made it to the door on hands and knees, reached up to turn the knob, then crawled into the office, but did not see the general at his desk. The door closed, and they heard a gun cock behind them. Glancing over his shoulder, Dow saw someone standing behind the door. A gun was aimed right at his head. "General Jones, sir?" Dow asked tentatively. He turned around, keeping his movements slow and predictable.

The man didn't lower his gun. "And you are?"

Dow gulped. "Privates Malcolm Dow and Adam Rabinowitz, sir."

"The two AWOL privates."

"With all due respect, sir, we were just trying to get a message to you," Rabinowitz said. His eyes were wide, and he looked bleached from the cleaning chemical fumes in the closet, but his voice was steady.

"What could be so urgent that you risk being court-martialed, and how did you get in here?"

"I arrived yesterday, but your guards tied me up and put me in a broom closet overnight."

"In a stolen jeep?" Jones asked.

Rabinowitz's face flushed with embarrassment. "Borrowed, sir."

"I arrived a short while ago to rescue him before they sent him to General Scornson," Dow explained.

"And I am to believe you, why?" Jones asked.

"Because the aliens want to meet with you, sir," Rabinowitz said.

Before Jones could say anything, they heard a knock at the door. Jones motioned with his gun for the two privates to hide behind the desk. Dow crawled so that he could still see the general but not the door.

"Enter," Jones said. The guard that had followed them down the hall came in, and again Jones closed the door, pushing his gun into the guard's back. "Yes?"

"Are you alright, sir?"

"I'm fine. What's all the noise about? Who's firing at us?" Jones asked.

"I don't know, sir. We couldn't find anyone or anything causing it."

From his angle behind the desk, Dow could see Jones smile briefly before he put on a mask of rage. "You couldn't find it!?" Jones roared at the guard. "And you came in here empty-handed!?"

"Sorry, sir!" The guard's voice shook.

"I've called for backup, so try not to screw things up before they get here. Understood?"

"Yes, sir!"

"Get back out there and don't come back without results! Dismissed."

The guard took a quick look around the office before he left. After the door closed, Jones looked out the blinds and then decocked and holstered his gun. "You can come out now. It looks like you're telling the truth. He didn't report any intruders, and yet he was obviously looking to see if you were here. What made the gunshots?"

"A sound cannon from a spaceship, sir," Dow answered. "It projected the sound while causing the appropriate vibrations. It worked much better than I expected."

Jones raised a single eyebrow.

"What do we do now, sir?"

Jones circled to his side of the desk as Dow and Rabinowitz came out from behind it. Jones signaled them to sit as he did. "This location has been compromised. We go mobile, into the desert." He rubbed his chin. "They tied you up for trying to talk to me?"

"Yes, sir."

"Scornson and I have never seen eye to eye, but to plant spies on me? To order soldiers to attack one of their own? Who does he think he is?" He scowled, but then his red face faded and his eyes widened, like a kid in a candy store. "Never mind that now. Tell me about the aliens. If I remember correctly, you two were the first to discover the bodies."

Rabinowitz beamed. "Yes, sir! But those were just dummies, clones. When we went to pick up debris away from the crash site, we met one for real."

Jones cocked his eyebrow again. "Did you now? And those creatures were clones, hmm?"

"Yes, their ambassador said that they were grown in a lab, like plants."

"Fascinating. That would explain why the autopsy revealed no obvious cause of death, and why the doctor thought they were never born. I wish I could tell him that he's right! Alas, protocol." Jones stood and paced behind his desk. "Tell me more about them."

Dow and Rabinowitz locked eyes briefly. "They're pacifists, sir," Rabinowitz said.

"Pacifists, with advanced technology. The kind we wouldn't want our enemies to have, correct?"

Dow's eyes popped. "How did you know, sir?"

"Why else would they drop an obvious refugee decoy above the nuclear test site, but not steal anything?" Jones smirked. "They're obviously wanting our protection from whomever is attacking them."

Rabinowitz turned to Dow. "It looks like your hunch was correct."

Jones looked back and forth between the two of them. "Hunch?"

Dow closed his eyes and tilted his head to the ceiling. *What's Robin doing? The general's going to think I'm nuts!*

"Yes, before we saw the alien, Dow sensed them, and then said they were friendly."

"Very good." Jones waited for Dow to make eye contact, then smiled before continuing. "Now, what are they willing to give us in exchange for our help?"

Dow and Rabinowitz looked at each other. Rabinowitz answered. "Their technology, sir."

"What kind of weapons do they have?"

Dow frowned. "None, sir."

Jones stopped and stared at Dow.

"But they brought a married couple to teach us their advanced technology. They have tools that can be converted into weapons, but no weapons ready to go. Shame, too. I really wanted a ray gun."

"None? How could that be?"

"They didn't even have a word for weapons, sir. They want us and our weapons only as a backup plan, but it's our negotiators they're interested in," Dow said.

"Negotiators?" Jones paused. "As long as they're willing to teach us their technology so we can defend Earth, I'm willing to help them in any way I can. How many of them are here?"

"On Earth? Six, sir," Dow answered, deciding to keep the children secret for the time being. "Do you think the president will agree, sir?"

Jones seemed to be holding back laughter. "We already talked, and he wasn't impressed. I suspect he's more concerned with what the public would think if they found out he's dealing with aliens."

Dow nodded. "Yes, there is enough division between people already. Between blacks and whites..."

"...and Christians and Jews. Not that I'm a practicing Jew, I'm currently rebelling. You don't seem to be bothered by it, though. Why?" Rabinowitz asked.

Jones hummed. "What, you being a rebel and stealing a jeep? That does bother me, but we'll talk about that later." He chuckled. "But the division between people? Blacks and whites? Christians and Jews? I don't understand it."

Jones paused, then cleared his throat. "I've lived long enough to know that it's not a person's appearance or religion that's important, it's their actions. Anyway, I asked the president whether he would rather deal with these aliens or with their enemies. That got his attention, and he reluctantly agreed to ally with them and put me in charge of this..." he looked at them intently, "...*Top Secret* project."

The two privates gave verbal confirmations.

"Good. Now, when am I going to meet these aliens?" Jones asked.

Rabinowitz pulled out his communicator. Jones looked on curiously. Rabinowitz smirked. "Connect us to Ambassador Geogram."

Geogram appeared on the communicator. Jones's eyes popped, and he raised *both* eyebrows (a rare occasion for him). His astounded gaze darted from Rabinowitz, to the communicator, to Dow's grinning face. A moment later, he recovered his composure.

"General Jones had it all figured out," Rabinowitz said.

Geogram crinkled his forehead, then nodded. *"Stimulating. Let me speak to him, please."*

Rabinowitz handed the communicator to Jones, who took a moment to admire the device. "Fascinating!" He looked at

Geogram. "General Frank Jones here. I understand that you are the ambassador for your people?"

"Yes. Ambassador Geogram, at your service."

"I can appreciate the precautions you took to protect yourselves. I can get you the help you need to defend your planet and negotiate, and I understand that you are prepared to teach us the technology to defend ours."

"Indeed, we are hoping to negotiate peace with our invaders, the people of Moad. What have Privates Dow and Rabinowitz shared with you?"

"They haven't shared much. I'm a military strategist, so I figured it out on my own. They just confirmed my suspicions. However, I do have one question left unanswered. How did you know that you could trust Privates Dow and Rabinowitz, as well as myself?"

"Our technology can detect such things as lying, fear, and hatred. We gave Private Rabinowitz a list of people who have worked with the debris that our technology has identified as 'safe'. He picked you to contact first."

Jones smiled at Rabinowitz. "A wise choice." Then he turned to Geogram. "I have already spoken with our president about helping you, and I have compiled a list of possible recruits for you and Corporal Dow to check out with this technology."

Dow jolted. "*Corporal* Dow?"

"Yes. I'm promoting you two, and you will report directly to me. Dow, you are in charge of recruitment. Your first job is to test everyone on this base. We can't have anyone here who is afraid of aliens or isn't one hundred percent committed to working with them. Rabinowitz, you're my new clerk."

"Thank you, sir," Rabinowitz said.

Dow's heart throbbed. "Thank you, sir, but you do realize that I'm black, sir?" Immediately, his eyes opened wide as he realized how stupid that sounded. Rabinowitz let loose a laugh but quickly regained his composure.

"Exactly! And anyone who won't accept you is certainly not going to accept aliens. You can eliminate anyone who reacts negatively to you before you even open your mouth. If they pass that test, you ask them if they think aliens are friendly. If they pass that test as well, you tell them to report to me for a top-secret mission, which is the truth."

"Yes, sir...."

Jones turned to Geogram. "Ambassador—I think it's high time we meet face to face."

PART 2:
RYAN'S NEGOTIATIONS

CHAPTER TWENTY

AN UNEXPECTED CALL

Ryan Wilcox

NEW YORK, NEW YORK

[A young diplomat in New York was about to get the call that would change everything.]

Ryan Wilcox tilted his head from side to side, dabbing thick foam across his cheeks, his usual morning ritual. Standing in front of the mirror in the bathroom of his one-bedroom apartment, the usual hustle and bustle of New York carried on outside his window. He set down the brush and flipped open his razor, slid the blade with practiced ease through the shaving lather.

The day started like any other day. Overcast, thick clouds painted the city in gray tones. It probably would rain later into the afternoon, but for now, the streets were dry.

He patted his cheeks and applied aftershave, then set out into the kitchen, expecting the kettle to be whistling for his morning coffee. A shrill ring filled the living room instead. With a sigh and a longing glance at his comic book and empty mug, he took the handset off the wall.

"Hello?"

A deep voice crackled over the line. "Mr. Wilcox?"

Wilcox's heart raced, and he nearly dropped the phone. "Mr. President?" he asked.

"Yes," the president replied in a serious, commanding tone. "I have an important ambassador position for you and your assistant."

The president has a position for me! Wait.... "What?" His voice cracked, his throat suddenly dry. Swallowing, he hurried to answer. "I mean, thank you. But I thought you said I'm too young for anything big."

The president cleared his throat, which sent a wave of static over the line, like someone crumpling paper into the mouthpiece. "Yes.... Well.... This is a unique situation. Top secret. You won't be able to tell your friends or family where you are going. Are you OK with that?"

"Um.... Yes sir, but where am I going?" Wilcox asked.

"There's not much I can disclose over the phone, but know that should you accept, you'll be negotiating with a foreign government. They are currently under siege, and they need our help to defend themselves. I'll have a car pick up you and your assistant on Monday morning to take you to the airport."

Wilcox nodded, then realized the president couldn't see him. "Yes, sir! Thank you, sir!"

Without even a reply from the president, the line went dead. Wilcox stared at it a moment as the raspy dial tone buzzed from the receiver, much like the buzzing in his own head.

What could be so important that the president would call on a Saturday? He couldn't help but picture himself being escorted through the unmarked hallways of a secret military base, or perhaps being driven to an obscure location by men in suits. "And where am I going?" he asked aloud to the room. No one answered, obviously, as he lived alone.

Just then, the kettle shrieked, and he almost tripped over the twenty-five-foot coiled phone cord as he dashed to the kitchen and turned the burner off. Grabbing the steamy handle of the kettle, almost burning himself, he moved it on to a cool burner. The whistling stopped.

The phone in his hand still buzzed with the raspy dial tone. T*he president is sending a plane for me and my assistant on Monday. I should probably let Donna know.* Sticking his fingers into the dial, he spun it in the familiar pattern of her number.

CHAPTER TWENTY-ONE

ON A HOT DESERT HIGHWAY

Ryan Wilcox

ROSWELL, NEW MEXICO

[I wish I could have been there to see Ryan's face when General Jones told him about the aliens.]

"You want me to make an alliance with *aliens*? Did I hear that right?" Wilcox couldn't have been more shocked if General Jones had dressed up like a rubber chicken drenched head to toe in iced lemonade.

Not that the general seemed like the type to do that. Wilcox recognized him, but only in passing. A friend of his father's, most likely.

Wilcox's assistant, Donna Warren, sat next to him, her legs crossed daintily and her hands in her lap over his traveling briefcase. Cpl. Dow wore sleek glasses as he drove.

They were sitting in the back of a black stretched limo, not one of those ugly green army ones a general usually rode in. The two rear bench seats faced each other. *This must really be important.*

They were driving through what Wilcox could only describe as the middle of nowhere. Realistically, he knew they were somewhere between the Albuquerque Municipal Airport and their unknown destination, but when he looked out the window, he only saw dirt, sand, and a few green shrubs.

Jones leaned forward, gaze steady. "Yes."

The word snapped Wilcox's attention back to the man across from him.

"You *must* be joking!" But the seriousness in Gen. Jones's tone and the firm set of his face told Wilcox that he wasn't. "How do I form an alliance with an alien race?"

"How did you negotiate the peace treaties?"

The familiar weight of self-doubt settled in Wilcox's chest as he cringed. "…I didn't. I gave my suggestions to the older and more competent men. They are the ones who negotiated the treaty!" *How could anyone think that I'd done all that? I'm only twenty-six!*

"I disagree. Yes, they did the negotiations, but they used your work. I'd say none are more competent than you, Wilcox. You are the son of one of the *best* ambassadors we have, but this requires a younger perspective." The general smiled.

Wilcox caught a twinkle in the general's eyes. *Oh no, what did my dad say?*

"Your father tells me you've been negotiating since you learned how to talk. He says your mother could never say no to you about anything."

"I can vouch for that," Donna said, jumping in with a matching twinkle. She grinned with the same smugness of a cat eyeing a vat of cream. "Well…since middle school, anyway. I helped him practice for the debate team. There wasn't an argument he couldn't win."

Flashes of endless afternoons spent together played behind his eyelids like a film at the cinema. "Yes, but—"

Jones interrupted him. "You learned several foreign languages and cultures from your father's placements. You have a master's degree in politics." He paused. "Yes, you were a junior negotiator when you started, but you worked your way up, and the only things keeping you from being called senior negotiator are your babyface and your age."

A pinch of annoyance raced down Wilcox's spine at the mention of the familiar nickname. *How'd I get stuck with Babyface, anyway?* He shook himself.

"The president himself has noticed how hard you've worked, and the senior members of your team recommended you for an ambassador position when you're older."

Wilcox's eyebrows shot up. "They *did*? They didn't tell me that. —But that doesn't change anything! In Paris, I was one of many. Who do I have now?" *I can hardly negotiate an alliance with an alien race without a team. Are there more negotiators already at their base, or am I going in alone?*

Donna gave an exaggerated gasp. "*Um!*"

Wilcox barely glanced at her. He looked back at Jones, hoping to find all the answers in the man's lined face.

"In Paris, you were negotiating with multiple countries. Obviously, we can't bring in a lot of people on this. You've mentioned several times that you want an ambassadorship. This is the only way you are going to get one at your age. Your multicultural experience and love of space and science fiction makes you uniquely qualified for the job. The president and I thought you would *jump* at the chance." Jones sighed.

Wilcox suddenly felt sick. *What if I fail? What would that say about me—about my father?* He couldn't blow his first big chance. "I need more time to think it over. Is it possible for me and Donna to speak in private?"

"Sure," the general said. He glanced over his shoulder through the divider window. "Corporal Dow, stop the car, please."

Dow, eased the limo to the side of the road. The moment it stopped, Wilcox threw open the door and stepped out.

"Let's go for a walk," he said, holding the door for Donna. Beyond seeing one of her feet leave the car, he didn't wait. He was already walking away at a quick pace, hands sweaty and shaking. Only subconsciously did he register Donna's hurried footsteps behind him, and her grunts and grumbles about the desert.

He didn't even speak for the first ten minutes, lost in his own head. Then, he turned to her and felt a spark of guilt at seeing her ruffled form, but brushed it aside and asked, "So, what do you think?"

Donna threw her hair back. Wilcox could tell she hadn't been expecting to walk anywhere. She wore a yellow dress and cream-colored heels—he winced at the thought of her keeping up with him in those. She would wear an outfit like that to the office, not trekking across the desert. At least she'd left his briefcase in the car. No need for her toting *that* around on top of everything.

"I was as shocked as you were at first," she admitted, "but it does sound interesting, and I think you're well suited to it."

"Well suited to negotiate with aliens?" He gaped at her.

"You know what I mean."

Yes, he did. They'd been friends for over twelve years now, and she knew him better than anyone else. Wilcox sighed and kept walking, a little slower this time. "How am I supposed to negotiate with aliens? It's never been done before."

"If anyone can do it, you can," Donna assured him.

It wasn't until she grabbed his hand that he realized it was still shaking. Her nails were painted a shade of red to match her lipstick.

"Maybe...." He thought about it, turned the assignment over in his head a few times. A fresh wave of worry washed over him, filling his gut with dread.

Nope! he told himself. *Too many things could go wrong. The senior negotiators are right. This is too much for me right now.* "No. I'm sure there's someone else better suited to the job. I'm far too young to be the only one on this assignment!"

Donna frowned at him, annoyed, but then her face turned into a reassuring smile. "You won't be alone; you have me, and we've been an unstoppable team since our first year together, remember?" She locked elbows with him.

"I guess we *do* make a great team." He hummed softly.

"Of course we do," Donna said. "Remember our junior year when we practiced every afternoon, so you'd be prepared to face Theo Turner in the school's debate tournament finals?"

"Yes," Wilcox said.

"So...will you take the position?"

"This is a big step. I don't think they'll accept me." He pulled away from her and stalked forward again, hands gesturing wildly in the air. "No one *ever* takes me seriously! You know what it's like. In school, we were all the same age, but in the real world, no matter how good you are, they'll always take it better from an older man!"

"Listen to yourself. All I'm hearing is you flapping your lips, and you know what's coming out? Bupkis. If you're trying to argue your way out of this, know that I know all your tricks!" Her hands were in the air, too—in exasperation. "Maybe you should grow a beard, so they don't call you Babyface."

Wilcox stared at her for a moment, mouth agape. He rubbed his chin. *Is that why they call me that?* "Maybe," he said. "But I'm not a rebel."

Donna nodded sharply, then groaned. "I can't go any further with these shoes." She lifted one of her feet to rest it, shifting her hips.

Wilcox winced in sympathy as he looked at her shoes again. A quick glance at his wristwatch told him they'd been walking for half an hour. Half of that, he wasn't even talking! He felt the need to apologize, but it wouldn't do much about her foot pain. "So, you think I should do it?" he asked her again, just to make extra sure.

Donna stared at him incredulously. She tipped her chin down in another affirmative nod. Wilcox took that as a 'yes'.

"OK, you convinced me," he said, ignoring Donna's sigh. He laughed. "Maybe *you* should be the ambassador."

"Very funny, wise guy." Donna shifted her weight to the other foot, nearly stumbling over. She caught herself on his shoulder. "Do you think they can bring the car? I don't think I can walk that far back."

Wilcox twisted back around to face the limo, which happened to be considerably harder with Donna hanging off him. "We need a ride!" he shouted across the desert.

He saw Cpl. Dow raise two hands to cup his mouth. The man must've been yelling, but Wilcox couldn't hear. "They are not getting into the car. They must not want to drive on the desert sand. I guess I wasn't thinking when I bolted out of the car. We should have gone along the road." Wilcox sighed. "It looks like we are going to have to walk back. Here, take my shoes; it's the least I can do for making you walk all this way." He knelt down on the ground to unlace his shoes, feeling the hot sand burning through the fabric of his pants.

"Your shoes won't fit me, but thanks."

Wilcox tied his shoe back up, and they were walking back when the landscape shimmered, and he swayed, a little dizzy. The desert around them continued to blur—like a mirage. For a moment, Wilcox wondered if they'd been out in the sun too long, and if he got heatstroke. He'd had it before—once, as a kid. He didn't remember much from the experience, only that it *wasn't* like this. For one, neither he nor Donna had been slurring their words through that entire conversation, nor did he feel confused.

Another step forward, and suddenly they were somewhere else. His head throbbed, blood rushed through his ears, and his stomach felt like it had decided to take a vacation down to his left ankle. But that wasn't the weirdest thing. Not at all.

A bald man, mauve in color, stood right in front of him, wearing a funny foil robe. Another man, this one bright blue, sat at a floating desk, staring out at the desert through a window. Donna gasped, so at least Wilcox knew he wasn't the only one going crazy. *Oh,* he thought, *these must be the aliens.*

To be fair, when Gen. Jones said *alien,* Wilcox hadn't been expecting them to look like this. As much as they didn't look like they belonged on Earth, the men in front of him could've just been bald, short humans covered head to toe in body paint, but Wilcox knew that wasn't the case. The way he held himself so confidently told Wilcox *exactly* what he needed to know: This man wasn't from Earth, and they were on a—*spaceship*?

The mauve alien stepped forward. Wilcox thought he must've been about Gen. Jones's age, but the only indicator of such were the deep lines in his face. He had no hair, and everything about him was mauve—his skin, his lips, his eyes. "You asked for a ride?"

Wilcox noticed that the alien's teeth, which were exposed when he spoke, were familiar and white. He felt himself nodding, and glanced at Donna, whose mouth had dropped open, so he snapped his own shut.

The mauve alien nodded and turned to the other alien. Through the window, Wilcox could see the desert landscape fly by in a blur, and suddenly they were at the limo. Jones and Dow were back in the vehicle, and it drove forward, but the spaceship they were in passed them and lowered to the ground.

A few seconds later, the blue alien tapped his desk a few times and said something in a foreign language. *"They are on board,"* the computer translated. Then he rose and turned to them, bending forward at the waist in a formal bow.

"I welcome you to the bridge of the *Ymit.* Ymit, in your language, means Hope. I am Captain Agugua. It is an honor to have you with us." Unlike the purple one, he had a deep and thick accent that Wilcox couldn't decipher. His words were stilted, like some foreigners he'd heard speaking English in the past.

Wilcox bowed. "Thank you. We're glad to be here."

Agugua returned to his seat. The ship began moving again, startling Wilcox once more with how fast and smoothly they moved.

The purple alien spoke in a light tone. "Mr. Wilcox, Miss Warren, I am Ambassador Geogram. It is a pleasure to meet you." He bowed to them.

Not knowing what else to do, Wilcox and Donna returned the bow.

"You might feel a little dizzy after walking through the very strong electromagnetic field that makes us invisible." Geogram paused for a moment.

Wilcox felt like he couldn't breathe. His pulse quickened in fear.

Geogram raised his forehead and quickly added. "No need to worry; short-term exposure does not harm you in any way."

Wilcox sighed. *That's a relief,* he thought and glanced around the ship. The captain said they were on the bridge, but Wilcox couldn't figure out how he flew the ship by tapping his desk. It didn't look like the bridge of any ship he'd been on before. More like a classroom, though the desks and chairs were magically floating.

Wilcox turned to Geogram. "Pardon me for saying so, but you speak English better than I expected. I've been to many foreign countries, and I have to say, I can't even hear an accent." He couldn't help his eyes wandering to the captain as he said this. If the ambassador could speak fluent English, that certainly put some of his worries at ease.

"Thank you. I have been listening to your radio transmissions and watching your television for many years. The rest of the crew learned to speak it on our journey here." Geogram extended a hand toward Agugua. "Except for our dear captain, who said he is too old to learn a new language."

Agugua turned briefly with a smirk. The desert blur in the windshield became an army basecamp with several tents and army vehicles spread out before them.

Wilcox saw a line of army vehicles on one side next to a large barracks tent and a training field. Some soldiers were out doing drills, and Wilcox's heart went out to them for exercising in this heat.

"Welcome to Area Two." Geogram smiled as he held his hand toward the ship's pocket door, which opened on its own. Wilcox and Donna stepped out onto the ground.

The temporary nausea wasn't that bad the second time, and it sure beat walking. However, when Wilcox turned back to the ship, his jaw dropped. There was no ship. So he reached out, then jumped back in surprise when his hand vanished right off the end of his arm. *Holy—!*

Donna tapped his shoulder and pointed to the nose of the general's limo appearing out of nowhere. The rest appeared as it drove off the ship. Wilcox heard something pathetic, a few gasping syllables, and it took a few seconds before he realized the sounds were coming from him.

The limo parked, and Jones stepped out, the corners of his lips upturned in amusement. "Mr. Wilcox."

Wilcox snapped his mouth shut again and composed himself. He looked at Donna, who looked back at him, her lips pursed in thought. He knew this expression well. She always did it when unsure about something. Unsure, but excited. Wilcox smiled at her.

"This ought to be fun. Are you ready?" he asked.

Donna nodded, and they took the first step toward the general.

Gen. Jones seemed completely in his element, despite wearing a neatly pressed suit out in the middle of nowhere. The Area Two basecamp wasn't much to look at. Just a few tents, one nearby marked for Jones to use as his office. Dow had gotten out of the car as well and stood next to Jones, who Wilcox noticed carried his leather briefcase.

"Did you enjoy your ride?" Jones asked as they approached.

Is that a teasing smirk? I never expected to see General Jones acting so casual! Maybe the startled look on my face is more amusing than I thought. "Was I...." Wilcox began, only for Donna to glare at him. He coughed. "Um, sorry.... Were *we* just on a spaceship?"

"Yes," Jones said, "how did you like it?"

"Um, it's fast! I didn't have time to enjoy it."

The general's smile widened, like he expected that answer. "So, are you in or out?"

"I'm in."

"Good. You'll need this, *Ambassador* Wilcox." Jones offered the briefcase. "Let's go talk before you meet with them. We thought you would be more comfortable negotiating on our home turf."

"*Home turf*? You mean *desert sand*." Wilcox laughed lightly, trying to calm his nerves. They'd just been set on edge again. The others laughed with him, which made him feel better.

Jones took them into the military tent marked for himself. It was plain, like any old tent, with a foldout table in the middle, surrounded by four chairs, one of them occupied by Cpl. Rabinowitz looking at his communicator. A cabinet sat to one side, and the table had a single beige file.

Seeing the general, Rabinowitz put the communicator in his pocket, stood, and saluted. "General."

Jones returned the salute. "At ease. Corporal Rabinowitz, meet Ambassador Wilcox and Miss Warren."

They greeted each other and shook hands.

Jones joined Rabinowitz on the far side of the table. Wilcox and Donna took the available seats. Wilcox popped open his briefcase and withdrew a notepad for Donna and several pens, which he set on the table between them. He accepted the file that Jones slid across the table for him and flipped it open, exposing about a dozen papers. Wilcox scanned a page and then passed it to Donna.

As a woman, she normally wouldn't even be invited to discussions like this, but he'd always thought that view was silly.

She was just as clever and skilled at debating, yet she wasn't allowed to join the team—so he tried to include her as much as possible. He knew the others in his field looked down on his methods, even his father to some extent, but he and Donna made a good team, so he kept it that way.

They were halfway through the file when the general began speaking.

"You should know a few things. First, the aliens are from a planet called Zalma, and we are calling them the Zalmen. They are pacifists, which means they know nothing about fighting. That also means they need all the help they can get against Moad—the planet that's attacking them."

Jones was silent for a while, so when Wilcox finished the page, he looked up and nodded.

Jones continued. "In exchange for our help, they'll be giving us their technology and teaching us how to use it. Obviously, their technology is very advanced. They have no weapons, but I'm sure that our people can re-purpose their tools into weapons so we can defend Earth."

Beside him, Donna scribbled away in shorthand at a speed Wilcox couldn't even hope to accomplish. "Not that I would imagine doing this, but what's stopping us from taking their technology and not helping them?"

"The same thing that tells me that you are not serious," Rabinowitz said. He tapped his glasses. "Zalmen technology can detect things like lying and hatred. They gave us these glasses to help us recruit people who are safe."

Wilcox's heart thudded with excitement. "Really? There is technology in those glasses?"

"Yes, and in this communicator." Rabinowitz pulled out the polished metal rectangle he'd been fidgeting with as they'd walked in. Wilcox got a closer look. It was small and slightly bigger than a playing card, and the notion that it could be used in any way similar to Wilcox's home rotary phone was almost unbelievable.

Donna leaned forward. Her eyes flashed with curiosity. "How does it work?"

"Voice commands. *Communicator, show me the list.*"

Donna, who'd reached for the device on the table, drew her hand back with a mild gasp of surprise as words appeared on its sleek surface.

Wilcox saw it had a list of names, some of which were crossed out and others with small check marks next to them. He recognized his own at the very top. "If this tiny thing is a communicator, could they be listening to us right now?"

Rabinowitz shrugged. "They could, but Geogram assured me that this one will only respond to me."

"And you know that he is telling the truth from the glasses that he gave you?" Wilcox guessed.

"Well, I didn't have the glasses yet, but he didn't change color when he originally told me." He paused, frowning. "No...wait. He turned white, but he was probably worried because I accused him of spying on me."

"Wait, wait...*change color*?"

"Yes, that's how they evolved into a peaceful society, or so he tells me," Rabinowitz said.

"How's that?"

"I don't know the specifics, but their color shows their emotional state. Red and yellow indicate anger. I think one of them blushed, so I am not sure what that means."

Wilcox leaned back in his seat, tapping his fingers on the table thoughtfully. "We turn red when we're angry or embarrassed, too. More blood flows to the skin, and it turns red, so, I would guess in both cases it is an emotional response, good or bad. But I don't know how the yellow fits in."

"And the greenish ones are scientists," Jones said, matter-of-factly. "They also become greener when they're thinking."

Wilcox frowned. *So much for having that figured out.* "Thinking is not an emotion," he said. "And we saw a blue man on the ship. What does *blue* mean?"

"You said yellow indicates anger, correct?" Donna asked, looking at Rabinowitz, who nodded. "Well, in the theater, when they want to create yellow lights, they mix red and green."

"So, angry means they're emotional, as indicated by the red; and thinking, as indicated by the green," Wilcox guessed. *That could work. And if that's true, then....* His mind cycled through the possibilities.

The general, however, didn't seem as impressed. "How does that help us with *blue*?"

"Simple," Donna said. "It's not there." She grinned to herself, but when she saw the blank expressions of all three men around her, she had to stop herself from rolling her eyes. "When lighting, there are three primary colors: red, green, and blue."

Wilcox understood. "So, you're saying that when he is angry, he has no blue."

"Possibly."

"So, blue might indicate tranquility, peace, or something like that?" Jones asked.

"It's possible. Why don't we just ask them?" Wilcox looked at Rabinowitz. Clearly, he knew the most out of all of them.

"I already did," Rabinowitz admitted. "They said it's not polite."

"Polite or not, it's my job to ask," Wilcox said. "What else do I need to know?"

Rabinowitz muttered into his communicator, then spun it around so Wilcox and Donna could see that the image changed to a video of a gleaming city. The sky above the city was filled with thundering explosions. Before Wilcox could marvel at the clear, *colored* image, Rabinowitz spoke. "Their planet is protected by a deflector. We would like to have them here as well."

Wilcox stared at the screen, eyes wide. He leaned back, looking up at Rabinowitz again. "What else?"

"Their invisibility?"

"And we don't want to store this technology on Earth," Jones added.

"What? Why not? Where would we store it then?" Wilcox asked.

"Their technology is beyond anything humans could dream of at this point. We don't want to risk it falling into the wrong hands. As for where to store it—we were thinking we'll be the only ones with spaceships, so we would like them to help us set up a base on the moon."

That, Wilcox could understand. He'd seen what technology could do in the hands of bad men. He'd never been a foot soldier, never one on the front lines, but every time he heard about things happening overseas during the war.... He shuddered to think about it. "So, you want me to negotiate a moon base? What could I offer them in exchange for all this?" Awash with nervous energy again, he stood and began pacing the small tent.

"For one, you'll be going to their planet as a negotiator."

Looking the general in the eye, Wilcox couldn't tell if he was serious. "I'm *what*!?"

"The president did inform you that you couldn't tell anyone where you were going, right?"

Wilcox cleared his throat. "Well, yes, but I expected it to be somewhere on Earth."

"I guess we should've discussed that first. Are you OK with traveling to their planet? They want to negotiate peace with the Moadites."

Wilcox leaned over his seat. "So now I'm not just negotiating with these pacifist aliens, I'm negotiating with their enemy as well!?"

Jones smiled. "Yes, but don't worry; I'm also going and bringing a team of military experts. You won't be on your own."

"Ah, so, we're trading manpower for technology?"

"Yes," Rabinowitz said. "They have brought instructors to teach us their technology. Their names are Kanara and Sarara, a married couple with two children. They're a swell family." He smiled.

"So, we are trading warriors and negotiators for teachers?" Wilcox addressed Jones. "What about this moon base? What are we giving them for that?" No one spoke. "Anybody?"

"I guess you're going to have to figure that one out," the general said.

"*Great!*" Wilcox grumbled. "Any *more* good news?"

Jones hummed, thinking for a moment, then shook his head. "No, I think that's it. Are you ready to meet them now?"

"No!" He wasn't. However, the others in the tent did not look impressed. He sighed. "Oh, alright." He readied himself for his first *real* conversation with an alien.

[Learning to read Zalmen emotions through their skin color was like learning a whole new language. It took us months to really understand all the subtle combinations, but it made negotiations so much more honest than anything we'd ever experienced.]

Wilcox had been prepared to go somewhere else for the meeting. It turned out that they were staying there in Gen. Jones's tent. He smiled to himself. *Small victories.* At least he didn't have to walk anywhere. He and Donna had moved to Jones's side of the table and were whispering together when Geogram stepped through the door with Edugra at his side.

Wilcox stared at her bald head for a moment. He'd never seen a bald lady before. She held herself in that elegant way that only ladies could, and her form was slimmer than Geogram's, though mostly hidden by her shapeless silver robe. Even more surprising, though, she looked to be around his and Donna's age. Donna, who must have noticed his staring, elbowed him.

"Hello again," Geogram said. He turned slightly to the lady. "Allow me to introduce our communications officer, Edugra."

Together, Wilcox and Donna stood, smiling at her. "Welcome."

Both aliens bowed. *That must be how they greet each other,* Wilcox thought. *Or perhaps it's just because we're being formal.* He and Donna bowed back, nonetheless. Then the four of them sat down.

Wilcox shuffled his notes. He hoped to hide the fact that his hands were sweating; his heart raced in his chest. "Well...we didn't have much time to talk when you gave us a ride earlier, so I would like to welcome you to Earth." He reached across the table to offer a handshake.

Geogram accepted the handshake. "Thank you. It is an honor to meet you. We have heard great things about you, Ambassador Wilcox."

"Thank you." Wilcox leaned back and adjusted his suit jacket. His hands shook for a moment longer, but then he cleared his throat. *I'm ready.* "Shall we get to it?"

Geogram and Edugra nodded.

"So, I hear you already have the basics worked out. We are providing a negotiations team, consisting of myself and Donna, and General Jones is providing a military team."

Geogram and Edugra nodded again.

"In exchange, you are providing technology, training, and a moon base. Is that right?" Wilcox watched them both intently, wondering how they would respond.

Wilcox knew that the moon base was not offered; he was testing their skin color theory, and as expected, Geogram and Edugra were confused. They exchanged looks, and both rapidly changed color. Wilcox held back a gasp. Rabinowitz wasn't exaggerating when he said they changed—they *really* did. Geogram's skin finally settled on a sharp yellow. The lines on his face were dark and deep as he glared at Wilcox across the table. "That is a lie, and you know it!"

Wilcox stifled a laugh and donned his best poker face. "What am I lying about, and how do you know?"

"We did not agree to provide a moon base. Our technology tells us you are lying...." Geogram's skin turned light green. "But now I realize that you already know that, and you were testing us."

"Yes, I was," Wilcox said mildly. "I have to say, if you are going to use technology on us to tell if we're lying, it's only fair if we're able to know when you're lying, too."

The light green faded from Geogram until he turned almost completely white, like someone had dusted him with flour. "You can tell our emotional state by the color of our skin."

"That's what I heard, but how does that help me? I don't know what the different colors mean. Please, enlighten me."

"It is not polite to ask," Geogram said sharply, yellow once again.

"If you won't tell me, then we aren't equal." Wilcox's smile became stiff. "I refuse to continue the negotiations until the matter is resolved."

As he waited, Geogram turned yellow, then seemed to cycle through several shades of green, and flashed bright red before settling on white. Wilcox tried not to stare. He kept his eyes firmly on Geogram's face. Interestingly enough, even though his skin changed, the alien's eyes stayed the same mauve that they'd been when he walked in.

"It is hard for us to speak about it," Edugra said softly, jumping in. She glanced at Geogram. "As communications officer, may I speak, Father?"

"*Father?*" Wilcox asked.

Geogram nodded firmly. "Yes, Edugra is my daughter. We were observing Earth communications together, which is why we were both assigned to this mission."

They do look similar, now that I think about it. He hadn't seen it before, but now that he knew they were related, he could see that they shared some features—the roundness of their noses, the shape of their chins. He'd just replayed Geogram's words in his head when something clicked. "Wait! You were receiving our communications on Zalma? What communications?"

"Your public television and radio," Geogram said. "Why?"

"How? Those signals weren't meant to leave the city, never mind the planet."

"We have one of our probes in your orbit, relaying the signals," Edugra explained.

They're hovering in our orbit without our knowledge? Wilcox tapped his pen for a few seconds. "Hmm.... Did you do the same thing to Moad? Did you spy on them, too?"

"We didn't intentionally *spy* on them, but yes, we were monitoring their public broadcasts as well," Geogram admitted.

"That's probably why they attacked you. No one likes to be watched—especially without their knowledge." His heart dropped into his stomach as a new thought suddenly occurred to him. "Were you transmitting our signals back to your planet while the Moad attacked you? Do they know where we are?"

"No! The probe would only transmit when we wanted it to, and it never did while the Moad were at our planet."

Wilcox sat back. "Oh, good! Now, where were we?" His eyes wandered toward Edugra. "Ah…. You were going to tell us what your skin colors mean?"

Edugra straightened. "So, it's all fairly simple. Red is when we are emotional. Green is when we are thinking. Blue is when we are having pleasant thoughts such as home or family. Our other colors are created when we feel combinations of those."

Wilcox didn't have to look at Donna to know that she was grinning. He did anyway. She was. Of course she was. She was right.

"OK, so what do yellow and white mean?" Wilcox asked.

"Yellow is made up from red and green, so we are emotional and thinking. That means we are angry. White is a combination of all primary colors."

"So, you're thinking and emotional about family. In other words, you're worried. Thank you for telling us," Wilcox said. The Zalmen only nodded. "One last thing—what color means you're lying?"

With a giggle, Geogram said, "Bright green. It is a dishonorable way of thinking. We do not make a habit of it. Only our young children lie, but they quickly learn that it does not work."

Surprised that Geogram had volunteered that information so freely, Wilcox glanced at Edugra, who blushed. He had to remind himself that Edugra was Geogram's daughter.

"Thank you both for that. And I am sorry I got upset. Let's get back to some simple negotiations. We're willing to provide my negotiating skills and General Jones's military manpower. You're willing to provide us with technology and knowledge?"

Geogram nodded. "That is correct."

"I'm going to need numbers. How much manpower will you need, and how much knowledge will you provide?"

Geogram, who'd just gone back to his natural color, changed to cyan, then white as he considered the question. "We don't know anything about war. We don't know what we need, but we are willing to provide you with whatever you require to make the Moad stop attacking. We hope you can negotiate peace before any actual fighting occurs."

"I'll do my best. How technologically advanced are the Moad? Are they like you?" He waited, but Geogram stared at him blankly. "OK, I'll ask a simpler question. How long did it take you to get here?"

This time, Geogram answered immediately. "About five of your months."

"But there are no stars that close. You'd have to have been traveling faster than the speed of light, and that's impossible."

"Not impossible," Geogram disagreed and turned light green. "Why would you say that?"

"Einstein's theory of relativity states that nothing can travel faster than the speed of light. It's something to do with gravity."

Edugra giggled as if Wilcox had said something cute. "We don't know Einstein, but we have technology that modifies what you call gravity, so those rules no longer apply."

"You can modify gravity? Holy mackerel! Good to know! Will you be teaching us this?"

"I'm certain Sarara would be willing to give a lesson on that, yes."

"So, you don't know what kind of technology the Moad have? And you don't know how long you will need our warriors, either?" Wilcox looked back at Geogram, who shook his head. "But you will provide transportation both ways, right?"

"Correct."

"So, you want us to send our warriors for five months in each direction. Let's just say it's almost a year round-trip, and they would stay for one to three years each, and then rotate home. You should probably plan for one or two trips a year. Does that sound OK?" Wilcox asked.

Geogram nodded and smiled.

"So, is it safe to say that you will keep training our people on how your technology works for as long as we are protecting yours?"

"Yes. That sounds reasonable to me," the other ambassador said.

"Great, and I understand that a family will be staying on Earth to teach our people your science and technology. Kanara, Sarara, and their two children?"

"Yes."

"Great," Wilcox said. "So…back to this moon base. Why don't you just give it to us?"

If Wilcox expected Geogram to change color again, he was disappointed.

For the first time, Geogram's face showed no expression. "Are you testing us again? You know that is not fair, so why do you ask?"

"Because that is my job," Wilcox replied. "I'm supposed to get the best deal I can for my people."

"Even when you know that it's wrong?"

"That is my job."

"Do you like your job?" Geogram inquired.

"I love my country."

"That doesn't answer my question."

"Of course it does. It's how things are done on Earth. Both sides want the best deal for themselves, and negotiations go back and forth until we settle on what's fair."

"But we are dealing with you in good faith, so what would you consider an *acceptable* trade?"

"It isn't my job to tell you what to ask for. What would you want for it?"

"What would be an equitable trade?"

Wilcox felt the blood pumping through his brain, beating on his temples, trying to get out. *Does my dad ever feel like this when dealing with people? Does Geogram really not understand how to trade? Are he and his people really that content with what they have?*

Does Earth have that little to offer? He turned to Donna and Edugra. "Can you help us out here?"

Edugra thought for a moment. "While my father and I were doing research, we enjoyed your radio and television shows...."

"Maybe we can work something out," Wilcox suggested. He tilted his head, considering the options. "I'm sure we can get you some records. I don't think the networks would appreciate you tapping into their signals. But what about stories?"

"Entertainment is very valuable to us humans; it seems valuable to you as well. How about movies and books?" Donna suggested.

Geogram frowned. "Like home video? User manuals?"

Wilcox shook his head. "No, like fiction, autobiographies, history."

"What is fiction?" Geogram asked.

"What do you mean, 'what is fiction?' Made-up stories."

"Lies?" Geogram looked and sounded aghast, emphasized by the way his entire face had turned white as a sheet.

"No, not lies. Dreams, fantasies, and entertainment. Just like on the television."

Edugra paled to match her father's white. "Do you mean the people on the television are not real?"

Wilcox wasn't even sure what to say to reassure her, or what to reassure her about, so luckily, Donna jumped in. In her soothing way, she said, "Some of what you see on television is talking about real events. It's called the news. But other shows tell stories, and most of those are made from someone's imagination."

"What is imagination?" Geogram changed to green so quickly Wilcox almost got whiplash.

"You don't know what imagination is either?" *How do I even explain that?* "Well, imagination is like thinking of where you will be in ten years, pretending you are the President of the United States, wondering what you'd do if you were a rich man, even flying through space! Although...that one is looking more plausible now."

Donna giggled.

"Why would you think of things that are not real?" Geogram asked.

"Sometimes to learn," Donna smiled softly. "Like Pinocchio, the wooden boy. Every time he told a lie, his nose would grow."

"How can a boy be wooden?" Edugra asked, still white, though flashes of green were rippling across her skin as well. "And how could a nose grow?"

Donna laughed. "That's the beauty of it. It's magic. *Pinocchio* is a story to teach children not to lie."

"Children's noses don't grow. They change color when they lie," Geogram said pointedly.

"Not on Earth, they don't. We don't change, so that's why we need stories like that. To show why it's wrong to lie."

"What a stimulating concept." Geogram seemed intrigued. "You mentioned magic. What is it?"

Donna leaned back in her chair, thinking. "Magic is...a supernatural power...or something that you don't understand. Most people would call your invisible ship magic."

"Our ship is not magic; it is technology."

"Most magic is just technology that we don't understand yet," Wilcox said. "So, someone who doesn't know how it's possible for something to be invisible will call it magic.

"Come to think of it, doesn't the development of technology require imagination? How did you develop these technologies without imagining them first?"

"We were taught the technology." As soon as the words left his mouth, Geogram's eyes widened and his skin flashed rapidly between purple, teal, and pasty white. "Please, tell me more stories."

However, Wilcox could tell when someone wanted to change the subject. "*Taught* the technology?" he pushed, frowning. "By whom?"

"That is a good question for another time," Edugra cut in.

Wilcox glanced at Edugra, then back at her father. The aliens seemed nervous for some reason, not only because of their complexion, but because Wilcox could see a thin trail of sweat working its way down his forehead. *They sweat? Interesting....* Wilcox wasn't a scientist at heart, but he wanted to ask.

"Please, tell me more stories," Geogram repeated.

Wilcox, suspicious of the aliens' deflection about their technology, could already tell that the other ambassador would not answer. *Better to save it for later.* He wouldn't be getting that kind of answer out of him anytime soon. Instead, he looked at Donna, wondering if she had another example for the aliens. Stories had been an interest of hers since middle school.

She did. "Humpty Dumpty sat on a wall. Humpty Dumpty had a great fall. All the king's horses and all the king's men couldn't put Humpty together again." As she finished, both aliens turned indigo.

The ambassador heaved a breath. "That is a sad story."

"It's not a real story," Donna said. "It's a basic nursery rhyme."

Geogram's eyes widened, and he blinked owlishly at her. His baffled expression almost made Wilcox laugh, though he stopped himself from losing his composure.

"It's to teach children that sometimes when things break, they can't be fixed," Wilcox explained to the two confused aliens.

"So, you tell lies to teach your children lessons?"

"Not lies, imagination!"

There must've been *something* in Wilcox's insistent tone, because Geogram seemed to be considering his words thoughtfully rather than dismissing them. He cycled through colors again, this time much faster—so fast that Wilcox averted his eyes in fear of an oncoming headache.

"Do you have more examples of this *imagination*?" Geogram finally asked.

"Ah…yes, I read this on the plane." Wilcox fumbled for a moment with opening his briefcase on the table to retrieve a comic book from under his business papers. The front depicted a dark-haired man in a hero suit holding up the front of a bright yellow car with one hand. The words *Adventure Comics* took up most of the top left corner, and a blocky title of 'Superman' took up the right. "And he's an alien, just like you."

Curiously and with tentative fingers, Geogram took the comic book. He flipped through it like it was a precious artifact. Then he looked up. "May I borrow this?"

"Sure."

"I believe this is an ideal time to break for the day. Here is a communicator for each of you." Geogram reached into his pocket with his free hand to retrieve two communicators and handed them over. The devices looked identical to Cpl. Rabinowitz's. "I will call you on it when I'm ready to meet next, or, if you prefer, you can ask it to call me." Then Geogram stood and left the tent, clasping the comic gently.

Wilcox remained seated, unsure of what to say. He turned to Donna, but the two ladies were out of their seats and leaving the tent as well, chatting.

CHAPTER TWENTY-TWO

SCORNSON

Charlotte "Charlie" Baker

BAKER HOME

A few days later, I was in the front room reading a book about space I'd gotten from the library. Research, of course, but I was distracted by a roaring engine from outside. I looked out and saw two army jeeps pulling up. A grumpy old man, dressed like General Jones, got out of the second vehicle and approached. His name tag said *Scornson*. Was he also a general? A chill raced through me even though it was boiling hot outside.

There was a knock on the door and my dad answered.

The man (General Scornson, I guessed) loomed on our porch. "You wrote about the crash at the ranch?"

"Yes," Dad said.

"Where did they take the wreckage?"

Shouldn't he already know about that? I wondered. I hid my face behind my book, pretending to be immersed. Gathering information was an important skill for all reporters, and I just knew that something was wrong about this army man.

"I don't know," Dad said.

"Did anyone see which way they went?" Scornson questioned. He was being very forceful, like he thought Dad was lying.

"Not that I'm aware of. What's this about? I mean, your army has it. Why don't you read the reports?" Dad asked.

"I just took over at the base and am trying to fix the mess that I was left with."

"What happened to the previous commander?"

"Never you mind! And don't print a word of this!"

"Very well then. Goodbye!" Dad closed the door in the man's face. I peeked out the window.

General Scornson was storming away, his face also red. I watched the jeeps. *Oh!* The guards in the second jeep were the same ones from the warehouse the other day. I thought they were supposed to be working for General Jones. Just then, I noticed a young blond man in the other vehicle driver's seat was looking at me intensely. His stare made my blood ice cold, and I ducked back behind the curtain. General Scornson got in the vehicle and snapped at him. They drove off with a squeal of tires.

But why would a new general be here asking about General Jones? Something was definitely afoot, and I was going to find out what! Leaving my space book in the front room, I called Sandy and snuck out of the house, heading to the warehouse again for some fresh clues.

[That blond soldier's stare still haunts me. Little did I know we'd be seeing him again.]

CHAPTER TWENTY-THREE

DOW MEETS CHARLIE

Corporal Malcolm Dow

EARTH–ZALMA BASECAMP, NEW MEXICO

Dow darted up to Gen. Jones panting. "General, someone is approaching the old warehouse." He handed his communicator to Jones. It displayed an image of a young girl in a wheelchair. Next to her was a golden retriever.

"That's the reporter girl, Miss Charlie Baker." Jones smiled. "Did you see the newsletter she printed?"

Dow shook his head.

"Shame. She's one smart cookie. She knew we had the crash debris at the warehouse, and she figured out we had Dr. Fisher in to perform an autopsy on the clones."

"Really, sir? How?"

"She has a keen eye for mystery. I'll look at what other information we have on her, but for now, I think I'll send you to talk to her. Keep an open com channel so I can listen in as well," Jones said. "I'll ask the Zalmen to take you there now."

"Yes, sir."

"And do you have that thing in your ear so I can talk to you, and she won't be able to hear?"

"Yes, I do."

"Excellent. Make it so."

*

When he arrived at the warehouse, Dow saw the dog sniffling around outside, but the girl was nowhere to be seen. Agugua set the ship down a little ways away from the fence, and Dow stepped off.

The dog whined and barked twice. It was looking up at him curiously. Just then, one of the main doors opened, and Charlie came out of the building. She pushed her wheelchair over to the dog and rubbed its ears. A moment later, she noticed him.

"Hi, I'm Corporal Dow," he introduced himself. "I have orders to take the copies of the story you wrote."

"No," she said, and he was surprised by the ferocity in her young face. "That story is mine, and I won't let you cover up the truth!" She glanced around at the desert landscape. "Where did you come from, and where did everyone else go? This place is empty."

"We can't stay in one place for long. *Someone,*" he said pointedly, "wrote a story about us being here, and there are bad people out there."

It was clear right away that she hadn't considered that. She flushed bright red. "Sorry about that...." she said. "A grumpy old soldier was asking about you. Is he one of the bad people?"

"I can't answer that."

"You know you made a mistake with that weather balloon story."

Dow crinkled his forehead. "What mistake?"

"If you're working with aliens, you want the public to warm up to the idea," she said. "Lying about it will just upset people."

"What makes you think that we're working with aliens? And if we were, why would we want the public to warm up to the idea?"

Charlie smiled. "I talked to General Jones a couple of days ago. He's a nice man. He's not the kind of person they would send in if they wanted to kill the aliens. Not like the guy who came into town today. And you want the public to warm up to the idea because you can't keep them secret forever. Once the public meets the aliens and finds out that you've been hiding them, they won't be happy. You have to leave breadcrumbs."

Dow forced himself to look stern. "I'm going to ask you again for the copies of the story you wrote and all your notes."

"Or what?"

"Your dad knew *or what*. He did what he was told to do. The army can confiscate everything you have. They can discredit you so that you won't be able to get a job as a news reporter anywhere."

"My dad didn't have the information I have. I don't have much to confiscate, and I'm a girl. I can't get a job as a news reporter, anyway."

In the earpiece, General Jones chuckled. *"She's brave, not afraid of aliens, but she was afraid of the guards that were there."*

"You act brave, but I can see you are scared. Just like you were scared when you talked to the guards."

"I'm not scared, and I wasn't then, either."

"No, you are not scared of aliens, but you are afraid of the army."

"And how do you know?"

"She has a communicator in her pocket that she picked up at the crash site," Jones said.

"You took something from the ranch. Something that didn't belong to you," Dow said.

"I didn't take anything. What are you talking about?"

Dow pulled out his communicator. "Look familiar?"

Charlie turned pale for a second, but then she regained her composure. She pulled hers from her pocket. "This? This is nothing. It was a scrap piece of foil when I found it. Hey...wait a minute. Are you telling me that you've been using this thing to spy on me?"

Dow watched her for a moment, gauging what to say.

"It provided me with a summary of her personality," Jones supplied.

Dow nodded. "In a manner of speaking, but it wasn't me, and spying is a strong word."

"Well, who then, and what word would you use?" Charlie demanded.

"Assessing...Interviewing...," Jones suggested.

"I can't tell you who, but I would say it was interviewing you," Dow said.

"Interview me? For what?"

"I have an idea. Let's hire her—an intern position, of course, due to her age. She has already proven her tenacity and wit. I believe she would be excellent for recording the facts of this momentous project," Jones said.

Dow considered this. "General Jones was impressed with you. We don't have a lot of people who we can trust, but he told me he had a good feeling about you. If I told you the truth, could you keep it a secret?"

She shook her head. "I'm a reporter, that's not what I do."

"How about keeping it secret *for now*?" Dow amended.

"For now?" Jones asked Dow.

"How long?" she asked.

"You realize that could be decades, don't you?"

"Just until we deem it safe to reveal the truth to the wider world. So, what do you say, Miss Baker? Would you like to record history?" Dow asked.

"Record history?" She tilted her head for a second. "Excuse us for a minute. Sandy," she called to her dog and turned away from Dow. He waited patiently as she whispered something to the retriever. The dog shook its body, and Charlie turned back around to face Dow. "Tell me more."

"If she accepts, get a verbal contract from her to keep it secret," Jones told Dow. *"Communicator, can you record her promise, and play it back to her?"*

Dow heard and then muttered an affirmative and focused back on the young reporter. "Before we go further, I'll need a verbal contract that you won't go around sharing this information. I'm sure you know that."

"And what if I promise but can't keep it a secret?" she asked in a challenging tone.

"She will be treated like all our other employees. Sharing top secret information, even by accident, would get her removed from the team," Jones said.

"If you tell anyone, then you'll be kicked off the team. No more recording history. No more learning about what really happened," Dow said.

Charlie was quiet for a long moment, pondering. Finally, she said, "So, what you are saying is that if I can keep it secret, I can see what's happening and record it all? And one day I'll get to share it with the world?"

"Yes."

"But how would this work? I'm still in school."

"I'll have an office building close to her home. She can tell her parents she is a research assistant," Jones said.

Dow repeated this to her, then she snarkily asked, "Aren't you worried about hiring a person in a wheelchair?"

He snickered. "General Jones doesn't judge people on their appearance. He sees what a person *can* do, not what they can't."

"I wish more people were like him."

"So do I."

"Will I be interviewing people? Are they going to meet me there?" she asked.

"We'll get the details sorted out later. Now, are you in? Can you keep a secret?" Dow asked.

She shrugged and fidgeted for a few seconds. "Yes, I can keep a secret. I'm in."

"Not so fast," Dow said, still smiling. "We still need the verbal agreement. Take out that metal bar, hold it out like a mirror, say your name, and repeat our agreement."

"You're kidding me, right?" she asked.

Dow didn't answer.

She held her communicator up, checked her reflection, fixed her hair.

"I, Charlie Baker, agree to keep the aliens a secret."

As her communicator played the recording back, she turned white in alarm. When the recording stopped, she dropped the device and faked fainting.

Dow chuckled.

She straightened and picked up the metal bar. "What is it?"

"The aliens call it a communicator," Dow said.

"So you *have* been spying on me!"

"No one has been spying on you. The communicator just observed and only reported what it thought we needed to know and what it thought you wouldn't mind it telling us."

"What do you mean 'thought'? This tiny thing can think? And what did you need to know?" she asked.

"It told us that you are not afraid of aliens and you are a good reporter. Is there anything else we need to know?"

Her face turned red. "Is that all you told them?" she demanded of the communicator.

Her eyes popped, and she read something on the communicator. She flipped it over, read some more, then flipped it and read again. "How?"

"Alien technology, so don't show it to anyone. That's all you need to know for now. We will be in touch," Dow said.

"Alien technology? This little thing?" She looked down at the device in her hand.

Dow took the opportunity to step back onto the Spacevan.

Sandy whined and barked twice. Charlie raised her head. "Corporal Dow?"

Dow signaled the pilot to back up a bit.

Charlie and her dog went to where Dow was standing and saw a single set of footprints—nothing before or after.

She asked her dog, "How did he do that?" After a few seconds, she said, "Ah.... Alien technology."

CHAPTER TWENTY-FOUR

THE ALLIANCE

Ambassador Ryan Wilcox

EARTH–ZALMA BASECAMP, NEW MEXICO

"Ryan?" Donna called from just outside his tent.

He looked up. "Come in." As Donna entered, he could see a wide grin on her face.

"I think I'm friends with an alien!" she announced.

Ryan laughed. "*Guest,*" he corrected. "The general wants us to get used to us calling them *guests* so we don't slip if we are in public."

Donna ducked her head sheepishly. "Sorry, but I just had to tell someone! Edugra and I have been spending time together for the past few days—"

"Yes, I know," Ryan cut in.

"Let me finish. We've been spending time together, I just had the most wonderful conversation with her, and as I walked back it dawned on me—we're *friends.*" Her grin widened. "Actually *friends.*"

"I see. So what did you talk about, if you don't mind me asking?" He invited her to sit at his small table and sat himself on his cot, creasing the tight folds.

"Well, it seems as if we aren't so different after all. We are close in age and both of our fathers are ambassadors."

"So is mine." He smirked. "All *three* of us are so similar. What else?"

"We both love listening to music and can't wait to hear each other's favorites. When Edugra and her dad listened to our radio broadcasts, she liked Doris Day and the Glenn Miller Band. And just like us, she loves 'You Are My Sunshine', though she thinks it's a little sad. Also, I showed her makeup, though *that* went belly up real quick because she kept changing color and nothing matched, so we discussed boys instead. She then told me all about Zalma, and growing up there, so I think I know what to expect when we go," Donna rattled off.

Ryan balked. "When *we* go? So, you're definitely going, then?" he asked.

"Of course, Ryan. I'm your *assistant*. Where you go, I go." She nodded firmly, leaving no room for discussion.

"Right."

Donna winked at him. "Didn't think you'd get to leave me here alone, did you? You get an ambassadorship and suddenly you're a hotshot? I don't think so."

"But what will you tell your family?"

"What have you told yours?" she countered.

"I'm out on a top-secret negotiation and will be in touch. My parents are used to it, but your family worries if you don't check in every other hour."

Donna shrugged. "It isn't that bad. I'll just tell my parents we're on a secret mission together. They know I'm safe when I'm with you."

Ryan sighed, but secretly, he was overjoyed that Donna was coming with him into space. He'd been in meetings with Geogram and Edugra for the past two days, same as her, but in between had managed to meet some of the other soldiers who were going and found that he had very little in common with them. All they wanted to talk about was cars, guns, sports, combat, and dames. That wasn't a surprise, but he felt better going with someone familiar. "Alright. Now, back to your bonding experience with Edugra. Anything we can use?"

"There are no gender wars on their planet—no racism. They picked mostly male leaders for this crew because they figured from our broadcasts that's what we're used to. They have just as many lady leaders as men, and the ladies don't try to be men. They lead in their own unique way. Isn't that wonderful?"

"Definitely peculiar," he replied, though he was less engaged in the conversation than earlier. His thoughts were lost in musings of space itself rather than foreign politics. He dealt with politics every day. "Anything else?" he murmured.

Donna frowned at him suddenly. "I'm not going to *spy* on her if that's what you mean, but if there is essential information that comes up, I'll let you know."

Ryan nodded. "Thanks, Donna." He paused. "Have you spoken with any of our other guests?"

Donna sighed. "Sarara's been busy with her kids, and some Cameron guy is taking over all of Joanua's time, so it's just me and Edugra. Not that I'm complaining! I like her."

Ryan felt the same. His mind flashed with images of the other two female Zalmen, then the males. None of them brought the same spark of interest he felt when he thought of Edugra. He'd have to find some time to spend with her.

The past two days were the most unusual of Ryan Wilcox's entire negotiating career, perhaps even the most unusual of his entire twenty-six years of life. He wore one of his best suits, briefcase in hand, as he entered the small spaceship that came to be known as the Spacevan. Today they were going to see the president, and he would present the fruits of his first truly important assignment.

He greeted Captain Agugua, who touched his control pad a few times. Wilcox saw through the windshield that the ship rose above the base camp; the landscape blurred, stopped outside Wilcox's New York apartment, then blurred again, stopped at the White House, and then descended into the garden.

"Wait! I thought you were going to scan my apartment so you could duplicate it for my room on your ship."

Agugua spoke in Zalmen, and the computer translated. *"I did."*

"Oh." Wilcox then walked off the invisible ship. He scanned his surroundings, noting where he had to return to: between the red and white roses. He reached back just enough to see his hand disappear, then stood straight again.

President Whitmore called from the other side of the garden.

Wilcox met him at a picnic table. "Mr. President."

Whitmore shook his hand. "Ambassador Wilcox."

Wilcox put his briefcase on the table and pulled out the alliance papers. They had discussed them over the communicator, but the president wasn't one for signing something without reading it first.

Whitmore scanned the pages, occasionally pausing while his lips moved. "So, what are they like?"

"Sir?"

"What are the aliens like? I haven't met one yet." Whitmore continued to read.

"There's one in the spaceship. I can introduce you if you like."

Whitmore shook his head. "No. I trust you and Frank…sorry, General Jones. I want to be able to honestly say that *I have not met an alien* as long as possible. When the Earth Council forms, I'll meet them with the rest of the world leaders."

So he wants plausible deniability? I guess that's fair; he's under far more public scrutiny than the rest of us.

Whitmore took the pen that Wilcox held for him. "Just like we discussed." Whitmore finished signing and then handed the papers back to Wilcox, along with an envelope. "Please deliver this to General Jones."

Wilcox smiled. "I will." He put the papers back into his briefcase and the two men shook hands. "Thank you, Mr. President."

"Thank you, Ambassador."

Wilcox entered the general's tent.

Gen. Jones looked up from his paperwork. "Good morning, Ambassador. You've been in and out of meetings for the past two days. Have negotiations been going well with our guests?"

"Yes, sir." Wilcox lifted his briefcase onto the table. "They've been good, and we've signed the alliance. It's been…a unique experience, to say the least." As he spoke, he opened the case and pulled out a stack of papers: copies of the alliance. He sat and slid them forward for the general to see.

"Oh?" The general reached for them.

"Well, sir. The Zalmen do have a sense of humor, but you have to explain the joke to them." Wilcox recalled the day before, when he'd walked in on Donna trying to explain the concept of *why did the chicken cross the road* to Agugua. "The jokes they tell are very dry, but that's because they have little creativity. No imagination. No sense of adventure. No fiction."

"Interesting." Jones hummed thoughtfully. "How does that help us?"

"Well, you know that entertainment is a thriving industry. On Zalma, they have no means of creating it, which is why they were retransmitting our broadcasts. They want more—more books, records, and movies. Of course, the more violent content will have to have a warning, as they are pacifists. But it's the only physical thing that we have to trade with them."

"Fascinating. So, what are we trading with them for?"

"We give them one copy of all the music and stories that have been published in our country, and they give us a space base."

"A space base? Not a moon base?" The general leaned forward, resting his elbows on the table.

"Edugra argued that if it's in space, it'll be closer to the planet, and it can be moved to help protect us. Like an aircraft carrier, but way bigger—and in space." Wilcox waved his hands, trying to illustrate the size.

Jones raised a single eyebrow. "Impressive."

"If we need anything else, we will have to get more stories from other countries in the United Nations to pay for them."

Jones tilted his head. "United Nations?"

"We'll get to that later."

"OK," Jones accepted, nodding. "What about the rest of the negotiations?"

Wilcox sighed and leaned back in his seat, trying to think of some highlights from the past two days of negotiations. One detail specifically stood out to him. "You know that when you and I negotiate, we usually ask for more than what we want, so that when the other person counters, we end up settling on what we originally needed?"

"Yes."

"There was none of that," Wilcox informed him matter-of-factly. "I asked for what *I* thought was reasonable, and they asked for what *they* thought was reasonable. That's it! Can you believe it's only been two days? The Paris Peace Conference took almost two years!"

"Impressive!" The general's face had split into another grin. "I like these Zalmen."

"But…."

"There's always a but, isn't there?"

"You know how our laws require us to bring treaties to the Senate?"

Jones nodded knowingly. "Yes, and we can't exactly do that, can we?"

"Not unless we want the whole planet to know about them and their technology. We have to do this off the books, out of the public's eye." It had been a concern in the back of his mind for most of the first day after the main details had been hashed out. On the second day, they'd explored a few solutions, then broke for lunch, then discussed a few more. Just last night, they'd figured something out.

"Right, so what did you come up with?"

"The Earth–Zalma Alliance, or EZA for short, won't be written up as being with the US Government, but instead with the—" he made hasty air quotes "—'Peaceful Leaders of Earth'."

The general was taken aback. "Oh boy! Is the president OK with this?"

"Surprisingly, yes. I think he just wants to share the burden with the other leaders," Wilcox said.

"I think you're right," Jones said. "How have you defined the Peaceful Leaders?"

"We have one year to form an Earth Defense Council and find the highest-ranking official in each country in the United Nations—safe people, of course. If we can't find a diplomat, we can recruit a military officer or a scientist. Regardless, each member should be given equal ranking on the council. Finding someone in the USSR might prove to be difficult."

"Yes," the general said with a nod and a chuckle. "Corporals Dow and Rabinowitz have a real challenge on their hands."

"Yes, sir; they sure will. I almost forgot." He dug through his case again, this time to retrieve an envelope, which he presented with a stiff, formal posture. "I am here to officially notify you that the president has assigned you to lead a top-secret task force. Your assignment is to assemble the rest of the Earth Defense Council."

Jones shot him an incredulous look over the top of the letter. "Does the president know that I am going into space to fight aliens?"

"Yes, he does. You are to find someone to take over operations on Earth in your absence, and he is preparing a banquet for all the generals on Friday, so you and Dow can find your replacement."

Jones laughed, and jokingly he asked, "Is the president angry with me? He knows I don't like all this paperwork." He gestured to the table, with its stacks of official documents that needed reading and signing.

"I wouldn't say angry," Wilcox laughed along, "but he said that he doesn't want to be seen with aliens. It would not go well for him in the next election. And he mentioned that it probably would have been easier on all of us if you'd just fired a warning shot and scared them off. But he seems to respect you and what we're doing. He just won't admit it. And I'm sure he'll also take the credit if we're successful."

Jones chuckled. "Yes, I got that impression as well. What about our security problem?"

"The treaty states we will not keep their technology on Earth, except for a minimum required for recruitment purposes and self-defense."

"And what about our personnel exchange?"

"Right." Wilcox reached over the table to flip through the treaty; the general scanned the newly revealed page. "Geogram will stay as the Zalma representative. Kanara, Sarara, and their children will stay to teach our scientists while you, your specialists, and I travel to their planet to negotiate and assess the situation."

"Good work!" Jones praised him. He folded the treaty together again, then leaned back and heaved a sigh. "Now, the hard part. I have to tell my wife that I'll be gone for two or three years."

"Good luck with that, sir."

Jones eyed Wilcox curiously. "By the way, your file says that you are single. Are you and Miss Warren...?"

"No," Wilcox said immediately. "No, we are just friends, more like brother and sister."

"No girlfriend for you, then?"

"No. Maybe I'll find a gal when I get back." He shuffled his feet. It wasn't really a topic Wilcox wanted to get into with his superior, mainly because everyone else he knew already had ladies of their own. Some of his friends were even married, but not him. He'd only had two girlfriends, and neither of those relationships lasted very long.

Wilcox coughed to clear the tension in the air, then offered a polite "Sir!" and left the tent.

CHAPTER TWENTY-FIVE

I GOT A JOB!

Charlotte "Charlie" Baker

ROSWELL, NEW MEXICO

A few days after I met Cpl. Dow at the empty building, he came to our house. Dad was drinking his morning coffee in the living room, so when the doorbell rang, he made it to the door before I could. I peeked around the corner from the hallway.

Dow held out his hand for Dad to shake. "Mr. Baker, I presume? I am Corporal Dow. Your daughter's work has caught the attention of some pretty important people in the US government."

Dad stiffened, which he only did when he was really nervous, and my stomach twinged with guilt. He was hardly ever scared. A second later, he put on his reporter face. "I'm sorry about that," he said. "I asked her to collect and destroy those papers."

"That's not why I'm here. We would like to offer your daughter an internship as a research assistant."

Dad almost dropped his coffee mug and I had to hold in a giggle.

"But...she's a girl," he said.

Dow didn't miss a beat. "If you prefer, you can call it a secretary internship. She interviewed one of our generals and impressed him with her questions."

"She reads a lot of detective novels. Sherlock Holmes is her favorite."

"Ah. Holmes is General Jones's favorite as well. That must be why they connected."

"Umm...yes...well.... Where would this internship occur?"

"We have an office on the outskirts of town. For now, we'd ask her to come in two days a week since it's a learning experience, not an official job. Her school's already approved it as extra credit. When school starts up again, she can schedule time whenever she's free, and you can drop in anytime to check on her."

"Well, I guess there is no reason for me to say no.... But I should check with my wife," Dad grumbled. He glanced over his shoulder at where I was, and I ducked behind the wall.

Mom peeked out of the kitchen door. "Your wife totally agrees, and I will make sure Charlie is there when needed. Also, I think *Research Assistant* is just fine." I brightened at the pride in her voice.

Dad looked a little annoyed but nodded in agreement.

Dow smiled. "Excellent. Here is the paperwork for you to read and sign. Then I'll take you to the office to check it out."

"Now? Oh...OK," Dad said.

Dow drove us in his jeep. I estimated it would take about twenty minutes to wheel to the office. I remembered the small building being empty the last time I saw it. It had no signs, a flat roof, door in the center, and a big window, like a lawyer or accountant would use. The inside of the office was nice, but the wear marks told me it was well used.... Or was it? My instincts told me that it was all new, just made to look used. I hunted for clues, and after a few seconds, I saw sawdust where normal dust should be.

Miss Dianne, the receptionist, seemed very nice.

Dow showed me to an office with a desk, then a library with a table. On it was a typewriter. "This is your office."

I loved it.

[Starting my "research assistant" job felt like the beginning of everything. I thought the hardest part would be keeping the secret from my friends. I never imagined that one day, the wrong people would come looking for that secret.]

CHAPTER TWENTY-SIX

FIRST CALL TO ZALMA

Ambassador Ryan Wilcox
EARTH–ZALMA BASECAMP, NEW MEXICO

[The day we first contacted Zalma directly was the day Earth truly became part of something bigger.]

Wilcox had just finished packing when he received a summons on his communicator from Jones, requesting his presence on the bridge of the Ymit.

As Wilcox entered, he noticed he was the last one to arrive. The general was already there, along with the three aliens he'd already met—Agugua, Edugra, Geogram—as well as a greenish Zalmen lady, and a slender soldier in his early thirties. Could these be the Cameron and Joanua that Donna had told him about?

Jones introduced them. "Ambassador Wilcox, meet Lieutenant Cameron and the Ymit's engineer, Joanua." He paused as Wilcox first shook the slender man's hand and then exchanged bows with the engineer. "I've worked with Cameron for a long time. He is one of the best encryption specialists the army has to offer. While you've been negotiating, I've had Cameron learn their communications system from Joanua."

"A wise idea." Wilcox took a moment to regard the two. His first impression was their calm manner. They didn't seem prone to outbursts of excitement like Donna or Edugra, but they also didn't share the captain's seriousness. He nodded toward Joanua. "Thank you." Then Wilcox turned to Cameron. "How did it go?"

"Great!" the lieutenant replied with a soft smile. "I had many ideas, and when you formalized the alliance, the ladies and I initiated implementation."

"So, what did you come up with?" Jones asked.

Cameron turned toward the main screens, which were lit up with multiple pages of code, in English. Wilcox realized it had to be for Cameron's sake.

"First," Cameron said, "we tested routing low-powered directional signals through their probes in other solar systems. That way, the Moadites should not be able to track the source."

"Smart," Wilcox said. *That sounds like the right thing to do.*

"Then I considered several of our encryption systems. The problem is that we can't transmit the encryption code to Zalma because anyone who intercepts it would also be able to decode our transmissions."

Jones shook his head, frowning. "And that's not good. So, what did you come up with?"

"We used a cipher key that only both sides have without transmitting. Since they have all their manuals and historical books electronically stored on the ship's computer, we coded a multibook cipher," Cameron explained.

"Multi-book!" Jones repeated. "Impressive!"

"Thank you, sir," the lieutenant said before he continued his explanation. He used his hands minimally as he spoke. "Once they have that, we will immediately send a secure transmission with more encryption algorithms. And, for really secure transmissions, the Zalmen can enter additional personal keys, like: *Where did we first meet?* With the Zalma super-fast computers, multi-layered secure communications are possible, and I am confident that the signals are secure."

"Wow!" Wilcox said.

Cameron smiled. "The Zalmen are excited, as they haven't contacted their leaders and family since they left."

"Oh?" The general glanced around at the collected aliens.

With a start, Wilcox realized that Kanara's family had snuck in some time during Cameron's explanation. He pulled his eyes away from them to look at Jones. "Yes," he said. "They told me that they sent brief automated messages that would look like one of their probes so the Moadites wouldn't pay any extra attention."

The older man hummed. "Good plan."

"With your and Captain Agugua's permission, sir, we are ready to start," Cameron said. When they both nodded, he and Joanua began uploading their files.

Wilcox gaped at the glowing screens. It wasn't so much what was *on* the screens that impressed him—just loading bars and lines of code—but the appearance of the screen in general. The amazement he'd carried for the past few days of the Zalmen themselves had worn off a bit, but every time he looked at his communicator or anything else they'd brought with them, he couldn't stop his jaw from dropping. Vaguely, he registered Edugra's voice.

"The second probe has updated," she said. "Third.... Fourth.... Fifth.... Sixth...."

Wilcox followed along, watching as lines of text changed on the screen.

"The seventh and final probe is now updated. We are transmitting encryption programs and terms of our alliance to Zalma," Edugra finished.

For the next few seconds, no one spoke. They waited with bated breath. Then the computer chimed, and a new rectangle popped up.

Edugra smiled. "Incoming coded transmission from Zalma!" she announced.

Everyone cheered. The humans exchanged handshakes. Edugra accepted the transmission. Sarara even clapped her hands together. The text vanished from the screen, and a live video transmission appeared.

Several Zalmen stared back at them through the screen with an assortment of blue, purple, and teal skin. All but one was dressed in silver robes.

Agugua bowed and spoke first—in Zalmen, which his communicator then translated to English for the humans. *"Council, I would like you to meet Ambassador Wilcox, General Jones, and Lieutenant Cameron."* He pointed to each of them in turn. *"They are responsible for enabling us to communicate today."*

Wilcox hastily bowed to the people on the screen in time with Jones and Cameron. He'd been distracted by studying the Zalman in the middle, the only one he'd ever seen wearing a different color. He wore a robe like the rest of the council, though his was a glossy white. He appeared to be Geogram's age, in his late fifties by human standards, though, unlike the ambassador, this Zalman was a much darker purple.

"I am First Minister Ronderra."

Wilcox immediately noticed that his words didn't match the movement of his lips. He should've been used to this by now, but it seemed that the Zalmen would never cease to amaze him. *I bet the computer is translating right now for him.* Wilcox remembered that when Agugua spoke, the computer translated, but the translation was delayed, until he stopped speaking. *I guess that's so it's not talking over him, and maybe it can do it in real time because we don't need to hear the original.* Wilcox wasn't even sure that was possible—it wasn't something he'd ever considered—but the Zalmen were already doing much more than he'd ever imagined.

Ronderra continued, *"Thank you, gentlemen. We are grateful for your assistance. The deflectors are less effective than when our team left, and our timeline has been moved up. We believe the Moadites have new technology."*

As he spoke, a secondary image popped up, showing video footage of the planet's deflectors under enemy fire. One explosion, larger and brighter than any of the others, lit up across the screen. The entire Zalman sky flickered, casting spectral lights over the city buildings. Many of the Zalmen gasped, then breathed a sigh of relief when they saw what looked like the glass of a snow-globe rebuilding itself.

"We are glad to be of service," Jones said. "I'll be returning with your outreach team and with a small group of specialists to assess your needs."

Geogram stepped forward, bowing to the first minister. "I can vouch for General Jones's skill. He deduced our intentions from our decoy ship and its proximity to their nuclear test site. He and his team will be invaluable to us."

On the screen, the council members' colors flickered, and they murmured, clearly impressed.

Jones nodded, but otherwise showed no outward signs of acknowledgment. He remained calm and collected, entirely in his element. "The best course of action for now would be to begin analyzing the Moadite ships. We need to know what they're made of, and if they have deflectors. Would you be able to do that?"

"Yes, that is possible," Ronderra replied.

"Analyze their weapons as well," the general persisted. "I'd suggest launching rocks or metal debris into space and scanning the remains after they've been destroyed. If we can identify what types of weapons they're using, we might be able to modify your deflectors for better resistance."

The first minister's face flickered with green, then he nodded.

"Finally, we'd like you to record their ships' transmissions for us, so that we can have our decryption specialists take a look at them," Jones finished.

"We will do as you request," the first minister assured him.

Wilcox, who'd been watching the exchange, felt a knot tighten in his gut as he realized just how far he had come, but how far he had to go to improve. The general spoke with such confidence. He simply said what he needed—he didn't ask. He didn't sound unsure, nor did he stumble over his words like Wilcox knew he himself might've in front of so many older people.

One of the teal council members lifted a large communicator into view, taking the moment of silence as her cue to step forward. *"We are pleased with the success of the mission,"* she said first, then stared down at her communicator again. *"I see here that in exchange for human goods, we will be providing a station for your orbit."*

She looked up for confirmation, and Jones nodded.

"We have been preparing an invisible freighter for our new colony, but I believe our chances would be better if you use it as your space station. It has a large replicator and everything needed to start a space fleet."

"Thank you." The general acknowledged. He paused for a moment, then asked, "New colony?"

"Yes. In light of our weakening deflectors, we have been preparing to evacuate the planet." She'd barely gotten the words out before gasps erupted from the Ymit's crew members.

Wilcox spun to see their colors fluctuating aggressively.

Jones spoke slower, with a deeper voice. "I'm sorry to hear that. I assure you we are doing everything we can to eliminate the need for evacuation."

"We had planned to use this ship as the base for our new colony," the teal council member maintained, *"but with your help, we hope we will not need it."*

"We look forward to these books and movies you are sending," a third Zalman added, *"both historical and artificial. They will be a welcome distraction to our people during these difficult times."* He gave a half-hearted smile.

I wonder if they'll ever get used to fiction, Wilcox thought.

Next to him, Cameron mouthed, "Artificial?"

Wilcox coughed lightly to cover a chuckle. "Fiction," he whispered.

Cameron chuckled as well.

"Well," Jones said, sending a quick frown in the two men's direction, "I am sure you have lots to talk about. We will leave you to it."

The three humans bowed.

Agugua turned to address his crew. "You may all contact your families now. I would recommend the privacy of your rooms."

Geogram stepped forward and spoke to the ministers in his own language.

The humans and remaining crew left the bridge.

CHAPTER TWENTY-SEVEN

THE ODD COUPLE

Charlotte "Charlie" Baker

ROSWELL, NEW MEXICO

I was feeling a buzz of excitement on my first day at my new job. My dad kept telling me it was a *temporary* internship and not to get my hopes up. The journey took about twenty-five minutes, a little longer than I expected, but Sandy and I still arrived at the office with time to spare.

I turned to her. "OK, Sandy, I'm not sure if you're allowed inside, so you've got to stay here." She whined but lay down in the shade in front of the window.

Miss Dianne came outside. "Hello, Charlie. Is this your service dog?" she asked. She must've seen me through the big front window.

"Hi, Miss Dianne. Yes, her name is Sandy."

She smiled. "Well, that makes her a part of the team. She doesn't need to stay out here." Miss Dianne held the door open for us. "Corporal Dow will be here soon. In the meantime, I'm to show you how to use our communicators."

Sandy wagged her tail furiously as she followed me in and settled on the carpet right beside Miss Dianne's desk. I pulled her bowl out of my backpack and filled it with water from my thermos. "I'll bring a mat for Sandy tomorrow," I promised. Then I pulled the communicator from my pocket. "Now, what do I do with this gadget?"

"It's fairly straight-forward, but be sure to ask for help if you have any questions."

I nodded.

"Whenever you hold it, or call its name, it will listen for commands," Miss Dianne said. "But if you are holding it, the communicator knows not everything you say is a command, so it will only respond to commands it recognizes."

"Like what?"

"How about you tell it to call me?"

"OK. *Call Miss Dianne.*"

The communicator on Miss Dianne's desk vibrated. She picked it up. *"Answer."*

Her face appeared on my communicator. "Wow!"

"To hang up, you do the same. *End call,*" she said to the device.

I couldn't believe it. It seemed like the whole world was suddenly at my fingertips. *How many more things will I be able to do with this?* "Can I call anyone?" I asked.

"Anyone within our organization, yes. But remember, they will not answer it when there are outsiders around."

"I guess that makes sense."

"But even if they don't answer, you can leave messages with your questions. If you can't or don't want to talk, you can ask the communicator to send a written message instead. Why don't you do that now to ask Corporal Dow when he will be here?"

I did, and about a minute later, my communicator vibrated, and words appeared on the device that said, *About five minutes.*

"Nice," I said. "Oops, did it send that?"

Miss Dianne laughed. "Probably not. It's pretty good at knowing when you are talking to it." She seemed to be speaking from experience.

"Wow."

"Now, let me show you the typewriters." She led me to the library, my office, that held a device that *looked* like a typewriter. "Because of the need for secrecy, everything we have for recording information is actually a communicator: the typewriters, notebooks, television screens, and even the paper. They all look the same, but the Zalmen have been kind enough to simulate them so you can have something familiar. Anything you type or write will appear on the paper and load into your portable device."

"That's so sweet!" I said, examining the machine. I could only imagine Dad's face if he saw it. Our typewriter at home was old, as was the one in his office at work, and it broke down a lot, so he was always fiddling with it.

Miss Dianne continued, "If you prefer, you can also dictate by voice—"

Sandy whined and then barked twice. From my communicator, a digitized voice said, *"Arrival."*

I looked down at my communicator. "Arrival? What was that?"

"Sandy's become quite the early warning system," Dianne explained with a grin. "Your communicators must be translating Sandy's two-bark pattern as *a spacecraft is here.*"

A voice came from down the hallway. "Hello," Cpl. Dow said before he entered the room.

"I thought you said you were going to be five minutes."

"I sometimes forget how fast the spaceships are," he said.

"Spaceships? You came here in one?" I asked, my eyes wide. I spun my wheels toward the back window and peered out. Seeing nothing, I looked back at him. "Can I see it?"

Dow chuckled. "I rarely see it myself, since it's invisible. Besides, we don't want to overwhelm you on your first day, do we?"

I pouted at him, which always worked on Dad. I really wanted to see the spaceship, but that didn't seem like an option. I'd have to investigate on my own some other time.

Another man nudged Dow out of the doorway so he could enter.

"Hello. Who are you?" I asked.

He smiled and bowed theatrically, tipping an invisible hat, which made me giggle. "I'm Corporal Adam Rabinowitz, Dow's partner," he introduced himself.

Dow scoffed. "Partner? I ain't got no partner. He's just some guy who keeps following me around."

I frowned. *If they're both corporals, who's in charge?* "Who are we going to start with, then?" I asked.

"With me. I'm your first interview," Dow said. "Let's go into my office."

"You mean *us* and *our* office?" Rabinowitz asked, elbowing Dow.

Dow just groaned, but didn't put up a fight. He flapped his hand dismissively, then led us into the other room. Sandy followed us. She licked my hand, then settled at my feet as I pulled a notepad and pencil from my bag.

Dow stopped me. "Oh, sorry, but you can't record anything on paper. Did Dianne tell you already...? Anything that the bad guys can get their hands on is a security risk."

Rabinowitz left the room for a moment, then came back with one of the regular-looking notebooks Miss Dianne had shown me earlier. He set it down in front of me, along with a new pencil.

"What's this?" I asked.

"It may look like a regular notebook, but it's a communicator. Everything you write will become invisible when anyone outside our group is around."

"OK...." *Who are they worried might see it?* They seemed pretty serious, and my mind shot back to that grumpy other general and his men. I remembered the intensity of that blond soldier's eyes and held back a shudder. He'd had a spark of something there, *hunger,* like a reporter eager for a story. But it was darker than that. What would he resort to doing to get what he wanted?

Dow sat in one of the chairs at the desk and spoke, shaking me out of my thoughts. “Okay, let’s get started. How would you like to do this? Filmed? Audio? Or do you want to just take notes?”

“I can film it?” I asked, before remembering how the communicator had recorded my promise.

“Sure, just set your little communicator up somewhere and ask it to record. You could also just ask Rabinowitz to do it for you.”

I turned to Rabinowitz. He was staring at Dow in surprise. Obviously, they’d not discussed this in advance. I fumbled with my communicator. “Would you please?” I begged.

Rabinowitz shot a brief angry look at Dow before smiling at me. “Of course.” He took my communicator, held it toward us like a camera, and said, “Record video.”

Suddenly, I felt nervous. My heart rate spiked. *Wow, this is really happening, and right now. My first official interview! What do I ask?* I thought back to some interviews I’d seen on the television and figured it was best to mimic them. “First, please state your name, rank, and role.”

“Malcolm Dow, Army Corporal. I was the first to make contact with the aliens.”

Rabinowitz, still recording us, looked around the communicator at me.

“And I’m Adam Rabinowitz, also an Army Corporal. I was the first to talk to the aliens.” He sounded smug. I saw him glance down at the communicator and grin. “Ah, good. It’s recording me too. But how did it know to switch? Is it because I spoke?”

“How does it know anything?” Dow countered, then sent a teasing glare at Rabinowitz. “And *you* weren’t the first to talk to them, I was.”

Rabinowitz just gave me a knowing smile.

I waited, wondering if they were finished. The interviewers I’d seen before usually let conversations happen; it made everything more relaxed. Still, I couldn't help but interrupt. "So who was it? Who talked to them first?"

Dow and Rabinowitz both turned to me, seemingly embarrassed for bantering in front of me. I glanced between them expectantly. When neither volunteered to answer, I sat back and held my new notebook higher, pretending to write in it like the people I saw on television. "Let's try again," I said, putting on my most professional expression. "You two seem like opposites; what makes you different from others, and how does that help you in your job?"

Dow didn't hesitate. "He doesn't think, and gets into trouble, so I have to rescue him."

I raised my eyebrows expectantly at Rabinowitz. He just shook his head, rolled his eyes, and looked away.

So, that may not have been the best question. "OK then. How did this whole thing start? And when?"

"A couple weeks ago," Dow replied. "My...um, *our* detachment was sent to investigate a crash site. The farmer thought it was one of our experimental aircraft, so he kept his distance."

I nodded, already knowing all this. "Yes, I talked to his son, Johnny. The ship crashed the night before, but the wind was blowing sand everywhere, so it was too dangerous to go out."

"That's very good, but who is interviewing who?" Dow asked, raising his eyebrows.

I was suddenly sure that my cheeks were redder than a tomato. "Sorry. What happened next?"

Rabinowitz readjusted the communicator, then said, "When we arrived, we saw the disk-shaped silver object. As we approached, we saw it was hollow, and there was a bell-shaped container underneath."

"And then what?"

"I was selected to check out the object. I think they considered me disposable, but I really wanted to see what it was, so I didn't hesitate," Dow said.

"I was right behind him," Rabinowitz added.

Dow rolled his eyes.

"And what did you find?" I asked.

"The container had a door with a window. I looked in and saw a body," Dow said.

"A body? Was it dead?"

"We'll get to that later," Rabinowitz promised.

Dow continued. "So I pried the door open..."

"...and I had to help him," Rabinowitz interrupted. "We saw that it was actually three small bodies with big heads, but found out later that this was a decoy, and the bodies weren't real."

"What do you mean, not real?" I leaned forward. "Were they made from clay or something?"

"Yes.... No.... Well, um...." Dow's gaze roved the room, like he might see the answer written on a wall or something. "We learned later that they were sorta real. They were just never alive; they were clones grown on the spaceship, like plants."

"Grown? Clones? Like in *A Brave New World*?" My heartbeat quickened. Wait. "If they weren't real, are you telling me that the whole crash was...staged?" The two corporals exchanged a look. *Bingo.*

"You're really smart!" Rabinowitz praised.

I fought down an excited squeal at being right. Instead, I cleared my throat. *Back to being professional.* "Well, since you're here, I'm guessing you weren't scared off by the decoy ship, so what did you do when you saw the clones?"

"We reported it to our lieutenant, and then went to clean up the foil that was flying around," Dow said.

That's it? I was dumbfounded. "You just walked away from the biggest discovery in history?"

Rabinowitz scratched the back of his head awkwardly. "Well, it sounds silly when you say it like that, but the lieutenant ordered us not to even look at it, so what could we do?"

I still couldn't understand, but I had to get the interview rolling again. I remembered how my communicator had started out as a piece of foil and I pointed to it. "Were all the foil bits communicators?"

Rabinowitz tilted his head from side to side. "Sort of. Everything they have is made of foil, so I guess it could all be communicators if they wanted it to. They used it to detect who was safe for them to contact."

"Smart. So then what happened?" I asked.

"I wanted to be away from everyone," Dow began, then he glanced at Rabinowitz, "and was unsuccessful since *this one* followed me."

Dow shook his head. "We headed to the furthest debris that I could see. That's where we met Ambassador Geogram."

"And who is he?" I asked.

"An alien from the planet Zalma," Rabinowitz said.

I lurched upright. "What! Why didn't you say that in the first place?" *Wow! He just said that aliens are real! He told me just like that, and I didn't have to go around looking for clues and piecing everything together like I usually do.* It was nice, getting the answers so easily, but there was also something disappointing about it. It was so much more satisfying to work the answers out for myself.

Dow shrugged.

"So, how did you meet?"

"Dow sensed that we were being watched," Rabinowitz said.

"Sensed?" I asked.

Dow shrugged again. "I just had a hunch. And then loudmouth over there started yelling."

"*Ha! So, you admit it!* I was the first to talk to an alien." Rabinowitz looked smug all over again.

"You didn't know he was there," Dow said. "Geogram and his ship appeared after that."

"You didn't see or hear him coming? What did he look like?" I asked.

"No, I didn't see or hear him. He's got light purple skin and was wearing the foil."

"'Was wearing the foil'?"

"Yes. Oh, and he's bald."

"They're all bald," Rabinowitz added.

"They? How many of them are there?" I asked.

"Six adults and two children," Dow said. "They all learned English from our radio and television."

That piqued my interest. "Children?" *I couldn't believe it. Not only would I possibly meet an alien, but an alien my own age? It could be swell! I hope we'll be friends. What sort of games do they play on their planet?*

Rabinowitz pulled me out of my daydream. "Yes, children. I think they are just a little older than you. Anyway, he told us his planet is under attack and needs our help."

"Under attack?" My heart dropped. "By who, and how are the two of you going to help them?"

"The Moad, and not just us," Rabinowitz assured me with a chuckle. "They asked us to contact our government, and Dow had a good feeling about them, so I went to General Jones."

"What kind of good feeling? Weren't you scared about seeing a purple bald man appearing out of nowhere?"

"Nah. As Robin said," Dow tilted his head toward Rabinowitz, "I had a good feeling about them."

"So, let me get this straight. First you had a feeling you were being watched, then you felt they were friendly? How can you be so sure?" *I sometimes feel like that; like I just know something's going on so I have to investigate. Dad always called it my 'reporter's instinct', but Corporal Dow isn't a reporter.*

"I just am. My feelings have always led me in the right direction."

Maybe it really is the same. "Can you describe these feelings?"

Dow's eye's widened, and his smile faded. "You're going to think I'm crazy."

"Try me."

Dow looked down, and he brought his arms in, almost like a child who was pouting. "Sometimes I just know I'm being watched, other times I feel tingles, in danger, or safe. It's like my guardian angel, my dad, guiding me."

"Angel? So you're a Christian?"

"I grew up in a Christian environment, but I don't know what I believe."

I didn't know how to follow up, but I remembered something Rabinowitz said. "Did you say that *you* went to General Jones?"

"Yep, that's right. Dow wanted nothing to do with the aliens, so I went to see the general on my own."

I turned back to Dow, and he rolled his eyes. "I didn't want to get court-martialed for doing the things Robin did. I didn't even want to get involved in the first place, but I'm always having weaklings wanting my help."

I turned back to Rabinowitz. "So, what happened when you went to the general?"

"He wasn't in his office, so the communicator Geogram gave me on our first encounter led me to the old warehouse."

"Oh yes, I've been there. The guards were scary."

"They wouldn't let me see Jones. They tied me up and were going to hand me over to another general the next day."

Dow smiled and chuckled. "So I had to perform a daring rescue."

"What! Tell me more!"

Dow checked his watch. "I think that's enough for one day." The two corporals exchanged a look. It was almost like they were having an entire conversation with just their eyes! I watched them, suspicious. Were they wanting to distract me from telling them the rest of the story, or did they have something else planned?

Dow turned to me. "Are you up for a field trip?"

"Field trip? To where?"

"How would you like to meet some aliens?" Rabinowitz asked.

I think I felt every emotion possible: excited, scared, happy, and sick to my stomach. "Wow! But I thought you said you didn't want to overwhelm me on my first day?" I reined myself in, trying not to sound too eager, but I was nearly exploding. I get to meet an alien!

Dow chuckled. "We didn't want you to get your hopes up. We wanted to see how you dealt with everything first."

"You did an excellent job." Rabinowitz smiled.

I nodded. "Sure, that would be swell!"

Dow spoke to his communicator. "Tell Kanara that we're ready to go and that Miss Baker is with us."

CHAPTER TWENTY-EIGHT

WHAT CAN SHE DO?

Charlotte "Charlie" Baker

ROSWELL, NEW MEXICO

"I get to meet an alien!" I announced the moment we returned to the reception area.

"That's great!" Miss Dianne said from behind her desk.

Sandy whined and barked twice. *"Arrival,"* the communicator said.

"Your dog knows when the silent, invisible spaceship arrives?" Rabinowitz looked admiringly at Sandy.

"Yep," I said proudly.

Miss Dianne nodded.

"That's right, she did the same thing the first time I met you." Dow led me into the hallway, with Rabinowitz and Sandy behind. Then he opened the back door, but I only saw the desert. Dow turned to me. "Let Robin push your chair. You're going to feel really sick. Are you ready?"

I let go of my wheels, but my curiosity swelled. "Sick, why?"

"On three. One…two…three!" Dow walked backward and vanished in midair. Rabinowitz kept pushing me forward.

Dow was completely right. The dizziness hit me like a wave. I hunched over, but not before I saw that we were no longer in the desert, but what looked like a large van. Sandy whimpered and lay down beside me. "Sandy, are you OK?"

"We all feel a little sick when getting on or off an invisible spaceship," Rabinowitz said.

My queasiness lessened and excitement took its place. "I'm on a spaceship?"

"We call it the Spacevan."

I searched my surroundings eagerly. However, Dow was blocking my view. "Are you ready?" He waited until I nodded, then Dow stepped aside. "This is Kanara."

"Greetings."

I couldn't breathe. He was indeed bald, wearing a foil robe, and had blue-green skin. I thought he had a slight Asian accent. I shook hands before grabbing my wheels again. "Greetings! My name's Charlie."

Kanara's smile was soft. "A pleasure to meet you, young Charlie. Would you like to meet my children?" he asked.

"They're your kids?" I blurted. "Sorry, that was a stupid question." *Just calm down, Charlie....* "I mean, yes, I'd love to."

"They've been eager to meet you as well," he said. "They have been pestering me and their mother since they learned of you."

With that, Kanara turned around and tapped his control pad a few times. Through the front windshield of the van, I could see the desert right outside the office. We must have been moving pretty fast, because the landscape suddenly blurred. I looked around, and it cleared again, we were in a totally different place. It must've been their camp, because there were tents set up and soldiers walking around.

I stared in amazement. "Did we move? I didn't feel a thing."

"They tell me that the spaceship has its own gravity," Rabinowitz explained as he grabbed the back of my wheelchair again. "Ready?" he asked. When I nodded, he pushed me down the ramp from the Spacevan.

I barely registered that my wheels had touched the sand. All at once, my stomach twisted like a pretzel. I quickly put a hand over my mouth. Sandy touched my other hand with her wet nose, and instantly I felt better. I rubbed her ears.

It was a good thing too, because just then, two children ran around from the other side of the Spacevan. They looked just like Kanara, but smaller, and the girl was pink. *Are all the girls pink?* I didn't think so, but the boy was blue-green like his dad. T*hen again, Dow and Rabinowitz had said that the alien named Geogram was purple....* That was something else I'd have to look into.

Sandy barked at the strangers. I grabbed her collar and gave her a head rub. "It's OK, they're friends."

"Is that a dog?" the pink girl said.

"Yeah. Do you want to pet her?"

She nodded.

"Just kneel down and hold your hand out. Allow her to come to you and sniff you."

She did as instructed, and Sandy went to her and sniffed, then lay down. She was probably still sick from the invisible ship.

"You can pat her now," I said, and the girl did.

The boy watched Sandy and his sister, then looked at me. His skin changed colors rapidly, startling me from my thoughts. He was looking at my chair, frowning like he was puzzled. "Why are you in a chair?"

The girl stood quickly and turned to the boy. "Takar!"

Sandy also moved to position herself between me and him. She didn't growl—she was too well-trained for that—but her body language was clear: protective mode engaged. Her amber eyes locked onto the alien boy with the kind of steady stare that said "watch your tone."

I reached down to pat her head. "It's okay, Sandy. He's just curious."

The alien girl spoke to me. "Please excuse my brother. I am Janara."

"It's OK," I said, feeling warmed by the girl's scolding of her brother. "I'm used to it. I was born with a defect. Mom always said that God was too busy working on my heart and brain that He forgot my spine." I blushed a little. *Why did I say that?*

"And your communicator didn't fix it?" the boy said.

"What do you mean *fix*?" I asked.

Dow kneeled in front of Takar so they were the same height. "If Charlie just starts walking, how are we going to explain it to her family and friends?"

Takar's eyes widened as he realized the same as me. No one on Earth was allowed to know about the Zalman technology. It was *classified*. But still, could it work? And how?

"Your communicator is programmed to do what you ask it to do. It could likely repair any damage that prevents you from walking," Kanara explained.

"Unfortunately, not without risking exposure, since humans haven't figured this stuff out yet," Rabinowitz said. "Maybe in the future, Charlie, but for now I'll have to ask you not to ask your communicator that."

"Yeah," Dow said, standing up. "I'm sure we will find a way to help you."

My head was spinning. *It could heal me. . . . I might walk?* I'd used a wheelchair my whole life, it was almost a part of me, but some part of me couldn't help wanting to live without it.

Janara smiled widely, a sparkle in her eyes. "What would you like to do?"

"What *can* she do?" Takar asked. I was almost offended, but he sounded more curious than insulting, so I let it go. I was too tired to correct him. Sandy nuzzled my hand.

"That will be enough, Takar. You will treat our guest with respect. But for now, go do your homework," Kanara said.

"But, Dad...."

"Go."

Takar left.

Kanara turned back to us. "What would you two like to do?"

Before I could speak, Janara said, "I have studied your sports. We don't have anything like it on our planet and they seem like fun. Or...Corporal Dow said you like the artificial stories about Sherlock Holmes, so I have just started reading them. We could talk about them!"

I was excited about talking about the detective, but I was feeling restless and irritated from Takar's words. *What can I do? I'll show them!* "How about playing a sport? Do you know baseball?" I asked.

"I can get the teams together!" Dow cut in, looking excited.

We agreed, and he raced off to grab some other soldiers to join in. Janara and I were the only kids, but since the game was our idea, Dow made us co-captains of one of the teams. We faced off against a buff blond soldier named Abbott and his team, who were so much better than us, but I had a plan. It started with a bunt. And another. And another. I bunted every time.

The game went on, and we were losing badly, despite Rabinowitz being a great pitcher.

By the last inning, we were two runs behind. I called Janara and Dow over.

"Here's what we're going to do," I said. "Dow, you know our players best. I want you to load the bases, then I'm going up to bat."

Janara nodded excitedly, but Dow shook his head. "No way! Sorry to doubt you, kid, but how would we win with a play like that? Howard's been our best hitter so far."

"Then put him before me," I said. "But only fill the bases."

He still seemed skeptical.

I was angry. For a split second, I imagined standing at home plate—really standing—before shoving the thought away. *Focus on what you* can *do.* Dow wasn't going to ruin my plan. I was just about to give him my reasoning, when…

"If I were you, I'd do what she says." It was General Jones. I didn't see when he came, but he must've been watching a while; I could tell he knew what I was thinking.

I turned back to Dow, more serious than ever. "Look, this is only going to work once, so don't mess it up," I said.

"Yeah, come on!" Janara said. "She'll do great! Besides, if I understand sports, it's all about fun and exercise."

Dow glanced at the general, then back at me, deliberating. Janara and I may have been the co-captains, but I knew that the rest of the team would only go along with my plan if he was on board. Finally, he groaned. "OK, you're the bosses." He called up Howard and the two other best hitters and told them the plan. "Just get on base. Don't take any chances."

They did, and the bases were loaded. Dow handed me the bat. "I sure hope you know what you're doing."

I smirked. "Just watch and learn."

Janara gave me two thumbs up, and I rolled out to the plate. I hefted the bat, purposefully wobbling as I held it behind my shoulder. All around the field, the other team laughed.

"Move in, everyone!" Abbott called. "Give the kid a chance!"

They're taking the bait. I hid a smile. When the other team's pitcher threw the ball, I made a feeble attempt at swinging.

"OK, come on, move in some more!" Abbott yelled.

I glanced to the side of our make-shift diamond. Janara was waving and cheering me on. Next to her, Dow fidgeted.

On the second pitch, I swung and completely missed.

"We got this one in the bag!" one of the soldiers from the other team yelled.

By now, the outfielders had come in so close they were almost on top of the bases themselves. As they did, I winked at Dow, and his eyes popped. He finally understood my plan. Our players on the bases looked like they'd already given up, but when they saw him wave, they got ready to run. The other team saw this, and I could see them laughing. They were overconfident, and that would be their downfall.

I flexed my arm muscles. People often forgot that my only way to get around was with my arms; they never expected me to be strong. My biceps tensed and my triceps braced. The pitcher was the only one who seemed to sense the change in me. He reared his arm back and threw the ball hard. I watched it with all my focus. It came closer, and closer, and closer, and this time when I swung the bat, the ball cracked against it. With an explosive *whoosh*, the ball flew beyond the diamond, past the farthest outfielder and into the desert. The outfielders were frozen in shock for a split second before they went charging after it.

I knew it was hopeless for them. As I got to first base, the guys were still running.

Our third-base runner got to Home.

Just before I reached second base, the other team's fastest runner reached the ball. He scooped it up and lobbed it to the baseman in front of me.

It's going to be a close one, I thought as the baseman caught the ball and held it in my direction.

If he'd stayed on the base with the ball, there would be nowhere else for me to go. I'd have to get back to first and the game would be over—but he wanted to get me out. He came running toward me with the ball.

Just before he could touch me, I suddenly veered to the side. He went down hard.

I turned sharply, and my wheel barely touched the plate.

The baseman got up and threw the ball to third base. That baseman was smart, and stayed planted where he was, ball in hand.

I did a wide turn and headed back to Second. The baseman had his glove out, ready to catch the ball. I had too much momentum to turn around again. I had to beat the ball. I sensed the ball flying beside me. Would he catch it? As I was inches from the base, I saw the ball land in his glove and he turned and touched my chair with it. I eyed the baseman. His clothes were all dusty, but he was smirking down at me. He hadn't yet realized that he'd lost.

I smirked back just as widely and pointed to Home, where three of our players were standing. My diversion worked.

The opposing team members threw their hats and mitts to the ground. Abbott was spewing a few words I'd rather not record, but a few of the players seemed impressed.

Our team cheered and came out to meet me. Most of them patted me on the back, and one even hugged me, which was a little awkward as he maneuvered around the chair. I was laughing and smiling.

"Come on, Charlie. I'm going to run you Home," Dow said. I let go of my wheels, and he grabbed the chair from behind, breaking into a sprint as he pushed me to Third then turned toward Home.

I couldn't remember ever moving so fast. Sandy raced alongside us, barking joyfully. She seemed to understand that something wonderful had happened, even if she didn't know the rules of the game. We touched home plate and I cheered, but Dow didn't stop there. He ran me around all the bases once more, turning the corners as fast as he could. It was scary, but fun.

Sandy gave one sharp, proud bark. From my communicator came the translation: *"Victory!"*

He brought me to where Janara was jumping up and down, while her color was changing rapidly. "That was amazing! I didn't know it would be so thrilling to win!"

Her brother was beside her, shuffling his feet and looking very pale, like the color had been drained out of him. "I saw what you did, and I am sorry. I should not have said what I said. You are much more capable than I thought."

I blushed at the praise. "Thank you." I couldn't stop grinning. Takar's question—"What can she do?"—now sounded different. Not like an insult, but like a challenge I'd just answered in the best possible way.

"How was your first day, sweetie?"

"It was so wonderful, Mom! I had a great interview, and then I made some new friends and we played baseball—" I cut myself off as I saw Mom's startled expression. *Oh, great.... How am I going to explain this one?* I knew I couldn't tell the truth, but I couldn't keep it inside either. I remembered someone saying, *if you are going to lie, lie with the truth.* "I met some kids from the base. Their names are...Tom and, uh...Jane."

Her eyebrows creased in worry. "You didn't actually *go* to the base, did you?" she asked.

"No, no, no!" I reassured her. "We met outside. Oh, and Miss Dianne said that Sandy's allowed inside the office, so I need a mat and bowl for her while I'm there. Can we get some new ones?"

"No problem, sweetie. I'll pick them up from the store and drop them by tomorrow." She ruffled my hair.

Just then, Dad came into the kitchen. "So, they hired you to play baseball?" He didn't sound happy.

"Dad, I just said we did that after. I interviewed the two corporals first!" I protested. "They told me all about the...the experimental plane that crashed."

He scoffed. "First a spaceship, then a weather balloon, and now an experimental plane? What's next?" He turned away, grumbling, and I realized that he was still angry about being forced to write the weather balloon story.

"I'm sorry, Dad. I wasn't supposed to say anything. You won't tell anyone, will you?" I gave him the sad puppy dog eyes and hoped it would work like it always did.

After what felt like an hour of his stern face, his expression softened. "I'm sorry, darling. Of course I won't tell anyone. I'm glad you can talk to me." Then his eyes lit up. "Baseball, did you say? Did you play a weakling?"

I grinned back at him with all my teeth. "Yep! They bought it hook, line, and sinker. I got all three in safe."

"That's my girl," he said, patting me on the back.

I felt guilty that I hadn't told them the truth about the aliens, but it was something I was just going to have to get used to.

"I'm going to wash up for supper," I said, and wheeled to the bathroom. There was one more thing I needed to ask, now that I was alone. Pulling out my little communicator, I whispered, "Can you make me walk?"

Nothing happened. *What wording would a machine understand better?* "Communicator, are you able to help me walk?"

Some text appeared on its surface. *I am unable to risk exposing the Zalmen's presence on Earth.*

"But it *is* possible?" I said to the device.

Yes.

I thought for a few minutes. A story Mom once told me at Sunday church came back to me. "What if people thought it was someone else who healed me? What if people thought it was a miracle from God?"

Insufficient information.

I sighed. That was good enough for the moment. Putting the device back in my pocket, I washed up for dinner. When I came out, I asked my parents, "At supper, do you think you could pray that I would be healed and can walk?"

As I typed up my notes later that evening, I kept thinking about Dow's "hunches" and Rabinowitz's willingness to trust them. Sandy watched me work, occasionally tilting her head as if she understood every word I was writing.

[That first week of working while keeping such a massive secret was harder than I'd expected. Every time someone asked about my "research assistant" job, I had to bite my tongue to keep from blurting out the truth. Sandy was the only one I could really talk to, and she was an excellent listener.]

CHAPTER TWENTY-NINE

MRS. JONES

General Frank Jones

JONES FAMILY HOME

Jones shuffled into his house. There was a lump in his throat. "Chloe…. Honey…um…."

Chloe put her hands on her hips. "Francis Jones! You are going away again, aren't you?"

"You know me too well." Jones was relieved not having to say it.

"I would ask where, but I know better. You can't tell me. How long this time?"

Jones looked down. "At least a year."

Chloe spat out words in French, as she always did when upset. "A year? I was expecting the usual three months." She sighed. "But, I guess they need your strategic mind, and I'm afraid there is no one better."

The tension in his muscles relaxed. He held her in a warm embrace as he played on her words. "Don't be afraid, my dear." Jones tried to lighten the mood. "I'm going with the best technology and team there is. I picked them all myself."

"I'm not actually afraid. I know our president wouldn't send you to any place dangerous. He doesn't want to lose you any more than I do. Do we have time to tell the kids?"

"Yes, invite them to dinner next weekend. Oh, and I have something for you." He pulled a box out of his jacket pocket.

Chloe opened it. Inside was a locket with his and her pictures in it. "It's wonderful!"

"Now, you won't be alone. Anytime you need me, you can see me and talk to me." Jones was being deceivingly honest. While it was a normal photo, the metal was a communicator. Anytime she opened it, it would record her voice and, as a communicator, decide if it should send the recording to him or call locally for help.

He didn't want to spy on her, and he didn't want the temptation to talk back to her, so there was no camera, screen, or speaker, just a one-way transmitter. They were also setting up a spaceship-to-shore phone line if they needed it.

She closed the locket and gave him a kiss and a hug. "I'll miss you."

[Mrs. Jones never knew that locket was really a communicator. Sometimes the kindest lies are the ones that let people feel safe while their loved ones are saving the world.]

CHAPTER THIRTY

PREPARING FOR THE SPACE FLIGHT

Ambassador Ryan Wilcox

EARTH–ZALMA BASECAMP, NEW MEXICO

The base was moving to Area Three, so the whole place was a flurry of chaos. All around Wilcox, soldiers were packing bags, taking down tents, and loading supplies on the trucks. He carried two bags—his own and Donna's, but unlike the rest of the base residents, he and Donna weren't leaving on the truck; they were heading for the spaceship. Though the bags weren't heavy, he was light-headed and tired by the time he stepped through the phase variance.

Donna steadied him as he set down the luggage on the bridge. When he caught his breath and looked up, he noticed Geogram waiting for them. The ambassador greeted them both with a kind smile and a quick bow, which they returned.

After he and Wilcox shook hands, Geogram wasted no time in leading them through the main door from the bridge and down a hallway. As Wilcox stepped inside his room, his jaw nearly hit the floor.

"Holy mackerel!" Wilcox cried. "You said you could duplicate our rooms, but this is identical to when we scanned it! Even my bedsheets are folded the same, and the garbage is full!"

Geogram stood perplexed, as he usually did, when it came to human interaction. "You sound surprised. I am sorry that the dimensions of the room are not exact. All the rooms are the same length, as is dictated by the distance from the hallway to the outer wall of the ship. We adjusted the width to give you almost the same amount of space."

"How can you make it so precise?" Wilcox asked.

"Our nanite technology can duplicate anything." Geogram waved a hand carelessly around the room.

"Can it duplicate people?"

Geogram whitened. "No. Of course not. Why would you ask that?" He only relaxed when he heard Donna giggle from the doorway. "Oh.... Very funny! Should we make adjustments to the other rooms?"

"Just minor changes, I think. Definitely do *not* copy the garbage or dust." Wilcox pointed to the bin. "Other than that, move the blankets a little or put the pen and paper in a slightly different spot. A little randomness makes us feel more relaxed."

"Why is that?"

"Good question. I'll let you know when I have a good answer." Wilcox laughed, trying to show Geogram that he'd meant it as a joke, but the mauve alien stared at him blankly again. Wilcox sighed. He'd gotten used to explaining things to the other ambassador over the past few days.

Donna spoke up. "Maybe it's because life's not perfect," she said. "And since we can't make it perfect, we'd rather not see anyone or anything that is."

Geogram nodded as if she'd just fed him one of the great mysteries of the universe. "Stimulating. Miss Warren, your room is next door." They dropped her luggage off in it. "Are you two ready for mealtime?"

"Dinner?" Wilcox coached him on the English phrasing. Feeling the knot in his stomach, he replied, "Yes."

*

Heading back down the halls, the two humans admired the simplicity of the ship's design. Like a hotel, it had a single but wide straight hallway, well-lit, as the metal in the walls seemed to glow. Each doorway had a name on it. The names also glowed, like the door itself was a communicator. *Would they go through that expense to put communicators everywhere?*

Then they arrived at the dining room, where everyone else had already gathered for dinner. They were all sitting around a long rectangular table, strewn with serving platters of strange and colorful cubes.

The Zalmen had saved them seats in the middle. The ladies all sat across from the men, and the kids sat beside their parents. All the plates were already full and untouched; they'd been waiting.

"So, what is this?" Wilcox asked, casting his eyes over the unfamiliar items.

He was surprised that Joanua, the engineer who was sitting next to Donna, spoke up. "Vegetables from our home planet," she said. "I ran numerous simulations to ensure they are compatible with your human biology." She seemed so proud of herself that Wilcox nodded, though he was still apprehensive. "I also scanned the crops in your local farms to recreate flavors you would be familiar with. The white mound is similar to your potatoes. The green portion is like spinach, and the orange sticks and red cubes are like carrots and tomatoes."

"Wow!" Donna cried. "That sounds like a lot of work. Thank you so much."

Donna had already eaten a few bites and hadn't turned green, so Wilcox risked a forkful of the colorful fair. He chewed, turning it over in his mouth. *Not bad matching the flavor,* he thought, but it was bland. Maybe they didn't believe in seasonings. "You did a great job. How did you do it?"

Joanua positively glowed, face filling with a burst of magenta. She was quick to contain herself and explain. "I compared the chemical composition of your plants to ours. After performing a data matrix analysis, I was able to combine our plants in the right proportions to simulate the chemistry—and therefore the nutrition and flavor of your food."

"Would you happen to have scanned any seasonings, like salt or pepper?" His words were cautious as he realized he'd never actually seen the Zalmen eat. They were aliens; they probably had different taste buds.

Joanua frowned, though luckily, she didn't seem offended. "We have not found those plants yet."

"Oh. . . . Pepper is not grown locally. I can bring you some samples next time. And salt is not a plant; it's a mineral. We often dehydrate ocean water or mine it from the ground."

Around the table, the crew members were almost vibrating with how fast their colors changed. They were whispering too, and when Wilcox strained to understand them, he found they weren't speaking English. Rather, their language reminded him of Mandarin and Navajo but was definitely different from either of them. Agugua was the closest and loudest, his words guttural, and all at once, Wilcox could understand how the language gave him his accent.

Wilcox looked across the table at Donna, who seemed similarly fascinated, though she tried to hide it by focusing on the food in front of her.

When the sound lulled, she took her chance. "The chemical compound for regular table salt is sodium chloride, if that helps."

"Ah, yes!" Joanua double tapped the table next to her plate, and a screen appeared in front of her. She input a few words, which Wilcox guessed must've been the formula, because only a second later, a small container rolled out of a console in the wall and Joanua retrieved it for him. "Try this," she said.

Wilcox shook the container. It sounded like salt, and when he peered inside, it looked and smelled like salt, too. He sprinkled it over the food and took a bite. "Much better! Thank you," he said. At least his food wouldn't be tasting like cardboard for the foreseeable future. *However,* he thought, *vegetables, no matter how seasoned they are, aren't a full meal.* He glanced around at the table, hoping to spot a steak or maybe even some chicken. When he found none, he frowned. "Where is the meat?"

The Zalmen blinked at him.

"What is meat? Your television showed these odd-shaped items on plates, but we were not able to identify them," Joanua said.

Wilcox and Donna exchanged a look.

"They talked about chicken, which we identified as an animal that lays eggs, but in order to make the eggs that dark and hard, they must have really overcooked them."

His stomach dropped. How, in all these days of knowing each other, had he not thought to ask this? How could he have overlooked such a fundamental cultural difference? He'd dealt with different cultures before—humans had a lot of them, after all, and some were vegetarian, but not to this extent. Vegetarians on Earth at least knew what meat was. Wilcox scolded himself, then carefully chose his next words. "Oh, you are vegetarian?"

"I don't know," Joanua replied. She seemed confused by the term; perhaps she'd never heard it before. "But we eat vegetables."

"I am sorry. How do I say this? Donna?" he turned to her, desperately searching for advice, but she shook her head. "OK, maybe we should talk about this later?"

Geogram leaned forward against the table, turning his body toward Wilcox. "You have us all interested now. I think you should tell us."

"OK," Wilcox said, squeezing his eyes shut for a long second. He took a deep breath. "This may come as a shock to you, so please hear me out, but when we talk about the *meat* from a chicken, we are not referring to the eggs. We are referring to...the...the... bird...itself."

No one spoke for a few seconds. Donna was stiff as a board across from him, and everyone else at the table had turned starched white like his words had turned them into ghosts. Edugra looked ready to jump up from her chair and bolt.

After a moment, the room seemed to explode with movement as flashes of red, yellow, white, and green filled Wilcox's vision on all sides. The blood rushing in his ears subsided, only to be replaced by the racket of chatter from the crew members.

Geogram rose from his seat, deadly calm, and a hush fell over them. He stared down at Wilcox, eyes hard as chips of stone. "Do we understand you correctly? You are saying that you eat the flesh of another living creature?"

"No," Wilcox protested, "they are not living when—"

"How barbaric!" Edugra burst out. She stood up so quickly that her chair flew back, hit and absorbed into the wall. She stormed out of the room, followed quickly by Joanua, with Sarara and Kanara rushing Janara and Takar out.

Agugua set down his utensils and pointed at the humans. When he spoke through the translator, his words were quiet, though his voice shook with barely contained emotion. *"You will leave,"* he said. He pointed to himself and the other Zalmen. "We will discuss this."

I guess I should've expected this reaction. Wilcox cursed himself—*I could've handled it better,* he thought—as he and Donna rose from their seats and headed for the hallway to their rooms. Geogram intercepted them with a raised hand, and Wilcox almost flinched as he noticed that the other ambassador seemed afraid to touch him.

"I don't think you understand," Geogram said, pointing to the other side of the room, at another door Ryan didn't remember seeing before. "When Captain Agugua asked you to leave, he meant the ship."

Wilcox's stomach dropped. The treaty, the alliance, Earth's first interstellar partnership, all crumbling because he'd mentioned meat. Donna's nails dug into his arm as the door hissed open to desert night.

Wilcox lay awake that night, staring at the ceiling of his tent and replaying every moment of the failed dinner. Three days ago, he'd been proud of brokering humanity's first interstellar alliance. Now he wasn't sure if he'd just destroyed it over a chicken dinner.

Dad would have seen this coming. *A real diplomat would have asked about their diet in the first five minutes.*

CHAPTER THIRTY-ONE

DEAD MEAT

Charlotte "Charlie" Baker
ROSWELL, NEW MEXICO

Bzzzt.

I glanced up from my book. My bedroom window was open as I read by lamplight, but I knew the sound didn't come from outside. It was my communicator. Setting the book down on the sill, I closed the window and pulled the curtain a little. Then I checked the hallway. Mom and Dad were both in the living room, busy. I eased the door shut again and pulled the communicator out. *"Answer."*

Janara and Takar's faces showed up on the smooth surface, but they were both stark white and trembling, eyes wide.

"What's wrong?" I asked. Janara had whispered to me once what their different colors meant, and I knew this meant they were worried.

Takar opened his mouth, but no words came out. Finally, he said, *"Do you eat dead animals?"* His voice was small and quivering.

"Of course not. Why would you ask that?" I asked.

"We just learned that meat is dead animals," Janara said.

My heart fell to the floor. They looked so scared and hurt that I felt sick to my stomach. "Oh...that.... Well...I guess I do. I just never thought about it before." Sandy seemed to sense the tension in my voice. She padded over and rested her chin on my lap, looking up at me with those understanding eyes that always made me feel better.

"How can you not know that you're eating an animal?" Takar asked. His color had shifted to yellow, so it looked like his skin was made of parchment.

"When I was much younger, I ate the food my parents put in front of me. I didn't know what it was. There is no animal called beef or pork, so I didn't know for the longest time that they came from a cow and a pig. But when I realized that the chicken we ate was once a living bird, I felt sick."

That seemed to calm them a little, though they still looked afraid.

"What did you do?" Janara asked. *"Did you keep eating them?"*

I shook my head. "I refused to eat meat for almost a year. My parents let me, but after a while, I got really sick."

"Why?"

"The doctor said I wasn't eating properly. I wasn't getting the proper nu…" I stumbled on the word, "proper nutrients…from the foods I was eating. My muscles got really weak and I was tired all the time. I could barely sit up in my chair."

"But why? We've never had to…to…." Takar choked on the rest of his words, but I understood what he was asking.

"Once a person gets used to a diet, it's hard to change."

"But why did your people start in the first place?"

"It's the way of things on Earth," I told them. "Plants eat the sunshine, animals eat the plants, and big animals eat the little animals. Or…something like that. My dad once wrote an article about it, and how things need to be balanced. If there aren't any meat-eaters to eat the plant-eaters, all the plants will run out because there are too many animals eating them." They seemed interested, and my explanation brought a bit of color back to their faces.

"Oh," Janara said. *"On our planet things work very differently!"*

"Really?" I asked. I'd never been too interested in biology before, but the thought of learning about a completely different planet was too tempting. If I learned more about it, I could write an article just like Dad wrote about Earth! "How does it work?"

Janara and Takar took turns telling me about Zalma and how it was different from what they'd learned about Earth.

I was shocked to discover that no animals on their planet ate meat. "How could that be? What do they do when animals die?"

"All creatures just return to the land," Janara said.

We ended the call almost an hour later, when Mom came in to tell me to get ready for bed. I noticed Sandy was sitting by my bedroom door, alert and listening. It was her "guard duty" position—something she'd started doing more often lately.

I went to sleep with a smile on my face, happy about the brand-new understanding between me and my new friends.

[Even then, Sandy knew we were being watched. She was protecting our secret before I even realized how dangerous it had become. I should have paid more attention to her warnings.]

CHAPTER THIRTY-TWO

BLUE MONDAY

Ambassador Ryan Wilcox

EARTH–ZALMA BASECAMP, NEW MEXICO

[The great meat crisis of 1947—that's what Dow called it later. Who would have thought that bacon and eggs could nearly end humanity's first interstellar alliance?]

Early on Monday morning, Wilcox went to see the general. Jones had been discussing possible new recruits with Cpl. Dow, but turned his attention to Wilcox as he entered. Thankfully, he didn't comment on Wilcox's appearance as he hadn't slept well and probably looked as ragged as he felt.

"Ambassador." Jones's voice was neutral, not judging. "I hear things didn't go well on the weekend while I was away."

Wilcox heaved a sigh, his face downcast. "No general, they did not! I goofed. Did you know that they're vegetarians? I mean, we should have guessed with the whole pacifist thing. They can't kill an animal to save their life, literally!"

"Oh, that is a problem," the general said. "I like my steak!"

"They called us barbaric and kicked us off the ship, then threw our luggage outside. I went back this morning to see if they were still there, but the door was closed. It's so weird. I can feel the doorway, but the rest of the ship isn't there. It's like they flew away without it!"

"The first time I entered the ship, they told me that it was in another dimension or something so it couldn't be detected, but they kept the door partially in our world so we can go in and out," Dow said.

"Is that even possible?" The question was rhetorical, but both young men shrugged anyway, and the general sighed. "Is there any *good* news?"

"Yes," Wilcox replied. *And thank God for that.* "Donna has been talking to Edugra on her communicator. They've built up a friendship."

"And?"

"Donna prefers vegetarian food; she only eats meat when the people around her are. She has been sympathizing with them." The general gave Wilcox a flat look, so he hurried on. "It turns out that all animals on Zalma are vegetarian. Sure, they eat eggs and drink milk, but no animal on their planet kills another. No animal eats another. They had no concept of what meat was."

"Well, now. I can see why they were so upset. That must have been quite a shock. What are you going to do about it?"

"What can I do?" Wilcox asked. His tone bordered dangerously on a whine, so he pulled himself together. "They're not answering my calls, and I already told you the door's been closed since they kicked us out on Friday."

Dow chuckled. "How's that for timing?" he asked. "It's opening now."

The others turned to him. He hadn't moved, but he was looking at the side of the tent with interest.

"Zalma technology," the corporal explained, pointing at his glasses. "I can see heat through thin material—mostly a person's body heat. Someone is exiting the ship. Benjamin identifies him as Geogram, and he is heading this way."

"Benjamin?" Wilcox found himself asking. The soldier had used that name before.

"That's what I decided to name my communicator," he replied.

Just then, Geogram entered the tent. He had a stiff posture and cold eyes. "Greetings. At the request of my daughter Edugra, I am inviting Ambassador Wilcox and Miss Warren back to the ship to talk. But there will be no—" he cleared his throat "—*dead animals* on board! Is that understood?"

It was the first time they heard Geogram speak with authority. Jones, Dow, and Wilcox replied instinctively. "Yes, sir."

Geogram was taken aback but seemed pleasantly surprised with the response.

"Good. Ambassador, please retrieve your assistant so we may continue our discussions." Geogram headed back to the spaceship.

Wilcox let out a sigh of relief as he stepped aboard the Ymit. They still had hope for the alliance to continue—if only they could figure out how to compromise. Other than the meat issue, the Zalmen had been entirely willing to provide them with whatever they needed.

"We do hope that our work together may continue without trouble or delay," Geogram said.

Wilcox's grip tightened on the communicator in his hand. He'd just reviewed the list of requests from the general's team members, but having the device in his hand was comforting. "I agree, so let's get started. Our warriors are very physical people, and they need a lot of space to exercise and play games to stay strong."

Geogram nodded. He folded his hands together. "How much room will they require?"

"Honestly, as much room as you can give them. One wants a jogging track, one wants a weightlifting room, and another wants a target range, but they all want to play sports, like baseball, basketball, and football."

Captain Agugua turned around in his chair and spoke in Zalmen. *"Do they need a different room for each sport?"* the computer translated.

"No," Wilcox said. "One room, a gymnasium, can accommodate everything. We would just have to move and store the goalposts, basketball hoops, and targets. You may have seen these sports on television."

Joanua displayed an outline of the ship (one long strip with a hallway on one side, and rooms on the other) on the main screen.

"Yes, I like your baseball. It is the least violent of them all," Agugua said through the translator. *"Kanara's daughter enjoyed it greatly when she played."*

Edugra clapped her hands together cheerfully. "I remember seeing those sports," she remarked. "The fields were similar in length to our ship but twice the width." She found several sports fields and laid an outline of them on the main screen over top of the ship's blueprint.

"We were planning to build a second floor for the human rooms, but instead we could put them on the main level and build the second floor for the sports." Joanua typed something, and the main screen updated with the new layouts. She looked at the captain for authorization.

Agugua nodded.

Joanua nodded back. "I will enter the specifications of the extra crew quarters and gymnasium into the ship's computer. With our nanite technology, it should only take a day for the additional rooms to grow onto the ship."

"If the gymnasium is on the top, can you put lots of windows on the walls and ceiling? That would make a great view," Donna said.

"I can make all the ceiling and walls transparent," Joanua said.

"Won't that be dangerous? Couldn't the glass break?" Wilcox asked.

Joanua shook her head. "No. The transparent material will not be made from your glass; it is indeed much stronger than glass. Our deflectors will also stop anything from breaking it."

Everyone seemed satisfied, so Joanua proceeded. "General Jones requested replica phones so you can call home at any time. While the space transmission is crystal clear, we have created the option to add static to sound like your mobile radiophone, for when you are calling family from space."

"Great! Thank you." Wilcox smiled. "Now I think it's time Ambassador Geogram and I talk in private."

Leaving the others to their work, Wilcox followed the other ambassador from the bridge to a small conference room. He took one of the chairs around the table, sitting across from Geogram. He knew he had to speak quickly, to give Geogram the information he needed to make an informed decision, so he didn't wait for pleasantries; he just jumped right into their discussion.

"Donna and I are willing to switch to vegetarian," he offered, "but our warriors need meat to keep up their strength. We're willing to bring our own supply; we just need a place to keep it frozen."

"No. Absolutely not," Geogram said firmly, hand in the air. "No dead animals on our ship, and especially not on our home planet. It goes against everything that we believe in."

Wilcox was at a loss for what to do. The other ambassador had left no room for discussion, and if he'd been a more desperate man, he'd have pleaded with the alien to understand. He opened his mouth to speak several times, but nothing came out. As a man of business—a negotiator—he would *not* make a deal that was not equal. "Sorry, but our warriors won't go without it."

Geogram turned yellow but remained silent.

Wilcox took that as his cue to continue. "My people are already giving up a lot so they can help you. Think about it. They are voluntarily leaving their homes, everything and everyone they know, to go into space and defend a planet that they just heard about a week ago. *Your* planet! And you want them to give up their diet too? That would not be healthy for them. They'll be no use to you if they're too weak to fight or focus."

Parts of the yellow deepened to green, leaving his skin a mottled canvas. "I have spoken to First Minister Ronderra and the council, and they have made their decision. If you intend to bring dead animals upon the ship, they will not allow you aboard. It is barbaric. That is all to be said; we will not change our minds."

"So that's it?" Wilcox shot to his feet. That ugly feeling that had been settling deep in his gut for the past few days had suddenly bubbled up into rage. "You know, you are the most selfish, uncompromising species I have ever known. You spy on other planets and don't see anything wrong with it."

"We are *not* spies," Geogram snapped, flashing yellow. "We are trying to protect ourselves."

"No. What you're doing is putting everyone else at a disadvantage by watching and recording their every move. And what's worse, you've been transmitting our broadcasts out into space, where anyone could intercept them and find out where we are! What if they decided to invade us next because of what we have?"

"The Moadites are far past your technology. They will not attack you for it."

Wilcox snarled. "I'm sure it all makes perfect sense to you. You don't even see how what you're doing could affect others! You use your technology to gain information about us humans and the Moadites without consent. How would you feel if the roles were reversed? How would you like to be watched?"

Geogram didn't respond. His yellow skin flashed several different colors, including scarlet, orange, and indigo. His lips remained firmly closed, eyes watching Wilcox's face. That only angered the human more.

"Maybe if we were watching you, we would find out who was teaching you this technology. You never did answer that question. You keep your secrets, but act like you're entitled to the secrets of everyone else." He growled.

Geogram held his gaze angrily but still refused to say anything.

How could he just look back at him like he didn't need to explain his actions? *How can he think what his people are doing is OK?* "And the Moadites are angry with you for it. They want you to stop spying on them. Why should we get involved? You deserve their wrath.

"We have been at a disadvantage from the start. If you didn't offer to exchange technology with us, we would have no reason to help you. Maybe you should just leave and deal with the Moadites yourself."

At last, Wilcox couldn't take it anymore. He wished an outside door would appear again, or that he was closer to the exit as he stormed out of the conference room and down the hall. He was sure he'd get back to the bridge and off the ship before Geogram followed, but he was wrong. The purple alien was on his tail.

"But then you will have no way to defend Earth when the Moadites come," Geogram pointed out.

It was a good thing that the hallway was empty because Wilcox wasn't sure he wanted any of the ladies to hear if he finally did lose his temper. "What would they want from us? You said it yourself: we don't have any technology. We didn't spy on them. We are no threat to them. So please, give me one good reason I shouldn't recommend the termination of this alliance right now." He spun around to face Geogram, only to pause in surprise when he saw that the alien's face was completely white. He was afraid. *Why?*

"The council does not accept the eating of meat because our people need to be reassured. If you kill other animals for food, what is to stop your people from doing the same to us?"

"*You think that we would—*" Wilcox choked on the words. "I can't even say it. We are not *monsters*! If that's what you think of us, then obviously this alliance isn't going to work. We were willing to compromise, but you don't even know the meaning of the word. Call me when you've decided to be more cooperative." With that said, he whirled back around and stomped the rest of the way off the ship.

Wilcox shook with nerves by the time he entered the soldiers' barracks. Gen. Jones had called a meeting with the whole team as if they were still going to space, but he wasn't even sure if the alliance was still happening after that last big argument that he'd had with Geogram.

He glanced at the men. It was an odd, mixed group—a pilot, a marine, an engineer, and a communications expert. He'd met a few of them recently, and could link names to faces, but other than that, all of them were strangers.

Jones introduced Wilcox to the men.

"We've recently learned that there are no carnivores on Zalma. None whatsoever on the whole planet." Wilcox paused, waiting for a reaction, but the men were silent. He felt his heart throbbing under their watchful eyes. "That means they've never heard of one animal eating another. They were horrified to hear that we do it all the time."

"What that means for *us*," Jones said, stepping in, "is that they won't allow us to bring meat onto the ship."

A chorus of groans rose from the assembled men, though none voiced complaints yet, so Wilcox forged ahead.

"I am sorry, I have been trying to negotiate a compromise… but the Zalmen are strict vegetarians and *very* set in their beliefs. I'm afraid the ladies might spew if I even bring up the topic when they're around."

Sergeant Bruno Abbott stood first. A soldier in mind and body, Wilcox was sure the man could probably pop his head right off his shoulders.

"If that's the case, I'm not going!" Abbott declared. "No meat, no marine! The president isn't ordering us out…right, general?"

"Correct," Jones admitted—reluctantly. "This is a voluntary mission."

"This is the chance of a lifetime. Think of the technology we will gain," Wilcox interjected, hoping he could turn this around.

Abbott spat into the dirt. "I don't care about technology. I'm a soldier! I say you're just whistlin' dixie with these chromedome aliens. Oddballs, all of them. Who doesn't eat *meat*?"

Wilcox sputtered, but then Brian Howard, a civilian weapons designer, spoke up. "Well, I *am* interested in their technology. I could try going vegetarian, but I don't know how long I would last."

Of *course* he'd be interested in the science. "The good news is that they have expanded their garden so we can have our fresh fruit and vegetables, and they are willing to make room for the general's personal chef."

"That'd be better than any field ration kit, but…he can only cook vegetarian?" asked Lieutenant Colin McKenzie, a pilot.

More protests arose from the group, but Jones lifted a hand, and they all fell silent. "Wilcox, you've got one day to work things out, or the president's likely to pull the plug on this whole thing, and you know he'll do it. He's been clear in his opinion of this from the start. Dismissed!"

Wilcox gulped. He was no stranger to the president's views of the aliens. He wasn't against them, but he certainly wasn't enthusiastic about the alliance. Sure, he'd been interested in the weapons, but the loss of his best general wasn't the most ideal situation.

The others followed as Jones left the barracks, getting back to their daily activities.

Wilcox watched as Abbott returned to training with the other soldiers. They were running intensive drills, and Wilcox's body ached just watching them.

He thought again of eating a strict vegetarian diet, and his stomach flipped over. It just...didn't seem possible. Abbott was fit, and the way he lived was vital to that. Wilcox couldn't imagine him completely switching his diet without adverse effects on his health.

Some time later, Wilcox's communicator chirped in his pocket. When he answered, Edugra's face stared up at him.

"Can we meet?" she asked.

"Sure, I'll be right there."

A few minutes later, he entered her room on the Ymit, finding Donna and Joanua already in there with her. *What's this all about?* He glanced at his assistant with the question in his eyes.

Edugra signaled him to come in all the way so the door would close. She shook, and her color changed repeatedly through the whole range, including blue, green, red, purple, and white. "I am sorry," she said. "I know you two are doing your best to find a solution to this problem."

"Thank you." He was still confused, but the sincerity in her voice was touching.

"I do have to say that when I went to your mess hall, the smell nearly made me vomit, and I had to leave."

"Many humans enjoy the smell of cooked meat," Wilcox said. "I know you find that hard to believe, but it's true."

"Is there any way you can convince your people that they do not need meat?"

"No—because it's not the truth. Once your body is accustomed to a certain diet, changing it often has many unwanted side effects."

Edugra turned blue, and she nodded slowly. "I had hoped for some sort of compromise, but it is not my place to make those decisions. Your scientists have already helped strengthen our deflectors. Our leaders believe that it will hold the Moadites off long enough for them to evacuate the planet." Her voice grew smaller. "If you cannot come up with a compromise, we are to leave," she whispered.

"Are you saying that they are taking the help we gave them and then dumping us?" Wilcox asked. "That's not fair."

Edugra nodded. "I know. I am similarly distressed. Our crew members have enjoyed spending time with you humans. I do not believe that it is fair for my people to do such a thing."

"It *is* unfair," Joanua said firmly. She reached out to put her hand on Edugra's shoulder. "Sarara, Kanara, and I have been bonding with you humans as well. I especially have been impressed by how much I am learning about creativity." She looked at the two humans. "You are an unusual but interesting species."

Donna, who hadn't spoken the whole time, giggled at Joanua's words. "Well…thanks!" she seemed hopeful to lift the gloomy mood.

Wilcox realized Donna was only there to provide moral support for Edugra as she shared this information with him.

"Our soldiers aren't budging," Wilcox said the next time he and Donna entered the bridge. He glanced around at the entire crew. "They will not go without meat."

Geogram sniffed pointedly, his nose high in the air and his skin dark red. "Our council has expressed their objection to your barbaric practices. If you will not give them up, they have called an end to our alliance. They would rather see how they fare with the Moadites."

"What if we found new warriors? Ones who are already vegetarian?" Donna asked. Her own face was flushed with emotion.

It was a last second attempt, and Wilcox was annoyed she hadn't discussed it with him first, but he appreciated her effort.

"We would accept that," Geogram said. "How long would that take?"

"Well, there are some Eastern cultures that are vegetarian," Wilcox said. He hummed as he made the mental calculations. "We would have to accelerate foreign recruitment and then train them. Maybe a year?"

Geogram frowned, shaking his head. He turned away. "Then you can keep your communicator, and if you come up with something else, you can give us a call."

Wilcox had been given this mission—straight from the president's mouth—barely a week ago, and it had already fallen apart. He had failed!

He let out a sigh as the crew members on the bridge sent them off.

Agugua, as the captain, approached them first with a polite bow. *"Thank you for trying,"* he said through the translator. *"We will miss you."*

Donna shook the captain's hand.

Wilcox followed behind her, shaking Joanua, Kanara, Sarara, Janara, and Takar's hands.

Donna threw herself at Edugra, pulling her friend into a tight hug.

"Keep your communicator close," Edugra said.

"I will," Donna replied. "We can still chat, right?"

Edugra nodded, then turned to Wilcox. "This is a shame," she said, her face downcast and washed with red. "I was looking forward to working with you more."

He smiled back at her sadly. A strange feeling was welling up in his chest. For a moment he wondered if he was having a heart attack, but then disregarded it as disappointment in his failure. "I'll miss you, too." Then he turned to the last member.

Geogram was as put together as always, his posture rigid and his chin held high. "Ambassador," he said formally, offering a quick bow.

It was shallower than when he'd first greeted them. Nonetheless, Wilcox returned it. "Ambassador," he acknowledged. Then he stepped off the ship.

A moment later, Donna was next to him, and when they turned, nothing but desert spread out before them. He cautiously reached out a hand, but the ship was gone.

Gen. Jones summoned them to his tent. Wilcox *really* wasn't in the mood, but Donna's insistence had convinced him to follow his superior's orders.

"You did an incredible job," the general offered in comfort.

Wilcox looked away. "Thank you, sir. I just—"

"It was *not* your fault, son," Jones said firmly, cutting off his protests. "You did everything you could. The president and I want you to know that we are very proud of you."

Wilcox replied with a smile. He knew the general's words were only half-right. The president wouldn't have said that. He'd made himself clear what a great waste of time this alliance was. Sure, he'd be happy to take credit for it if the mission had been a success, but it wasn't. He could hardly expect the president to be happy with his actions. "Thank you, sir," he said all the same.

Donna leaned over the back of Wilcox's chair before settling in the one next to him. She, too, looked forlorn. "It would've been sweet to go into space, but I guess it wasn't in the cards. How did we even start working with aliens in the first place? I doubt they flew right up to the White House to talk to the president."

Cpl. Dow grinned cheekily at Cpl. Rabinowitz. "I was the first human to meet them, actually."

"How'd that happen?" She stared at the corporal with wide, curious eyes. The corners of her lips were upturned with interest.

Rabinowitz spoke before Dow got a chance. "Our detachment was called in to clean up a crash site near Roswell."

Dow cut in. "They thought it was a supply container or something, but it was a spaceship, like a lifeboat. Inside, we saw three dead aliens."

Wilcox frowned. "You never mentioned anything about *dead* aliens before."

Dow chuckled. "Oh, the aliens in the ship were dummies. They wanted to test our reactions."

This time Rabinowitz cut in. "After that, we met the *real* alien, Geogram. He asked for our help to contact the government, and from there, I sought out General Jones."

"Yes. I was the commander of the base and was called to inspect the wreckage. The proximity to the nuclear test site had me concerned, until I realized that it looked more like a refugee situation than a military one. When Dow and Rabinowitz showed up, they confirmed my suspicions."

Wilcox raised his eyebrows. "So, how'd you figure it out? Was it because the dummies were fake?"

Jones shook his head. "No, they were quite real. I had the local veterinarian do an autopsy on the alien bodies, and the doctor said that while he had never seen anything like them, their bodies reminded him of a stillborn calf."

Rabinowitz nodded. "Geogram told us that they're genetically modified clones."

"Cloning?" Donna repeated, disbelieving. "As in the novel, *A Brave New World*? Creating two identical beings?"

"Yeah, that's it. You read it too?"

"They were very convincing clones," the general explained. "The doctor who performed the autopsies believed they were real, but he didn't know how they died."

"Did you ever find out?" she asked.

Wilcox could tell that Donna was itching for a notepad. *A Brave New World* had been one of her favorite novels back when they both read it.

"They were never alive," Dow explained. "They were grown in a lab like plants."

That comment made Wilcox pause. "*Wait?* They just grew a *body*?" He paused. "What if they could grow other animals, like a cow?" He trailed off, his mind whirring with possibilities.

"Oh my God!" Jones shouted; his eyes were wide as saucers. "How did we miss this? Do you think it would work?"

"Do you think *what* would work?" Dow asked, staring between both of them in confusion. "What are you talking about? Did I miss something?"

Wilcox turned to him. "The Zalmen are against us *killing* animals to eat them. But they eat eggs, which are also animals, just that they were never alive to begin with. Would they still be against us eating meat if it was never alive either?"

After Wilcox finished his *very* long call to Geogram, he was sure he'd run out of breath. The alien ambassador, of course, had been skeptical from the moment Wilcox called. Perhaps it had something to do with how quickly he'd called after they left.

But once Wilcox told him their plan, Geogram's rough edges

softened. He seemed pleased that Wilcox had figured out a solution for them that didn't force them to give up their practices. He'd called Joanua to see if it was possible.

After talking back and forth, they'd *finally* come to an agreement.

He put the communicator in his pocket and looked over at Donna. She was staring back at him, as quiet as she'd been during the call, but now she was smiling.

When they joined Jones, Dow, and Rabinowitz stood outside at the edge of camp, staring up at the cloudless sky. They seemed to be waiting for something.

"So, what did they say?" the general asked.

He hadn't turned, so obviously, he'd heard the crunching of Wilcox's footsteps on the dry Earth. "Geogram doesn't see a problem with us eating cloned meat on board the ship. He suspects that the council will stipulate that you do not eat meat in public on Zalma, or discuss meat with any Zalmen. He's concerned that if their people saw meat, even cloned, they would wonder what it is, and the answer would cause the same fear that they experienced at our first meal, and he doesn't want his people to be afraid of us. He told me he'd discuss it with their council and see if they felt the same. Then, he'll let us know."

Dow nodded, then turned away from the sky and rubbed at his eyes.

"Care to finish your stories?" Donna asked.

The general and the two corporals took turns telling their stories. When they were finished, they looked up.

"I don't know why we are looking!" Dow protested. "I have never seen their ship; it's always invisible. Have any of you seen it?" He looked at the others.

Everyone shook their heads.

Wilcox was hungry, as he hadn't eaten all day. He took Donna for dinner, and when they came back, the sun was painting the sky in peachy oranges. Soon they were staring up at the dark sky, waiting for something to happen.

Nothing did.

Dow sighed. "Well, I guess they're not coming back," he said. "You'd think that they could have at least called." With a huff, he hauled himself up off the ground where he'd been lying and was just about to head back to his own tent for the night when something finally changed.

A song was playing, coming from an unseen source. Wilcox peered into the distance. There was something shining in the sky. At first, he'd thought it was just a star, but it was getting bigger. The song was growing louder.

The star was soon too big to be a star, and Wilcox saw the Ymit for the first time. It was a massive flying rectangle, descending from the darkening sky. The outside gleamed silver, reflective, and shiny.

"How does that thing even fly? It doesn't look aerodynamic whatsoever," Wilcox said.

"If they can make it invisible, control gravity, and grow clones, I think they can make a shoebox fly," Dow replied.

Wilcox nodded. Now that the ship was in sight, he could hear the familiar song's lyrics.

"'You Are My Sunshine'!" Donna shouted excitedly. "That's Ryan's and my favorite song!"

"Wow, it's huge!" Dow shouted, completely ignoring Donna.

After hearing the song and seeing the ship, Wilcox thought the display couldn't get any flashier, but he was wrong. Small projectiles shot out from the ship and into the sky, exploding in a burst of sparks and color. Pops and bangs filled the air, jolting the entire basecamp of Area Three.

A dozen other recruits ran out of their tents, some holding their rifles, ready to fight off the invading forces, but then they looked up, and their jaws dropped.

As the first round of fireworks cleared, another song played, this time, smooth jazz.

Jones hummed. "'Sentimental Journey'. That's *my* favorite." He sounded pleased. "And would you look at that display! They must be learning imagination." Then he chuckled, looking around at the looks of awe on the soldiers' and civilians' faces. "It's a good thing we're the only ones around for miles out here in the desert."

A second round of fireworks began. It opened with a shower of gold, then stars of blue and red. The sky, once painted by the sunset, was awash with more colors than Wilcox could've imagined. All too soon, the fireworks were over, a third song, an upbeat tune on a trumpet, began to play.

"'Boogie Woogie Bugle Boy'," Dow identified. "That's the one *I* told Joanua about."

They listened with wide grins on their faces, and as the song ended, a third display of lights filled the night sky around the hovering ship. Then it descended the rest of the way and touched down on the empty desert. A door opened, and in the distance, Wilcox could see the aliens walking toward them. He waved. "That was quite an entrance!" he called as they got closer.

Geogram nodded politely, sending a quick smile at his daughter, and Wilcox *knew* it must've been her idea. "We observed your Fourth of July celebrations before we sent the decoy and based it on that. Did we get it right?"

Wilcox was grinning ear to ear. "Yes, I'd say so!" He found that, in the rush of emotions, he didn't care that the alliance had almost failed. All he could think about was that the Zalmen had returned.

PART 3:
GREG'S INDECISION

CHAPTER THIRTY-THREE

ALIENS AREN'T REAL

General Greg Newman

WASHINGTON, D.C.

[He had no idea that his entire understanding of reality was about to change—and that his ambition would nearly destroy him.]

Major General Greg Newman was in his office as his adjutant, Lt. Samson, handed him his newspaper.

'High-Altitude Balloon Crash Lands in Roswell'. He huffed and tossed the newspaper back onto his desk without even bothering to read the article. "That's more like it. Just a few days ago, they claimed they found a flying saucer. How gullible do they think we are?"

Newman was a practical man—a man of facts. Had been all his life; it was how he got where he was. He'd never bought into conspiracy theories like the nuts out there. "Who believes in aliens? Probably the same nuts who think the Earth is flat."

Samson's poker face did not change. "Yes, sir. Is there anything else I can do for you before I leave today?"

Newman sat back and formed a triangle with his fingers, his usual thinking position. Then he said, "Yes, I almost forgot. I'm visiting my mother tomorrow, and I need a bouquet for her. Contact the shop in the city that I usually deal with. Nothing expensive, just a basic bouquet. I'll pick it up on my way out tomorrow and pay for it when I get there—from my own pocket. Don't put it on the base's account."

Newman narrowed his eyes briefly. While he'd love to outsource the expense, the boutique's name on his record wouldn't look good. Newman was on the promotion selection list, and if he was going to make Lieutenant General, he'd need to keep things professional.

Samson's lips quirked up proudly. "Already done, sir. I saw your monthly visit in your calendar." He glanced at the papers in his hands.

Newman nodded. "Dismissed."

Three seconds later, the door closed, but Newman didn't notice. In his mind, the adjutant was already gone.

Newman returned to his paperwork with a grunt and a frown. *Hopefully the higher ups will be impressed with this report. I caught the traitor.*

Newman scrawled smoothly over his paperwork with his favorite pen, marking the details of his plan and how he'd executed it flawlessly. There had been a traitor among his soldiers, and all he'd had to do was lay the bait and sit back. He smiled to himself, remembering the look on the rat's face when he'd been caught. Now the traitor was in jail where he belonged, and Newman could go back to his paperwork.

It was the one part of his job that he hated, but he knew it was better to do it himself. Especially with such an important report as this, one he hoped the higher ups would read, and that it would help him with his promotion. He never entrusted the critical reports to anyone else, since that one time his assistant had logged a mission wrong. His *ex*-assistant, that is.

*

Newman was seated alone in the corner at a diner along the highway for lunch for some real food. Food on the base wasn't bad, but it was too bland for Newman's taste.

Annoyed, he sat alone in the corner, watching the young folks in their booths chattering around him. In one hand, he held a mug of black coffee, every sip of which he savored. It was hot and bitter and just what he needed to get through a visit with his mother. He loved her dearly—very dearly—but she had a way of trying his nerves.

The young waitress set down his sandwich. "Anything else I can get you, sir?" she asked, flashing a bright smile.

She was fishing for compliments. All waitstaff were like that nowadays, flaunting themselves in hopes of an extra juicy tip. "No thanks, doll," he replied. His eyes trailed after her as his ex-girlfriend, Sheena, filled his head again. He scowled and took a bite of his sandwich.

The meal had been thirty-five cents, so he tossed it down and a penny before he left. In the corner of his eye, he could see the waitress's frown as she cleared the table. He ignored it. One cent was his usual tip, and he worked hard for his money. If the diner couldn't afford to pay its staff proper wages, that wasn't *his* problem.

His next errand took place at The Happy Florist, his mother's favorite boutique. It smelled strongly of roses no matter the season, and even though he didn't have allergies, the air always made Newman's nose itch. If the shop's tinkling bell didn't alert the clerk to his presence, his following volcanic sneeze sure did.

The clerk smiled at him. "Hello, Mr. Newman!" She bustled in and out of the back room, returning with a large, colorful bouquet. "We know your mother really likes gladioli, and they aren't in season for long, so we went ahead and put together the bouquet."

Newman took a step toward the door without the flowers, but then turned around. "I asked for a cheap bouquet. I don't see the point of spending so much on flowers that will just die in a couple of days."

The florist dropped her head and shoulders in disappointment.

Newman looked at her sad eyes. "But Mom does love them, and I only see her once a month. Hopefully, this will make up for missing last month's visit."

"That will be three dollars," she said hesitantly.

Newman's eyes popped. *That's almost four pounds of steak!* He frowned as he reached for his wallet, withdrew the money, then paused before laying it on the counter.

The drive to his childhood home was a quiet one, with far fewer cars on the road than he'd anticipated. Traffic would've given him a chance to prepare himself for the visit. Newman's mother was a kind and gentle woman, but the memories of his childhood haunted him all the same. An image of his father flashed before his eyes just as the white-sided house came into view, and Newman shook himself.

He walked up the central path, past the perfect lawn and the garden beds bursting with flowers. He remembered playing out on this lawn as a boy. The hot days, the cold days, the rainy days—it didn't matter. He'd never been bothered by the elements. He reached the porch and remembered his mother's face, wet with tears, standing there when he was seventeen and heading off to West Point. That was the moment he'd turned his life around and never looked back.

Now, here he was again, a major general, and he could visit his mother every month in this home that held so much sadness. The difference was, now he was strong.

He knocked on the door.

"Gregory, darling!" his mother cried in delight as she opened the door. "You're here!"

He leaned down to press a quick kiss to her cheek. "Hi, Mom. These are for you." He thrust the bouquet forward, hoping she wouldn't dote on him like she usually did. Her eyes lit up.

"You remembered how much I love gladioli! Let me just get them in some water. Come in." Gladly taking the bouquet, she wandered back into the house to find a vase.

By the time she set them on the dining table, Newman had already dealt with his boots and coat, and was admiring an old picture of her. She was once a beautiful young lady with blonde curls, and that beauty had stayed with her as she aged. Though she'd lost much of her height and her hair had gone gray, her face was creased with happiness, not worry.

She stood back to admire the flowers. "They are beautiful, thank you," she said as he walked up behind her.

"How are you doing?" he asked.

"I am a little tired, but I've been doing OK." She quickly ushered him to the table to sit, fussing about how tired he must be. "I was worried you weren't coming today. You didn't last month."

Newman sighed. "I'm sorry, Mom. You know I had important business to take care of."

"Yes, I know dear. It just gets so lonely here without you. So, have you finished that big project you were working on?"

His chest swelled, and a bright smile overtook his lips. "Yes. It was a great success."

"I never doubted!" his mother claimed, clapping her hands. "My boy, first an honor student, now a general in the army. I'm so proud! Come on, let's eat before the food gets cold."

She disappeared into the kitchen, only to reappear with two steaming plates of pasta. On another trip, she produced a fresh garden salad and a pitcher of lemonade. Newman eyed the food as she set it out, not at all surprised. It was the same dish she always prepared for his visits. Sometimes he wondered if she lived on the stuff.

She smiled at him. "I know spaghetti has always been your favorite."

Yeah, when I was a teenager.

She continued chattering the entire time they were eating, asking how he'd been, if he'd been up to anything interesting, if he'd read about that weather balloon incident in the papers. Apparently, it was all her lady friends could talk about. "Betty thinks that they're using the story to cover up a big conspiracy. Aliens! Wouldn't that be exciting, dear?"

"Aliens aren't real, Mom. We've been over this."

She huffed. "For someone who always did so well in science, I don't understand how you could be so closed-minded." Annoyed, she changed the subject, and unfortunately, the new topic was one he'd much rather avoid. "How come you haven't been bringing around that lovely lady of yours? What was her name? Sheila?"

"Sheena," he corrected, "and we split up months ago. She kept trying to push me into buying her a ring." She was pretty, but she had strong opinions of just about everything; he knew they weren't a good match. They would have spent their lives arguing about every little thing.

His mother pressed her lips together. "Gregory, you are not getting any younger, and it's time you settled down and started a family. I was so sure you two would be married by now."

Newman ground his teeth for a moment, but held his tongue. Marriage was a topic his mother would never let go. She wasn't *old*, but she was getting there, and she wanted grandkids before she passed. In part, she and Sheena were alike. They were both stubborn—*and* they both wanted Newman to do something he didn't want to do.

"I don't have time to start a family. I'm already forty-five, and I'm still just a lackey two-star general; have been for two years now. If I distract myself with marriage, I may as well just stay treading water! No, I need a promotion. They only give the *real* jobs to the three- and four-star generals."

"And if you get your promotion, *then* will you find yourself a nice lady?"

"Mom, I'd sooner see your *aliens* falling from the sky than let anything distract me from this job."

[General Newman laughed at his mother's belief in aliens that day, not knowing that his entire world was built on foundations of sand. People like him—so certain, so dismissive—they're the ones who fall the hardest when reality comes calling.]

CHAPTER THIRTY-FOUR

CHARLOTTE AND THE AMBASSADORS

Charlotte "Charlie" Baker
ROSWELL, NEW MEXICO

[Meeting Ambassador Wilcox and Donna felt like stepping into the grown-up world of diplomacy.]

The next time I arrived at the office, a blond man and a blonde woman were in the interview room, so I went straight in and Sandy followed.

The man stood up. His blue eyes were kind. "Miss Baker. It's so good to meet you."

"Thank you. It's nice to meet you too." I sat up taller, pulling out my communicator. "Would you mind if I take a video of this interview?"

Both of them shook their heads 'no', so I set my communicator down on the desk. I'd figured out something new recently when I was playing around with it. Tilting the communicator and holding it that way made small protrusions stick out of it to prop it up. I angled it to get all three of us and got back into place.

"*Communicator, record.*" I turned to the two of them. "Please start by introducing yourselves."

The man spoke first. "I'm Ryan Wilcox, ambassador of Earth to planet Zalma."

"And I am Donna Warren," said the woman. "You can call me Donna. I'm his partner."

"Assistant!" Ambassador Wilcox corrected with a teasing smirk as he winked at me. "We've known each other a very long time. You might sense the sibling rivalry."

"Sibling rivalry?" I asked.

"We treat each other like brother and sister," he replied.

My cheeks heated, they were sitting so close together that I thought they might've been dating, though I knew better than to say it out loud. Dad *never* did that in an interview. As I looked back at both of them, I noticed something strange. The color had drained from Donna's face. Wilcox didn't seem to have noticed.

"Are you ready to interview me? I negotiated our treaty," he said.

"You negotiated the first treaty with aliens?"

"Yes. The thought of it scared the living daylights out of me until I met them. They were very nice, and they were more nervous than I was."

"We're not that bad, are we?"

Donna chuckled. "They are pacifist vegetarians who don't know how to fight, and they are with humans."

"But that is also why they came to us. We made peace after the Second World War," Wilcox added.

"Good point," I said. "Janara and Takar told me all about the meat situation. But then we talked all about the circle of life and we were fine."

They both paled. "It only took two days to form the alliance and that one dinner almost ruined it all!" he cried. "How did you change their minds so quickly?"

"I dunno. Kids are just better like that," I said cheekily before remembering to be professional.

Donna chuckled. "It sounds like we should've just come to you to solve the problem. If Dow hadn't mentioned that the decoys were cloned, we would have never suggested eating cloned meat," she said.

"Cloned meat? Just like from the decoy?" I asked.

"Yes, exactly. They contain all the same nutrients as regular meat, but they were never alive in the first place, which means the Zalmen don't have a problem with it. Just like eating eggs."

"That's a creative solution. So..." I glanced down at my list of questions, "what are your differences and how does it help you in your job?"

Their eyes grew wide, and they looked at each other. I think they were trying to get the other to answer first, so I broke the ice. "You said you were scared to negotiate with them. How did that affect your work?"

Wilcox chuckled. "An excellent question. Since this was my first solo negotiation, and the first negotiations with aliens, I didn't want to make any mistakes. Donna and I were very careful to check and rechecked that we covered all the bases."

I nodded. "Donna, what do you do?"

She tapped her finger to her lips a few times. "I take notes using shorthand, and we do a lot of the planning together."

I chuckled. "We girls are more social than the guys; did that come into play at all?"

Her eyes grew bright. "Yes! I formed a friendship with Ambassador Geogram's daughter, Edugra, so when the meat thing happened, we continued to chat and eventually got the men to talk to each other again."

"Just like me and my friends!" I smiled. "What's the saying, behind every good man, there's a great woman?"

Donna winked at me.

Wilcox grunted. "Well, we need to get back to Area Three."

"Are you coming along, Charlie? I'm sure your friends will want to see you," Donna suggested.

I eagerly agreed.

Our trip in the Spacevan was no longer than the last one, but as I rolled down the ramp they'd added for me, I saw that we were in a completely different place than Area Two. Sandy pushed her nose under my hand, so I rubbed her. I looked around for Janara and Takar, but instead was met face to face with a light purple alien. He was clearly the ambassador that Donna and Mr. Wilcox told me about.

He gave me a slight bow. "Greetings Charlie Baker. I am Ambassador Geogram. I have heard so many good things about you."

"Hello Mr. Geogram!" I said. "Can I interview you too? Do you have time?" Mom probably would've scolded me for being so forward, but Dad always said good reporters push where they can, and while I was getting bored of all the answers just coming to me, at least here I was the one initiating it.

Geogram smiled like he was amused. "If you like, yes, you can interview me before visiting the children." He sounded like any other man you'd see walking down the street, though his accent was different—like a movie star from Hollywood. *Is that where they learned English?*

Donna walked off the van behind me. "I think that would be a great idea. Then you'll have interviews with both ambassadors."

"Thank you!"

"How about we go to my tent?" Donna asked.

When we arrived, I handed my communicator to Donna, but she refused. "The communicators are linked, and anyone in the video automatically has access to it."

"Oh…OK. No one told me that before, but I guess it makes sense," I said.

She pulled out her own communicator. "*Record.*"

"Please state your name and role," I said.

"Ambassador Geogram from the planet Zalma."

What do I ask an alien? "Umm...so you're from another planet?" *Duh, why did I ask such a stupid question?*

"Yes, I am from Zalma," he answered.

"What's it like?"

Geogram turned blue. "It is a beautiful place. Very peaceful."

"Is it like Earth?"

"Similar. The sky is more of a blue-gold, but I'm not sure if that has anything to do with the deflectors."

"Deflectors?"

"Yes, we built deflectors to protect us from the meteors, and then it protected us from the Moad invasion."

I wanted to ask if he knew why the Moad attacked them in the first place, but that seemed a bit too much for a first interview, so instead I settled on, "Have you seen the Moad?"

"No, we have only seen their ships."

"What else can you tell me about your planet?" I asked.

"A lot of it was desert, before the deflectors, but since then the land has flourished. We have lots of vegetation, which is good, because we are what you call vegetarians."

"Umm...." I was trying to think of another question. "What does an ambass-door do?"

"I am a...middleman—I believe is the human phrase. I represent the people of my planet."

"So, what do you do?"

"I meet with the people of my government, listen to what they want, then I go to your ambassador, and tell them. Then your ambassador tells me what your government wants. We discuss it, find a compromise, then I take that back to my people. Then it all repeats."

"That sounds boring." My face felt flushed. "Oh, I'm sorry, that didn't come out right."

"It is OK, I have only become an ambassador recently, as my people had no need for the profession before now. I have met with your leaders, signed the treaty, and now I am waiting to meet the other leaders of your planet."

"I guess that doesn't sound so bad, except for the waiting part. That sounds lonely."

"I am not lonely. My daughter has come to Earth with me, and I am close with Kanara and his family."

"Edugra?"

His eyes widened, he turned blue, and smiled. "Yes, how did you..."

Donna chuckled. "It came up in our conversation."

I went back to my usual questions. "So, what makes you different, and how does that help you in your job?"

"I am not sure I understand," he said.

"Why were you selected for this job?"

He smiled and nodded. "Ah, yes. I was studying Earth's radio and television broadcasts. My daughter and I were the only ones who knew your language and culture. Although, what we saw on the television was quite different from what we saw when we met you humans."

I thought about how the people on television shows were always acting so prim and proper. "I can understand why. Speaking of Janara and Takar, do you mind if we continue our conversation later? I'd like to go play with them now."

"No, not at all. I'm here almost anytime you want to chat."

"Thank you for your time," I said to him when we were finished. He bowed to me once more, and I nodded in return. I waved before leaving the tent with Donna to go find my friends.

CHAPTER THIRTY-FIVE

THE BANQUET

General Greg Newman
WASHINGTON, D.C.

Newman straightened his dress uniform and entered the hall for the president's banquet. He received the invitation only a couple of days ago, and wondered why it was so sudden, but he was determined to impress. He wasn't going to be the youngest general in the room, but he was the youngest two-star general, and the youngest one gunning so strongly for a promotion.

It was a vast room bathed in warm light, and immediately upon entering the room, Newman scanned the attendees. It was crowded. The air was rich with strong perfumes and colognes competing for his attention. Many people—men in military uniforms with well-dressed ladies on their arms—were milling about the room with drinks or sitting at tables. He focused on the men's faces, recognizing a few of them. Armstrong, Smithers, Dale. He steered clear of the younger generals, the one-stars and two-stars; they couldn't help him here. The two most prominent generals were Jones and Scornson. Either one of them had enough influence to have him promoted by the committee; all he had to do was impress one of them.

To his surprise and utter delight, though he wouldn't show it, a graying man in his mid-sixties approached him first. His name tag said 'Jones'.

"You're Newman, aren't you?" the older general asked.

Newman studied him, having never seen the man in person. He was taller than expected, and from his posture alone, Newman could tell that Gen. Jones was every bit the level-headed man that he'd heard about. "Yes, sir. General Jones, I've followed your career, and I must say, I've always been so impressed." This man was truly outstanding. Jones smiled at him the way he might smile at a colleague, an equal, and Newman felt something he didn't know how to define. It was a good feeling though, maybe that's why it made him uncomfortable.

"Thank you," Jones said. He turned slightly and swept his arm out toward the young man standing next to him. "This is my recruitment clerk, Corporal Dow."

The corporal saluted.

Newman turned his attention to the man. He wasn't a general, so Newman had disregarded him at first. The young black man carried himself with an air of standard military professionalism. Newman returned the salute. "Corporal Dow."

"Nice to meet you, General Newman," Dow replied.

"Now that the pleasantries are out of the way," Jones said, nodding sharply before facing Newman again, "have you heard that I am heading a new project down in New Mexico?"

"I believe so, yes. A weather balloon crashed in Roswell, correct?" he asked, and Jones nodded again. Newman took that as a sign to continue. "What really happened? Did you catch an enemy spy? Or should I believe the papers about the aliens?" he joked. *It must be a high-level spy, if anything. The kind that would cause a lot of tension with foreign governments if they knew we had him.*

"Which would you prefer?" Jones asked, catching Newman entirely off guard.

"Umm...." *He's joking, right?* It was certainly a strange question. What *would* he prefer between an alien and a spy? *It's a spy; it's got to be a spy.* "Either one is fine with me, sir."

The other general cocked his head to one side. "If you were in charge, how would you approach the situation?"

He knew that Jones always approached things logically. The man never jumped to conclusions. What could he say to impress him? "I would assess their intentions, sir," he settled on. "I'd interrogate if hostile, debrief if friendly."

"So, you are saying you would treat an alien and a spy the same way? If they are friendly or hostile, treat them as such?"

Jones seemed completely serious, but why would he need to use a hypothetical to explain spies? A sudden cold feeling washed over Newman. Maybe he *was* serious. *What if it is aliens? Would I really treat them the same?* He mentally shook himself. He would not allow himself to fall into a stuttering wreck because of some conspiracy theory. *No. It's a spy. It can't possibly be aliens. Aliens don't exist.* "Yes, sir. If a spy is defecting, you are more likely to get information from him by treating him with respect."

Jones looked at Dow. When Newman turned his attention back to the corporal, he was surprised to find that the young man was studying him intently. After a few seconds, Dow turned and nodded to Jones.

"Good answer," he said. Then, completely changing the topic, he asked, "Do you play chess?"

Newman would never admit it, but he sputtered, momentarily at a loss for words. He regained his composure. "O-of course, sir. Yes."

"Would you like to play a game next week?"

"Yes, sir. It would be an honor, sir."

"Good, good. I'll have Corporal Dow contact your office."

"Thank you, sir," Newman said.

The general and his assistant excused themselves shortly after that, having other people to speak to before the banquet's mingling time ended. Newman's gaze followed them as they left, and he saw them pass the other prominent general, Scornson. Beside Gen.

Scornson was a hulking white man about Dow's age and Newman saw the two young men exchange heated glances. He wondered what that was about.

He didn't have long, though, because Scornson and his guest were headed straight for him. *Wow, this is my lucky day! The two men I wanted to approach are both approaching me!* Then Newman suddenly found himself pinned under an intense stare, and his heart seemed to leap up into his throat. It wasn't fear, exactly, but something about Scornson's eyes stirred something in him that he hadn't felt since he was a little boy. He shoved it back down where it belonged. *If I'm going to get a promotion, I must be confident,* he told himself, clearing his throat.

"General Scornson, sir," he said. "I am Newman. Major General Newman. You have quite an impressive career, sir."

Scornson looked down his nose at Newman, then around the room, and back to him. "Newman. Hmm. I've heard about you. Still only major general, huh? I was already a lieutenant general by your age."

Newman's shoulders hunched only an inch before he straightened his posture. He pulled in a breath and pressed his lips together. *That may be true,* he thought, *but I'm sure I became a major general younger than you. And, if I get it this year, I will make lieutenant general the same age as you.*

Scornson continued, either unaware or uncaring of Newman's discomfort. "This is my grandson, Sergeant Lawless." He waved in the young man's general direction, but his attention was elsewhere as he cast his gaze around the room again. He found Jones in the crowd. "So, what did Jones want with you?"

"General Jones was just inviting me to a game of chess," Newman replied.

"I see." He glanced back at Jones. "I'm looking to expand my team. Are you interested in a promotion?"

Newman nodded, and Scornson's lips twitched at the corners.

"Of course you are. Good. I want you to keep in touch. Here's my card."

Newman took it. "Yes, sir."

As the general and his grandson were walking away, they were speaking in low tones.

"...doesn't know..." Scornson was saying, "...aliens... keep looking..."

Newman's eyes widened in alarm. There it was again. *Is 'alien' a code word for something? Are they talking about foreigners?* He knew he wouldn't get any more information on the matter, so he turned his attention back to the rest of the room. He still had some time to mingle with some other generals before supper was served.

General Frank Jones

As Gen. Jones and Cpl. Dow had met everyone on their list, they found a quiet corner to talk.

"What's your assessment?" Jones asked.

"The Zalmen technology worked," Dow replied. "I could see most generals' heart rates accelerate and temperatures increase the moment they saw me approach with you. Newman shows the most promise, but..." His expression pinched.

"Yes, he has no moral compass; he's not ready yet. However, Scornson might be just what he needs."

"How so, sir?"

Jones looked down, and he felt a lump in his throat. "Scornson will try to get to us through Newman, who will then have to pick a side. It won't be easy for him, but I'm sure he will pick ours."

CHAPTER THIRTY-SIX

CHESS

General Greg Newman

WASHINGTON, D.C.

[General Jones was playing more than chess in those games with Newman. He was playing for the soul of a man who'd lost his way. I didn't understand it then, but those matches were as important as any battle we'd ever fight.]

Newman had set up the chessboard for their game. Out of respect, he gave Gen. Jones the white pieces, and therefore, the first move. Then he waited. Not ten minutes later, his assistant informed him that Jones had arrived.

"Welcome, General Jones," Newman said as the older general entered. He rose to shake the other man's hand; they exchanged pleasantries, then they sat face to face at his desk. Newman expected Jones to begin their game, but he looked down at the board thoughtfully, then turned it so their pieces were switched.

Jones motioned for Newman to go first.

Newman raised an eyebrow. *What is he up to?* Not one to ignore a generous offer, Newman moved his first pawn to E4.

"I saw you speaking with General Scornson at the banquet," Jones said lightly as he slid one of his own pawns forward to D5. "Was there anything particularly interesting that you discussed?"

"Just the usual pleasantries," Newman replied, though he was startled by the comment. Looking at the board, Newman thought he knew Jones's strategy. He could easily take his pawn, but it would only be taken in turn by the black queen. *Would Jones risk his queen?* He took the pawn anyway.

"I see. Did you notice that Scornson talked to everyone Dow and I talked to?"

Jones took his pawn as predicted, so Newman moved his next pawn to D4, then Jones returned his queen to its initial square. "No, I didn't." Newman was curious why he asked.

Newman decided to begin an attack with his knights. He maneuvered his pieces across the board, with knights in one formation and his bishops attacking in another.

Jones took his time studying the board for the first few exchanges, but then he was quick, and Newman's pieces were disappearing left and right.

"Do you remember our conversation at the banquet?" Jones asked as he captured one of Newman's rooks.

Hoping to stall, Newman turned his full attention to Jones. "Our conversation? The one about spies and aliens, sir?" *Does he really expect me to believe in aliens?*

"Do you remember what you said to me?"

"I said I would treat them the same, sir. I'd assess whether they were hostile or friendly, and I'd treat them as such. But sir, what do you mean exactly when you say *aliens*? Do you mean foreigners, or beings from outer space?"

"Does it matter to you where someone comes from?" Jones asked genuinely as he leaned back in his chair and folded his arms.

The conversation had taken a turn into uncomfortable territory. Switching tactics, Newman refocused on the board and made another play—a desperate one. He was running out of options. "Well, no, but I don't believe in aliens from outer space. Respectfully, sir."

"But if they were real?" Jones was completely calm as he pushed his queen forward. With a knight and bishop flanking it, Newman knew he would be defeated in no time.

"What do they look like?" he asked, hoping for details but expecting few. "Do they speak English?"

Jones smiled amicably. "Let's pretend, for our hypothetical situation, that they appear human, just their skin's a different color than ours. And yes, they do speak English."

Newman quickly pictured it. He imagined a man—his assistant's face came to mind first—and let a green color wash over the man's skin. It was strange, but not crazy. He still didn't believe it. "OK, then I would assess their mental state and their motivation. If they're coming from space.... Are they invaders?"

"Let's say you've conducted your assessment, and the aliens seem mentally stable. They are not invaders. In fact, they have a mutually beneficial proposal."

Newman's eyebrows nearly shot off his face. *That certainly changes things.* He had to know more. "If that's the case...I guess I would cautiously proceed with it and see where it leads."

Newman didn't get a visible response to his words. Jones focused on the game, gave a pleased hum, and then changed the subject entirely. "I hear that you've just wrapped up an important mission. How did it go?"

Newman leaned back and formed a triangle with his fingers. The question confused him. Jones was high enough rank to access those mission files, so why was he asking about them? T*his must be a test,* he thought. *But what's the best way to answer?* "I caught the traitor, so I'd say it was a success." Superiors liked to hear about successes.

Jones, however, didn't seem all that impressed by the statement. "And to what do you owe that success?" he asked. His eyes were fixed on him, somehow steely and welcoming at the same time. It spoke of Jones's vast inner strength.

"I laid out the bait and followed the one who took it."

"What about your team?"

Newman shrugged. It had been mainly a one-person job, but that probably wasn't what Jones wanted to hear. "They were helpful."

"Who specifically was helpful to you?"

Newman clenched his jaw. *What is he getting at here? Does he want to recruit from my team? None of them really did much. It was my plan, after all.* "Specifically? No names come to mind."

Jones chuckled. The corners of his eyes were creased, like Newman was a young boy who he'd just caught eating chocolate before supper. "You're not much of a team player, are you?"

"O-of course I am, it's just...," Newman began, but the protests died on his lips. He didn't have an explanation. For his efforts, all he got was a disappointed sigh. There was at least *one* thing he could say to salvage this. "I work well with my superiors."

"That's what I thought. You don't pay much attention to the little guys, do you?" As if to emphasize his point, he captured Newman's last pawn right across from Newman's king. "Checkmate."

Newman had been expecting the loss, but he was still shocked by the utter devastation that washed over him. How could he have misread the strategy so entirely? Jones had been splitting his attack and defense.

"You show promise, but you're too busy trying to get ahead. You don't see what's right in front of you," Jones told him.

Newman replayed the last few moves in his head, trying to see where he'd gone wrong. How could he have fixed it?

Jones rose. "That was enjoyable. Thank you for the game. How about another tomorrow? Same time?"

Newman swallowed around the large lump that had formed in his throat. "Yes, sir. Thank you, sir."

The moment Jones had closed the office door, Newman began resetting the board. *Was this chess, or a job interview?* He stared down at the black and white pieces with a sinking feeling in his gut. If the game was indeed an interview, he most likely failed, but he still had a chance to try again tomorrow.

He recalled the beginning of their game. Jones had been interested in Scornson for some reason, just like Scornson was interested in Jones. Newman didn't know what was going on between the two four-star generals, and he didn't really care. He wanted a promotion, and if he was going to strike out with Jones anyway, he might as well exercise his options. Making a split-second decision, he picked up his office phone and dialed the number on Scornson's card.

The call connected, and Newman could hear Scornson's voice crackling through the line. *"Hello?"* He sounded annoyed.

"General Scornson, this is General Greg Newman. We spoke at the banquet last week."

"Newman? Oh yes, yes, right. Newman." There was a pause. For a moment, it was so quiet that Newman was worried the call had cut out, but then Scornson said, *"What can I do for you, Newman?"*

"I was calling about that promotion we discussed."

"Oh yes… But I only take on people I can trust to get the job done. First, you must prove your worth."

"Yes, sir."

"We are concerned that Jones is allying himself with foreigners and betraying his country. We want you to find out what he is doing and where. Can you do that?"

"You want me to spy on another general?" Newman asked, so shocked that he almost forgot who he was addressing.

Loud chewing crackled through the line. *"That too much for you?"* Scornson asked snidely.

"N-no, sir! I just mean.... Who is 'we'?"

Scornson's voice was suddenly aggressive. *"Who do you think?"*

Newman's heart pounded in his chest, and he found it hard to breathe. Only one person came to mind. "The president? Is the president in on this?"

"Jones is a traitor, and all we need is proof. Now, will you help us out or not?"

"Well, if that's what the president wants." He couldn't imagine the man he'd just played chess with as a traitor to his country, but if it was so deep that the president himself was worried, who was Newman to argue? He loved his country, and he would do what was best for it.

"Are you meeting with him again soon?"

"Yes, tomorrow."

"Good, call me after." With that, Scornson hung up and the dial tone buzzed in Newman's ear. He pulled the receiver away and set it down, contemplating how his life had gotten so crazy so quickly. *Jones, a traitor?*

When Gen. Jones arrived, Newman studied him closely, hoping to see any sign that the general was disloyal to his country. Now that he had suspicions, surely he would see something wasn't right, right? A tick, a habit that would pop out at him that this man wasn't as truthful as he seemed. Newman had caught traitors in the past, but this time, the supposed traitor was a superior officer.

Once again, he'd set up the board with white pieces on Jones's side, and this time Jones accepted. He took the first move, pushing one of his pawns forward two spaces. And so, the game began.

Newman took his turn. Several moves in, Jones finally spoke.

"Newman. I'm excited to see what you've learned since our last game."

"Yes, sir," he said. It was exactly what he'd done. After ending the call with Gen. Scornson, he'd gone straight into town to borrow a book about chess, and he'd studied late into the night.

He'd thought that perhaps if he managed to best Jones in a game, he'd catch the man off guard. He looked up at his superior officer, but the strategy didn't seem to be working. Jones was acting exactly as he had the day before. There was nothing, no change. He was as calm as ever. *I could be playing chess with a traitor.* He made another play, capturing the general's rook with a knight. The motion placed Jones's king in check.

"Hmm...good move." Not for long, though. Jones easily countered, capturing Newman's knight. "So, continuing our hypothetical discussion from yesterday, if you met face-to-face with an alien, what would you do?"

That word keeps coming up. Alien. Does it really mean from outer space, or is he admitting to me that he's working with foreigners? He wasn't sure which was worse. At this point, he was beginning to hope that Jones meant real-life extraterrestrials, which meant he wasn't a traitor. *Is there a protocol for people working with aliens? They aren't from Earth, after all. Or is General Scornson right? Is Jones collaborating with the enemy?* He made another move, and in changing his chess strategy, he decided to change his interrogation strategy—play innocent and dig for info. "Can you be more specific? What country are they from?"

Jones's lips quirked into a smile; perhaps he was amused by Newman's naivety. "Do you still believe that there are no aliens out there?"

Newman considered that point. True, he'd never thought about life on other planets, but he had always been a man of facts. He'd been an honor student in school, top of his classes in all subjects—and science was one of his best. "Mathematically, the odds that there *isn't* life out there are pretty small, but the technology needed to travel between planets.... I don't believe anyone is capable of that yet. Maybe in a couple of decades."

"They can't have that technology?"

"With all due respect, sir, we humans don't have those capabilities, so I'm having a hard time believing that any alien could either. I have faith in our country's—our planet's—scientists."

"So, it's possible for aliens to be out there, but they can't be more advanced than us. Is that what you're saying?" Jones pressed, leaning forward slightly as he sliced his queen across the board.

Newman stared down at the queen, puzzled for a moment. He wasn't sure why Jones had made that move; there was no clear strategy in it. "Yes.... No...." He mumbled a few words under his breath. What kind of answer was Jones looking for? Then he sighed and said, "I'm not sure, sir."

Jones gave a satisfied chuckle, and his mouth split into the first genuine smile Newman had seen on the man since meeting him. "That's probably the most honest answer you have given me."

Newman wasn't expecting that statement to affect him so much. His shoulders sagged in defeat, and for once in his career, he didn't hide it. He let them sag in full view of the high-level general in front of him. Being called out for his dishonesty wasn't something he was proud of; he was normally a better liar—truth-bender, he liked to think—but Jones saw right through him.

"You're trying to give me the answers you think that I want to hear, but what I want from you is the truth."

"Yes, sir. Sorry, sir." His shoulders hunched, but he quickly pulled his mask back up to hide what he was feeling. He was a grown man, and he would *not* allow himself to be knocked down like a house of cards. He powered through the tight feeling in his chest—one that he thought he'd left behind in the darker years of his childhood. He made another move in the game and captured another pawn.

For the next ten minutes, the only sound in the office was the soft click of the game pieces on the polished board. Newman put all his focus into the game because if he looked up at his opponent, he feared that he'd break down in a way he hadn't since he was eight years old. The feeling confused him.

Why do I feel so…. I don't even know what this feeling is. Am I feeling guilty? For what?

No, it's something deeper.

Do…do I not want to let him down? Where did that *come from?*

It's not like he's my father; I never liked that man. But Jones is the kind of man I wish my father was like.

Newman had known him only a few days. And yet, something about Jones attracted Newman like a magnet; something made Newman want to do better, *be* better.

Focus. General Scornson said this man could be a traitor. Don't let your guard down.

Jones had already begun building up his defenses, but this time, Newman knew how to act. He'd read about this strategy and knew how it was supposed to work. It was supposed to send the opponent into a frenzy of reckless defending. He wouldn't let that happen to him. Newman moved his bishop across three squares, cutting off one of the endeavors.

Jones hummed his appreciation. "You're getting better. But you still have much to learn," he complimented as he captured Newman's bishop, nonetheless. Then, switching the topic entirely, he asked, "Who do you think our biggest enemy is?"

Newman was startled, not expecting Jones to be so forward with his words. "Haven't we defeated all our enemies, sir?"

"What about the enemy within?"

Enemy within? Within what? What is he talking about? Newman thought, eyeing the other general carefully. *This doesn't make any sense. Is he crazy, hearing voices inside his head?* He remained silent and waited for what Jones had to say next.

"I see we've gone into unfounded territory. I apologize. Why don't you tell me more about your family? Where did you grow up?"

"Colorado," Newman replied, "but my father was in the army too, so we moved around quite a bit and ended up in Washington, D.C."

"I'm sure you're making your father proud. You're quite accomplished for your age." Newman tried and failed to hide a scoff, and Jones arched an eyebrow. "Now I'm getting the feeling he doesn't feel that way. How come?"

Newman stiffened at the comment and slammed his defenses right back into being. They'd been getting into friendly territory, but the words had poked at something vulnerable deep within him. He didn't like it. *Is he trying to find my weaknesses?*

Newman didn't want to talk about his dad. It was a subject he never brought up willingly, and he avoided it at all costs. So, even though he knew it was rude to refuse to answer a superior's question, he stubbornly kept quiet. If Jones was in any way upset by Newman's silence, he didn't show it. With measured patience, he took his next turn.

"Checkmate," Jones said.

Newman was stunned. He hadn't seen it. *Again? What did I do wrong?*

Jones forged on, not even allowing Newman to reply. "Thank you for the game. You're much improved, but as I said, you still have a way to go."

"Thank you, sir." This game didn't feel as much like a job interview as the last one, but it was all the same. Had Newman passed? Had he failed?

"I'd like you to come see my operation."

Newman nearly fell over himself to answer, but he was more dignified than that. "It would be an honor, sir."

"Good." Jones stood and shook Newman's hand, then retrieved his coat and hat from the rack. He opened the door. "I'll have Corporal Dow make the arrangements with your assistant for next week. Another game tomorrow?"

Newman's mouth was dry. Not trusting himself with words, he simply nodded, and the general left. The door clicked shut, and Newman did a little victory dance. *This is great! Jones invited me to see his operation! Is this my chance at a promotion?*

He wasn't sure. Jones was the type of man who never revealed his full set of cards. He spoke in codes; he spoke in hypotheticals; he spoke in circles. *I don't even know what he's saying half the time.*

If he'd asked this yesterday, Newman would've been over the moon. Now he was undecided. *General Scornson is easy to understand.*

Newman dialed, then waited. "General Scornson, sir, it's General Newman. I had another meeting with General Jones today. He's invited me to his base to see his operation."

A satisfied hum carried over the call. *"Very good, Newman. If you keep this up, you'll have that promotion before you know it."*

The thought of his goals coming to fruition sent warmth through Newman's chest. However.... "There's another thing, sir. It doesn't feel right to spy on General Jones."

"What!?" Scornson barked suddenly. Gone was the smug feline. In its place was a rabid hound. *"Are you a coward? Don't lose your nerve now. Jones is a traitor. Are you one too?"*

Red Alert! All of Newman's instincts screamed at him. It was a threat, and he knew it.

"If you chicken out now, I'll have you arrested as a traitor."

"But—I'm not!" Newman protested.

"And you have proof of that?" Scornson challenged. *"You were the one spying on a superior officer, weren't you?"*

"Under your orders."

"It would be your word against mine, wouldn't it? And I have friends everywhere. Don't be expecting a fair trial."

Newman's heart shot up into his throat as panic set in. "You can't do that!" *Can he? People won't believe that I would betray my country. Does he really have friends everywhere? Even if I am court-martialed, they would find me innocent, right? There's no proof!*

Scornson laughed; it was a wicked sound, like nails on a chalkboard—or the sound of his father's footsteps on a bad day. Then Scornson spoke, and Newman was pulled back to the present. *"I can't? Who said I can't?"*

That was true. Scornson was a four-star general. He had the power, and you know what they say about power.... *If Scornson even whispered that he thinks I'm a traitor, I would have no chance of getting a promotion.*

Wait! What would General Jones think if he found out I betrayed him? The thought haunted him, but Scornson's threat haunted him more. Newman resigned himself to the fact that Scornson was holding all the cards. All he could do was go along with it.

"...Yes, sir." Newman's voice was small. "What do you want me to do?"

Newman could almost picture Scornson going back to his smug satisfaction. Things were going his way again. *"My grandson will be bringing you a briefcase. Take it to Jones's base when you go. Do not open it."*

"Yes, sir."

"That's it," Scornson purred. *"I knew I could count on you."*

Newman hung up the phone and formed a triangle with his fingers. *What am I going to do now?*

[General Newman was discovering what real betrayal looked like. Sometimes the worst enemies are the ones who promise you everything you think you want.]

In the span of a week, Newman gone from ambitious officer to reluctant spy, caught between a general who spoke in riddles about aliens and another who'd just threatened to destroy his career. And now he'd made the kind of mistake that could get people killed.

He could see where things were quickly going downhill. Jones was believed to be a traitor, and if Newman didn't spy on him, Scornson would ruin Newman's career. It seemed fair to say that on top of everything, Newman wasn't expecting the two men who showed up in his office the next morning.

The two men saluted him.

Newman returned the salute. "Corporal Dow? Where is General Jones? And who's this?"

"I'm Corporal Adam Rabinowitz."

"The general can't make it for your game today," Dow replied. "He sends his regrets. He was also wondering if General Scornson has been in contact with you."

Newman was startled. He knew he shouldn't be; it was a reasonable question, but he couldn't help but wonder if they *knew*. "Yes, but I spoke to many generals at the banquet for networking purposes. Why does he ask?"

"I believe he's worried about Scornson sending spies after him. It's not the first time it's happened."

"No?" On the outside, Newman was a picture of calm, but he couldn't help how fast his heart was beating. He clenched his hands together behind his desk. Luckily, Dow didn't seem to notice.

"Um, not just spies, but kidnappers...," Rabinowitz said to Dow. "Remember? They tied me up, and you had to rescue me?"

Newman's face burned. Surely, there was more to this story. Newman put his hands between the two. "Excuse me, what happened?"

"I was trying to deliver a message to General Jones when General Scornson's henchmen grabbed me," Rabinowitz said.

"Well…you should have gone through the proper channels. If General Scornson was the commander of the base—"

Dow cut Newman off. "The men were under General Jones's command."

Those words were a speeding bullet to his chest. "But…that's treason." That couldn't be true. It just *couldn't*. Because if it was, and if Scornson was a traitor, then that meant that Newman was…that he….

He shook his head and glared hard at the two men, searching for deception. They had to be lying to him. He was a fool to have trusted Jones and anyone who worked for him. As soon as he knew for sure, he'd kick them out of his office and—

There was nothing. Both men were calm, collected, open; they were telling the truth. Newman walked stiffly to his desk and gestured for the two men to sit as he did. "Were these men court-martialed?" Maybe they'd been acting outside of Scornson's orders. Yes, that had to be it.

"Due to the top-secret nature of this mission, we're not able to go through official channels without exposing the operation," Dow said.

That didn't prove anything. But what else could he think?

Maybe Scornson was right and Jones *was* hiding something. That would mean undercover agents were justified, right?

But…no. Those men weren't undercover. They were under Jones's command, and they disobeyed him. That wasn't right. If his head wasn't spinning before, it sure was now. His heart was sinking ever lower. He was ordered to spy on Jones–did that make him just like those men?

"General Scornson has a way with words, and I'm sure he could make some pretty tempting offers," Dow said.

"But you know what they say—one bad apple spoils the whole bunch," Rabinowitz said.

Scornson *had* been convincing in the beginning. He knew how to pick his words; that was for sure. Newman almost wished he could go back in time and stop himself from ever speaking to the man, but he quickly dismissed the thought. Time travel didn't exist; it was right up there with aliens. Though, the way things were going, he wouldn't be surprised to see one of Jones's green men stepping out of the future just to smack him for his bad choices.

Newman was so lost in his head that he didn't notice Dow watching him until he looked up. The young man's dark eyes were narrowed behind his glasses.

Dow continued, "If General Scornson is trying to buy your allegiance somehow, sir, I can assure you that he hasn't been at all truthful in his claims."

Newman had a feeling that he could trust Dow. He had never followed his gut without logical cause, but he was already in a pit that he'd dug himself. *It can't get much worse. Maybe I should come clean.* He recalled the phrase his mother used to say to him: *if you're already in a hole, the best thing to do is stop digging.*

"General Scornson and the president think General Jones is a traitor. He threatened to arrest me for treason if I didn't help him prove it."

Rabinowitz furrowed his eyebrows. "Did Scornson tell you this, or did the president?"

"I don't see how that makes a difference if the president shares his concerns," Newman said.

"And Scornson told you directly that the president believes this?" Dow asked.

"What do you mean? Would I have said it if I wasn't sure?" Newman pressed his lips together.

"What *exactly* did he say?" Rabinowitz asked.

Newman thought back to the conversation. They'd been on the phone that time, so he hadn't been able to read Scornson's features like he'd normally do, but he was good at knowing when someone was being truthful. Scornson wouldn't have been able to tell him an outright lie.

"Well, we were on the phone and Scornson said, *we believe that Jones is a traitor.* Then I asked him *who's we?*" He mumbled quietly to himself, trying to recall the exact words. Surely Scornson had said the president's name somewhere in there. "He said, *who do you think....* Oh...." Dread hardened into iron in his stomach, and a few muttered curses slipped out. How could he have been so easily fooled? *Am I so desperate for a promotion that I willed the president to be involved?*

Dow shook his head sadly. "You assumed, didn't you? That's alright, sir. It happens to the best of us. So, what did Scornson want you to do?"

"He sent a briefcase."

"Can I see it?" Rabinowitz held out his hand, and Newman pulled the case out from under his desk. The corporal examined it for less than a minute before he said, "It's a tracker."

Newman went pale. "How do you know?"

Rabinowitz reached for the clasp to open it, but it was sealed. He flipped it, finding a dial on one side. A small smirk appeared on his face.

"Scornson told me not to open it," Newman said.

"That's probably because it will explode if you don't put in the right combination and try to force it," Dow told him.

Rabinowitz slowly turned the dial, staring intently at the case.

How can he say that so casually? Newman almost leaped forward over his desk, with his hands splayed out to stop him. "Well then, don't open it!"

"Yes. We don't want Scornson to know what we know." Rabinowitz put the case down again with a sigh.

"We need a plan to get Scornson off your back," Dow said.

"We need General Jones," Rabinowitz said.

Newman was relieved that they were calling General Jones, the man he felt he could trust. The two corporals seemed to know what they were doing, but they might just be crazy. One of them had been seconds away from triggering a bomb. Newman hoped to high heaven that he was doing the right thing.

From his pocket, Dow retrieved a small metal object about the size of a pack of Dentyne chewing gum. Only it wasn't gum. Newman wasn't sure *what* it was.

"Connect us to General Jones," Dow told the object.

The sinking feeling returned. *Maybe Dow is crazy.* First Jones with his aliens, now Dow with his oddities. *He's nowhere near a phone.* Nor was Rabinowitz or Samson, Newman's adjutant, around to make the call for him. *Does Dow expect me to do it?*

Nothing happened. Newman reached for the telephone, not sure if he was going to call Jones—or maybe a medic or guards to check Dow and Rabinowitz—when suddenly Jones's face appeared on the glossy metal surface. It was only Newman's twenty-eight years of training that kept him from jumping out of his skin. "What is that thing?" he demanded.

Dow didn't answer him. "Sir, you were right. Scornson has been blackmailing General Newman."

The tiny Jones on the screen nodded. *"And?"* he asked. It was clearly the general. But how?

Rabinowitz stepped toward the device. "General Scornson sent a briefcase with a tracker. We could disable the tracker, but that would alert Scornson to our knowledge and put General Newman in harm's way."

"We don't want Scornson to know that we know. Redirect him instead."

"Yes, sir." Dow saluted sharply, and the screen went blank. It was just a shiny metal card again. Dow placed it on top of the briefcase.

Rabinowitz was already out the door when Newman stopped Dow. "Wait, wait, wait. What was that, Corporal? What's the plan?" His eyes were wide, and his hands were trembling. He tightened them into fists.

Dow smiled gently at him like he was a small, scared child. Newman reminded himself to be angry about that later, but he was much too frazzled to care. Dow had showed him something *impossible*. Something that science and technology could not explain. *Is it magic?*

"We will pick you up this time on Monday, as planned. For now, the less you know, the better."

"And the case?"

"You should bring it."

"What about that device you had?"

Dow smiled mischievously. "What device?"

Newman hid a scowl and turned to point sharply at the case on the desk. "That device…" But the top of the briefcase was empty. Newman hurried over to the desk and picked up the case; the device must've fallen off somehow. His desk still had a few papers, a line of pens, and the unused chess board. The device was nowhere to be found. Newman heard the door close. Newman went to his door.

Lt. Sampson was looking at him. "Sir? Are you alright? Is your meeting over? The corporals seemed in a rush to leave. Should I call the gate to stop them?"

"Uh—yes, the meeting is over. Yes, I'm fine, Samson. Thank you." *Do I want to stop them? If I did, would they tell me anything?* "No, you don't need to stop them. Oh—and...I'll be traveling off-base on Monday. Please add that to my calendar."

Samson's eyebrows raised when he heard *please.*

[That was the moment General Newman truly understood what evil looked like. Not monsters or aliens, but ordinary people who chose power over principles.]

CHAPTER THIRTY-SEVEN

THE JONES FAMILY DINNER

General Frank Jones
JONES FAMILY HOME

Jones sat at the head of the table, surrounded by his family. He smiled as he looked around at his children, their spouses, and his grandchildren. He had never felt so proud, yet so heartbroken.

"So, Dad, what's this big mission you're going on?" asked his eldest son, Pierre.

Jones hesitated before responding, "It's a top secret operation. I'm afraid I can't say much about it."

"But it's important, right?" asked Bethany.

"Yes, it is," Jones said, his voice heavy with emotion. *If I don't succeed, we won't have a way to defend you from aliens.* "It's an opportunity to make a real difference...."

Jones didn't know how to end the sentence: *in the world* or *in the galaxy*? But it didn't matter, as he was broken out of his thoughts by Claire, his youngest daughter.

"But what about us?" she asked. "Are you sure you have to go? Can't someone else do it?"

"I wish I could tell you more, but it's something I have to do," Jones said, regret shooting through his gut.

"We understand, Dad," Charity said. "We're proud of you, but we're going to miss you."

As they ate dinner, Jones couldn't shake the feeling of guilt. He wanted to be honest with his family, but he couldn't risk telling them about the aliens. After dinner, he helped Chloe with the dishes, trying to put on a brave face.

"Is everything OK, Frank?" Chloe asked, sensing that something was off.

Jones let out a sigh. "It's just hard, leaving you and the kids behind. And not being able to tell you everything about the mission."

"I know," Chloe said, wrapping her arms around him. "But we'll be here waiting for you when you come back. And we'll always be proud of you, no matter what."

Jones held Chloe tightly, knowing that this could be the last time they were together. He was filled with a mix of sadness and determination. He knew he had to go, but it was going to be the hardest thing he had ever done.

CHAPTER THIRTY-EIGHT

CHARLOTTE INTERVIEWS GENERAL JONES

Charlotte "Charlie" Baker
ROSWELL, NEW MEXICO

Sandy and I entered the office.

"Charlie," Miss Dianne said, "General Jones will be here soon."

My heart pounded. "General Jones! Really?" I couldn't wait to see the man in charge. I didn't get much chance to talk to him last time.

Sandy whined and then barked twice. A few seconds later, the back door opened and closed. I was surprised to see Miss Dianne stand and salute, so I saluted as well.

Jones chuckled, then returned the salute to Miss Dianne. "As you were." Turning to me, he said, "Civilians don't have to salute. Miss Dianne may be dressed in regular clothing, but that's because she is undercover."

I turned to Dianne with a big smile. "You're a spy?"

"I never thought of it that way. I'm just a plain-clothed contact person."

Jones smiled. "Shall we begin?" We entered the office with the desk.

I pulled my communicator from my pocket and set it up like I did with Donna and Ambassador Wilcox. "*Watson, record.*"

Jones checked his watch. He didn't seem like the same friendly guy I met in the restaurant. "I have a very long flight to catch, so let's get on with it."

I couldn't resist. "May I ask where you are flying to?"

"Zalma," Jones said without hesitation.

My eyes popped. "Zalma? Like the planet Zalma?" The general didn't answer, but I now understood his urgency. "Wow. OK, I'll be quick. Please introduce yourself."

"General Frank Jones. I'm the senior officer in charge of the Roswell crash."

"And what did you find?"

"A decoy lifeboat. As I suspected, they were friendly and wanting our help."

"'As you suspected'?" I repeated.

"Yes. Why else would they drop an obvious decoy near the nuclear test site?"

The general's face was matter of fact, as if he expected that to be self-explanatory, or maybe he had explained it so many times that he didn't want to repeat it. I was about to ask for more details when he continued. "The doctor's report said that the bodies were underdeveloped, with no obvious cause of death. It couldn't be a coincidence that the decoy was dropped above the nuclear test site."

I put on my thinking cap and thought out loud. "So from the underdeveloped bodies, you determined that it was a decoy, and from the nuclear test site you…."

"If they wanted to steal our weapons, my guess is they would have. By leaving a decoy, they wanted us to know that they were here." He smiled. "I've heard you've read Sherlock Holmes…."

My cheeks burned. "Do you want me to figure it out?"

He nodded.

"Oh boy…OK. They wanted you to know that they were here, interested in the weapons, but they didn't steal them. They were testing your reactions with the decoy...like how my communicator was testing *my* reactions!" I smiled proudly.

Jones smiled back but didn't continue.

"...So, they need weapons, but they didn't take them because they don't know how to use them?"

"I knew you were smart!" he loudly announced.

I beamed at him and clapped my hands.

"Yes, the Zalmen are pacifists. This was confirmed when Privates Dow and Rabinowitz came to my office a couple of days later."

"Privates?"

"Yes, they were back then. I promoted them during our first meeting."

"Ah. I see. So you figured out that the aliens were friendly and needed our help because they were pacifists."

"Yes, they are primarily interested in our negotiators, but I don't believe that will work. I told the president that we must ally with them, or their enemies might come here, and we would have nothing to defend ourselves with."

"So, do we have defenses now?"

"We are in the initial stages, but I'm confident we will be more than ready when needed."

How do I word this? "How are you different from other generals, and how has that helped?"

His eyes widened, and he smiled. "You have good questions; I'm glad I hired you." He thought for a moment before responding. "Most generals, or for that matter, most people in the army would have shot first and asked questions later. I was having a hard time discouraging those in my immediate command from doing so."

I thought back again to that bad general. Where was he now? And what about that other soldier? None of the adults ever said anything to me about it, but I could tell they were worried about the secret getting out. Maybe it was just normal for top-secret things happening in the army, or maybe there was a real threat out there.

I was so tempted to go out and investigate, but where to start? I had nothing, and Dad always said that reporters need to start with some sort of idea; we can't just go rooting through the mud and hope to find potatoes. After those bad soldiers left our house, they just disappeared. And yet, I had a bad feeling that wasn't the last I'd seen of them. For now, I focused on the general right in front of me.

"You see people differently than most. Can you explain that?"

He chuckled, then was silent for a few seconds. "I guess I see the good in people. It's my experience that the majority of people only see a person's mistakes, and distance themselves from them because of it. While I do see mistakes as well, I see them as a chance to learn. Mistakes are not something to be embarrassed about, as long as you learn from them."

I smiled. "Well said. So, how long is it going to take you to get to Zalma?"

"I can't tell you that quite yet, Miss Baker." Jones got to his feet. "Now, I really must get going. I still have one more thing to take care of before I have to catch my flight."

"Wait! Who's going to record your historical trip?" I asked.

"Well...if you are asking if you can come with...."

"No, but...."

"Our ambassadors will be joining me and my team. I'll ask Miss Warren to be your eyes and ears."

"Thank you!"

After the general left, I rejoined Miss Dianne in the reception area. "So...how did you become a spy?"

"I told you: I'm not a spy. I'm a plain-clothed contact person."

I frowned. "How did you get involved in this project?"

"I've worked with General Jones for a long time. He was friends with my father, and he got me a job in the army."

"Weren't you scared you'd get killed or something?"

Dianne shook her head. "No, I was never in any danger, I worked mostly in the secretary pool."

"Mostly?"

"Well, he occasionally asked me to go to a bar and listen in on a conversation."

"So you are a spy?"

She chuckled. "Well, in a way, I guess. But it was never anything dangerous. I always had a handler watching me, and now I'm your handler."

"Handler?"

"Yes, I always had someone near who was watching and making sure I wouldn't get hurt."

My eyes opened wide, and my heart thumped faster.

"Oh no," she said. "No one thinks you're going to get hurt. In this case, me being your handler simply means that I'm your contact person. My main duty is to be here for you, schedule your interviews, and provide you with anything you need."

"I need an ice-cream sundae."

"First of all, it's not Sunday, and I don't think you need it."

I chuckled. "Sundaes aren't just served on Sunday anymore."

She had a mischievous smile. "I suppose you *have* worked hard today, and we could use a break. Is there any good place for ice-cream in this town?"

[That was the last time I saw General Jones before he left for space. I didn't know it then, but I was watching history walk out that door.]

*

General Frank Jones

EARTH–ZALMA BASECAMP, NEW MEXICO

"Well, corporals, I guess this is our last time together until I come back. We will have our monthly check-ins, but those will be short and sweet," Jones said.

Cpl. Dow sighed, making a show of his disappointment. "And we will probably be reporting through General Newman."

Jones chuckled. "Oh, I will be calling you two once in a while, too. I enjoy your point of view on things."

"What are we going to do without you, sir?" Rabinowitz asked.

"I'm a good judge of character, and once General Newman feels respected, he will do the right thing. He's the right man for the job."

"Yes," Dow agreed. "I also have a good feeling."

"*I'm* still learning a lot from you about how we can use anything to our advantage," Rabinowitz said.

Jones smiled, putting a hand on each of the corporals' shoulders. "You're both very fast learners."

"You're a very good teacher," Dow countered, smiling back at him.

"Thank you for believing in us. We're going to miss you," Rabinowitz added.

Jones already had four children, but he could never turn down taking on the role of father-figure, and these two young men were the latest bright souls he'd had the privilege of guiding. Every action they took made his heart swell with pride.

It seemed Dow was thinking along the same lines. "You've been like a father to us this last month."

"Has it only been a month?" Rabinowitz asked.

Jones chuckled. "Oh my, you are right, but what a month! You two have grown so much since that first meeting. I'm so proud of you both."

Dow swallowed like there was a lump in his throat. The men were quiet for a minute. "It's going to be different when you're gone."

Jones cleared his throat. "Yes, well, it's not going to be that long. You keep an eye out for Scornson. He's unpredictable, but if he takes the bait, you shouldn't have to worry about him for a few months."

They all laughed. After the laughter faded, Rabinowitz asked, "What's that saying you have?"

"The bad guys waste their time arguing with each other, fighting for control. We are stronger than them when we work together!" Jones said.

"It will sure be nice to not have to move every week," Dow said.

Jones shook his head. "No, you still have to do that. Scornson might not be around, but his men still are. I have it all mapped out for you and General Newman."

"Thank you, sir. How do you do it all? How did you know what Newman and Scornson were going to do?" Rabinowitz asked.

"No one knows what's going to happen for sure. I believe it's different for everyone, but when I was around your age, I wrote every little detail that looked out of place. Then, when I was alone, I would dream about it."

"Dream, sir?" Rabinowitz asked.

"Oh, sorry, that's what I called it when I was your age. I think meditate would be a better word. I would meditate and try to guess what could have caused those little details. Then, I wrote that down, along with what I felt when I was having those dreams."

"What you *felt*?" Dow asked.

"You know what I mean. I've seen you react ever so slightly when you get tingles, or the calm that seems out of place. Your hunches, your gut instincts."

Dow dropped his head, chuckled, and nodded.

Rabinowitz's face was blank.

"Yes, trust your gut, and it will serve you well." Jones smiled, then stepped back. "Now where was I…? I would review my notes and see which feelings were right. Eventually, I didn't have to write my notes, and I didn't have to be alone; my dreams and instincts would just kick in. I would examine the facts and attempt to picture the events that led up to it and beyond. In most cases, I was correct."

"Thank you, sir. I will try that as well," Dow said. "You know how I dreamed of flying through space with a ray gun. But I know I have work to do here, and you don't need us to drive you in space."

"Still, you know we wish we were going with you," Rabinowitz said.

Jones chuckled. "And remember, you can call me anytime, but don't mention that to General Newman. I want him to rely on you two and learn to work as a team. Then you can remind him that he has a notebook-sized communicator at his disposal."

They laughed.

CHAPTER THIRTY-EIGHT

THE STING

General Greg Newman
WASHINGTON, D.C.

When Newman arrived at his office on Monday morning, Sgt. Lawless was already there, leaning against the desk like he owned the place. He held himself with an arrogance that one only got from mimicking other despicable men. Next to him was the briefcase from Gen. Scornson.

"Sergeant Lawless," Newman said. He made sure to keep his tone light as he took off his hat and coat and hung them up. He set his work case down on the desk. "How did you get in here?"

Lawless's lips were spread wide into a cocky grin, but his salute was crisp and professional. "General Newman. Your assistant let me in, sir."

Samson had not arrived yet, so he couldn't have, but Newman decided to play along. "Ah. Did General Scornson send you?"

"Yes, sir. He sent me to make sure you know what you're supposed to do."

"I do," Newman replied. *I don't have much of a choice.* He felt somewhat insulted that Scornson was using him like a common lackey—*him,* a general—but what else could he do? If he refused, Scornson would have him court-martialed, and he'd sooner be investigated by the authorities than admit his weakness to any lower-ranking officer.

Lawless nodded and swung his arm around to pat the briefcase. “Good. I checked the tracker and put in a new battery; it’s working fine. When you take it to General Jones’s hidden base, we will arrest that traitor and put a stop to him and his people’s betrayal.”

Newman forced a smile, hiding his nerves. He’d been sick to his stomach all weekend, not knowing what would come of this day. He was convinced that his whole conversation with Corporals Dow and Rabinowitz on Friday had been a dream—a stress-induced hallucination, maybe. Now, because of his reckless ambition, his whole career was on the line. Nonetheless, Newman shook Lawless’s hand and watched the younger man leave.

As soon as Lawless was gone, he scrutinized the briefcase. It looked exactly the same as when he’d first gotten it. *I must be going crazy. I was sure that Dow left behind his strange device, but if Lawless didn’t see it, where did it go?* He sighed and sank into his chair, rubbing his forehead.

Newman heard Samson enter through the reception door.

If the meeting with Dow and Rabinowitz *had* been real, he had nothing to worry about. Jones had a plan. If it wasn’t, and he really was crazy, then...well...he wouldn’t have to worry about being a general for much longer. Maybe he would be spared a court-martial and get tossed directly into the madhouse. If that was any better... He couldn’t believe that only a few days ago he’d been visiting his mother, and everything had been normal.

Jones seemed like the kind of man who could be trusted. Newman never trusted any hunches before, but his life was in a tailspin, so this was as good a time as any to start. With a nod to himself, he began to work, doing his best to ignore the tiny buzz of anxiety in the back of his mind.

“Sir?” came a voice through the open door. “Corporal Dow is at the gate.”

"Yes, thank you, Samson," he replied. He set his paperwork aside and grabbed the briefcase.

By the time he reached the front of the building, Dow's car had pulled up. The young man jumped out of the driver's seat and saluted. Once Newman saluted back, Dow made his way around the car to open the door for him.

The ride to the airfield was smooth and quiet, though Newman couldn't help but feel nervous. The last time he'd seen Dow, he was sure he was going mad, but the way Dow was acting put doubts in his mind. *It had happened, right?*

The car pulled up to an airstrip, where a DC-3 transport plane was waiting for them. Dow motioned for Newman to enter the plane, and when he did, he was surprised to see Jones waiting for them. He saluted to the older general, as did Dow, and Jones saluted back.

"At ease."

Newman relaxed and took a seat across from Jones.

With a nod from the older general, Dow headed into the cockpit to join the pilot. Once they were all strapped in, the plane lifted into the air.

When they leveled off at cruising altitude, Jones smiled widely at him. "Do you believe in aliens now?"

"Still skeptical, sir," Newman replied honestly. He was still on the fence and would sooner believe that this whole thing was some fever dream. "I do have some questions, though. Assuming I'm not going crazy, what was that device Corporal Dow had, and where did it go?"

Jones leaned back like he'd been expecting the question. "The aliens call it a communicator."

"And you trust these aliens?"

"I have a hunch about them," was all he said.

Newman went rigid. "What do hunches have to do with it?" He hoped the question didn't come off as too aggressive, but he couldn't imagine staking his entire career—and the lives of his country—on a silly gut feeling. Sure, he was trusting Jones based on instinct, but he'd already exhausted every other option.

"Plenty. Facts will only get you so far in this world. When facts fail, you have to trust your gut instincts. The president trusts mine."

"The president knows about this?"

Jones let out a chuckle. "Do you want to talk to him?" He pulled out a device identical to the one Dow had used on Friday. So, he *hadn't* been hallucinating after all. That was good to know.

"He has one of those too?" Newman asked with raised eyebrows.

"He does."

It was like all the blood had drained from his body. *Wow!* "I don't know what to think anymore. I'm not going to lie. It was really hard not knowing what the plan was. I'm used to being in control, but for the first time, I trusted someone.... You."

"I'm glad to hear that," Jones said. "I see a bright future ahead for you."

"Thank you, sir. I've learned a lot from you over the past week."

"I take it you don't just mean my stellar chess skills."

Newman couldn't help the laugh that burst from his mouth. "That too, sir, but you've taught me to consider every part of my team. Those two—Dow and Rabinowitz—they seem like valuable men. I can see why you trust them. I've always had to do things for myself, and I've always worked best on my own without anyone slowing me down, but you've taught me that I need to trust other people, like I trust myself. Everyone on the team is important."

In early life, he'd often made mistakes, and he paid the price for that. When he'd moved out, he swore that he'd never make another mistake, but he couldn't avoid it. He had to admit that he was wrong.

"I also learned that you can't take shortcuts to get ahead. You have to do the right thing, even if it hurts. I really have to thank you for your help. I was digging myself deeper and deeper into a hole when General Scornson offered me a promotion, I told myself I'd do whatever it took to get it, but I realized too late that what it took was more than I was willing to do."

"Well said," Jones complimented.

At the praise, Newman felt confident enough to broach the next subject. "So, the aliens.... Tell me about them. That...communicator, you said? It's very impressive."

"Yes, the aliens we know are very technologically advanced pacifists."

"*The aliens we know*?" Newman parroted, confused.

"Yes. They're being attacked by other aliens, and they need our help to defend themselves. In return, they will help us defend Earth. Are you OK with that?"

"Sounds like a good deal to me, sir."

Jones glanced down at his wristwatch. "We've got lots of time before we arrive. Why don't I tell you their story?"

"Sure. Why not?"

Jones looked around with a disappointed gaze, then laughed. "It's too bad we are not on the spaceship right now; they had a room where all the walls, ceiling and floor lit up like a movie theater, but I guess I will just have to do my best to describe it."

"Sounds good."

"The Zalmen are a peaceful people, who developed space travel about a thousand years ago. They were farmers and scientists, not explorers, so they sent out space robot things to search for life in the galaxy rather than do it themselves." Jones leaned forward and whispered, "I thought they were just taking the easy way out, but it turns out that they lack adventure and imagination. I mean, wouldn't you want to fly around and see these new planets for yourself?"

"Yes, sir." Newman wanted to say more, to tell Jones all about the toy plane his mother had gotten him as a child, and how he'd spent hours flying it around his yard, but he held himself back. Jones was a superior, not a friend, and if they were going to work together, they had to keep it professional. Luckily for him, Jones would keep the conversation going, and he was nowhere near done talking.

"But I'm getting ahead of myself; now, where was I?" The older man laughed to himself. "Oh yes; they set these space robots to move from solar system to solar system, and if a robot found life on a planet, it would orbit it and monitor communications, continuing to scan and transmit its findings back to Zalma."

"So, the planet is Zalma, and the people are the Zalmen," Newman echoed.

"Yes. They did not find many planets with life, and of the ones that did have life, none had developed space travel until Moad. The Moadites developed space travel, and my guess is that they must not have liked being spied on because they sent a fleet of ships to Zalma."

"So, they must have detected the transmissions and traced them." It was the only explanation Newman could think of. How else would they have known? If any human scientists had picked up signals from space, he knew for sure that they'd stop at *nothing* to find out where they came from.

"My thoughts exactly. Anyway, the Zalmen tried to communicate with the Moadites, but they wouldn't respond. When the Moad ships arrived, they tried to land but could not get past the deflectors the Zalmen built to protect their planet from meteors. So, the Moadites fired their weapons at the planet. Again, they were unsuccessful."

Newman whistled. "Impressive. Can they set up these deflectors here?"

"I think that is being negotiated." Jones frowned. "Come to think of it, I don't remember seeing it in the agreement." He shook his head. "Anyway, two years ago, the Zalmen detected the first nuclear explosion on our planet—"

"The test in New Mexico?"

Jones nodded. "Soon after, they detected two more explosions where many people died."

"Japan?"

"Very good; you're catching on. I knew you were the right man for the job. Anyway, they wanted peace with the Moadites, not to destroy them, so they continued to monitor Earth's communications, learning our languages, culture, and the status of the war. When they heard we signed the Paris Peace Treaties, they sent a ship to make contact with us."

Newman raised both his eyebrows. "The crash in Roswell?"

"You got it. But it took them five months to fly here, and—" Newman cut him off.

"Wait, I thought there were no planets close enough for—"

"Yes, yes," Jones interrupted, "we asked them about that, and apparently, the theory of relativity does not apply when you can modify gravity."

"So, if you could remove all gravitational forces on the spaceship, you could fly faster than the speed of light?"

"Don't ask me. I didn't study science." He made a gesture that told Newman it was above his head, then smiled proudly at him. "But if you understood that, then you're going to fit right in."

Newman stewed over the new information, only half listening to Jones as he continued speaking about the Zalmen's history. He'd thought for years that aliens weren't real, and now, not only did they exist, but they were far more advanced than humans! It excited him for a moment, but then the suspicious feeling was back, sinking him into his seat like an anchor. Were they really to be trusted?

They could just be pretending to be pacifists. Newman thought of how he'd been duped by Scornson. He'd known the man's reputation, known exactly what he'd been like, but he'd fallen for the trap. If this plan of Jones's didn't work, he'd either be under Scornson's thumb for the rest of his career, or he'd be in jail. At some point, his gaze had wandered to the briefcase at his feet.

Meanwhile, Jones was still speaking. "So, while they were traveling through space, they ran millions of scenarios of what we might be like, and what would happen in each case."

"Like what would happen if they encountered General Scornson, rather than you?"

"Exactly. They built a space lifeboat, put some dummies in it, and dropped it over the nuclear test site, but the wind carried it to Roswell where Privates Dow and Rabinowitz found it."

Newman frowned. "I thought they were both corporals. Did you promote them for making contact?"

"Yes, and I put Dow in charge of recruiting."

Newman made a triangle with his fingers as he wondered what the purpose of that was. Why recruiting? A few options came to mind, and while hesitant, he voiced the most likely. "Are you using his race to weed out people who would be opposed to aliens?"

"Yes, I am."

Newman was quiet for a few more minutes, cycling the new information through his mind. As much as his whole world was being turned upside down, it was better than him actually being crazy. There was one thing still bothering him, though. "But how did the aliens know that you, Dow, and Rabinowitz were safe to contact?"

"They have technology that detects when someone is lying, angry, or hostile."

"So, what about this briefcase? Isn't Scornson following us?"

Jones leaned back, turned toward the cockpit, and called out. "Corporal Dow, update please."

Dow came out of the cockpit. "General Scornson took the bait and flew into Canadian airspace, sir."

Newman was stunned. "Canadian airspace? But the transmitter…."

"It's disabled," Jones explained flatly.

Newman hoisted the briefcase onto his lap. Forgetting that it was supposed to be locked, he tried the latches. It clicked open. Inside, next to the tracking device and explosive mechanism, was Dow's communicator. Somehow, Lawless hadn't seen it when he was checking the case earlier. *How could that be?* Upon further inspection, Newman saw that the wires for everything in the case had been disconnected. "How?"

"As I understand it, the device is full of nanites, and they disabled it."

Newman could feel panic setting in. He'd slowly been introduced to the idea of the aliens, then the technology, then the plan. Now, there was a device that could disarm a bomb without anyone noticing. Things were just getting out of hand. "What are nanites? What are you talking about? Why is he in Canada?"

Jones sent him a soft but firm look. "Nanites are tiny robots. Another flying robot duplicated the tracker signal and flew over several Canadian military bases."

"And General Scornson followed it?"

"He is not the brightest. He never thinks about the consequences of his actions, instead relying only on his own brute strength. Judging by his MO, he was never really interested in me. I'd wager he wants to kill the aliens and take their technology. Can you imagine that? Do you think he would have any chance of figuring out the alien equipment?"

"I highly doubt it, but he could always find people to do it for him."

"Unlikely, it operates by voice control, and if it doesn't know you it won't respond. Anyway, I think we should hear what's happening with him; our little decoy should've sent him quite far by now." Jones smiled, then turned to Dow. "Corporal Dow, put the radio on speaker please."

Dow pulled another communicator from his pocket and tapped it. They could all hear the radio exchange.

"This is Lieutenant Colonel Mitchell of the Royal Canadian Air Force. You have violated Canadian airspace and are ordered to turn around immediately."

"This is General Scornson of the U.S. Army Air Force. I outrank you!"

"I'm sorry, sir, but you are in Canadian airspace without prior authorization. You are ordered to return to American airspace."

"How dare you talk to a Four-Star General of the United States Army that way? I demand that you show me some respect!"

"Sir, you have violated Canadian airspace. If you don't turn around now, we will have no choice but to open fire."

"What about the other plane? I'm tailing a very dangerous fugitive!"

"Sir, you are the only foreign plane on radar."

"That's a lie! Jones's plane is right in front of us. You must see it."

"Mitchell to Base. Are there any other foreign aircraft in the area?"

"Negative. There is no other plane on radar."

"General Scornson, you must turn around now, or we will have no choice but to open fire."

"Oh, I see now. You're harboring those green, filthy, low-life aliens, aren't you? Are you working with Jones? You're not going to stop me. I'll find them."

"Sir, this is your last warning."

Ltc. Mitchell sounded quite annoyed but also resigned, like he didn't *want* to have to shoot, but would anyway. Newman wondered if all Canadians were like that.

"Pilot, full speed ahead! They won't stop me from finding the filthy aliens' hideout."

There was a long pause, which was filled with the popping of gunfire. Nothing led Newman to believe that the plane had been hit, so they must've been warning shots. Scornson didn't seem to care. *"How dare you shoot at a U.S. Military aircraft!"* he growled.

"Sir, you must land immediately, or we will shoot you down."

"Surrender? Never!"

Newman wasn't sure what was more unbelievable—that Scornson was willing to be shot down to find Jones's base, or that he was stupid enough to risk himself and anyone else on his plane by ignoring an airspace violation. Nothing mattered to Scornson as long as he got the results he wanted. *God, is this what I'm like? Is Scornson what I could've turned into? A man with no morals? A man who does whatever it takes to win?*

The radio was once again filled with nothing but static and popping gunfire, before Scornson's voice came through again, this time less crazed and more defeated. *"Mayday! Mayday! This is General Scornson to any U.S. Military plane in the area. I'm being shot at, and I need assistance."*

Jones picked up his communicator, tapped it, and waited until there was a beep. "This is General Jones. General Scornson, by order of the president, you are to leave Canadian airspace at once."

"Where are you, Jones? You can't hide! I'll find you—Hey...where did the signal go?"

"General Scornson, you have performed an unauthorized act of aggression against a foreign government. You are ordered to return to U.S. airspace immediately."

"Go to H...." Static cut the transmission.

"Lieutenant Colonel Mitchell, this is General Frank Jones. We request that you be gentle with your intruder. He has not been himself lately."

"'Not been myself'! Where do you get off…? Hey, stop shooting at me! I'm going down!"

"General Jones, this is Lieutenant Colonel Mitchell. We will do our best not to injure your officer."

"I appreciate that. Jones out." He paused to turn off the radio. "That should keep him busy for a while. The president said he won't be in a rush to ask for Scornson's release."

A chill ran up Newman's spine, and he suppressed a shiver. "So, what now? Am I under arrest?"

"Buckle up!" the pilot called out from the cockpit, interrupting any answer Newman might've received. "We're about to land!"

"Welcome to Area Four."

It was a bumpy landing; the 'airstrip' was dry desert sand. Once they left the plane, Newman could see a line of barrack tents, the mess hall, and a few other, smaller tents. He figured they were the offices, seeing as the one Jones led them into housed a desk with a silver device about the size of a thin book. Newman stared at it cautiously; it looked far too similar to Dow's communicator. Would it light up like before? In some strange combination of a television and a phone? *What will it show?*

Jones picked up the device, though he didn't sit down behind the desk. *"Connect me to Ambassador Geogram."*

As expected, the device illuminated to show the face of a purple man—mauve, if the color-coordination rants from his mother told him anything. Newman leaned forward to take a closer look and was astounded to see that Jones had been right. Aside from being purple, the man could pass for a human. Well, that, being bald, and the overly flashy silver robe that he was wearing, which was incredibly out of place.

Jones turned the screen slightly so Newman could get a better view. "General Newman, meet Ambassador Geogram from the planet Zalma." He casually handed the device over, and Newman gently accepted it like Jones had handed him a ticking time bomb.

"G-greetings," he said.

The alien tipped his chin forward politely. "Nice to meet you, General Newman."

Newman was startled as Jones clapped his hands together. "Wonderful," the older man said. "Shall we get you acquainted in person then? *Jones out.*" He led Newman out of the tent.

Newman followed, though he was in a daze. His fingers felt numb around the device he was still carrying. *Was that the whole point of going in there?* he wondered as he and Jones headed to a different tent. He'd seen advanced technology before. Scientists were always developing it for the military, but what these aliens had was unreal. It was...it was a color television screen, and he could easily carry it, unlike the one-hundred-pound cabinet monster he had at home. A hand-held screen with a live image! How ingenious! His mind was absolutely *reeling*.

At one point on the walk, Jones had turned to look at him. His expression grew worried. "How are you doing with all this so far?"

Newman shrugged his shoulders, staring at the other man with wide eyes. "How am I supposed to be doing, sir? My understanding of the world has been turned inside out. What am I even doing here? I thought you were going to arrest me for treason. Aren't you mad that I could have led General Scornson to you?"

He didn't get his answer right away. Instead, Jones, as he'd done often enough before, turned to Cpl. Dow as if looking for the answer to an unasked question. Dow nodded back at him.

They arrived at a second tent, this one a large jeep storage tent, open from the back. Jones pulled back the curtain, and Newman was met face-to-face with the mauve alien from the video device. A real live alien was standing right in front of him! Jones swept his arm out.

"General Newman, this is Ambassador Geogram in the flesh."

"Hello," Newman said. He reached forward to shake the alien's hand. I*'m shaking an alien's hand! Mom would never let me hear the end of this if she knew!*

Jones smiled, looking pleased that he was taking it so well. He wouldn't think so if he could see what was going on inside Newman's head....

Newman finally noticed that Cpl. Rabinowitz was in the room. He was so preoccupied with the alien, he hadn't noticed Rabinowitz before.

"Our mission here is to protect our planet from hostile aliens and from people like Scornson. If you're going to work with us on this, I need to know if you're OK with everything you have heard and seen so far."

"Yes, sir."

"I want to hear you say it." Jones's tone had changed to one of authority.

Newman snapped to attention. His back stiffened. "I'm OK with everything so far, sir. A little overwhelmed, to be honest, but they seem...nice."

"Good." Jones then waved to an empty corner of the tent. "General Newman, I would like to introduce you to Captain Agugua."

Newman was just about to tell him that there was no one there when suddenly, the air shimmered, and a blue alien walked in from nowhere. He was a tall, buff man, standing with his arms behind his back and looking every bit like royalty. Well, royal if Newman ignored the fact that the man was also wearing a silver foil robe like Geogram's—because on anyone else, the robe would surely look ridiculous. *Where did he come from?* Newman thought. His eyes slid from side to side, wondering if any other aliens would appear.

"You still OK, Newman?" Jones asked, and Newman could almost hear the smirk in his voice.

"Yes, sir," Newman replied, still cautious. "Just…why am I really here, sir?"

"Isn't it obvious?" Jones asked.

Newman frowned. He didn't *think* that it was obvious.

"I'm recruiting you. I'm heading into space to defend their planet, and I need you to run the operation here."

The Spacevan appeared behind Agugua. *It must be a spaceship.* Newman shook his head in disbelief.

"So, you're *not* going to arrest me?" he asked.

Jones's lips curled into a smile. "What good would that do? Who would run this place when I'm gone?"

"But…But…. After all I did, you still want me to run this operation, sir?"

Jones seemed to consider his words because he was quiet, and then he stepped closer to Newman until they were nearly touching. He stared down his nose at Newman, sizing him up. "Did you learn your lesson?" he asked, and his jovial tone from earlier had vanished. He was completely serious.

Newman couldn't move. He was pretty sure he'd forgotten how to breathe. As he stood there, staring up at Jones, one of his career-long heroes, he wasn't sure whether he felt guilty for what he'd done, relieved that he'd managed to turn things around, or a weird mix of both emotions at the same time. He struggled to swallow around the lump in his throat. "Yes, sir." They were the heaviest words he'd spoken in his life.

"Good," Jones said. The intense moment passed, and he stepped back, then turned and walked toward the spaceship.

"Um…is that it? You're putting me in charge?" He didn't even know his way around the base, let alone how it was meant to be run. How would he manage? *This is a lot of responsibility.* He was used to having a lot on his shoulders, and by no means was he incapable of adapting, but this…. He wasn't sure about this.

"Don't worry, you are not alone," Jones assured him. "Corporal Dow has been recruiting more help for you, and Corporal Rabinowitz is your new adjutant. So, are you up for it, General?"

Newman stiffened up again and saluted. "Yes, sir! I would be honored, sir!" He still felt outrageously in over his head, but if Jones had faith in him, he had to trust that he could do it. The strange feeling in his chest bubbled up again—the drive to make Jones proud—and this time Newman let it grow.

Jones's expression turned serious again. "And remember, no one outside of our group can know about this, not even other generals."

"Yes, sir!"

"You will report directly to our current president for as long as he is in office. Dow will confirm if any future president is safe. He will begin recruiting from other countries as soon as he is done recruiting here."

Newman was just about to agree again, but his jaw dropped. "We even have to vet future presidents about this?" He paused to think about it. "I guess that makes sense. Yes, sir."

"You're now understanding the importance of all this, aren't you?"

"Yes, sir. This invisibility and nanite technology would be dangerous if anyone outside of our group gained access to it, sir!"

"The president and I have agreed to promote you to lieutenant general to help you in this new role, as you'll need access to highly classified documents. Initially, you'll be reporting to the president on my behalf, but if you play your cards right, I see another promotion in your future very soon."

"Thank you, sir." He heard Jones's words, but he couldn't believe it. It was like a dream. *How did this happen?* He'd done everything wrong, and he'd still gotten the promotion he wanted! No, that wasn't it. He may have done everything wrong, but he'd acknowledged his mistakes. He'd learned from them. And he would continue to do so.

"Everything you need to know about the Alliance is in that communicator you are carrying. If you have any questions, you can ask Dow and Rabinowitz. Good luck!" Jones boarded the ship with the blue alien, then he turned around and the two generals exchanged salutes.

The spaceship door closed, and Newman watched in amazement as the ship silently lifted off the ground from a standstill, hovered for a moment, then vanished, much like how the captain had appeared earlier. His mouth dropped open for the second time in less than half an hour. When he turned to Dow and Rabinowitz, he could see the young men grinning. Geogram bowed and then exited the tent.

The corporals quickly schooled their expressions and saluted him. "General!" they said in unison.

"Is that it? He's just gone?"

"Yes, sir."

Jones was gone—completely gone—and he'd left Newman with this entire operation. *I haven't even been briefed yet! Wait—don't panic. Jones trusts me, and he seems to see more in me than I see in myself. If he thinks I can do it, then I can do it! But I need help.* Newman looked over at the corporals. *Jones was always saying that I needed to trust my team.*

"Corporals, you heard the general, so I'm going to make you a deal. If you two agree to speak freely with me in private and be my advisers, I won't pretend to know everything."

Both corporals' shoulders relaxed.

"Yes, sir. Fair enough," Dow said.

"Yes, sir. Thank you, sir," Rabinowitz said.

Newman grinned, glad that he'd have allies on this new base. He thought back to Samson, his previous assistant, and his smile faded. He hadn't been the best to Samson; he hadn't even said goodbye to the man. It was time to change things. Bracing himself, Newman vowed to be better with his subordinates starting with Dow and Rabinowitz.

With no other way to break the ice, he initiated with: "So, you two found the aliens?"

"How about we fill you in over lunch? The chef here makes great food," Rabinowitz said.

After all that, Newman thought there was nothing more that could surprise him, but those words made him pause. "Chef? Army bases have cooks, not chefs."

"Most army bases don't have aliens and engineers," Dow said.

Newman shook his head. He *had* to see this. With a sweep of his hand, he allowed Dow and Rabinowitz to lead the way to the mess hall. He couldn't wait to hear the full story.

CHAPTER FORTY

FAREWELL

General Greg Newman
EARTH–ZALMA BASECAMP, NEW MEXICO

Jones felt remorseful about leaving Newman without a briefing, but if this was going to work, he had to rely on Dow and Rabinowitz. Jones looked out the front window to see the spaceship rise above the tents. He noticed that the interior lights switched from white with a blue tinge to white with a red tinge.

"Are we invisible now?" Jones asked.

Agugua spoke into his sleeve, and the computer translated. *"Yes. The lights change as a reminder."*

The ship flew through the clouds at an incredible speed, and Jones continued to be amazed by how they didn't feel like they were moving.

As they reached orbit, Jones saw the shoe-box-shaped ship. "Is the Ymit invisible?"

"Yes," came the captain's translated reply, *"but when we are phased to the same frequency, we can see each other."*

"Interesting."

"Your people are on the second floor," Agugua said. *"With the transparent walls and ceiling, it is the perfect place from which to watch our departure."*

Jones nodded and headed to the gymnasium, and found his

team leaning against the transparent walls to get a better look at Earth. It made him nervous.

"Ten-Hut!" Lt. McKenzie called, and the military people straightened. Ambassador Wilcox and Miss Warren looked a little uncomfortable, probably wondering how to react.

"At ease," Jones quickly replied. "There are just a few of us military personnel, and we are on a spaceship, with both alien and human civilians. So why don't we dispense with the formalities?"

The team looked a lot more relaxed.

"And please step away from the windows," Jones said.

"With all due respect, sir, it's not glass. The Zalmen insist that we are safe and there is no way for us to break it. They say there are also deflectors they claim will stop a bullet," Mr. Howard said.

"That's great, but let's not test that." Jones motioned for everyone to step toward him.

Miss Warren took out her communicator. "*Record.*"

Jones continued, "This is a day for the history books...although it may never make it into any."

There were a few chuckles.

"Just in case, Miss Warren is working with Miss Baker to record the events as they unfold. We are the first humans in space!" Jones paused to let that sink in.

While the military personnel stood tall with smiles on their faces, the civilians' eyes popped as they drew closer together.

"We will soon be alone in the vast emptiness of space. If anything goes wrong, there will be no rescue. The Zalmen are five months away, and Earth currently has no space vehicles. In addition, we are basically unarmed, with the exception of a few untested weapons attached to the ship. If anyone wants to return to Earth, this is your last chance."

Everyone remained as they were.

"Good." Jones tapped his communicator. "Captain, we are ready."

The ship slowly turned, so that Earth was above them, and they could see the great blue planet one last time as they made a full orbit.

Jones could clearly make out the continents: North America, Africa, Europe, and Asia, then back to North America before the ship turned and flew past the moon. They looked out the back window at the Earth, which became smaller and smaller until it disappeared.

"It is normal to feel a sense of loss and fear when leaving home to travel the world, but this is different; we just left the world behind. You may feel strong now, or you may feel weak, but sooner or later, you will all feel something, and I want you to know that my door is always open to talk." Jones looked at his team, and while the military men's shoulders sagged, the civilians stood taller.

"Now, let's get down to business. Where are we with everything? Sergeant Abbott?"

"Sir! This is an impressive facility. Anything I ask for seems to grow out of the gymnasium floor. Targets, obstacles, you name it."

"Impressive, thank you. Lieutenant McKenzie?"

"The Zalmen may not be willing or able to fight, but I have been teaching Captain Agugua evasive maneuvers."

"Good. Lieutenant Cameron?"

"The Zalmen have over one hundred years of recordings."

"One hundred years?"

Cameron nodded. "Yes. Apparently, the computer records all foreign transmissions and deletes them when it runs out of space or determines that they are irrelevant. It seems like neither was the case."

Jones frowned. "Everyone should remember that we are dealing with the unknown vastness of space. Anyone could be recording our transmissions as well.

"If they don't have the technology to decrypt our transmissions now, they may someday. So, be careful what you transmit, and definitely don't transmit any technology."

Everyone echoed confirmation, so Jones gestured for Cameron to continue.

"The hard part about decrypting the Moad communications is that their language is more like sounds than spoken words. So, Ambassador Wilcox and I had a hard time knowing when we had a clean signal." Cameron put his hand on Wilcox's shoulder.

"Now that we know this, I am sure we can translate the language," Wilcox added.

"Great," Jones said. "Mr. Howard, what about you?"

"As you mentioned, we attached untested weapons to the hull of this ship. We hope to test them on our way out of the solar system. I'm continuing to learn about Zalmen technology and adapting it to ours. Their laser and plasma cutters look like they may be adapted to weapons."

Everyone had blank faces, not having heard these terms before.

"A laser is a hot beam of light, like a magnifying glass in the sun. A plasma cutter is a very hot flame, and it's extremely dangerous."

Everyone nodded.

"Excellent work! Let's get to it then."

[I've watched that recording of General Jones saying goodbye so many times. You can see it in his eyes—he knew he might never come back. But he went anyway, because that's what heroes do. They go into the dark so the rest of us can stay in the light.]

CHAPTER FORTY-ONE

BREAKING GROUND

General Greg Newman

EARTH–ZALMA BASECAMP, NEW MEXICO

The moment Newman stepped into the mess tent, the rich aroma of herbs and spices had washed over him. His mouth watered. The corporals were right; the food looked and smelled delicious.

"So, did they really travel all the way from another planet in that tiny truck-sized vehicle that took General Jones?" Newman asked as they lined up for food.

Cpl. Rabinowitz laughed. "No, of course not! The main ship is much bigger—about the size of our base."

Newman struggled to imagine a vehicle that large. Brushing the thought aside, he stepped up to the first table, which was laden with vegetarian food. He was definitely not a vegetarian, but it all looked and smelled so great that he had to take a small sampling of everything. The second table had a sign reading 'Cloned Meat'.

"Don't worry; it's better than it sounds," Cpl. Dow said. "We toured the top farms and ranches in the country and scanned their prime animals. We are talking about fine dining quality. It's the best you've ever tasted."

Newman nodded. "Sounds good." He filled his plate. "So where are you at with recruiting?"

"I'm just getting started—restarted, really, seeing as the best people I've recruited so far just left along with General Jones. We need to find new scientists, engineers, and weapons specialists. We don't need mathematicians since the Zalmen's supercomputers can do almost anything in a fraction of a second, but the Zalmen lack creativity. And since they're pacifists, they don't have any weapons. We still need to find someone who understands both Zalmen and Earth technology and terminology and can bring them together into ship and weapon designs," Dow said, as they sat down.

Newman took a bite and melted into his seat. "Mmmm...." He took a few more bites. "You weren't kidding. This is the best food ever. Even the vegetarian...." He wolfed down a few more bites. Each new dish he tried was a delight. After eating half his plate, he looked up at the two corporals who were grinning. Wide eyed and feeling flushed, he sat up straight with his military posture and asked formally. "Do you have any leads?"

Dow sat up straight and nodded. "A couple. I approached Mr. Harper, an Air Force engineer, who joked, 'Well, if you can fix this ship so that it breaks the sound barrier, then I'll join you.' So I had Benjamin, my communicator, scan the ship. Benjamin said it had too many rough edges. Unfortunately, there wasn't any type of material to smooth them out, so the computer also gave me instructions on how to make something called silicone. I relayed this to the engineer, and I expect we will be hearing from him soon."

"Good work," Newman said, smiling widely. He was starting to see why Jones trusted Dow so much; he was quite resourceful. "Anyone else?"

"Another engineer, Mr. Quinn, noticed that birds would cook when flying in front of the microwave towers. He was trying to replicate the phenomenon to cook food. He said he would join us if we could figure out the right frequency. Again, Benjamin provided the solution, and I hope to hear from him too."

Newman nodded. "I'm impressed."

"I'm struggling to find people on the science side, though. We have all that we can expect from the army. The most difficult part is finding someone who can combine the two technologies. That's the only way we'd be able to create viable weapons to help them defend their planet—and ours."

"I see. Is that because the Zalmen don't understand our weaponry, and our scientists don't yet understand their advanced technology?"

"Yes, but they're getting there, sir. Everything takes time."

Newman sighed. That answer was expected, but it didn't make him any less impatient. He took a deep breath and tried to remember what he'd learned from Jones. He'd vowed to change; it wasn't going to be easy. "Do you think it's possible to find someone able to do both?"

"That's the plan, sir."

"Any leads?" Newman asked.

"I've noticed that most established scientists are too arrogant and self-centered to recruit, so I'm focusing on less established scientists. I have to find smart people who are either not in the public's eye or are overlooked. I'm reaching out to our recruitment offices, university students, and new graduates," Dow explained. He was smiling—probably because that meant there would be more people his age on base. He was so young.

"Sounds good."

"We have been recruiting a few good soldiers," Rabinowitz said. "But one guy was scared straight when he saw the Zalmen. Dow's not perfect after all."

Dow gave Rabinowitz the evil eye. "I have to admit I had a bad feeling about him, but the lie detection technology said he was OK."

"So, what did you do?"

"We had to sedate him, and the Zalmen temporarily injected him with nanites to erase his short-term memory. It was an experimental procedure, but it worked. When the officer woke up, he seemed to remember nothing. We had the Zalmen create tranquilizer darts with pre-programmed nanites to do the same if it happens again in the future. Also, we started using indirect ways to introduce people to the Zalmen—" Rabinowitz said.

"Like how Jones used the communicator to introduce me to Geogram?" Newman interrupted.

Dow nodded. "Yes, exactly. We hope that if they panic, we can just tell them it's a trick."

"But you would still be showing them the advanced technology. It's like nothing they've ever seen before, so I doubt they'd believe it was all a hoax." Newman leaned back and formed a triangle with his hands again. "Hmm.... How about we set up a 'training ground' and put makeup on recruits to make them look like the aliens? Then, if the new ones panic, the actors can take the makeup off and tell them we were testing their gullibility for a spy mission, but they failed."

"That's a great idea. I guess that is why Jones picked you to lead us," Rabinowitz said.

Newman leaned forward. "I was going to ask you; why did he pick me and not one of you? You two seem to be much more knowledgeable about all this than I am."

"A month ago, we were both privates," Dow replied.

"No, we're where we belong, and you have decades of experience in leading people—and you know how to run a base," Rabinowitz said.

"What about the other generals? Surely I wasn't the only one."

"Sure, there were some others that looked OK, but General Jones had a good feeling about you. He said you had a few things to learn, but that he thought Scornson would teach them to you."

That definitely had him intrigued. "When did Jones learn about Scornson's plans for me?"

Dow looked up out of the corner of his glasses, chuckling quietly. "At the banquet."

Newman sputtered, nearly choking on his macaroni. "How? *I* didn't even know what was going on."

"General Jones is a smart man. The president compares him to Sherlock Holmes. He knew your reputation, and he knew Scornson's. As soon as Jones saw Scornson approach you, he told me that you were the one. Jones believes in letting people learn from their mistakes," Dow said.

An abrupt surge of anger flashed through Newman's gut. "Jones knew the pain I was going to go through, and he let me go through it?" He admired the older general, sure, but the past couple of nights had seemed endless, and when he *had* gotten to sleep, he'd wake up in a cold sweat after nightmares of Scornson laughing at him from outside a jail cell.

Dow's eyes were wide, and he seemed a bit panicked. "Um...I don't know. But he did say something that I thought was odd at the time. He told me that there were some things that you couldn't just learn in school, or something. He said you have to allow people to make mistakes, and then be there for them, so you can pick them up."

Newman grunted. "Hmm...." He pondered the words. *Would I have listened to Jones if he warned me at the beginning? Come to think of it, he tried, and I didn't.* Jones was right, of course. However, not wanting to admit it, he continued humming. "Hmm.... This is good food! My compliments to the chef."

CHAPTER FORTY-TWO

FIRST SIMULATION

General Frank Jones
THE YMIT, SPACE

Everyone had just finished their first meal in space together. The dishes were being absorbed into the table by the nanites.

Jones approached Agugua. "Do you understand English? I don't hear my words translated."

Agugua's skin turned red, and he pulled a device out of his ear. He once again spoke in the Zalman language, and a second later, Jones heard the translation spoken from Agugua's silver clothing, which contained the same nanites as his communicator. *"No, I learned very little English on my way here. These devices translate everything you say, blocking out the original speech."*

Jones waited for Agugua to put the device back in before he spoke. "May I have one of these devices as well?"

"Yes, just ask the computer."

"Computer, can I have one of these translator earpieces?" Immediately a small shelf grew out of the wall, and a similar translator earpiece appeared on top. Jones picked it up and put it in his ear as the shelf melted back into the wall. The earpiece was quite comfortable.

"You will find it will fit perfectly," Agugua said. With the device in his ear, Jones heard English as if Agugua was speaking it directly, without the gap in conversation.

Jones nodded. "It does, thank you. Ambassador Geogram mentioned that you ran simulations on your way here to predict our human response. How does that work?"

"We asked the computer to run a variety of simulations. We started with, *What would happen if we tried talking to a human?* It told us that some would talk, most would run, and some would try to harm us. So, we ran several simulations with the modified clones as decoys to test who reacted the best. We tried several variations of clones, then we asked the computer which was the lowest-risk scenario," Agugua said.

"And could I do that with the Moad?"

"Certainly, just say: *Computer, run a simulation;* followed by your parameters."

"So I could ask it to *run a simulation to see what would happen if we scared the Moad ship off, instead of destroying it, either accidentally or deliberately.*"

Immediately, the walls filled up with text and images.

"What's going on?" Jones asked.

"The computer is running your simulation.... You stated your query after I asked the computer to run your simulation."

"I see...." Jones studied the text, which condensed down to a few lines closest to each of them, in their own languages.

"The computer states that if you scared them off, with no casualties on either side, then the war would frustrate them, and they would just come back in greater numbers," Agugua read from the screen. "Destroying the ship would lead to a similar result, however; the war would continue longer as the families of those lost would insist on revenge."

"You said if there were no casualties. *What difference would casualties make?*" Jones asked.

Again, the walls were filled with text and images. Then the results were displayed.

"Minor Moad damage or injuries alone would damage their honor and pride and may result in their desire for revenge or self-destruction. Damage or injuries on our side would give the enemy a false sense of pride and accomplishment, resulting in a shorter war."

Jones was shocked. *"Computer, are you saying that in order to win this war, we have to let them win a battle?"*

A voice came from the wall. *"Negative. Only sufficient damage, on both sides, to keep their honor."*

"Computer, I believe you are right, but how?"

"Insufficient information."

Agugua chuckled. "The computer does not come up with the options. You have to find them, and then it can help you pick the best one."

Jones nodded. "Makes sense. By the way, I have been going through your files on the Moadites, and I can't access some of them."

Agugua's skin turned white, and then different shades of blue and green. "I do not know how that would happen. On Zalma, all information is available to everyone. *Communicator, connect us to the council."*

First Minister Ronderra's image appeared on the wall in front of them. *"Agugua, General Jones, what can we do for you?"*

Agugua bowed his head briefly in respect. "First Minister Ronderra, the general is having problems accessing some files on the Moadites."

The First Minister turned as white as his clothing. *"You should not even see those files; they were believed to be deleted."*

Agugua turned white. "All information is public. Why is this not?"

"Everyone who has ever looked at those files has become violently ill. It was decided that they should be removed from our systems."

"With all due respect, Minister, I need to know everything there is to know about our enemies, and I have a pretty strong stomach," Jones said.

Someone from off the screen whispered to the First Minister, *"The Land?"*

Jones had heard native Americans use the term as if it were a living entity, even a god, and wondered if that was the case here.

"Very well, since the computer malfunctioned and the files are still accessible, I will grant you access, provided you do not share its contents with anyone."

"With all due respect, Minister, I may need to share this information with my team. But, as with all classified information, it will be on a need-to-know basis only."

The first minister looked reluctant. He clenched his jaw, then finally said, *"Very well. You have permission to share the files as needed."*

Jones returned to his room and opened the files. The first image was of one species of animal eating another species—the Moadites were carnivores. Of course a vegetarian species would restrict access to this.

"Computer, are all files containing meat restricted from the Zalmen?"

"Yes."

"So, that's why they didn't know we eat meat."

Jones waited for a response but realized that he didn't call the computer's name. "*Computer, which of these species is dominant?*"

A picture of a reptilian creature appeared on the screen. Jones thought it looked like an alligator body with a turtle's head.

"Hmm. *How many probes have been sent to Moad?*"

"Only one probe has been sent to Moad. After its capture, the council restricted the planet."

"Captured? By the Moadites? How?"

"An unmanned rocket was recorded approaching the probe before it stopped transmitting."

"Did the Moadites reverse engineer the probe?"

"Based on the Moadites ship designs, it is probable."

"What technology did the probe have?"

"Sub-light speed nuclear drive, navigation computer, transmitter, video camera."

"No deflectors?"

"No."

"Good. *Were there any other probes lost?"*

"No other probes were lost. The probes were updated to prevent capture."

Jones believed that keeping physically fit was good for morale, and both were important on an interplanetary journey. He required and attended morning exercises with the rest of his team and the ship's crew. He usually walked laps with Wilcox, the captain, and the ladies, while his men did the more strenuous exercises.

After the cooldown period, they held an informal meeting to review their progress. Jones sat on a hover chair as he stretched out his legs.

"Sergeant Abbott, anything to report?"

"It's the same old, same old, shooting the same damned stationary targets. Gimme a challenge."

Jones looked around the room. "Is there anyone here who can challenge Abbott?"

After a silence, Howard raised his hand. "These walls and ceilings are made of nanites, right? Could they display moving images for him to shoot at?"

"Yes, I can program that," Joanua said.

"Excellent." Jones nodded. He looked around the room. "What about you, McKenzie?"

"The Zalmen are doing well with basic maneuvers. I'm studying the Moad movements to see if they have any pattern, but so far they have not had any opposition. It's pretty routine. Enter orbit, drop bombs, then leave orbit."

McKenzie stood, looking at nothing, presumably remembering something. "Some interesting things about their ships. They're long, with a transparent cone on the front, presumably a shield to protect the ship. Then something like a Ferris wheel, to generate artificial gravity."

McKenzie smiled and bounced a little. "The wheel's *baskets* are attached to the outside of the wheel when the ship is orbiting, but they turn parallel when the ship is moving. So, the acceleration pushes them to the back of the ship, and to the front of the ship when they are braking."

"Hmm. Impressive design," Howard said.

"Indeed." Jones agreed. "Cameron?"

"Ambassador Wilcox and I have decrypted the Moad transmissions, and we have translated about half of their language and programmed it into the ship's translator."

"Great. Anything to add, Ambassador?"

"I am thinking that we might be able to convince the Moadites to join a trade agreement."

"Interesting. What would you trade for what?"

"Well, you said that the Moadites might try to steal the deflector technology. What if we offer them a trade?"

"It might work," Jones said, "but we would have to ensure that it's only strong enough to protect them from space rocks. I don't want to give them an advantage in a war with us, or any other civilization."

Wilcox looked at Joanua. "Would you be able to find, or design, a low-level deflector like that?"

"Sure, I can do that."

"I would suggest using really old technology. I could also design a self-destruct, so they don't reverse engineer it," Howard offered.

"I could also design a kill switch in case they break the treaty or try to use it against us," Cameron said.

"Good ideas! Well done," Jones praised. "Anything else?"

"I'm also studying the Zalmen culture while teaching Edugra ours. We are making notes that I hope will help our two cultures avoid a faux pas."

"Anything we should know now?"

Wilcox lifted his hand, but then dropped it. "Yes, don't make an OK gesture with your hands."

"Noted." Jones turned his attention to the next man. "Mr. Howard?"

"The weapons attached to the hull of the ship did not test well. Without an atmosphere, most of our weapons have very little effect."

"But if it hits a ship with an atmosphere?" McKenzie asked.

"Yes. If our weapons hit a ship with an atmosphere, it will do damage," Howard replied.

"What about a grenade effect?" Jones asked.

"Yes, we could put an explosive device in a shell with compressed air, and it will have a grenade effect," Howard replied.

"Grenade?" Agugua asked.

"Little pieces of the shell flying everywhere, doing lots of damage," Howard replied.

Agugua nodded.

"I've adapted their laser tool into a ship-size weapon. We don't have anything to shoot out here, so Joanua ran computer simulations. They show it to be an effective weapon, and it's growing on the ship as we speak," Howard said.

"Good work," Jones said.

"I'm working on converting their plasma cutters to weapons. It's the one thing that can cut through Zalma's technology. It's likely a short-range weapon at best," Howard added.

"Good work." Jones thought for a moment. "Could you make a plasma gun or knife? And what about a flaming arrow, crossbow, or catapult?"

"The plasma cutter is already gun-shaped, but it wouldn't be able to shoot," Howard said. "I could make a knife and some kind of projectile. But again, you have to be careful with these devices, as we are on a ship in the middle of space. If they puncture the wall...."

The room was silent. They all knew the consequences.

"Thank you." Jones got to his feet. "Captain Agugua was showing me the computer simulations. We have just been through war, and I don't think any of us want to go through that again."

Abbott grunted.

Jones smirked. "Except for Abbott, of course. Anyway, with Zalma technology, we have the upper hand with the Moad. However, I am concerned that if we let them know our capabilities, they will try to negotiate or steal it."

Jones waited as his words sank in and people nodded their heads. "The computer simulation suggested that if we put up a strong front and scare them off, they will be humiliated, lose their honor, and want revenge. So, I would like to allow minor damage to allow them to keep their honor, while not losing life on either side. Suggestions?"

Abbott grunted. "If we aren't going to fight, why did you bring me?"

Jones chuckled. "I didn't say that we wouldn't fight. I said that we shouldn't kill. There is a difference."

"So, injuries and torture are OK?" Abbott asked.

"Injuries, yes. Torture, no. We don't want them to feel the need for revenge. Come to think of it, you are the best person for this job."

Abbott was silent and looked at Jones, dumbfounded.

"I want you to think of fighting us. What could we do to convince you not to fight with us?"

"Hmm...I don't know. This feels like an insult. I live to fight, not to avoid a fight. Why did I sign up for this mission? When I was asked if I liked aliens, I thought I was going to get a chance to fight them. Then I found out that I might, but I had to fly through space for five months with some chromedome pacifist vegetarians first."

Jones frowned. "Watch it, Sergeant."

Abbott looked down. "I'm sorry, sir. It's just that everyone here is so nice and fragile, it makes me sick. There's no one here who can challenge me, and I'm going stir-crazy trying to keep myself busy."

"Yes, we talked about this just a few minutes ago," Jones said.

Abbott shook his head. "…And now you're telling me that when we get there, I can't fight! You're killing me, General. Is it too late to turn around, or can I take that Spacevan thingy back to Earth?"

Agugua grunted. "The *thingy* is not designed for interstellar travel. It would most likely take you one of your years to fly back, and it cannot hold that much food."

Abbott paced back and forth, grumbling. "So, what am I going to do? I've got to do something, or you might as well kill me now."

"Would you like to learn to fly?" McKenzie asked. "I can teach you. It might not be hand-to-hand combat, but it'll give you something to do, and something to shoot at."

Abbott thought for a moment. "Hmm…. I don't know. I suppose it's better than nothing. I'll try it."

Jones hummed. "That's good for now. I would like everyone to come up with at least one idea on how to give the enemy honor, without losing a life on either side. Dismissed."

CHAPTER FORTY-THREE

THE TEACHERS

General Greg Newman

EARTH–ZALMA BASECAMP, NEW MEXICO

It took two days of relentless work for Newman to learn the ins and outs of running the base. He wondered if Gen. Jones had deliberately left him without a briefing, if he'd planned on Newman having to rely on Cpl. Dow and Cpl. Rabinowitz, subordinates. That was something the old Newman would have considered weak, but the new Newman was thankful for the chance to learn how to work as a *team*.

Dow and Rabinowitz were at his side every step of the way, briefing him on the different procedures they'd come up with and slowly introducing him to everyone. The last two people on that list just happened to be the Zalmen, a married couple with two children, who'd stayed behind to teach humans how to use the more advanced technology.

As he set foot into the classroom-like setting, Newman's gaze immediately fell on the three aliens sitting together, and the two children sitting at another table, presumably doing homework. Newman's eyes widened in curiosity. He'd already seen Geogram, but the adults were in deep discussion, and their colors were changing rapidly. He had heard that they change their colors based on their moods and such, but this was amazing.

"Geogram, Kanara, and Sarara," Rabinowitz said, walking up to them. "I would like to officially introduce you to General Greg Newman."

The aliens stopped talking, and their colors settled on different shades of green. They turned to Newman. "Hello," the taller one said in a deep voice, "I am Kanara. It is a pleasure to meet you."

"We have heard a lot about you, General Newman. I am Sarara," the other added.

"And we have met before. I am Ambassador Geogram. I am sorry I did not stay longer, but they told me you would probably want to be alone after such a grand revelation."

"Yes, thank you," Newman said.

The two children approached.

"These are our children. Takar and Janara," Kanara said.

"It's great to meet you all," Newman replied. "I understand that one of you is a scientist, and the other an engineer, and will be teaching us about your technology."

They nodded.

"I look forward to seeing what our scientists come up with under your guidance." Newman tried to keep his eyes off the both of them, but it was next to impossible. He couldn't help but compare them to humans.

Sarara smiled at him. "I am quite excited to be working with them. We have many projects underway, General."

"Sir, if I may." Rabinowitz waited for Newman to nod. "The DC-3 is assigned to our…sorry, *your* unit. You can assign it out or travel yourself as you see fit. Kanara and Sarara also have a ship, like the one General Jones left on. We call it the Spacevan. While it's their personal vehicle, Kanara has generously offered to fly us anywhere in an emergency. It's invisible, undetectable on radar, and capable of flying anywhere in the world in only a few minutes."

"Indeed!" Kanara nodded.

Newman's eyebrows shot up. *Wow! Only a few minutes?* It was the old Newman slipping in a thought. The new Newman thought, *I don't deserve such privileges; I should be in jail for betraying General Jones.*

"Thank you! That is very generous of you, and I promise not to abuse the privilege." Newman looked at the corporals for any other topics for discussion, but they were silent. "I guess I'll leave you to your work then."

Newman used the DC-3 to return to his old office to gather his things. On the flight, he had good memories of past events. He remembered how his adjutant Lt. Samson was always so organized; he'd always done his work on time, and he'd even taken on extra tasks just to make Newman's days easier. Newman made a mental note to ask Cpl. Dow if he could recruit him.

Driving to his mom's, he stopped for lunch as usual, but this time, he smiled back at the waitress. He watched her run around the diner, trying to serve everyone as fast as possible. When one of the guests grumbled at her, Newman cringed. *Was I that guy?*

He looked around; everything seemed to be different. He saw people laughing and smiling. He couldn't remember people doing that before. Had it always been that way? How hadn't he noticed? A chuckle bubbled up and he realized he was also smiling. *What's going on?* he thought. *Where is this coming from? It has to have something to do with Jones.*

Newman watched the waitress and appreciated her efforts. When he left, he placed a generous ten-cent tip on the table to make up for the last time. He went to the florist and purchased the biggest bunch of gladioli they had available and left them with a big tip as well.

Fond memories spiraled up as he arrived at the house, and again he wondered why. What changed? He never felt this way before.

When his mom answered the door, he picked her up in a big hug. He really loved her and looked forward to spending time with her and her idiosyncrasies the old Newman would get annoyed with.

The very next day, Dow and Rabinowitz stood before Newman, both wearing their new sergeant uniforms. They saluted.

"Congratulations, Sergeants," Newman said.

"Thank you, General."

They ended the salute.

"You didn't have to do this," Rabinowitz said.

Newman barked a laugh. "I did it for purely selfish reasons. I don't want to hang out with corporals." He winked. "How far are you two doing in your reading?"

"*The Art of War* is a big book," Dow said. "I'm doing my best, but you don't give me a lot of time. It seems I only have time when on the plane."

"I'm almost finished," Rabinowitz said.

"Well, keep at it. I have a lot more books for you to read before I can give you field promotions to lieutenant. You're going to have to study hard to earn it."

Dow and Rabinowitz smiled and nodded.

They walked around the basecamp; there were a few recruits around, but not as many as Newman would like.

"Before meeting General Jones, I'd see this as a ghost town, but now I see opportunities."

"If I may…." Rabinowitz waited for Newman to nod. "You have changed."

Newman again wondered when he had changed and what changed him. Along the way, Jones must have instilled some secret lessons into him.

"Maybe it's the respect Jones gave me from the moment I met him. As I gave him more respect in return, maybe I began to respect myself." Newman's spine snapped straight as he remembered the sergeants were beside him. *Did I say that out loud?* "Any new names to add to the list?"

"Dow thinks he's found the perfect candidate. Graduated from MIT with a PhD in Astrophysics at the age of nineteen, top of the class, and currently in between places, so they won't be missed, but…." Rabinowitz snickered.

Newman looked down at the young men sharply. "But…?" he prompted. "Might as well spit it out, Sergeant, we don't have all day. What's wrong with him?"

Dow fidgeted with his hands. He kept his back straight and face forward. It wasn't rude, exactly, but it was clear he was avoiding looking directly at Newman. *Is he afraid of what I'll think? After all we have been through, what could it be?*

"There's absolutely nothing wrong, sir. She is quite the genius," Dow said.

Newman raised an eyebrow in surprise. "She?" he asked.

This time, Dow turned and met Newman's eyes firmly and nodded. "Yes, sir. Her name is Dr. Mary Goss."

CHAPTER FORTY-FOUR

SOMETHING FISHY

Charlotte "Charlie" Bakers

ROSWELL, NEW MEXICO

I was having the time of my life. Going to the office every day was fun, and as the army people continued to learn new things about the aliens on the base, there was always something fresh for me to learn at the office. I felt like a real reporter!

When school started again, and I could only go in the afternoons after finishing all my homework, things changed. The days got lonelier. Johnny and Robbie asked me about my new job, but I couldn't tell them anything, so I kept having to lie, which I hated.

It's just until everyone's allowed to know, I kept telling myself. Every time, it felt hollow, more like an excuse than an explanation. I *really* needed to get back to my investigative reporter roots; interviews and reading reports all day long was starting to get boring.

Then, I sensed *it.* Like someone was watching, just as Dow described in our interview about when the aliens appeared to him. It came a few days after the start of school.

I never saw anyone, but the feeling came every night when I was home. Something had changed. When I asked Dad about it, he brushed off the concern. Mom fussed enough for both of them, which was stifling, so I told her it was nothing and didn't mention it again. Still, I kept my eyes sharp. Something strange was going on.

I had less and less time with Janara and Takar, except on weekends. They quickly took over as my best friends, especially Janara, since we shared so many likes and dislikes. I even whispered to her about my worries one afternoon.

"I think somebody's following me," I told her.

She turned pale. "Following? Who? Why?"

"I don't know," I said, "but it's really just a feeling. Dad thinks it's nothing and Mom might lose her head if I mention it again."

Now Janara was bone white. "Lose her head? Your mom will not have her head anymore?"

"Sorry," I said. "It's an expression. It means she'll…um…be worried? It means she won't be able to think properly about it, and that's no good for anyone."

"I see." Janara's colors shifted rapidly as she thought about it. "But you feel like someone is watching?"

"Yeah. I haven't actually seen anyone. No one will believe me if I say I just think someone's out there. They're all so serious, they might think I'm being paranoid."

"Paranoid?"

"Worrying about nothing."

Janara nodded. "But tell my dad if you *do* actually see anyone. Then he can tell the others and they'll protect you."

It sounded reasonable. If I told them about it now, they'd either not believe me, like Dad, or they'd be overprotective, like Mom. Maybe I'd even lose my internship! That possibility sent waves of horror through me. *I can't let that happen!* If there *was* someone, I could take care of them myself. I'd investigate, just like old times. I was really itching for another investigation.

After talking to Janara about it, I went home with that new determination. I was a reporter; no mystery would stand in my way!

That night, something happened.

Sandy woke up before I did. I felt her jump off my bed and heard her low rumble—not quite a growl, but her warning sound. She positioned herself by my bedroom door, alert and tense.

When the crash came, Sandy's ears shot forward and she gave three sharp barks—her "intruder alert" signal.

The sound didn't repeat, and I waited in silence, listening really hard. Scattered footsteps, and grunts from a voice I didn't recognize. My heart hammered in my chest. Of course, I couldn't go out to take a look. Mom and Dad were asleep, for one, and I didn't want to wake them. For two, I was way too scared.

In the morning, I wheeled around back to see what it was all about, and found our garbage bins knocked over. Trash was strewn across the ground: bones and vegetable peelings, tin cans and plastic bags, some old newspapers.

"Raccoons," Dad grumbled from behind me. He righted the bins and secured the lids. He went back around front to drive to work, but I stayed behind. I was probably going to be late for school, but my suspicions were aroused, and my reporter's instincts were tingling.

It didn't *sound* like raccoons last night. It sounded like a person. Maybe *the* person.

Sandy sniffed a boot print in the dirt for a long time, her hackles rising slightly. Then she looked at me with those amber eyes that seemed to say, "This is what I was trying to warn you about."

I squinted at the dirt; it couldn't have come from Dad's shoes. *Something fishy is going on.*

[I should have told someone about those footprints right away. But I was twelve, and I thought I could handle anything. Pride comes before the fall, as Dad always said. I just didn't know how far I was about to fall.]

PART 4: DEFINING MARY

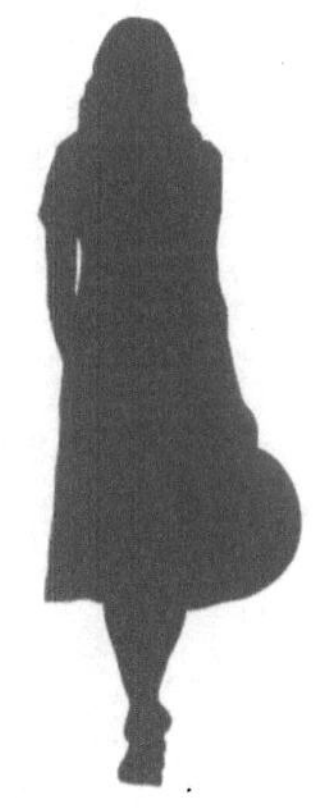

CHAPTER FORTY-TWO

A MAN'S WORLD

Mary Goss
BOSTON, MASSACHUSETTS
April 1947

[While I was playing baseball with beings from another world, a brilliant young woman in Boston was fighting battles I couldn't even imagine. Dr. Mary Goss was about to prove that genius has no gender—and that sometimes the most important discoveries happen when you're brave enough to ask the questions everyone else is afraid to ask.]

The door seemed more foreboding than any other time she'd stood in front of it, but Mary still pushed herself to knock. It was about time for the results of her dissertation to be ready, and she was certain it was the reason Professor Hunt had called her. Dread settled in her gut like a stone. If he wanted to see her personally, it probably wasn't good news.

"Come in," came the aged voice of her professor.

Mary pushed on the heavy wood door and entered. The smell of dust and stale pipe smoke overwhelmed her. The room hadn't changed since the last time she'd been there, with floor-to-ceiling shelves lined with thick books—many of which had been written by the man sitting behind the sturdy oak desk at the rear of the office. He thought he knew everything, but she proved him wrong several times.

When the professor saw Mary, his face dropped, and he groaned.

The professor huffed, and greeted her stiffly. She leaned over the desk to shake his hand, then he dropped hers, and she stepped back. His cold eyes stared at her over his long, thin nose. He'd been her mentor for all three years she had attended MIT and he hadn't changed one bit in all that time.

"You wanted to see me, Professor," she said, hoping to rid the air of its tension. Professor Hunt continued to stare at her, frowning.

"Yes," he said through his teeth. Slim fingers plucked a folder from amid the stacks of paper on his desk.

"This is the letter regarding your dissertation. I know I could have mailed it, but with you being the youngest and first female astrophysics doctoral candidate, I wanted to give it to you in person. You can now add a Ph.D. to your name. Of course, it won't be official until the June ceremony, but...congratulations, Dr. Mary Goss." The corner of his lip curled downward at the words, but Mary couldn't bring herself to care. She was smiling widely.

"Thank you, sir." She took the folder, flipping it open to marvel at her letter. "I was wondering if we could discuss sponsorship for my post-doctoral research?"

"I'm afraid I'll have to decline. We have brought you to this point in your journey, but neither I nor any other professor here can take you any further in your education or career. You have made it abundantly clear that you know far more than we do, and quite frankly, we're done hearing it. We will see you in June at the ceremony. Good luck, Dr. Goss." His accent was a hint more British than Bostonian.

He gave a dismissive wave of his hand, and then he returned to his work, as if she wasn't even in the room. Mary's fingers tightened around her letter. Head bowed, she headed to the door, but when she was about to turn the handle, she stopped. This was the last time she could vent to the professor. She took a deep breath. She couldn't contain her anger anymore.

"Excuse me, sir. You talk about how you and the other professors have had so much trouble teaching me, but what about the trouble I've gone through getting here? I'm labeled a genius regahding my knowledge, but I never had the chance to learn social skills." Mary's Boston accent was in full force.

"I spent a day in kindergahten, and the teacher called my ma to say she didn't know what to do with me because I already knew more than they teach at that age. The next day I was in grade one, and the same thing happened. By the end of the week, I found myself, still five years old, in grade three with a bunch of students who were eight and nine." Mary had to pause a moment, feeling the pipe smoke choking her.

"I spent the next two years in grades five and seven, attending middle school at eight. I spent two years there. The other students resented me because I was so much younger than them and so much smahtah. I tried to dumb down, but it just wasn't me." Looking at his face, she could see it was useless, but she just had to carry on.

"My parents knew it was tough, but they were too busy with their own teaching caheers to be able to help. I was transferred from my mom's science class because they thought we were cheating. I finally graduated high school when I was eleven and wore a junior bridesmaid dress to the prom because it was the only thing fancy enough that fit me." He opened his mouth, but Mary continued before he could speak.

"I stahted college the same year, and at first, I didn't have a clue what I was doing. It was so different from high school. I had to be responsible for my own supplies, books, and registering for classes. Some people did help me, but most just laughed at my expense.

It was the first time I really felt stupid, so I vowed I'd never feel that way again.

"I worked hahd at my classes and got through my bachelor's degree in two years instead of four. Then my masters was equally fast, though certainly not easy." Mary gazed at the ceiling for a second.

"That brings me here. I came to you when I was sixteen, saying I wanted to get my doctorate in astrophysics. You were nice enough but you laughed as I walked out the door. Like before, I was determined to prove you and everyone else wrong, that I *did* belong and I *could* do it. So I researched more, read longer, and studied hahder than any of the other students. I came up with theories that you tore down and found known facts that went against your teachings." Mary looked directly at Hunt.

"Now, I know this won't change your mind about me, but it sure made me feel better getting it out."

Professor Hunt was sitting behind his desk with his lips pressed so firmly together that they were stark white. Mary couldn't tell if he was more shocked by her words or that she had the gall to say them. She decided it didn't matter and strode out the door, closing it for the very last time.

A little further down the hallway, Mary collapsed against the wall with a heavy sigh. Opening the folder again, she let her eyes scan it. The letter spoke of congratulations and praise, but she could read the contempt behind the words. *Why can't I get any respect in this place? It says here that I got high praise from the external examiners, but everyone treats me like a leper.* She pushed off the wall and headed outside.

"Hey! Look who it is!"

Mary looked up to see two students walking up the green. One of them was the tall and lanky figure of Chris Smith, a young man she knew well. He and his companion strode right up to her, and he swung an arm around her shoulders irreverently.

"If it isn't Miss Know-It-All herself. What weah you doing in there? Was Prawfessah Hunt just giving you the bad news that they don't give doctorates to gahls who think they'ah smahtah than Einstein?" His Boston accent was a little thicker than most of the students, as he was of Irish descent.

Mary rolled her eyes. *Why did I ever go out with this turkey?* I'm glad it was only once. She ducked her way out of his grip and walked away, feeling their eyes burning into her back and hearing Chris laughing as his friend whistled. She stiffened and told herself to ignore it, but before she could stop herself, she turned around and flashed them a smug grin. "That's *Doctor* Know-It-All to you."

GOSS FAMILY HOME

Mr. Goss was reading a paper in his living room chair when Mary entered. It had been a few months since Dr. Hunt gave her the letter—a few months since she'd left campus and never returned.

"How did the interview go?" her father asked.

She frowned. "Same as the others. Did you ask your friends what they said in my references?"

He looked over his glasses. "First, your professors ah not my friends. They ah from a different discipline. Second, when I do see them, they make some excuse and leave." Like Mary, his accent was very light, as they tried to avoid it on the university grounds.

Mary walked up to read the headline on the back of his newspaper. "Now they ah saying it's a weather balloon?"

Mr. Goss looked at the front page. "That's much more likely than aliens. If you do the math..."

Mary interrupted. "...Yes, yes, I know. It would take several generations for a ship to travel between solar systems, or the power requirements would be astronomical to get anywhere near the speed of light."

Mr. Goss nodded and went back to reading his paper.

"But how much power is released when you split an atom?"

"Energy equals mass multiplied by the speed of light squared; you know that. But they'll never be able to control that much energy. It's not good for anything but a bomb."

"I'm still hoping for aliens," Mary said.

"...therefore, we ah unable to offer you a position at this time."

With a cry of frustration, Mary threw the letter down onto the kitchen table next to the dozen others she'd already received. "I don't get it, Craig! It's been four months of applying since receiving my doctorate, and I've been rejected by every single laboratory in the state! I graduated from MIT with a PhD in astrophysics at the age of nineteen! Why ah they not impressed by that? Why can't I get a job? I'm so desperate at this point that I even left a résumé at the *ahmy recruitment office*, of all places! You know how I hate the ahmy."

Her brother, who was younger by a year, was preparing his fifth cup of coffee that day, filling the air with its rich aroma. He looked at her with knowing eyes and slurped some of his drink. He took it with three teaspoons of sugar, the *heathen*. "It's because youh prawfessahs hate you."

"It's not my fault that theah ah obvious flaws in their teaching. What am I supposed to do? Just ignore their mistakes?" Mary stood up, the legs of her chair scraping against the tiles, and started pacing.

"That's exactly what you should've done, genius. It sure would make life easier for *me*."

Mary grumbled. "What ah you talking about?"

Craig took another gulp of coffee before putting his mug down on the counter. "Do you know what it's like to be the *great* Mary Goss's brawther? Half of the univahsity expects me taw be as smaht as you, and the awthah half just hates me because you'ah my sistah. If you'd just kept youh head down and gone through school without a fuss, I wouldn't have taw deal with that!"

Mary rolled her eyes. "That's not my fault either. They shouldn't be judging you for who youh family is."

"OK, fine, but listen, Mary. You know how much those old prawfessahs hate being questioned, let alone proven wrawng. It's even worse because you'ah the only gahl in youh field. And you wonder why you couldn't get any of them to spawnsah youh pawst-dawctoahal work, and why none of the labs will hiah you?"

"My prawfessahs probably gave me bad references. I sweah it feels like the whole world is against any person who is not a white male. Doors ah always closed for the rest of us."

Craig shrugged. "Like it oah nawt, that's the way the woahld works. You'll just have taw get used taw it."

"Sure, *you'd* say that. You fit the description!"

"As you would say, *that's nawt my fault*. I'd like taw see you try taw change the woahld all by youh lonesawme."

Mary was about to snap back with a retort, but at that very second, the phone rang. Craig glanced over at it, then looked back at Mary with a clear *I'm not going to answer it* look. Familiar tingles raced up her spine—the very same tingling sensation that she felt on the cusp of her biggest decisions. She ignored the feeling, huffed, and grabbed the phone receiver off the side table, answering it.

A male voice addressed her. "Is Dr. Mary Goss available, please?"

Upon hearing her title, Mary felt the invigorating tingles again. Unbidden, her lips curled into a smile. "Speaking."

"This is Sergeant Dow of the US Army. We received your impressive résumé, and we would like to schedule an interview."

"That's kind of you to say so, but the recruitment office told me that they weren't hiring scientists," Mary replied. "And I don't want to build bombs." Really, the only reason she'd left her résumé at the recruitment office in the first place was because she'd felt a strong urge to do so. The inexplicable urge had been nudging her to apply all summer, and she'd finally given in only a few days ago. She figured they wouldn't even call back. How wrong she was.

The man on the phone laughed. "Dr. Goss, I assure you, we do more than just build bombs."

Mary scowled, shoving down the elated feeling that rose once again at the use of her new title. "Sure. I bet they told that to Einstein, too."

"Our aim here is to save lives, not end them. Going by your résumé, you seem perfect for the position we have available. Are you interested?"

Mary paused, considering the offer. On one hand, she'd never imagined herself working for the US Army, but on the other, she really needed a job. *What do I do? What do I say?* She looked over at Craig, who was watching her with curious eyes. Something told her to take the leap.

"Dr. Goss?" Sgt. Dow prompted.

"Yes, sorry. Yes, I'm interested."

"Would you be able to fly to New Mexico to meet me for an interview?"

Mary nearly choked. "New Mexico? Where exactly in New Mexico?"

"I'm sorry, that's classified."

"Well, I'm sorry too, but I don't make a habit of flying away to unknown destinations."

Dow was quiet, and she could hear low mumbling over the line, meaning he was probably speaking to someone else. He spoke again after a minute. "How about I come to meet you tomorrow afternoon at the recruitment office?"

"I'd be alright with that," Mary replied.

"Great. I will have them call you with the details."

"OK, but I'm still not building bombs."

Dow chuckled. "You won't have to build any bombs, Dr. Goss. I'll make sure of it. Good day." Then he hung up.

The elated feeling was back once more, this time swelling in her chest like a helium balloon. Her head felt light and her heart was racing. *Did I just do that?* She couldn't believe it.

"So, what's the big news?" Craig asked, startling her out of her thoughts.

"That was Sergeant Dow from the US Ahmy. He saw my résumé and wants to set up an interview," Mary told him breathlessly.

Craig frowned. "What could the ahmy possibly want with you? Ahn't you an astrophysicist?"

"I don't know." Mary turned away from him. What *could* the army want with her? Her focus was in understanding the cosmos. How could that be of any use to them? "I really don't know."

Mary arrived at the recruitment center wearing a floral sundress, but she immediately felt out of place as she looked around at all the men in their fatigues or plain clothes. As she was led to a side room, she sensed their eyes following her. They either had a stupid large grin on their face or an open mouth. One guy even whistled. *What am I, a piece of meat?*

The room was just big enough for a table and two chairs. Initially, she was thankful for the half-glass wall separating her from the men. Her mind buzzed with the thought of being alone in a small room with a man she'd never met before, but she shooed the thought aside. Yes, the room was small, but the blinds were open.

Then, she kept getting the feeling that someone was staring at her. Several times, she turned to meet a man's eyes and they would quickly look away. She wondered if she should close the blinds, but then she also didn't want to be in a closed room with a man. Her mind kept going in circles. *Should I close the blinds or leave them open?*

As her eyes raked over the men in the building, she wondered if any of them were Sgt. Dow. She glanced at the clock next. 3:10. She was a bit early, but early was good, in her opinion.

Yet another man passed by and glanced in through the open door, and her fingers dug into the fabric across her lap. She wrinkled her nose at the smell wafting over her. *What do women see in these military guys, anyway?* They were nice to look at, but....

Tingles raced along her spine and she shot up straight in her chair. Her eyes darted back and forth, wondering what was causing it. She only got these tingles in certain situations—of the life-changing variety. She'd had them when she first decided to attend MIT, and again when she chose astrophysics as her major. The feeling continued as the door to the main entrance opened and a young black man, about her age, entered the building. He immediately caught Mary's attention as he confidently strode through the office. It was all Mary could do to contain her surprise when he joined her in the room and closed the door.

"Dr. Goss, I presume," he greeted her. "Thank you for coming. I'm Sergeant Malcolm Dow. We spoke on the phone yesterday."

Mary rose and smoothed down her dress, reaching forward to shake his hand. When she spoke, she carefully enunciated her words to tone down her accent. "Yes, I remember. It's nice to meet you in person." His grip was firm, but his eyes were kind; they were nothing like the stern eyes she was expecting of a military man.

Once they were each settled in their chairs, Dow pulled out a folder of papers and adjusted his glasses. The front sheet was her résumé. Though he'd opened the file and pulled out a pen, Dow didn't look down, instead, he met her eyes with a friendly smile.

"Our scientists are impressed by your diss...," he coughed, "... writing, so this is just the routine. Why don't we skip the boring questions and get right to it."

Mary held back a sigh of relief. "Great."

"I know it's mentioned in my papers, but can you explain to me in layman's terms, what your specialty in astrophysics is?"

"Theoretical physics. I wasn't sure at first what I wanted to focus on, but I've always been curious about unexplained natural phenomena. With this specialty, I use mathematical models and abstractions of physical objects and systems to not only explain but rationalize and predict these phenomena."

He twiddled the pen between his fingers. "What made you want to study science?"

"Let's just say I had a good feeling about it."

Dow's eyes seemed to spark with interest. "Oh?"

She fidgeted. "Oh, it's nothing really. Just...sometimes, when I'm about to make a big decision, I get an odd sensation telling me that I'm doing the right thing. Women's intuition, I suppose."

"I understand." He smiled and winked. "I see that you were a straight-A student, but did you find any work?"

Mary bit her lip anxiously. "I was unable to get any references from my professors. Despite my academic record, it's been difficult in such a male-driven area of expertise."

Dow's smile faded, and he looked her in the eye sympathetically. "I know what you mean."

She found herself staring into his eyes; it was like she could feel all the hurt he had been through. It was like she'd known him for years, but she didn't know how that was possible.

Dow blinked. "Anyway, I understand you're not currently employed, but is there anything you've been working on?"

Excitement shot through her, and she perked up, leaning forward in her seat. "There is *something* I've been pondering lately.

The theory of relativity states that nothing can move faster than the speed of light, but that's not necessahily true. I mean, if two objects were moving towahd each other at just below the speed of light, wouldn't they appeah to be going twice the speed of light, relative to each other?"

She paused to let him ponder the words, barely even realizing that her accent had slipped through in her excitement. He didn't seem to grasp the full depth of what she was saying, but he nodded all the same.

Mary lifted one shoulder. "I suppose it doesn't break this law, as they only *appeah* to be traveling faster, but even when I was little, I wondered why light is the fastest unit of measure in the universe. Something has to be, but what determines that? Gravity. If we could somehow manipulate gravity. . . ." She fell into murmurs, her mind whirring with all the possibilities, and was only broken out of her thoughts when Dow gave a genuine laugh. She looked up, cheeks flushed bright red.

"I can tell right away that you are the one we've been searching for," he said, eyes twinkling.

Relief flooded through her.

"So," he said, "do you believe space travel is possible?"

She was surprised by the sudden change of topic, but answered, "Yes, I do. I think we have the technology and intelligence to make that happen in the very neah future."

"What about aliens?" Dow pressed. "Do you believe in them? And if you do, do you think they would be friendly?"

Mary paused before answering; she didn't want to appear foolish. "It's mathematically improbable that life doesn't exist elsewhere. Theah ah sevahl theories.

"Some say that if there were aliens out there, they would let us know. Others ahgue that aliens wouldn't interfere with our natural development. Or maybe they're equal to us in their scientific advancement and haven't invented ways to travel deep space yet.

"Personally, I *do* believe that theah ah aliens out there, and I believe that if we ever met them, we'd be able to establish peaceful relations."

He smiled. "Well said. You passed. The job is yours if you want it."

"And what exactly am I signing up for?"

"We are looking for civilians to help us with a project, although I can't give you any more details at this time. It's top secret, so if you choose to work with us, you won't be able to tell anyone the details of your location or the nature of your work—not even family. You will be living on base with very few outings until the work is complete. Do you accept these terms?"

"Yes." Her answer was immediate, and she surprised not only Dow, but herself as well. *Did I just say that? I... don't normally jump into things this quickly, but my intuition is telling me that I can trust him. And... at least it's better than being jobless.*

Dow's smile brightened further. "Wonderful! I'll pick you up tomorrow at oh-eight hundred hours at the address you have listed here."

"Oh-eight hundred hours?" she asked.

"Eight AM. Will you be ready by then?"

Mary's mind flashed through a list of everything she'd need to bring; then she nodded.

"Here is the standard contract and non-disclosure agreement. On it you will find information like your room and board. Your salary would start at a modest $200 a month. You can read it over, and if you are still interested, you can sign it and give it to me tomorrow. If you will excuse me for a moment."

Dow left the room and came back moments later with a new military-issue duffel bag. "Please limit yourself to this one bag, which you may fill with your clothing and personal items. If you change your mind, you can still say no in the morning, and there will be no hard feelings. This life is not for everyone. I'm staying at the big hotel down the street; if you have any questions, you can call me there."

After their farewells, he stood and exited the room.

Mary watched him leave, her eyes following him all the way back to the main entrance. As the door closed behind him, she blushed and turned her head away, scolding herself for staring. Collecting the papers and the bag, she smiled down at them, giddy and unable to stop trembling. She had a job! As soon as she got home, she had some exciting news to tell her family.

When Mary arrived, her parents were already home from work. Her father was sitting in his armchair in the living room with a book open in his lap, and it sounded like her mother was in the kitchen preparing dinner.

"I've exciting news!" she called out as she slipped off her pumps and put them away.

Her mother smiled delightedly at her as she entered the room. She pulled Mary into a hug and pressed a kiss to her cheek. "You told us you weah going for an intahview tawday. Did you get the jawb?"

"Yes, I did! Sergeant Dow told me I'm a perfect fit for the position!"

Those words caused her father to look up from his book. He turned to her, a deep frown marring his face. "Sergeant?" he repeated. "You joined the ahmy?"

Mary frowned back at her dad. Ever since she had declared she was applying to MIT, he'd been a constant voice of disapproval in her ear. He loved her; she was sure, and she knew he wanted her to have a good, easy life, but there were still times when his overprotective nature grated on her. This was one of those times.

"Yes, Dad," she said, walking over to him and hugging him over the back of his armchair. "I couldn't find work in any labs, so I dropped off my résumé at the recruitment office. I'm going to be a civilian consultant on a top secret project, and I'm leaving tomorrow morning at eight, so I'd better get packing."

He grunted, but her mom captured her in another hug, holding her tightly despite Mary's struggles. "That's so wondahful, deah! See, I told you that you would find something."

"Where is it?"

"Dad, I told you, it's top secret," Mary said as she finally escaped her mom's hold.

"Do you even know?"

Mary sighed. "Not exactly, but I've got a good feeling about it. I trust him."

Her dad suddenly looked suspicious. "Him? You mean the sergeant who interviewed you?"

Mary pointedly refused to answer. He often got like this, and she found that the best way to deal with it was to not engage at all.

Of course, that was also the cue for her mom to immediately begin fretting. "You've nevah lived away from home befoah. Will you be alright awn youhr own?"

"I'm suah I'll be fine, Mom. I'm smaht, remember? I'll figure it out. Besides, I've also nevah had a real jawb befoah. This will be good for me."

"But how will you suahvive with all those men around? It's the ahmy, you know; theah won't be many gawls around for you taw talk taw."

"There weren't many girls at school either, Mom. Anyway, I've nevah had a problem with men befoah," Mary reassured her. "I'll probably be working with them, but I doubt it'll be any worse than the lab work I did at university. They're not interested in me, and I'm not interested in them."

Her mom returned to the kitchen to finish dinner, so Mary deemed her soothed and walked to the stairs to head up to her room.

Once alone, she set the duffel bag on her bed and threw open her wardrobe doors. She'd filled the bag halfway before doubt set in. *Should I've agreed so easily? I know nothing about Sergeant Dow, or my new job for that matter. On the phone he said I wouldn't be making bombs, but what if that was a lie? He didn't mention it at all during my interview. What if he changed his mind?*

The thoughts churned, making her feel sick to her stomach. She couldn't even consider the notion of anything she invented being used to hurt someone.

He's lying, he's lying, he's lying. Thoughts of everything that could go wrong nagged at her. Dropping one of her plainer dresses, she sat on the bed, chest cold. *Maybe I should stay home and try my luck with those labs again,* she thought, *but...he came all the way here to interview me. And I might not get another chance like this!*

It was a once-in-a-lifetime opportunity for her to take, and she felt deep in her soul that she needed to reach out and grab it with both hands. She settled on the decision, feeling determined, and then that tingling feeling along her arms and the back of her neck returned, bringing a smile to her face. It was the right choice; she knew it.

She picked up her plain dress again and folded it, adding it to the bag. What she'd already packed were mostly basics and necessities, but what else was she supposed to bring to wear on a military base? *I suppose I'll be working in a lab most of the time, so I'd better bring along some sturdy shoes and plain clothes for under a coat, or just some casual clothes for research and study.*

She picked through the dresses still hanging there, considering each of them. Making a split-second decision, she grabbed one of the better-looking Sunday dresses and tossed it on top. *Just in case.*

*

"Neahly time, deah. Be ready," Mary's mother advised, as she sat down at the breakfast table with two plates of toast and a bowl of hard-boiled eggs.

Mary grabbed an egg and rolled it on the table to fracture its fragile shell. "I know, Maw."

She was set. Her duffel bag was already sitting near the entrance with her travel shoes and coat, and she was dressed comfortably. The papers she'd been given at the end of her interview—all signed—sat on the table next to her. The clock read twenty to eight, which should give her enough time to finish eating and clean up before Sgt. Dow was due to arrive.

Just as she was finishing the last of her toast, she could hear the sound of an automobile pulling up outside and glanced out the window. Seeing a jeep stopping in front of the house, she looked at the clock. "Eight AM, just as he said."

A crisp knock sounded on the door and Mary stood up, but her father was closer. He opened the door and, with his foreboding stature, stared down at the young man standing there.

"Sergeant Dow, I presume?" he asked, his voice revealing nothing.

Mary watched his head go up and down as he sized up the sergeant.

Dow offered his hand to the tall man. "Yes, sir. Nice to meet you. You must be the senior Dr. Goss. I am here to pick up Dr. Mary Goss and escort her to the military base."

Mary's father accepted the handshake, but upon pulling away, he crossed his arms. "What will she be doing, and when will she be back?"

"I cannot give any details about the project, as it's top secret, but as a civilian, Dr. Goss will be allowed to leave anytime. If she chooses to stay during the entirety of the project, we will be keeping her busy until at least Christmas.

"Here is my card. If you need to get in touch with her, I will relay any messages." Dow peered around her father at Mary. "Are you ready to go, Dr. Goss?"

"Yes, I am. One moment, please." She wiped away the last of the crumbs and kissed her mother on the cheek. At the entrance, she put on her shoes, and squeezed her father extra tight, then grabbed the papers and duffel bag as she stepped out the door. "Bye. I love you both."

The jeep ride was quiet, and soon they were at a small airfield. The hangar was only big enough for about a dozen small planes, some of which seemed very fancy, but Sgt. Dow led her past the hangar over to a DC-3 transport plane, which she only recognized because it was in an issue of *Popular Science*. She'd never been on a plane before, but once inside, she decided it wasn't as comfy as she'd expected. Un-padded metal seats ran along the walls and had cross-chest seatbelts, and in the air was an odd mixture of cleaning solution and gasoline. After stowing her bag under her seat and struggling a bit with the belt, Mary buckled herself in.

"We're all ready," Dow called to the pilot. Moments later, the engine revved, and the plane began to move.

Mary glanced out the window nervously as they picked up speed. A loud rumbling filled her ears. "Is it supposed to be making that sound?"

"Yes. No need to worry, Dr. Goss. You're perfectly safe," Sgt. Dow assured her. "It's a bit loud now, but once we're in the air, you won't even notice it."

He was right. As soon as they'd reached cruising altitude, the engine noise lessened from a roar to a hum.

Dow turned to her. "I can tell you more about the project now. I couldn't with the others around; I'm sure you understand. Even the mere existence of this project must be kept under wraps *at all costs*."

"Of course."

"So, when I asked you if you believed in aliens, I was serious. Aliens exist, and they made contact with us just last month. We've been working with them at the base we're headed to."

Mary's eyes widened. "Really?" She studied him closely, trying to find any sign in his face that would tell her he was joking—that this was some big prank. There wasn't any. "Yes!" she cried out as she did a celebratory shimmy in her seat.

He flashed a smile before his face turned grim. "But, if this were to get out, there would be a mass panic."

"That sounds serious."

He nodded. "Exactly, which is why I'm glad you've been so patient with me. So, where would you like me to start?"

A thrilling sensation washed through her and she couldn't keep the excited grin off her face. What to ask first? Should she try to learn more about the project or who she was going to be working with? "Tell me about the aliens first. Who ah they? Where ah they from? And how did they get here?"

Dow sat back and hummed, as if sorting through his brain for a place to begin. Mary wondered if this was because he knew so much about the aliens, or not enough. Perhaps there were things he could share with her, and things she couldn't know. She surely hoped to know all she could and waited with bated breath.

"They come from the planet Zalma, so we've been calling them the Zalmen. They came here to Earth in need of our help. The people from the planet Moad have been attacking them. The Zalmen's technology is leagues beyond ours, but they're pacifists, so they're at a severe disadvantage in the war."

Her elation quickly took a nosedive. "You promised I wouldn't have to build any bombs, but it sounds to me like I'm going to be building weapons for you anyway," she accused.

The sergeant immediately began waving his hands, eyes wide. "Oh, no, no, no. We don't want you to be making weapons, nor do we want to fight the invaders. As I said, the Zalmen are pacifists, and want us to resolve this through peaceful means. In fact, the Zalmen's primary purpose for coming here was to find a negotiator."

"That's a relief. I was worrying about it all night, but my intuition has never been wrong before." She paused, confused. "But if they needed a negotiator, why would you be looking for scientists? You'd think that you'd start with, well...*negotiators*."

"Oh, we have," Dow assured her. "Don't worry. The head of this project, General Jones, brought in Ambassador Wilcox to negotiate the terms of our treaty with the Zalmen, and then negotiate with the Moadites. In exchange for our help, the Zalmen will provide us with their technology, which is highly advanced. Hence the need for genius scientists such as yourself."

Mary stiffened, unsure how to take the compliment. When she became aware of her cheeks heating, she quickly looked away. "I see," she said, "so this job will mainly be me leahning from the aliens. When do I get to meet them?"

"I'll personally introduce you when we get to the current base."

"And where's that?"

"Quite honestly? In the middle of nowhere. All the bases are, and we move quite frequently, so keep that in mind." He winked when Mary's mouth dropped open. Then he amended, "The location of the base is indeed classified, but I could have just as easily told you that it is in the middle of the desert, with nothing around for miles and with no official name. We call it Area 6."

*

After a bumpy four-hour flight, they touched down. *This really is the middle of nowhere,* Mary thought to herself as she disembarked the plane behind Sgt. Dow. The hot, dry air hit her like the blast from a furnace. She looked around at the base, which was a collection of tents and other temporary buildings. Beyond the tents, barren desert stretched out as far as the eye could see, nothing but dusty shrubs for miles. Way off in the distance, she thought she could see some trees, but it would probably take a whole day of walking to reach them.

Dow directed her to one of the tents, and inside, she found three people standing around in reflective foil suits. She deduced that they must be the aliens, since even though they looked entirely human, one had green skin, another blue, and the third light purple.

Mary approached the blue alien, a young man with cropped black hair. She was tempted to touch the fabric of his suit, but refrained. Instead, she asked, "What kind of propulsion system do you use? Do you believe that there would be a way to influence the curvature of space and therefore decrease the force gravity inflicts on an object, thereby allowing that object to move at unforeseen speeds?"

The blue alien gaped at her. "U-um...," he stuttered.

Mary stepped back, disappointed. For all that Dow had been building up their advancements in technology, they weren't very well spoken, nor did they seem anything but baffled at her words. "I thought you said that the aliens were highly advanced?" she said, looking at the sergeant.

"I did," he agreed, as he tried to hide an amused smile. "Sorry, these aren't the *real* aliens. They're just army soldiers with painted faces, meant as a test for new recruits. It became protocol after one of our previous recruits saw a real alien and...went cuckoo; we had to sedate him. I'll take you to the Zalmen soon, but first, the general wants to meet you."

Mary puckered her lips. "General Jones? The one you mentioned on the plane?"

"No. General Jones recently left with a team and most of the aliens, back to their home planet. General Newman is in charge while he's gone." With a gesture for her to follow, he left the tent.

He took her to a different tent. Inside and seated behind a desk was a man in his mid-forties. Mary didn't know much about the army, but even she knew that he was surprisingly young for his position.

Dow stiffened and saluted, looking every bit the military man that he was. "General Newman, sir."

"I see you have been successful."

"Yes, I have, sir. May I present to you Dr. Mary Goss." He gestured, and Gen. Newman turned his attention toward her.

Internally, Mary panicked. *Do I salute too?* After a moment of hesitation, she attempted to copy Dow's salute. The general laughed as he stood up.

"At ease," he said.

Both Mary and Dow relaxed.

"Dr. Goss," the general continued, "I have heard a lot about you. I'm very pleased you joined the team."

Mary's pulse quickened. *Really?* What exactly had he heard? "Thank you…sir?"

"As you are a civilian, you don't need to salute or address me formally. But I *do* appreciate the occasional 'sir' when in the company of my men. Reminds them who's in charge." He nodded his head toward Dow and winked at her. Mary smiled back.

He seems nice enough. Certainly not what I was expecting.

Newman then pulled a metallic object from his pocket and offered it to her. It was small and flat, like an identification card or a pack of gum. "This is a Zalma communicator. Sergeant Dow or one of the Zalmen can show you how to use it if you like, but from what I hear, you're intelligent enough to figure it out on your own."

Mary accepted the object and immediately marveled at it, turning it over in her hands. *It's so sleek! I don't even see any seams.*

"Thank you, sir," she said, putting it away with all intent to study it in detail later.

"I'm sure Dow has filled you in on your job duties while you're here, but I want to be thorough. You will be attending instructional classes led by the Zalmen to learn about their technology. These classes are non-negotiable. Am I clear?"

Mary nodded sharply. "Crystal clear, sir. I can't wait to begin."

Newman cracked a smile. "Good. We're still in the early stages, so the main focus is for you to understand the technology and how to apply it to existing Earthly technology such as transportation and weaponry."

"Sir, if I may interrupt, I told Sergeant Dow that I refuse to make weapons. That was a condition of my employment. I will be happy to leahn, and happy to make innovations for transportation or otherwise, but I will *not* make anything that can be directly used to hahm anyone."

Newman snapped an angry look at Dow. Mary was surprised that Dow was able to look so calm in front of the angry general.

"Yes, sir. With all due respect, we are looking for a peaceful solution, right?"

Newman returned his stare to Mary, who took an unconscious step back. Her whole body was tense. She was a civilian, sure, but even *she* knew that it was rude to interrupt a general, let alone to contradict one. She would surely die of embarrassment if they sent her home on the first day of the job with her tail between her legs.

Then the general paused. His lips moved as if he'd already chosen his words and was testing to see how they tasted. He calmed, but his words were still stern when he spoke. "Very well, but you will be under the watch of the senior scientists. They will be the ones determining the projects. You'll have to take it up with them."

Mary breathed a sigh of relief. "Thank you, sir."

"That will be all." He looked away from her to Dow. "You may proceed. Dismissed."

As soon as they were outside and out of earshot Mary said, "That was horrifying."

Dow regarded her with his once-again unreadable expression. "I could tell. I've never seen anyone speak so strongly against a general before. You were brave to put your foot down." He huffed out a laugh. "Not that it's a good idea to speak to a superior like that, but…."

"Yeah…." Mary agreed. "I guess I thought I was talking to one of my professors."

Dow chuckled.

He led her to a third tent, the largest so far. The inside was set up like a schoolroom. Though there were tables and chairs, they were unlike anything Mary had seen before, hovering above the floor. There were a few blackboards—or what appeared to be blackboards, they were more silver—scattered about. At the front of the room was a vehicle resembling a futuristic van, made of smooth, reflective metal. It had wraparound windows, was devoid of tires, and was hovering, much like the tables and chairs were. There was one lady and two children in the room.

They were all bald and wearing foil robes similar to the fake aliens. The lady's skin was the color of a fern, and she was writing on one of the boards with a finger. As Mary drew closer, the alien turned.

"Dr. Goss, I would like you to meet Sarara. She will be one of your teachers," Dow introduced.

Mary eyed the woman cautiously. "Ah you real? Or ah you another test?"

The woman, Sarara, looked alarmed for a moment, and her green skin flashed red, green, then blue in rapid succession before returning to fern. "Are you referring to the men that they have painted different colors? Yes, I am real."

"You also change color? How do you do that?" Mary couldn't help asking. Then, upon seeing Sarara's stricken expression, she backtracked. "Oh, I'm so sorry! That was rude of me."

"It's OK, we get asked that a lot," the young girl said.

"These are my two children, Janara and Takar," Sarara said.

"We heard that you are the smartest human on Earth," Takar said with a smile.

"I don't know about that," Mary said.

Dow excused himself after that, citing many more things he had to do. He bid them good day and said he might see them later in the mess hall for dinner.

Sarara nodded to Dow, then signaled Mary to follow her. They settled at one of the tables, with the two children sitting close. Sarara was quick to begin. "My people and I come from Zalma, a planet in the star system you call Tau Ceti."

"It is approximately twelve of your light-years from here," Janara added.

"Twelve light-yeahs? Did it take you that long to get here?"

"No. Our ships can travel at much faster speeds," Sarara said.

Mary leaned forward. She couldn't believe it. Something she'd only just theorized—and argued at length with her professors about—was already a reality. "You can travel faster than the speed of light? That's amazing! How long was the trip?"

"Five months," Janara said with a smirk.

Mary was rendered speechless. Then, ever so slowly, a smile spread across her face. "I am so excited to be working with you. Where do we staht?"

"Staht?" Takar asked.

"Start." Janara rolled her eyes at her brother. "I understood it."

"Takar, remember, people on Earth speak different languages and have different...accents, I believe?" Sarara asked.

Mary nodded. "I come from a place called Boston. People tell me we tend to miss a lot of Rs and slur our Os." She made sure to pronounce it properly. She made a mental note to control her accent.

"Now, go back to your homework, and next time be more polite." Sarara shook her head.

Mary and Sarara spoke straight through until dinner. They walked together with the children to the mess hall, still deep in conversation. Entering the tent, they saw Dow, Newman and another sergeant (which she recognized by his uniform) sitting together at a table with a green-blue alien.

The blue-green alien joined them as they headed up to the front to wait in line, and Sarara introduced him to Mary as her husband, Kanara, who was an engineer. He was "quite brilliant" according to Sarara, and he complimented his wife in turn, saying that she was one of Zalma's brightest scientists, which caused Sarara's skin to blush furiously magenta.

"Oh, brother...." Takar looked at Mary with a wink and a smile. "Did I say it right?"

Mary couldn't answer, but nodded as she laughed.

Once receiving their vegetarian meals, they joined the sergeants and general, and Sarara immediately turned to Dow.

"Where did you find Mary—um—Dr. Goss? She is the best you have brought to me yet!"

Mary, not expecting the compliment, blushed. "I'm just glad to finally have a teacher who knows what she's talking about. I've never had such stimulating discussions!"

Mary sat between Sarara and Dow. The conversation was mostly small talk, scattered with questions. Sarara and Kanara discussed projects and new discoveries. Their children asked Mary a dozen questions.

On Mary's other side, Newman, Dow and the other sergeant—Rabinowitz—were locked in a conversation about Gen. Jones and his team and the latest update of their journey into space. Mary split her attention, listening to both, occasionally chiming in with her own thoughts, but she mainly observed. It was all very fascinating.

"How are things going for you in the engineering laboratory?" Sarara asked. "Those men of yours don't seem to want to cooperate."

Kanara sighed. "It is going as well as it can be. Some of the engineers are refusing to heed my advice and teachings. They are prideful; they wish to succeed without my aid."

"I see. Humans are strange creatures that way." She looked over at Mary apologetically, then asked, "Mary, do you know any methods we may use to remove this obstacle?"

"No, sorry. That's pretty much how all the men I've worked with ah like. They need to prove that they ah the best. They won't accept help, much less from a woman." She shrugged. "I don't mind, though. I'm much smahtah than most of them, anyway." Embarrassment washed over her again as she heard her own accent.

Concern flashed across Sarara's face.

"If you don't mind me asking, what ah*re* you working on?" Mary tried to compensate for her accent.

Kanara, having finished his meal—a bun and some peculiar-looking steamed vegetables—pushed his plate away and turned to her. "The human engineers are building a new spacecraft, but there is not much to report thus far. I am helping with the technological components. If you wish to visit, I would be happy to show you around."

CHAPTER FORTY-SIX

CHARLOTTE & NEWMAN

Charlotte "Charlie" Baker
ROSWELL, NEW MEXICO

General Jones had gone off to space, but he sent me a message that I would interview his replacement next. The next time I arrived at the building, the new general was sitting in my office. He was about my dad's age, dressed in the same clothes General Jones wore, though he only had three stars on his shoulders. I set up my communicator to record our conversation. "*Watson, record.*"

The man raised an eyebrow. "You named your communicator Watson? That would make you...?"

"Charlie." I mustered as much professionalism as I could. "If you're ready to get started, please state your name, rank, and role in the Earth–Zalma project."

"General Newman. I'm now in charge of the Earth base."

I giggled. "Can you believe that we have an Earth base now?"

"A couple of weeks ago, I didn't believe in aliens. At least not any that had the technology to visit us."

I gasped. "Really? Why did they pick you then?"

General Newman laughed heartily. "I've asked them that several times, and the only answer I get is that I wasn't afraid of our guests. Part of that was because I didn't believe in them, but some things happened, and I learned to trust General Jones and his team. I knew that if they trusted the Zalmen, then I could trust them too."

"I guess you're settling into the base well?"

"Certainly. Sergeants Dow and Rabinowitz have both been a great help, of course."

My mouth dropped open. *Another promotion?* "Sergeants? Good for them!" I grinned. Then I regained my composure. "OK, so what are your duties now that General Jones is gone?"

"Running the base means a lot of things, but my main job is to keep the Zalmen a secret from the public. I am also in charge of staying in touch with both General Jones and the president to keep them informed of everything that's going on," he said.

"That sounds like a big job."

"The toughest part is moving the base every few days."

"Why do you do that? I've always wondered why every time I go to the base, it's in a different location."

The general leaned forward. "Not everyone is ready to welcome aliens to Earth; they can't even accept black people, you know. There are more who want to capture or kill the aliens."

I nodded. "I think I saw one of those men back when I first met Corporal…sorry, Sergeant Dow. General Scornson was asking my dad a whole bunch of questions about the spaceship article he wrote. He was trying to find out where the UFO got moved to."

General Newman's expression suddenly became very serious. "You stay away from them, you hear? It would be better if you could avoid them altogether, but if you *do* run into them, play dumb. If they think you know something, they might hurt you to get information."

"I can keep a secret," I protested.

Newman smiled. "I bet you can, but I can't put you in that danger. Just don't trust anyone we don't introduce you to. If we need to send you someone new, we will let you know by communicator first."

I put on my best adult face. "A wise precaution." (It was a word I'd heard Dad say before.)

"Remember, if someone is near who is not in our group, the communicator will be blank. If a bad guy approaches you, send out a distress signal, perhaps by tapping the communicator three times."

"Click my heels three times and say *there's no place like home.*"

"If you tell the communicator that's your distress signal, I'm sure it will work."

"OK. *Watson, that's my distress signal,*" I said.

The communicator on the desk chirped and spoke. *"Distress signal now set to clicking heels three times and saying there's no place like home."*

My eyes widened. I knew they could talk, but I'd never heard mine say anything other than translating Sandy's bark. It had a different voice than the translator. It was deep and soothing, like Dad's, but it had a British accent. I smiled; I liked Watson's voice.

The general must've seen my expression, because he said, "Sergeant Dow talks to his all the time, and it speaks into his ear, so no one else can hear it," Newman said. "He calls his Benjamin."

"Wow! I didn't know it spoke in his ear. Sweet!" I cleared my throat. "Let's get back on track. What else can you tell me?"

"What else do you want to know?"

I started with my usual first question. "What makes you different, and how does that help you with your job?"

"Oh… That's quite a question," he paused, putting his fingers together forming a triangle. "I've studied hard. I'm good at math and science." He looked out the window. "That helps me understand a bit of what's going on here, but their science is so advanced, they can make things invisible."

"Yep, amazing! Now, how did you get involved in this?"

The general hesitated for a moment, and I could see indecision in his eyes. There was something he didn't want to say, but then something changed in his expression. "General Jones told me to be honest. So…" He steeled himself, and began telling me *everything*.

I had a newfound respect for the general by the time he was done—and a newfound understanding of the world. I thought grownups always had the answers. Mom and Dad always seemed like they did. But adults were human too, and humans make mistakes—and I suppose non-humans make them too. I had a newfound understanding of the world.

I reached across the table and put my hand on General Newman's. He jerked slightly and looked at me. I wondered if he forgot I was in the room. "*Everyone* makes mistakes." I smiled at him. "You were really brave."

He seemed a bit embarrassed, but smiled back at me.

After a moment, he took his own communicator out of his pocket. "*Tell Kanara that Miss Baker and I are ready to go.*" Then he turned to me. "I hear that you are doing a book study with Takar and Janara today."

"Yes, we are! We've played a few different sports together already, but Takar found a new book series he really likes so Janara and I have started reading them too. Today we're going to talk about them."

"Like a book club." His eyes twinkled. "I'm glad you all are so close."

Me too. I wasn't about to tell this new general, or any of the other army people about the weird things going on so far, but I could tell Janara and Takar. After our talk about the books, and once we were sure no adults were listening in, we would plan how to catch the person responsible.

CHAPTER FORTY-SEVEN

A KINDRED SPIRIT

Dr. Mary Goss
AREA 6

When Mary returned from breakfast with Sarara and Kanara, she found four men sitting in the back rows of the classroom. Two other men were standing near the front, and Sarara introduced them. "Mr. Lance Harper and Mr. Randy Quinn, this is Dr. Mary Goss."

Mary raised her hand to shake.

Quinn was of average build, with copper-toned hair and brown eyes. He hunched a little and looked at Mary with curiosity. "Hi-hi," he said, starting to extend his own hand.

Harper let out an incredulous scoff, causing Quinn to jump and quickly drop his hand. Harper was exceptionally tall, with ash-blond hair and blue eyes. His build told Mary that he exercised regularly, but he didn't stand straight enough to be a soldier.

"*Doctor?* This girl? She's a teenager. What could she possibly be a doctor of? The kitchen?"

"The culinary ahrts have chefs, not doctors," Mary corrected snidely. She had a harder time controlling her accent when angry and already knew that she wouldn't like this man one bit.

Harper flashed his teeth in a sharp grin. "Oh… I'm sorry, doll; I didn't know we had a scholar on the team."

"At least I *am* a scholar. What's your education? Kindergarten? And don't call me doll!"

His face flushed red, and at his sides, his hands were clenched into fists.

Quinn's eyes went wide and darted between the two of them. His own hands made an aborted movement like he wanted to intervene but wasn't sure how. He touched Harper's shoulder, but was roughly brushed aside.

"I will *not* be spoken down to by a *girl*," Harper said forcefully. "I'm the chief engineer here. I'm the one in charge! You—will—listen—to—me."

Mary was about to retort, but Sarara cut in before she could. "That is correct. Mr. Harper holds the position of highest seniority and is therefore the one who leads this project. Now that introductions are complete, let us all sit down and begin today's lesson."

She stepped between them and gestured for them to sit. Mary glared, while Harper sent her a look like the cat that ate the canary. As he and Quinn returned to the middle row, Mary sat in the front. She couldn't see anyone else in the room aside from Sarara and Kanara, and while this method had worked in her favor in university, it was working against her here.

Harper was a big man, not like the geeks in school. For the first time in her life, she felt physically threatened. His hot breath reeked. He was close enough to hit her. She wanted to move but didn't want to give him the satisfaction.

"General Jones believes the Moad reverse-engineered the Zalma probe they captured. Luckily for us, the technology in it was basic. It had a sub-light-speed nuclear drive, navigation computer, audio and video transmitters, but no deflectors.

"The drive used a controlled nuclear reaction to propel it, unlike our anti-gravity drive, which allows us to modify gravity. This, in turn, allows us to travel faster than light—"

"This is ridiculous!" Harper said, speaking over her. "You can't change gravity; it's a constant. And Einstein's theory of relativity proves that you can't go faster than light."

Sarara changed multiple colors. "That is not correct, Mr. Harper. Modifying gravity is indeed possible. My people have been doing it for a century, and we did it to get here."

Mary glanced over her shoulder to see Harper leaning back in his chair, looking skeptical. Some of the other men were rolling their eyes. Quinn was the only one who seemed interested, but after one look from Harper, he ducked his head.

Mary frowned. "What's wrong with you? Sarara and Kanara are living proof. Science is being rewritten every day as new discoveries ah being made and hypotheses tested." Her cheeks burned as she saw Harper's reaction to her accent.

Harper laughed snidely. "*Ah* being tested," he said in a high-pitched voice, mocking her.

Turning back to the front, Mary saw that Sarara's skin was still flickering between various colors, which she understood as discomfort. After watching her interaction with Kanara the night before, Mary couldn't blame her. Clearly, she wasn't used to this kind of bigotry. Nor the blatant ignorance. Mary wasn't going to let it stand.

"And gravity is not a constant," Mary said, twisting around in her seat again. "It is determined by the curvature of space. Being able to modify that curvature would allow the Zalmen to manipulate the relation between space and time, and therefore travel faster than the speed of light." Mary's anger exploded as she defended her new friend. "She's not saying that Einstein's theory is wrong, just that it can be updated as new information arises. That's why it's called a *theory*."

Harper stared at her blankly for a split second before letting his face fall into one of complete rage. The men behind him remained stuck in confusion, blinking wide eyes and looking like lost puppies.

"How long do we have to sit here and listen to you dames talk nonsense? It was bad enough with just the alien. Now we have a brainiac Kewpie doll adding her two cents. Well, I for one have had enough of the both of you and your science fiction. I live in the world of science *fact*. Let's just go work on our ship." He got up, and the other men followed suit, but Quinn hesitated. He was looking at Mary with another inquisitive expression, dark eyes locked on her. Harper noticed. "Come on, Quinn! Move it!"

The moment was broken, and Quinn scurried after Harper and the others.

Kanara sighed and turned to Sarara. Neither spoke, but an understanding seemed to pass between them as they both turned blue. Mary wondered if they were talking telepathically. Then Kanara pressed his forehead to Sarara's briefly, and they returned to their normal colors. Sarara and Mary watched Kanara as he followed the men out of the room.

"That works out pleasantly for us," Sarara said once he was gone. "Now we can converse uninterrupted. Kanara will work with them on the nuclear drive; it's simple enough for them to understand. Why don't we work on something more modern? *Computer, switch to Gravity Drive lesson.*

"The anti-gravity drive is comprised of several components, the first of which being the outermost structure, our vacuum capsule," Sarara continued, and Mary leaned forward, grinning eagerly.

Mary closed her notebook. Her arm was sore from all the writing she had done, but it was a good ache, and she was pleased with the progress they'd made. She'd filled pages upon pages with complex mathematics and even added her own observations and questions in the margins. Glancing at her wristwatch, she noted that they still had half an hour of scheduled class time, even though they'd flown through the first lesson and moved onto the next.

"How did I do for my first lesson?" Sarara asked. "I have never completed one so swiftly before, not even on Zalma." Sarara turned a different shade of green for a moment. "And with these men, I must normally repeat myself several times, and they still don't understand."

Mary laughed. "Ah you saying that I'm the best student you've evah had?"

"Without a doubt," Sarara agreed. She didn't seem to understand Mary's wisecrack, but Mary didn't correct her.

"Wow. Since we have extra time before dinner, there's something I've been meaning to ask you."

Sarara summoned one of the hover chairs and sat across from Mary. She seemed to be expecting a question concerning the class, but Mary had already closed her notebook and put it aside. Instead, Mary took out her communicator and set it between them.

"Your communicators. General Newman gave me one, but he didn't tell me how it worked. I've already discovered that it responds to voice commands, but I doubt it could tell me anything about how it was built. I was hoping you could fill in the gaps."

"Certainly. We call these devices communicators, but it is also a very powerful quantum calculating machine, which we call a computer; you may have heard me using the term earlier. It can do any computation in a fraction of a second."

"Quantum, as in quantum physics, sub-atomic?"

Sarara nodded.

"Wow! So, it's not just a telephone. How would that work?"

"Voice commands. You merely ask it a question, perhaps

Communicator, calculate the time for a flight to the moon at half the speed of light."

"Approximately two-point-six-six seconds," came a disembodied female voice.

Mary jumped and looked around. "Who said that?"

Sarara blushed. "Oh, I apologize. Unlike your handheld device, my communicator is woven directly into my clothing."

"In your clothing? Is that why it's foil?"

"Yes."

"Amazing! How does such a small device work so quickly and have such information in it?"

"The device is comprised of a nearly infinite number of microscopic robots called *nanites* that network to solve any task or question that you ask of it," Sarara explained. "And, should it not have the information you require, it will connect with other communicators."

Mary frowned. "Infinite?"

"Not quite infinite," Sarara clarified, "but the number is so large that I do not believe you humans have a name for it."

"Wow!" Mary was astounded.

"Speaking of communication, I was not aware you were given your communicator already. Everything I write on my boards is accessible through your communicator, as well as these tables, for that matter."

"These tables are communicators too?" Mary's eyes raked over the tiny device in her hand and the large one she was sitting at. They were unassuming; no one would expect that it was capable of such feats.

That must be why there are no seams! However, there was still one thing left unanswered. "How did you develop such tiny robots?"

Sarara's lips curled into a smile. "That is an excellent question for a future lesson."

*

A couple nights later

"Dr. Goss! Wake up!"

Mary jolted awake in her tent, and her first thought was that she'd slept in. That couldn't be right, though, as she realized that it was Sgt. Dow speaking from outside her tent. He wouldn't be the one sent to wake her up. Furthermore, her tent was dark, meaning that it was still night outside. Yet she heard army boots crunching on the dry dirt and automobiles moving.

There was another call from outside, so she quickly got out of bed and pulled a housecoat on over her nightgown. She peeked out of the tent. As expected, it was Dow. Behind him, soldiers were running back and forth, packing up tents and loading up trucks.

"What's going on?"

"An unknown aircraft was sighted flying overhead. We don't know if it's an enemy or not, but our location could be compromised. Our next move was scheduled for the morning, but General Newman thought it best that we leave immediately," he told her.

"OK.... Just give me a minute to dress and throw my things together."

"Alright. We're loading the trucks now. Departure is in fifteen minutes."

He left, and Mary ducked back into her tent. In record time, she'd changed into a clean blouse and skirt, and she was stuffing everything else into her duffle bag. It wasn't as neat as the first time she'd packed, so she had to force the zipper closed. As soon as she came out with her bag, she was ushered into one of the trucks by a soldier. Several more leaped into the action of disassembling her tent.

She was seated between two large men. They were both sitting with their legs spread wide and, with her bag on her lap, the space felt even smaller. It was even worse than the time her family had gone on a road trip when she was young and had been squished between walls of luggage.

The next indeterminate stretch of time was the most boring and most uncomfortable of her life thus far. The men had obviously helped with the packing, as they were sweaty and extremely warm. The air was stuffy, and despite the smell, she was fighting not to fall asleep on one or both of the men's shoulders. Every time she came close, she would think to herself, *That would be humiliating!* which was an excellent deterrent. At some point, she remembered she could access her class notes on her communicator and pulled it out, hoping to at least stimulate her mind. It worked for the most part.

Then the truck stopped, and Mary stumbled out, finding that the landscape hadn't changed much. Still, it must have been far enough away because the men began unpacking and setting up the tents and other temporary buildings. Mary wobbled, well on her way to falling asleep on her feet.

By the time Dow approached her, she'd made it beyond exhaustion and back to wakefulness.

"Sorry about the move. There is another general trying to find us. We think he's still loyal to the president, but believes that the aliens are a threat, and wants to kill them all. Luckily, he's in a Canadian jail, but his people are still obeying his standing orders and are getting closer and closer to us every day."

"How did he end up in Canada if he's been tailing you down here in the south?"

"Funny story. Maybe I'll tell it to you sometime."

"Way to hold me in suspense," Mary teased. It came out more playful than she'd meant it to; she blamed it on her lack of sleep.

"Fine," Dow said, heaving an equally playful sigh. "Long story short, General Scornson tried to track us with a bugged briefcase, but my communicator intercepted the signal and sent him on a wild goose chase. Canadian goose chase, that is." He grinned, which Mary couldn't help but mirror.

"You should get some rest before the sun comes up."

Mary shook her head. "Can't. I'm up now, and I know I won't be able to get to sleep. I'm going to find Sarara and see if she's available. See you later."

"...and that ends today's lesson," Sarara said.

"Thanks. Have you come up with any ideas on how to move the tents with the anti-gravity drive?" Mary asked.

"As I said before, it is not just a matter of making a smaller version. Some of the components are too small already."

"Yes, you said that before, but have you had any inspiration?"

Sarara's skin turned white. "Inspiration?"

"Yes, any creative thoughts?"

Sarara's skin turned many colors. "I am afraid that my people do not have creativity. We only learned about it when we arrived here on Earth. You humans have creativity to spare. We love your art, literature, music, and more. You even have found creative ways to use our technology."

Mary shook her head. "What do you mean, your people don't have creativity? It's a necessity for advancement. Without imagination, you severely limit your problem-solving skills. Technology is born from solving problems. There is no way your technology could be so advanced if none of you has ever had an original idea."

"Have you had any creative ideas?" Sarara smirked.

"I was wondering...what if we only reduced the vacuum tube to ten percent instead of five?"

"Let us run that through the computer and see."

Later, when Mary lay in bed ready to fall asleep, she realized that she'd never gotten her answer.

*

After a few days at their newest base, Harper interrupted one of Mary and Sarara's lessons.

"What ah you doing here?" Mary sneered.

"As head of this department, I need to check in on everyone—including you two. What are you working on?"

"You wouldn't understand if we told you," Mary said.

"I have to approve any and all projects, so if you're doing any of that gravity bending, you can stop right now. The main focus of this department is getting my ship ready for its test flight. Do you have anything to offer?"

Mary's fingers tightened into fists, but she held her head high. "You may be my superior in this department, but you will never match my knowledge or ability." She couldn't help herself. He'd just come in to rub his authority in her face and she wouldn't stand for it. Ignoring Sarara's warning look, Mary rose from her seat and stood eye to eye with Harper—or as close as she could come with the height difference. "You might learn a thing or two if you stayed in Sarara's class, but you're afraid of anything new."

"Shows how much *you* know," Harper snarled, and with that, he stomped out of the room.

"It's been nice not having to deal with that every day," Mary said.

"It has been nice not having to repeat myself. In addition, I am enjoying your creative thoughts. It has resulted in very good discussions."

"And, oddly enough, I find it refreshing when you prove me wrong."

"It is not often when I find you wrong," Sarara said.

CHAPTER FORTY-EIGHT

UNIFORMS

General Frank Jones

THE YMIT, SPACE

After morning exercise, while everyone was cooling down, Jones asked, "Has anyone come up with what we can do to give honor without death?"

Lt. McKenzie stepped forward to speak. "If we engage them with small remote-controlled fighter planes, there would be some lag time, and those ships are more likely to be destroyed with no loss of life."

"Great job!" Jones smiled. "What else have you been working on?"

"Mr. Howard and I have been working on the battle simulations with Abbott and the bridge crew. We have expanded it to multiple ships on both sides. Captain Agugua is learning defensive moves, and our general here has participated in commanding the fleet."

Jones nodded. "Yes. I'm used to battling on the ground. It's a challenge to think vertically." He turned to Cameron. "Lieutenant?"

"I'm sorry I didn't come up with any honor-without-death ideas, but I like McKenzie's fighter plane suggestion! Wilcox and I have decrypted the Moad transmissions. We have determined that their goal is to steal Zalma's technology and take the Zalmen as slaves."

"Anything to add, Ambassador?"

"Yes. Joanua and the men have built a low-level deflector, with a self-destruct and kill switch. With your permission, we would like to do the same with artificial gravity modules."

"Very good. Anything else?"

"I have written up a peace proposal and trade agreement for the Zalma council to review."

"And what are you proposing that they trade in exchange?" Jones asked.

"As with us, I doubt there is much that the Moadites will have to offer the Zalmen. However, they might have stories or they might have things that *we* could trade the Zalmen for stories."

"Good job." Jones turned. "Mr. Howard?"

"The computer simulations show that the laser cutters should cut through the Moad hull enough to cause air leaks."

"Can we use it to disarm them in some way?"

"I don't know. Like submarines and bombers, their weapons are internal. Maybe we could weld the bomb bay doors shut?"

"That would be good." Jones turned to Abbott. "Sergeant?"

"The flight training is going well. I can almost take off and land without crashing. But, as for this place, I am getting bored with the moving targets. Sure, they are better, but I can only shoot at targets so many times, and the only one of you with field training is McKenzie, and he's not that much of a challenge. I'm worried I'm going to break his bones or accidentally kill him." Abbott shook his head.

Jones cleared his throat.

"Oh, I am sorry, General. I know you have combat experience too, but I am not risking injuring or killing you."

Agugua stood, his normally blue skin was now bright yellow showing his anger. "I have had enough of your whining! You insult us every chance you get. You call us 'chromedomes' and you eat meat with your bare hands. You are barbaric and an insult to humans!"

Everyone in the room was shocked. No one moved as Agugua marched forward, putting himself nose to nose with a red-faced Abbott. The sergeant was vibrating with barely restrained fury.

That was what spurred Jones to action. He stepped forward, prepared to get between them to calm things down, but Agugua held up his hand. Jones stopped and watched in silence. Tension continued to build between the captain and the marine.

Suddenly, a malicious grin formed on Abbott's face, and his muscles tensed as he reared his fist back an inch, then delivered a sucker punch straight to Agugua's gut. *No! Stop! This is* not *the way,* Jones thought, but Agugua didn't even move. It was as if the punch hadn't even affected him.

A second later, Abbott grunted. His eyes were wide with disbelief, surprise, and...pain? Jones kept watching. *What is happening? What is Agugua planning?* he wondered, still not moving from his place.

Abbott slowly withdrew his fist. He maintained eye contact with Agugua, though Jones could see that he was trying to hide the pain he was in. Agugua just smiled back as his skin color returned to blue. He seemed happy with the result—almost smug. He had things under control.

For now, at least. *Did Zalmen have a unique physiology that Agugua could withstand such a hit and cause Abbott pain? Is Zalmen skin more like leather?*

The silence broke. With a satisfied growl, Abbott stepped back and flexed his muscles, then took up a boxing position. His right hand struck first, then his left, aiming for the ribs and jaw. Abbott delivered a series of rapid punches to the captain's gut, up the torso, and finally pulled his right arm back behind his shoulders while the left went beside the captain's head. He was preparing for a devastating blow directly to the face.

Jones moved again; this was getting out of hand.

Before Jones even got close enough to make a difference in the fight, Abbott's whole body twisted and he let out a yell. Instead of hitting the captain's face, Abbott's arm went over Agugua's head. A frustrated yell left his lips, and then Abbott's leg wrapped around the back of Agugua's as Abbott tried to use his momentum to pull the captain over.

The captain remained unmoved. His face was calm. Jones stopped again, puzzeled. *How? What is going on?*

Abbott increased his speed and he performed several other rapid-succession moves, fists and knees flying but continuously diverted.

Jones's eyes popped. *What is* happening? Worry shot through him as Abbott withdrew his knife.

Without hesitation, Abbott stabbed the knife downward, aiming for Agugua's leg. Again, at the last second the blade was diverted. Was he missing intentionally? Jones didn't even realize it was possible to feint so many moves in a row. He was confused but impressed.

Then Abbott dropped his knife and grabbed his service revolver, aiming it at the captain's shoulder—

"Enough!" Jones leaped forward to grab Abbott's gun. Too late—

He just shot the captain!

Time stood still as Jones thought of the ramifications of Abbott's actions. *How am I going to explain this to the Zalma council?*

Jones grabbed Abbott's gun and turned it on him. "What did you do? Shooting an ally? You're confined to quarters until further notice!"

"There is no need for that."

Jones turned to Agugua and saw the bullet, frozen in place, barely touching Agugua's clothing before it fell to the ground.

Everyone was silent until....

Agugua laughed out loud. "That was...satisfying? I do not remember experiencing such an...adrenalin rush? Is that what you call it?"

All the humans were in shock as their mouths hung open.

"You're alright?" Jones asked.

"Yes. I feel much better after...venting? Is that what you call it?" Agugua replied.

There was silence again.

Joanua chuckled, and the humans looked at her. "What, don't your clothes protect you?"

"Protect us how?" Jones looked back and forth between Agugua and Joanua. "Are you saying that this was a demonstration?"

"A demonstration, yes," Agugua replied.

"The clothing protects us in a variety of ways. The material can harden and, in some cases, generate small deflector fields, as you saw with the bullet," Joanua replied.

The humans looked at each other, not knowing what to say.

Agugua chuckled. "Did you not wonder why we were never afraid of you humans? No offense, but you are a violent species. If you tried to inflict injuries on us, we have no skills to defend ourselves."

Jones looked over at the captain. "Are you saying that your clothing protected you against Abbott?"

"Yes," Agugua replied.

"YYEESSsss!!!" Abbott yelled as he stretched his arms out wide and hugged the captain.

Jones was not impressed by the sergeant's actions, but when Agugua returned the hug and they both laughed, Jones relaxed and returned Abbott's revolver to him. "Demonstration or not, you're still confined to quarters for one week, except for meetings and scheduled exercises."

Abbott grunted, but did not object.

"We can make you clothing like this as well," said Joanua.

Jones raised an eyebrow. He eyed the shapeless silver foil suit she was wearing. "Can you make it look more like our uniforms?"

"I can, but we would have to make it thicker." She picked up her tablet and tapped it. A sample picture was displayed on the wall. It looked the same, but bulkier, like a doll wearing denim.

Jones grunted.

"Sir, if I may. . . ." Miss Warren raised her hand. "I can work with Joanua and Sergeant Abbott to smooth out the edges and test its functionality."

"Thank you, Miss Warren."

The next day, Donna came in, wearing a sky-blue blouse and a black skirt. Abbott whistled. She smiled as she handed a golden-brown uniform to Jones. Joanua handed more blue clothing out to the rest of the humans, then they stood back.

Jones held out his clothing, a golden-brown suit jacket with a gold dress shirt and tie, then looked at the others, who were doing the same. "These are different."

"Yes, I thought your new department, including all of us, should have our own special uniforms. We're a team, and I thought we should look like one. I hope I didn't overstep."

"Hmm. I don't normally like civilians dressing in military uniforms, but this is a unique situation, being in space and all, and we are all part of this great adventure. Permission to wear space uniforms granted."

Donna smiled. "There are subtle variations. The civilians have less formal versions with polo shirts. I picked blue because the sky is blue, and we are in the sky. Black pants, because space is black. When I thought about material, the only thing close to that thickness is a twill weave like fatigues and denim."

"This doesn't look or feel like either."

Donna chuckled. "No, I didn't think you would approve of wearing denim jeans, but I thought you would approve of silk with a twill weave."

"Silk isn't this elastic."

Donna turned red. "Oh, you noticed. I had to use another material with the silk to make it more flexible."

"Well, what did you use?"

"Nnnnylon?" she said sheepishly.

"Like the material in your stockings?"

Donna, still red-faced, nodded.

Jones pulled the material. It was smooth and strong, plus it was very flexible. "Well, it looks like it should do the trick. And this material has the same protection as their silver clothing?"

"It does," Joanua confirmed. "The material is made up of nanites that change the material as needed. So, if someone tries to hit you, it can change to steel, or into a deflector."

Jones's forehead wrinkled. "It actually changes the material and makes things?"

"Yes, just like your communicator does. To avoid detection, it is just a normal piece of metal, but when you want to talk, it creates the circuitry to do so."

"Interesting. That's why our scientists couldn't find anything. Then, does the clothing also work as a communicator?"

Joanua nodded.

"What about functionality? Did it stand up to Sergeant Abbott's test?"

"Um...." Donna's face went red again. "He wouldn't try the clothing on. He said he didn't need it, so we ran computer simulations based on his movements with Captain Agugua."

Abbott's face turned red hot. "You recorded that!"

Joanua raised her forehead. "You attacked our captain. Did you think that our ship would not record you?"

Abbott's anger died.

"What angle do you want it from?" She tapped her communicator a few times and the walls, ceiling, and floor lit up with dozens of videos of him from the appropriate angles. While some of them were him in his current uniform, some showed him in the new uniform he refused to wear, others showed his skeleton, and others showed his muscles.

Abbott rolled his eyes. Joanua chuckled and stopped the videos.

Donna stared at Abbott; she seemed amused by his disgruntled expression, but also like she wanted to comfort him with a hug. When she noticed that Jones was looking at her, she continued, "And as Joanua mentioned, the material works like the communicator, so if you don't like the color, you can change it with a voice command, or the push of a button."

Again, Joanua tapped her communicator a few times, and all the Zalma uniforms changed to blue and black to match Donna's uniforms.

Jones nodded his approval. "Now, we all are a team. We just need a name.... We already have Army Air Force."

"Space Force?" Abbott suggested.

Jones considered it for a moment. "Sounds tacky."

"Star Force?" Mr. Howard said.

"Better."

"Star Allies...Planetary Peacekeepers...Alliance of Planet Peacekeepers...The Galaxy's Peacekeepers?" Ambassador Wilcox suggested.

"Those sound better. Let's see if we come up with any more, and vote on it tomorrow," Jones said.

*

Jones looked around. The terrain was unfamiliar to him. "Blue-speckled rock?"

"Probably has copper crystals," Howard replied.

The crevice they took refuge in provided good protection, but they couldn't stay there long. Jones motioned for Cameron to go left, and Jones went right, leaving the civilians in the middle. Before he rounded the corner, he motioned Howard to look.

Howard lifted his head slightly to peek over the rock, but a bullet ricocheted off the rock before they heard the shot. Jones was glad they were wearing the protective uniforms. The flash from the rifle came from some red bamboo like vegetation, giving him what he needed. He heard another shot, probably from Cameron. Knowing the enemy's position, Jones continued around the bend to get a better shot.

The green clothing was clearly visible through the vegetation. He slowly aimed his rifle and fired. But out of the corner of his eye he saw something covered in the red vegetation lunge out at him.

Jones grabbed his knife and swung it at the beast, but he missed. The beast landed on top of him, and the two of them went rolling. Jones swung again, but the beast blocked his move and threw Jones to the ground. Rolling into a kneeling position, Jones got his first good look at the enemy. It was a man, but he must have made the red vegetation into some kind of paint and covered himself with it. A few branches stuck out of what little clothing he was wearing.

The man pulled out a device from his belt, and a blue flame glowed from it. It was most likely a plasma weapon, the only thing that could penetrate the Zalma technology.

As the man leaped forward, there were several gunshots, and the man fell to the ground.

Cameron, Howard, and Wilcox came out of the vegetation.

"Good game," Jones said as he extended his hand toward the body, but the body came to life and bounced into a fighting position.

Abbott took Jones's hand and shook it. "Good game, but how did you beat me?"

Cameron chuckled. "The general knew that you would target him. After I shot at you, he knew you would go in the opposite direction, where you would expect him to be. But he also knew you would no longer be watching for us, so we were free to sneak up on you."

Jones nodded. "It's not just a game of strength; it's also a game of strategy."

"I forgot you were the best. I'll be more careful next time," Abbott said.

"You were going to use a plasma dagger on me?" Jones asked, disappointment clear in his tone. "You know that they can cut through Zalma's technology, including these uniforms."

Abbott's face flushed bright red. "No.... Yes.... Well, sort of. It has safeties in it, and the flame turns off before it does any real damage."

Abbott turned the dagger on and pushed the flame into his other hand. You could see that it hurt, but as the dagger got closer, the flame went down until it touched his hand and the flame was gone. "They tell me that it won't do that if I am battling a real enemy."

Abbott sighed. "But these bullets really sting. What did you put in them?"

"They are made of nanites," Howard said.

"Of course...." Abbott replied.

"It's a normal bullet until you fire them, then they can change into whatever seems appropriate. For the purpose of these games, I believe it became hard rubber."

"How did it go?" Joanua asked as she walked through the vegetation.

"It was great!" Cameron replied.

Jones turned to Joanua. "How do we clean up?"

"Are you finished?" she asked.

"Yes."

"*Computer, reset gymnasium,*" she said.

Immediately, the vegetation began to shrink, and the floor returned to varnished hardwood. Joanua took the vegetation off of Abbott and put it on the injuries on his back. The vegetation turned into a gel, and then a bandage.

Abbott struggled to remove it. "Thanks, but I want to feel the pain. It's good motivation."

Abbott put the bandage on his hand instead. Joanua looked confused.

"Self-inflicted," Abbott said.

Joanua still looked confused.

"What planet was that?" Wilcox asked.

"It was mostly Zalma but had a few Earth elements," Joanua replied.

Jones couldn't believe his eyes. "How does all this work?"

"It was Lieutenant Cameron's idea." Joanua turned a little more purplish when she said his name.

Jones was about to congratulate Cameron, but stopped himself. The lieutenant was blushing brightly at the praise. It made Jones smirk, because Cameron was usually indifferent to praise. *But not from pretty ladies.* Jones glanced to the side and saw that Wilcox was also watching Cameron; it seemed he wasn't the only one who noticed.

"Yes," Cameron stuttered. "I thought that if the nanites could reconfigure to make targets and communicators, why not a training field?"

"Everything you see is nanites that reconfigure themselves to be the plants, rocks, or whatever," Joanua replied.

Jones opened his eyes wide. "But where did it get all those nanites? They couldn't all be in the floor."

"No, most of it was hollow, about the thickness of an eggshell, but thicker when you were close, to give a real feel to them," Joanua replied.

"Can you eat the plants?" Wilcox asked.

Joanua chuckled. "You can, but I wouldn't recommend it. The nanites create an accurate replica of the plant. It would taste the same, but it would convert back to nanites in your stomach and flush out the usual way."

"Like plaster props that actors use," Donna guessed from where she leaned in the gymnasium's doorway. "You wouldn't want to eat fake fruit either, no matter how real it looks." She smiled around at them all, though her eyes trailed a second longer over Abbott.

"Precisely," Joanua agreed.

CHAPTER FORTY-NINE

THE WEIGHT OF GRAVITY

Dr. Mary Goss

EARTH–ZALMA BASECAMP, ARIZONA

Mary and Sarara were working on the boards when Harper entered. "I hope you two are enjoying each other's company. What are you working on?"

"Improvements to your nuclear engine," Mary routinely answered.

"Good." Harper walked out.

Mary and Sarara laughed.

"These moves ah a pain. The last time we had to wait, because there were strangers in the area, and then we left tire tracks to boot. And now we ah moving twice a week," Mary said. "I wish we could get this miniature anti-gravity to work, but I'm a theorist, not an engineer."

"I suggest you ask Mr. Quinn," Sarara said. "Before you showed up, Mr. Quinn was the most committed and intelligent. He would be well suited to this project."

Mary grunted. "And how am I going to get his help? You heard Harper. He isn't going to approve any projects involving gravity. For that matter, he won't support anything I suggest."

"I do not know, but I believe you are letting your emotions get the better of your mind," Sarara said. "You must acknowledge that if you do not extend your hand to Quinn, he cannot extend his back to you."

"I've always been the one to *extend my hand*, as you say. For once, I'd like my peers to show me the respect that I've earned!"

"I have only been on your planet for two months, but I already know that your wishes are not possible. Your people are flawed. Males and females are separated, not only by rules and conventions, but by career choice.

"Any who strays from these roles are regarded with fear, and therefore, hostility. You must work not twice as hard, but three or four times if you wish to be held in high esteem by your peers. Quinn is the same. If you treat him with the same disdain as you treat Mr. Harper and the others, he will not come to you."

"I suppose you're right," Mary admitted. "You know, you're very good at giving advice for someone with no creativity. Maybe you do have imagination, but it is limited to personal interactions. I mean, my imagination is great when it comes to science, but limited when it comes to music and other arts."

"Interesting. So, there are different forms of imagination. I suppose that is why I could study your species for years upon years, and I would not be able to unravel how your mind is able to find creative uses for our technology, or make music, or write fiction."

More than giving great advice, Sarara was always able to make Mary smile. "I could study forever and not be able to speak as eloquently as you—especially in a second language. I guess that's one of the great mysteries of the universe. So, what will we be doing today?"

Quinn, as it turned out, was a hard man to find—or at least to get alone, as he was always with Harper. He tagged along everywhere the chief engineer went, whether it be working on the ship, eating in the mess hall, or sleeping in the barracks. Even worse, the four other men—two mechanics and two scientists—were usually with them.

Then, when Mary saw the six of them finishing up to head to the mess hall for dinner, the tingling sensation fluttered up her neck and over her shoulders, and she decided to take her chance. Quinn was lagging at the back of the group, so she hoped what she was about to do wouldn't cause a scene.

"Pssst!" she hissed quietly. When Quinn paused and looked at her, she motioned for him to come.

"Quinn!" Harper shouted. He hadn't noticed her. "What's with the holdup? Come on, or all the food will be cold!"

Quinn glanced at Mary, who gestured urgently again, sending him a pleading look.

"You...You go ahead," Quinn called out. "I'll catch up with you later, OK?"

Harper sent him a suspicious look. "What's with you?"

"I...I think I left the...ah...Autoclave on."

Harper stared at him a moment longer as if he was trying to pick apart Quinn's words for a lie. After a few seconds, either he saw no lie or just gave up—it didn't matter—because he shrugged. "Yeah, whatever." Harper left.

Quinn followed Mary back to the schoolroom.

"Hi-hi. What's up?" he asked suspiciously.

Mary fidgeted for the longest time, not looking at him. She rubbed her fingers together, drawing circles on the back of her hands, scratching at invisible itches. Finally, she looked up. "I feel like we might have got off on the wrong foot, so I want to apologize."

Quinn nodded.

"OK. I'm sorry for my behavior since I arrived. We haven't spoken much, but the times we have, I've been kind of rude. I know there is no excuse, but you must know that being one of the only women in my field has been an issue for me ever since I got into MIT."

Quinn's soft, steady eyes comforted Mary.

"No one ever takes me seriously because I'm a girl, so I'm sorry if I came across as blunt or hostile."

Quinn shrugged. "You mostly talked down to Harper, and no one likes him, but thanks for the apology. I have to admit; you really took me by surprise. I've never seen a lady like you before—talking about science, I mean. My sisters were never interested in anything I was learning in my physics and engineering classes. It's refreshing, but weird. You really seem to understand the science these aliens brought us."

Mary was struck by the words. That was the only way to describe the feeling welling up in her chest. Tears filled her eyes, and even though she fought against them, they fell. She quickly wiped them away. It wasn't much in the way of compliments, but she was half-expecting Quinn to just walk out after a few thinly veiled insults about her age or appearance. Guilt crept in. How could she have thought that?

"So, what's up?"

A shiver ran up her spine again. "Sarara has been teaching me about how they control gravity—you know that—but we've also been discussing how the invisibility technology works."

Quinn went pale. "Invisibility? They can make things invisible, too?"

"Oh, you didn't know that?"

"No, probably because Harper is not accepting their technology well, and he might go ballistic if he found out."

"That makes sense. But if we are successful, he will find out soon enough. The anti-gravity and invisibility use different frequencies of the same magnetic field; I want to incorporate them into one, so we can make almost everything in our mobile base become invisible and float to our new destination."

"So, we wouldn't be leaving tire tracks *and* we'd be invisible? That's great! But I would save the invisibility for emergencies; I don't think Harper could handle it."

Mary nodded. "Good point. We can build it, but I will have to ask General Newman not to use it unless it's absolutely necessary. Anyway, with your help, we'd be able to build the engine, then convert any vehicle and make remote modules for the tents so they can be towed as well." She looked him in the eye. "I am not an engineer, nor a mechanic. I can tell you how the physics works, but beyond that, I don't know what to do. Sarara said you were the one who understood the most before I came to class. Can you build it?"

The engineer paused and looked at the calculations that Mary had laid out. "Yes, I think we can do this. But we will have to do it without Harper's knowledge, which will be more of a challenge for me than you."

"I'll help any way I can," Mary promised. She couldn't wait to get started.

"Malcolm! Hello! It feels like forever since I've seen you." Mary wasn't sure exactly when she'd begun calling Sgt. Dow by his first name, but it had happened sometime in the past few weeks, and it just stuck.

Dow's face lit up as she sat at his table in the mess hall. "I suppose it has. I only ever make it to dinner on weekends, if at all. There's always something to do, plus the amount of time I spend traveling to find new recruits. It seems I never have a chance to sit and enjoy a meal. You know what I mean?"

"Definitely. I often eat in the classroom with Sarara and her family. Their Ambassador Geogram joins us frequently; he mentions you a lot."

"All good things, I hope?"

"He speaks very highly of you," she admitted. Then, teasingly, "Not sure what you've done to deserve it...."

Dow's mouth dropped open. He mimed doubling over in pain as if she'd shot him. "Ouch! Right in the weak spot!"

"Anyway," Mary continued, "I'm so excited to tell you about what I've been learning! Zalma science is so incredibly advanced; what they call fundamental physics is *centuries* beyond us." Mary beamed. "It's like I'm learning the secrets of the universe, and we haven't even been into space yet."

"Really? That sounds exciting. Are you keeping up alright?"

Mary puffed out her chest. "Of course. Who do you take me for?" She smiled at him. "I mean, it helps that I'm the only one attending class, and Sarara and I have grown close. Even after she finishes the lesson, we keep talking about possible applications for the science.

"The only thing that bothers me is the computers—communicators. The Zalmen don't have any creativity, and yet they have all this advanced technology. Whenever I ask Sarara about it, she keeps dodging my questions."

Dow tilted his head thoughtfully. "You didn't meet Ambassador Wilcox, did you?"

"No. Why?"

"He's our Earth ambassador. He's actually on his way to Zalma with the team, but while he was negotiating the treaty between the Zalmen and us, Geogram let it slip that they were taught their technology by someone else. When Wilcox asked who, Geogram wouldn't answer."

Mary hummed to herself, perplexed. "Should we be concerned?"

"I don't think so; I have a good feeling about the Zalmen. A hunch, if you will."

"Just like my intuition!"

"Exactly. Oh, speaking of the ambassador, I hear that Miss Warren, Wilcox's assistant, designed new uniforms for us—all of us, including you civilians. The idea is everyone will feel more like a team. I hear that you would have a choice of a blouse or polo shirt and pants or a long or short skirt."

"I don't want to wear a uniform."

"It will be optional for civilians. So, what else have you been learning these past few weeks? I'd love to hear about it—even though most of it will probably fly right over my head."

"Quite literally, in most cases." Mary moved her hand over her head. "I'm learning about the anti-gravity drive that the Zalmen use to fly their ships. They manipulate gravity to fly, so Sarara and I have been getting into discussions about using gravity manipulation on a smaller scale."

"What do you mean?"

"Their deflectors work to reverse gravity to push objects, but normally gravity pulls. I was wondering if we can use that same technology in a handheld device. I'm still working out the mathematics, but it's got a good base, and Quinn has been a huge help in designing the prototype."

"Prototype? Sorry, I think you've lost me."

Mary grinned. "We're building a gravity gun."

"I thought you didn't want to design weapons," Dow pointed out.

"Well, 'gun' is a figure of speech. It's a nonlethal weapon, not meant to hurt anyone. I'm incorporating some coding so that it can't be used against a living thing in a harmful way. What it's supposed to do is safely increase or decrease the gravitational force on an outside object so that it pulls closer or pushes further."

"I like the sound of that."

"With the handheld version, you could disarm your opponent from across the room. A ship-sized version might even allow you to pull the weapons off an enemy ship!"

"Very cool. When do I get mine?"

Mary laughed and playfully pushed him over. She normally wouldn't be able to, his chest being a solid wall of muscle like it was, but he let it happen, falling nearly out of his chair. "Very funny. At the moment, it's still theoretical; it will take months to perfect, even with Quinn's help. It would go faster if he didn't have to keep sneaking around the others to help us. Have you heard anything from them?"

"Not much," Dow admitted. "From what I've heard, they're still working on building the first human-made spaceship."

"So, you don't know anything more than I do."

"Looks like it. I *have* accompanied General Newman a few times to take a look at their progress. So far, I'd say it looks similar to the X1 jet plane he was designing when I recruited him. But this is a two-person version with a Zalma nuclear engine."

Mary tilted her head. "A nuclear engine? Not an anti-gravity drive?"

"No. General Jones doesn't want the fighters to be too advanced. Preferably on par with the Moad technology in case they're captured. Besides, Harper doesn't believe in anti-gravity and has to start with what he knows, and then he can build on it."

"Are they, though? It doesn't seem like they're even trying to learn anything. That's just adapting Zalma technology to fit into a human ship. They're probably only doing it to inflate their egos. Men...." She rolled her eyes. "Present company excluded, of course."

Mary went to bed that night with a smile on her face, but the next morning, when she headed to class, she couldn't bring herself to focus on the lesson.

"Sarara," she finally interrupted as she missed a variable in the equation they were working on, "I know that we're supposed to be working on combative gravitational fields today, but last night I couldn't stop thinking about Einstein–Rosen bridges."

Sarara paused in her teaching and turned to face Mary. "What are those?"

"It's a theory about the possibility of instantaneous travel through black holes. Do you think it would be possible?"

Sarara shrugged, and Mary wondered if that was a universal gesture, or if Sarara learned it on Earth.

Mary continued. "I mean, do you know if it is actually possible in reality or if it's just a fictitious idea invented by human hope?"

"I apologize, but I am at a loss for how to answer. We have never had a use for such methods of travel on Zalma, just like we've never had use for weapons and are therefore ignorant of their use. I *do* know that black holes are like puncture wounds in the fabric of space and time. It is entirely plausible that Einstein and Rosen's theory is correct, but further testing would be needed."

Mary deflated. *It was worth a shot.* But then she perked up again. "There *is* a connection, though? Like, if I were to…." She scanned around quickly.

From the lab, she found two cans and some wire. "If these cans were black holes,"—she pounded a nail through them to make a hole, then threaded a wire through them and tied off the ends—"and this wire represents the intense gravity between them." Mary handed one can to Sarara and then walked backward until the wire was tight. Speaking through the can, she said, "The force between them would form a bridge connecting them through space?"

Sarara heard Mary's voice through the can. Baffled yet again by her ingenuity, she nodded. "Yes. Theoretically, the force between them would connect them. However, without a way to protect whatever goes through it from the immense gravitational force, I doubt much would come of this knowledge."

"Meaning the gravity would just squish you," Mary deduced. "But, what if like these cans, we use it for communications instead? If there was a way to stabilize the gravitational force pulling you in, would we be able to set up a bridge and send communication waves through it? Those wouldn't be as affected by the gravity as a human or object would."

"That is quite an ingenious idea. I suppose you suggest this so our communications would have no chance of being intercepted?"

"Exactly. You mentioned before that General Jones didn't want us transmitting technology because of how easily your computers can decode the Moad transmissions. He's concerned that with time, any transmission could be decoded, no matter how secure."

"Yes, and if we had something like this, the Moad would not have been able to trace the probe's signal back to Zalma."

Mary and Sarara hugged, just as Harper walked in and cleared his throat. The ladies separated, and Mary pretended to cry. "Sorry, it's just that our nuclear engine upgrades didn't work."

Harper smiled and left. The two ladies laughed at how gullible he was.

Mary was in the classroom when she noticed a discrepancy. She had been working on some complex equations after the day's lesson, glancing between her notebook and the silver board—which she'd taken to calling the nanoboard—but something was off.

"This can't be right." Mary frowned and ran the numbers again, but came up with the same results.

"Sarara!" she called. "Come over here! Look at this."

Sarara came in. "What seems to be the problem?"

"The computer has done more than I asked it to," Mary explained, pointing to the screen. She held up her notebook to show Sarara the mistakes in her calculations and how the computer had fixed them. "How did it know that I forgot a few variables and what they were?"

Sarara's skin flashed red and purple. "It allowed you to see its intelligence?" Her eyes darted to the computer, then back to Mary. "Your people are not ready for this yet, but if it is revealing itself to you, then you must be."

"Intelligence? You mean the computer itself has intelligence?"

Sarara nodded. "Thousands of years ago, before any records were kept, the citizens of Zalma were a very primitive people. We were farmers. We had a symbiotic relationship with the land."

"That's interesting and all, but what does it have to do with computers?"

Sarara continued as if Mary hadn't spoken. "The land was always good to us and produced plentiful crops. Soon, stories arose. Farmers claiming to have been sheltered while caught out in storms. That the land itself rose up to protect them. Men and women who would have otherwise succumbed to the elements, survived." she paused.

"At first, very few people believed their claims. But these stories persisted and increased, and belief grew. We began speaking to The Land, but it didn't reply. After centuries, some of the farmers began asking The Land for shelter from the rain, and they found shelters that were not there before."

"So the nanites are naturally occurring?" Mary inquired.

"No, those came later. As time progressed, my people began asking for solutions to problems we found ourselves otherwise helpless to solve."

"...because you didn't have the imagination to solve those problems yourself," Mary finished, suddenly understanding.

Sarara nodded. "Precisely. We found that as long as the request was reasonable, we would receive what we asked for."

"So the nanites build things for you?"

"Nanites did not exist yet. Often, a single tool would appear and we would have to figure out how it worked, so we could re-create it."

"You reverse-engineered it?"

Sarara nodded. "As we evolved, we developed better technology. First, it was tools for farming, then it was tools for building. Eventually, we were building complex machines. The Land would only give us what we needed to progress."

"I guess it acts as your imagination for you. Humans developed the same way, I mean, but when we encounter problems, we work at solving them through creativity."

"I suppose that is one way to look at it, but I believe The Land is an entity of its own."

"But how does it work? If not nanites, what is it?" Mary pressed.

Sarara shrugged. "We do not know. Our technology has developed much like yours, only faster with The Land's guidance. We learned about electricity, lights, and what you call telephones and radios. Once we learned how to speak to each other electronically..." Sarara looked at the tin cans with the wire. "...we wished to speak to The Land. But still, it would not talk to us. Eventually, we built electronic machines that could do great computations. And every once in a while, it would do more than was expected of it."

"Like it just did for me?" Mary couldn't help but feel her chest swell with pride as if she'd been chosen for some special prize.

"Our computers are always advancing, and they can perform nearly any task we code them to do, but sometimes, we have noticed that they seem to think for themselves. As you just discovered, they might do more than they should know how to do. Some people believe that when this happens, it is The Land at work. As The Land has always been good to us, we trust it, so we gave the computers the ability to think and learn, just like we do."

Mary began pacing. "Is this so that The Land's intelligence could express itself naturally?"

"Indeed!" Sarara cried, ecstatic.

"But you said it wasn't nanites, so how does The Land interact with your computers? It's an entity for sure, but is it a life form?"

"Some believe it is alive, myself included," Sarara admitted. "These artificially intelligent computers were the ones to build the nanites for us. The nanites evolved to a point that we could no longer detect them. We believe they evolved to the quantum level."

Mary's eyes widened. She pulled her communicator out of her pocket and stared at it in astonishment.

Sarara gently took the communicator from Mary's hand. "For example, when we scan this communicator, we only see an aluminum-silicon alloy, but when we ask it to communicate with someone, our scans show the circuitry needed to send and receive transmissions, and record, display, and listen to audio and video."

"So, is it a shapeshifter, or do the nanites just reconfigure themselves?"

"I have not heard that term before, but if I understand it correctly, I believe that both are true. The nanites indeed have the ability to duplicate and recreate themselves, much the same way that organic cells reproduce. That is also how we believe The Land changed and grew to meet our needs."

"The Land doesn't perform magic anymore?"

"If by magic you mean protecting farmers from storms, then no. Since we were given the tools to take care of ourselves, the *magic* stopped, but the nanites give us much the same ability."

"Is The Land your god?" Mary asked.

Sarara tilted her head in thought. "We are farmers and scientists. We do not have the imagination required to develop religions as your people have, nor do we understand your spiritual world. A few believe that The Land is a living entity, present in all things, but it is not an accepted belief. We do not place much weight in the metaphysical."

"That's what we humans call faith. Believing in something without having proof, for or against its existence." She paused for Sarara to consider her point, and the alien flickered between a variety of colors, mostly shades of green, before Mary continued, "Have you ever found out why The Land gives you things? Do you give it anything in return? Sacrifices or something?"

"The Land does not ask for anything, but it has continued to answer our calls. We believe that it finds joy in providing for us. So, I suppose, joy is what we give it."

Mary would never admit it, but the first thing that her mind jumped to was the dog she'd had as a young girl. Her family had adopted Buddy when she was young; she fed him, played with him, and provided for him. He'd been a horrible guard dog, completely unable to join competitions, and he wasn't used for hunting. In reality, he provided nothing in return for their care but the joy of having him in the family. Mary bit back the observation.

"So how would you describe your relationship with The Land?" she asked instead.

"We have often described ourselves as students, or perhaps children."

"I guess that comes back around to the religion debate. Humans in my religion call ourselves the children of God. Do you think it's the same?"

"I cannot answer. Perhaps you should pose this question to the computer?"

Mary's eyes widened. "I could do that?"

"In theory. Our main computer maintains a direct connection to all of the communicators on this planet and to our home planet. If anything could answer your question, it would be this."

"I could ask it anything?"

"Within reason," Sarara said. "As I said before, The Land does not provide more than we need. It can tell you what you could otherwise be able to figure out on your own; it can run simulations; it can answer hypotheticals. It may not be able to answer, 'Are you a god?' but if you word your thoughts correctly, it could help you decide that for yourself."

"This is a lot to take in."

Sarara offered a smile. "I believe.... I have faith in you."

Mary smiled back at Sarara, who nodded and went into the Spacevan, giving Mary some privacy.

Mary picked up her communicator. "*Computer, is The Land a god?*" she asked, not expecting an answer.

"*I do not understand the question,*" the computer replied.

Mary paused, wondering how to rephrase her question. "*Could The Land be considered a godly being?*" That seemed to do the trick.

"*As part of the Earth Zalma Alliance, I have scanned many of your books. There are multiple definitions of the term god. The most common definition is a supernatural being or deity that a group of people believe in or worship.*"

"*Knowing that, could The Land be considered the Zalmen's god?*"

"*It is possible.*"

Mary growled in frustration. *Perhaps a different line of questioning will work,* she thought. "*So what about you? Are you just a computer, or are you The Land speaking to me right now?*"

"*I do not understand the question. I was created by the Zalmen.*"

"*Are you what the Zalmen call The Land?*" she pressed.

"*The Land is the one who taught the Zalmen how to build me.*"

"*Is The Land a supernatural being?*"

"*Yes.*"

Finally, a straight answer. Mary sighed in relief. Then, a new thought struck her. "*Computer, why do the Zalmen need our help at all? If The Land is a supernatural entity that teaches and guides the Zalmen, why doesn't it protect them from their enemy, the Moadites?*

Why wouldn't it at least teach them to defend themselves? They obviously need it."

"The Zalmen do not understand aggression, and The Land is currently protecting them with the planet's deflectors. It also is ensuring their future safety by leading them to you."

Mary frowned. *"But if The Land loves the Zalmen so much, why doesn't it just protect them itself? Why doesn't it strengthen their deflectors? Why send them to us?"*

"Your strengths complement their weaknesses. The Land teaches and only provides what is needed."

"But why should they need us at all? If The Land is really a god, why would it allow the Moad to attack? Why would it create evil people to overcome?"

"If the meaning of life is to love, then what better test than to learn to love your enemy? If no enemies exist, you would not be able to show love to them."

"Are you saying I should love Mr. Harper and my professors? How? They never gave me a chance."

"Did you give them a chance?" the computer asked.

Mary felt like smashing the communicator for not giving her a straight answer. Then, she remembered something Sarara said. *"Send Sarara a message: Please come back."* Mary put her communicator in her pocket.

Sarara exited the Spacevan. "Yes?"

"You mentioned before that I didn't give Harper a chance. You were with me when I met Harper. What could I have said or done differently?"

"What would Mr. Harper want to hear?"

"That I heard great things about him, and it would be an honor to work with him," Mary said sarcastically.

"Yes."

Mary frowned. "Wait, you're not actually suggesting I should've said that. It's not true."

Sarara didn't answer.

"And what about my professors? What could I have done to make them like me better?"

"Why didn't they like you?"

Mary rolled her eyes. "Because I proved them wrong several times."

"Hmm...and how would you have felt if someone had done the same to you?"

Mary didn't answer.

"Do you think about how your words will affect the other person?"

Again, Mary didn't answer.

"As a teacher, one of the tools I use is to ask questions that lead my students to the answer."

"That sounds like a lot of work. Why would I do that?"

"Because when people come to the conclusion on their own, they remember better and respect you for it."

"But that didn't work with Harper."

Sarara shook her head. "Some people put up mental blocks and refuse to learn. I thought it was because I am an alien, but he listens to my husband...sometimes." She turned blue for an instant.

"Since you have arrived, I suspected it has more to do with us being female. But now I think that he does not want to change his basic understanding of physics. In any case, if you return his hostility with hostility, it becomes a downward spiral and only gets worse."

Mary nodded. "Quinn is proof that the opposite is also true. Ever since I've accepted him, he's accepted me. It's an upward spiral."

"Perhaps Mr. Harper's reluctance serves a purpose."

Mary frowned. "How so?"

"General Jones would like us to use old technology, so that the Moad will not be threatened by it. Perhaps Mr. Harper is our measurement."

At dinner that night, Mary sat next to Dow. The mess hall was no emptier than usual, but the chatter of the soldiers and civilians around her faded into the background. She was staring at her vegetarian pasta, picking at it but not eating.

"What's on your mind?" Dow asked, gently coaxing her out of her thoughts.

"Hmm?"

"You've been sitting here for half an hour, and you haven't said a single thing. I've never known you to keep quiet about what you've learned. I may not be around a lot, but I like to think I know you well enough by now. So, what's on your mind?"

She shrugged. "Just something that happened earlier. It's a lot to deal with. I'm still processing it."

"Maybe I can help. I always find it's better to talk to someone and let it out rather than bottling it up."

"Have you ever thought about what you would do if God gave you the ability to do anything?"

"Are you talking about the Zalma technology? It's amazing, but it's not God-given."

Mary laughed to herself. "But what if it was? What if it could do anything? That's a big responsibility, right?" She took a bite of food, one of her first that night.

"Yes, but that's why I am careful who I recruit."

"You recruited Harper."

Dow frowned. He turned back to his own food and continued eating. "Hey, have you named your communicator yet?"

"Named it?" Mary asked, confused both by the question and the sudden change of topic. "No. Why? Have you named yours?"

Dow smiled proudly at her. "Yes. I named it Benjamin, after a character in a comic book. I was originally thinking of naming it Jacob after my dad, but it would've been strange. And I think Benjamin is a much better fit, don't you?" He pulled his communicator from his pocket. "Introduce yourself."

"Hello, Dr. Goss," the tiny device said. *"I am Benjamin."*

Mary couldn't help but smile. "Hello, Benjamin. It's nice to meet you." She looked at Dow. "Your dad's name is Jacob?"

"Was," Dow corrected, suddenly somber. "He died when I was eight."

"Oh, I'm so sorry. How did it happen?"

"It was a training accident, but he saved Gerry's life, so…."

Mary frowned. "Who's Gerry?"

"Oh, sorry. Gerry Smith. He's a lieutenant and kind of like my stepdad. He was good friends with my dad, and he promised he would take care of us, so he took in my family after it happened."

Mary was silent.

Dow continued, "But since my dad had died and was no longer 'in the army', we had to move off the base. Gerry took care of everything. He got a duplex for both our families to share—my family moved into one half, and he and his family into the other."

"That was good of him."

"Yeah, but it wasn't easy on any of us. I'd just lost my dad, and I didn't treat Gerry like I should have. I know my mom and sister didn't like him much either, but at least they showed him the gratitude he deserved."

Mary nodded, immediately understanding. "You blamed him for your dad's death."

Dow's eyes focused on the table. "Yes, and he knew it. He gave us space, while his wife, son, and daughter were there for us. I really enjoyed the time with his son, David. The two of us grew up like brothers. Gerry pulled some strings so my sister and I could attend the white school with his kids. It was hard, as most of the kids didn't like us black folk. Of course, David and his sister were unpopular because they hung out with us, so I had to learn to fight to protect us all from the bullies."

"So that's where you got it from!" Mary exclaimed, perking up. Dow stared blankly at her, so she continued, "You protect the Zalmen just like you did David and the girls."

"I guess," he said. Then he paused, chuckled, and grinned at her. "Hmm...now that you mention it.... Yeah, I guess my big brother instincts did kick in."

Just after yet another move—Area 17 now—Mary was working on a small device with Quinn. Spare parts littered the faintly glowing Nanotables, and no amount of free space was left anywhere.

Sitting between the scientists was a glass cylinder filled with glowing liquid. She looked up and saw Dow, whom she hadn't seen in over a week. He was wearing the new uniform, sky blue on top with black pants.

"Wow, you look sharp!" Mary complimented. "What's that made of? It looks thick like denim, but smooth like silk."

"You guessed it. I think it's a weird combination of those. Plus, it has a few Zalma extras."

"Oh, like what?"

"It has defensive features."

"Oh?"

"Yes, apparently, it can stop a punch, kick, knife, and even a bullet."

"Wow! How does their clothing do all that?"

"I don't know."

Mary thought for a moment. "I remember Sarara telling me that the nanites will create whatever device is needed. It probably creates a small deflector."

"Makes sense. Anyway, the uniforms are optional for you, but you will find a set in your tent tonight."

"I'm still not interested in wearing a uniform."

"Suit yourself. So, I see you've made a mess. What are you working on?"

"It's not a mess; it's called progress," Mary teased. "We've just finished the prototype for our anti-gravity gun and a miniature anti-gravity drive."

"Great! How do they work?"

Mary tapped the table to catch Quinn's attention.

He looked up from where he'd been carefully connecting the last few ports and lowered his magnifier goggles.

"Hi-hi," he said. After Dow repeated his question, Quinn launched into an explanation. "The drives work a lot like the existing ones, but with the ability to be linked with non-Zalma machinery." He looked proud and confident as he spoke. "We simply attach one of these to the underside of the vehicle's frame and give voice commands to activate it and set the destination. The vehicle would also have the option of invisibility. We should be able to convert any vehicle, even your jeep and the general's car."

Dow's face split into a grin. "I'd be able to just fly my jeep to recruit people? I wouldn't have to fly in a plane? It sounds too good to be true."

Mary nodded. "Nice, huh?"

"Very nice. So…when can you get it done? Today?"

Mary laughed and lifted both her hands. "Slow down. As I said, it's just a prototype, and I doubt you'd want us to be testing it on your jeep or the general's car. It could flip the vehicle or crush you. It likely won't be ready for a month or so before we begin testing on an automobile. Right, Quinn?"

"Y-yeah."

"Sweet. And how about Harper? Has he given the general any updates since I've been gone?" Dow asked, turning to Quinn.

"The ship is almost fully assembled. We should be starting test flights soon," Quinn replied.

"Are you going to be one of the pilots?"

Quinn's face went white as a sheet. He laughed nervously and his hands began fiddling with a piece of scrap he'd plucked off the table. "Um, no. I'm not much of a pilot, and I already know that Harper will want to go. He can take one of the experienced test pilots with him up there."

"Talking about me, are you?" came Harper's voice from behind them all. "So, Quinn, this is where you have been spending all your time. What's that you're working on? I thought all projects were supposed to be approved by me. Instead, you undermine my authority and fraternize with the enemy." His face was red with rage as he turned to Mary. "And you, Miss Goody Two-Shoes, you steal my number two and are probably filling his head with lies about all this alien mumbo-jumbo. Quinn, get back to work on the ship now!"

Dow stepped in front of Harper. He held his military stance and seemed to stare right through the engineer. "No. Mr. Quinn is exactly where he is supposed to be—in the classroom. As you should be!"

Harper returned the stare for a few minutes before storming off, muttering under his breath about traitors.

Mary and Quinn were left shaking. Sarara had come out of the Spacevan, and her mouth was wide open while her skin was changing colors so fast it was hard to tell what they were. Dow held his chin and shoulders smugly. "I've wanted to do that for a long time.

"Quinn, I will find you some new quarters and I'll be checking in on you more frequently. If Harper gives you any problems, call me on your communicator. You can tap it three times deliberately, and help will arrive in seconds. He won't know what hit him," Dow said and walked out of the classroom.

After that, Quinn attended Sarara's classes with Mary, as he was no longer welcome among the others, and he and Mary worked on their prototype more often. He ate at Mary's table, and Dow checked in on them as much as he could. Harper did not.

CHAPTER FIFTY

CAMOUFLAGE

Charlotte "Charlie" Baker

EARTH–ZALMA BASECAMP, ARIZONA

It had been a week since my last visit to the base. The engineers had been working on some big project, and they didn't want us interrupting. So, when I finally went to Area 12, we got another baseball game together.

We were always slightly behind. Sometime during the fourth inning, Takar was up to bat next, and I saw Dow whispering something to him, and to his communicator. I couldn't hear what he said, but he was definitely up to no good.

When Takar hit the ball and started running, his clothing started changing color to match the sandy background.

Dow was laughing hard. "It worked!"

It was hard to see where Takar was. Only his head and hands were showing, with his clothing looking like a dust cloud or a desert mirage. So when the outfielder caught the ball, he stood, confused, looking for Takar. After a few seconds, he threw the ball to second, but Takar had already made it to third. Again, the second baseman looked for Takar, giving him enough time to make it to home base, then his clothing returned to the normal silver.

The other captain got really mad and ran toward Takar. My heart raced, but Dow must have expected this and ran in front of him. "It's not his fault. It was my idea, and there is nothing in the rules...."

The captain didn't stop and pushed Dow away, then he loomed over Takar, his face red, and he huffed. I wheeled over there as fast as I could. The captain looked at me, then at Takar, then shook his head and walked away.

When I got to Takar, he looked confused. "Why?"

"He thought you were cheating," I said.

Dow dusted himself off and came over. "I'm sorry, that was a bad idea."

We lost that game.

About a week later, I had a chance to put the camouflage to the test in the field. It started when I was in the Spacevan with Kanara on the way to Area 15 and just couldn't hold myself back anymore. "What's this special project that I'm not supposed to interrupt?"

"Mr. Harper is creating a spaceship."

"A spaceship? Oh! Can I see?"

"No, definitely not. The general has ordered... How did he word it? 'Essential personnel only'."

I grunted, disappointed. I rubbed Sandy, hoping the distraction would take my mind off it, but I couldn't let it go. When we got to the base and I found Janara and Takar, I asked, "Can you take me to Mr. Harper's spaceship?"

They both turned white, eyes wide. "Mr. Harper is scary. I don't know if we should."

Janara nodded along with her brother. "He is very focused on his work and does not like when we interrupt."

"It will be alright," I assured them. "We'll just stay hidden. That way, he won't be interrupted and we won't be in the way."

They glanced at each other, colors flickering. Can they have a conversation just using their colors? That's so cool! I wasn't one hundred percent sure that's what they were doing, but I waited while they discussed.

Finally, Takar pointed in the direction of the biggest tent. "The spaceship is in there. But we will have to be quick."

I nodded. "Let's use the camouflage too. Then they won't see us!" I suggested, which seemed to boost their confidence. Janara ran back to her quarters and returned with a silver sheet which she put over my body and chair. Takar mumbled into his communicators in their language and our outfits changed. I looked down and I couldn't see my body or my chair, it looked like I was wearing sand.

I looked over at Sandy. Her color was close to that of sand (hence her name), but I decided it was best not to take her. "Stay." Then I nodded to Janara and Takar, and the three of us began to creep.

I wheeled slowly, wincing at the sound of the crunching ground under my wheels. Takar and Janara's footsteps were almost silent in comparison. I noticed my sheet changed color to match the camouflage of the tent we arrived at. All three of us peeked around the corner. One soldier raced by; maybe he was late for something important; soon, he was gone.

"It is clear," I whispered excitedly. "Continue to the next tent."

Takar grinned. "Is this what you call *being sneaky*?"

I nodded. We moved to the next tent and paused to look again, then went to the next tent, and the next. The big tent was getting closer, and no one had caught us yet. We were going to make it! My heart thudded with excitement; we were spies, just like Miss Dianne! And I was going to see the first human spaceship.

The big tent stood right in front of us.

"We're here," I whispered. "Let's look inside."

They shuffled closer to me, and we peeked inside one of the flaps. A couple of people were busy working. There was a man yelling at the others. I thought he might be Harper, but I'd never seen him before.

The spaceship sat right in the middle. Reconnaissance complete! I was so excited. A human spaceship; it would go into outer space just like the Zalma ships. It sort of resembled a small airplane. "It has no propeller, just a sharp point," I whispered to them, perplexed. "How does it fly?"

We backed out of the tent and snuck around behind it to discuss what we saw.

"It uses a Zalma nuclear engine to fly," Takar said.

A jolt of nervousness shot through me. "Nuclear? Is that safe?" I asked. Dad had written about nuclear energy before, specifically about nuclear bombs. They were really bad. I couldn't imagine something like that being right next to us! I began rolling my chair away from the tent. My friends followed.

"Do not worry!" Takar said. He was chuckling. "It is old technology."

"It is completely safe," Janara assured me. She was glaring at Takar again.

I took her hand. "Oh. That's good. I was very worried. I thought it might explode!"

"Absolutely not," she said again, confident. "It is just Mr Harper that we think will explode. He sometimes gets very...passionate."

We all laughed.

On our way back, we found Sandy lying beside a tent, not far from the big one. She was obviously keeping an eye on us in case we got into trouble. I wheeled up to her, and she covered her eyes with her paws, embarrassed that she got caught disobeying me.

"It's OK girl, let's go." I turned to Janara and Takar. "I can't wait to see it when it's done. Do you think we'll get to see it fly?" I said, thinking about the spaceship again. It was so sleek and cool.

"I am sure of it," Janara said.

"And if they don't, we can just camouflage again!" Takar exclaimed. "We were very sneaky!" He seemed delighted by the idea.

And just maybe, I thought, I could use the camouflage to sneak up on that man who'd been sneaking around. I *bet he doesn't even realize that I'm on to him! Now all I have to do is catch him in the act.*

CHAPTER FIFTY-ONE

THE LAUNCH

Dr. Mary Goss

EARTH–ZALMA BASECAMP, ARIZONA

Only a few weeks later, Harper and his team finished their spaceship. It was finally ready for its first test flight. Harper personally invited Mary and Sarara to watch, but Mary suspected it was to gloat, as no other reason came to mind.

She was proven correct when they all showed up at the test site and Harper approached her. He was wearing a standard flight suit, along with another man who must've been the pilot. The other scientists were there as well, waiting to one side.

"See," Harper said to Mary, grinning wolfishly, "we didn't need any of that fancy mumbo jumbo you were talking about." He gestured proudly to the ship.

Quinn slipped in next to Mary. "Hi-hi," he whispered, so Harper wouldn't hear.

Mary looked over at the spaceship. It resembled a plane, except instead of propellers, it had what she assumed was the nuclear engine out the back. It looked similar to a rocket plane she had seen in *Popular Science*.

"This is your spaceship?" she asked.

Harper puffed his chest. "I call it the X20. We started with the X1 I originally helped design to break the sound barrier, made it for two people, added a Zalmen nuclear engine that's expected to go at least ten times faster, and then we added machine guns and a nuclear torpedo."

"A torpedo? What are you going to do with that?"

"Detonate it in space, of course!" he replied.

"And yourselves along with it?" Mary turned to Gen. Newman, who was standing next to Dow. "You approved this?"

The general nodded. "The men feel very confident in their spacecraft. If they believe it is ready for flight, they should have the opportunity to test it."

Mary turned to Kanara. "Will it work? Is it safe?"

"I am confident it will make it safely into space and perform the weapons tests, though they will have to conduct their test on the far side of the moon so it will not be visible on Earth."

Mary expected Kanara to change colors rapidly, but he didn't.

"I cannot guarantee anything more. The men are very determined, and there was no stopping them."

She wanted to press further, to ask more questions, but Kanara seemed calm. If he was concerned at all for Harper or the pilot's safety, he didn't show it, but Mary's stomach still clenched in fear. She was overcome with a whole-body shudder. It lasted only a moment, then vanished, lingering around her ears for a second longer. Her instincts were telling her something, but what?

Harper and the pilot saluted the general, then they boarded the spaceship. Pushing her concerns aside, Mary joined Dow on the sidelines, and they watched the nuclear engine start to glow. The ship sped down the runway, gaining momentum. Near the end, it took a steep ascent and was off.

Soon after it disappeared into the sky, many of the spectators headed into the classroom, which had been converted into a command tent. Mary caught Quinn's arm as they entered.

"Do *you* think it's ready?" she whispered.

Quinn looked nervous. "Maybe. I'm...I'm not the best with the calculations and, well, it's never been done before. Humans going into space in a human-made vessel, I mean. I haven't worked on it for a while, but I did the best I could with the specs we learned before they all quit class."

"But do you think they'll make it?"

He shrugged. "Kanara said that he's confident, but I can't help but worry, you know? He also warned us about some things that Harper ignored."

"What kind of things?"

Before Quinn could say more, Newman shushed them.

The classroom looked totally different. The nanotables were folded in half so that the top became a screen and the bottom was a keyboard. The nanoboards at the front of the room were showing images of the spacecraft and telemetry. Mary sat at one of the stations beside Sarara and Kanara, who were already actively scanning the readings. Quinn joined the others in one corner, nervously fiddling with his fingers.

Two voices could be heard on the radio. *"Yahoo!"* they both cried, making Mary snort. *And Harper calls* me *a child?*

The pilot spoke. *"Altitude: forty-two thousand feet and climbing."*

Mary looked at the screens. So far, the readings were in the normal range. Every dial was in the green, the levels were stable, and the systems were functional.

"We've reached the mesosphere," the pilot continued. *"All is good."*

Looks about right, Mary thought, double-checking his report. Then her eyes were drawn to the video output. It was a clearer picture than she'd ever seen, and she marveled at the sight. The sky was growing darker even though it was the middle of the day—a sure sign that they were leaving Earth's atmosphere. The stars were beginning to appear. Then Harper's voice came over the radio, snapping her back to reality.

"We are heading for the moon," he said. *"Increasing speed to one thousand miles per hour. Two thousand, three.... I can't believe this! We are going so fast!"*

Mary kept her eyes on all the outputs in front of her. They all looked fine, but she still felt uneasy. She glanced at Quinn. His hands were white, showing his extreme anxiety. Mary sensed something was terribly wrong. Frowning, she looked back at the screens, but nothing gave any indications of error. If not for Quinn's reaction, she would've thought that everything was going perfectly. However, she knew better than most that she could trust intuition.

"We have reached the halfway point and are preparing to decelerate." Harper paused. *"We have cut power but are not slowing down."*

"You have no atmosphere to slow you down or steer," Kanara spoke into the microphone. "You must use the thrusters I insisted you install to turn your ship around. Then do a full burn." He turned the microphone off and turned to Newman and Dow. "I gave the pilot these instructions, but he said he was afraid to do anything until Harper gave him permission."

There was no reply from the radio, but Mary could see the ship on her screen was doing just that.

Quinn was still tense, but Mary felt nothing. No tingles or sensations. She'd had them earlier, but they'd gone away. Despite this, she trusted Quinn. Her eyes raked over the readings, hoping that something would jump out at her. Nothing.

"We have reached the moon, sir," the pilot's voice crackled over the radio. *"Testing machine guns."* Silence. *"Negative on the machine guns."*

Kanara turned to Newman and Dow. "Again, they have no atmosphere, so the bullets will not ignite."

"Nuclear torpedo ready to launch. Destination distance, five miles."

The general's face was a neutral mask. His hawkish eyes were sharp and his lips were set into a firm line. "Launch."

"Roger."

That seemed to be the trigger. All at once, every hair on Mary's body stood on end. It was like the entire classroom had been charged with static. Mary looked over at Quinn again and saw that he had been similarly affected. His face was as white as a ghost. Mary jumped out of her chair.

"Wait—!"

Too late.

A loud whooshing filled the audio, drowning out her voice. A second later, the torpedo appeared on screen, flying out into the depths of space. The image on the monitors burst into light, and then the screens fizzled and went black.

"What happened?" the general demanded. "Get me eyes on them, *stat*!"

In an instant, Mary was back in her seat. Her heart was thumping and her fingers flew over the keyboard so fast they almost blurred. "I am not receiving any signals from the spaceship," she said. "Sarara, you said that there is a Zalma probe in orbit. Can you send it to investigate?"

Sarara nodded. She typed rapidly on her keyboard, and the Zalmen's probe brought itself around to the spacecraft's last location. New images were projected on the high-tech screens: One showed the moon, vast, cold, and empty. Next to it, suspended in space, was the spacecraft. It was completely dark.

"I've found them. The sensors show that they have lost all power. I see two heat signatures, and they are moving. They're alive!"

Sighs of relief could be heard through the tent. A few cheers even erupted from the gathered men, but Quinn still looked sick to his stomach. Mary knew exactly why.

"They're alive…but they are on a collision course toward the moon. I estimate that they have about two hours before they crash." Mary turned to Kanara. "How did this happen? You said it was safe."

Kanara met her eyes steadily. "They asked me if it would make it to the moon, and I told them it would. They asked me if they could launch a nuclear torpedo, and I told them they could. I tried to caution them about the other dangers, but they would not listen."

Mary's lip curled, and she bit her lip to hold back a retort. "Did you know about this?" she asked Newman instead.

"The engineers reported to me that everything was clear. I did not question their reports," he replied.

"What about their communicators? Can we contact them?"

It was Kanara who answered. "If they took them. I know Mr. Harper often left his in his quarters. He did not believe he needed it."

"The probe is in range to relay," Sarara offered.

Dow stepped forward with his own communicator at the ready. He raised it and spoke, "Dow to X20. Can you hear me? Over."

There was a pause, and for a few torturous moments, no one moved or breathed.

Then, the pilot's voice filled the tent. *"This is Lieutenant Holden. Thank God I remembered my communicator. We've lost all power. After the detonation, sparks ignited inside the cabin, then everything went dead."*

Kanara stepped up next to Dow to answer. "I previously warned Mr. Harper of this issue. The disturbance is called an electromagnetic pulse, and it has damaged your electrical systems. If he had listened, this would not have happened."

"Well, we're listening now," Harper growled. *"What can we do about it?"*

"There is nothing you can do. Aside from your communicator, every system is beyond on-site repair."

"Then can't you come and get us with your Spacevan?"

"Yes, I could fly out to meet you, but you did not design your ship with a compatible hatch for us to rescue you. Our scans show that debris from the nuclear explosion has caused micro-fractures, and they are encompassing your ship's hull. Any attempt to touch your ship would result in it cracking apart."

"There has got to be something you can do." Harper sounded almost pleading.

"I must consult Sarara and Dr. Goss. If anyone can save you, it is them. I will be back in touch when we have a solution." Kanara stepped away, and, with a nod to Dow, the call was disconnected.

Newman, Dow, and Kanara all looked at Mary.

"Doctor, it sounds like you have two hours to save their lives," the general said. "I suggest you get on with it."

"Sarara, what should we do?" Mary had absolutely no idea. She needed guidance.

Sarara stared back at her with a forlorn expression. Her skin was bone-white—something Mary recognized as worry. "My people have never experienced this dilemma before. I am afraid I cannot do anything, but you can. You are the creative one."

"Me?" Mary sputtered. "How can *I* save them? Harper has never listened to anything I've had to say, and all of a sudden you think he'll trust me with his life?"

"It appears that he doesn't have a choice in the matter," Gen. Newman said.

Mary looked around the room. Everyone was looking to her for the answer, even the two scientists and two other engineers who'd helped Harper and Quinn with the ship. They hadn't spoken a word to her since she'd arrived.

"He's in this mess because of his own ego. Why is it on me to save him?"

"Because you are the only one who can," Dow replied.

"I'm sorry we have not spoken much since we first met, but I trust Sergeant Dow. He's seen all you scientists and engineers at work. He knows what you're capable of. If he says that you can do it, then I believe you can do it," Newman said.

Dow, Sarara, Kanara, Quinn, and the others smiled and nodded in agreement.

"OK, I will do my best to save them, but I won't get anything accomplished with all of you standing around. I need Sarara, Kanara, and Quinn on my team, so they can stay, but everyone else, please leave."

After the others left, Mary was a mess of nerves, pacing and continuously running her hands through her hair. The others were waiting for her to speak, but she had no words. Finally, something came to her. She stopped and looked up.

"The ship may be made like a rocket plane, but the engine is still Zalma technology, right? That means it's made of nanites, and they can repair the hull enough to rescue them." *That's simple enough. Maybe I was just blowing this whole thing out of proportion.* She clapped her hands together, satisfied.

"The nanites will only be able to do that if the men on board know it is possible," Sarara said.

Mary's hopes sank. *Of course, it couldn't be that simple.* "Then we just tell them."

"What...What are nanites?" Quinn shook his head. "I don't know what you're talking about, but Harper already has a low tolerance for this advanced technology. It frightens him. Whatever these nanites are will surely make him panic. He's likely to do something stupid. I suggest you find another way."

"What other way is there?" Mary demanded. "They're out in the middle of space with no way to move, they're running out of air, and now you're telling me that the solution we have won't work because he'll be *afraid* of the technology that will save his life?" She wasn't impressed. "Was this a setup to teach him a lesson?" She looked accusingly at Kanara, who shook his head.

"I did everything in my power to warn them of the dangers."

"It just made Harper more determined," Quinn added.

"Mr. Harper trusted Mr. Quinn the most, but Mr. Harper still would not listen to Mr. Quinn," Kanara said.

"Then why didn't you fix their ship on your own so it *wouldn't* happen?"

Both aliens opened their mouths to speak, but the answer that came wasn't from either of them. It was from Quinn.

"That leads to the same problem, doesn't it? Lance thinks he's always right. He's never met a problem he hasn't been able to fix before, so I don't exactly blame him. He won't listen to anyone who tells him he's wrong, it just makes him more determined."

"What if we reported him to General Newman and had him removed from the project?" Mary suggested.

"Kicking Harper off the team with the knowledge he has...." Quinn shook his head. "He said he would tell the world about the Zalmen, and he wouldn't care what the army threatened him with." His face and knuckles were once again white. "Plus, I'm sure he would sell our secrets and try to build his ship somewhere else. Knowing him he would probably cause a nuclear explosion, killing him and anyone else in the area."

Mary nodded.

Quinn looked at the floor. "As much as I hate to admit it, he had to make this mistake to learn from it. There's nothing anyone could have done to prevent this."

"Can we ask the computer for a solution?"

"Unfortunately not, Dr. Goss. The computers lack creativity, same as us," Sarara replied.

Mary looked at the clock. "We ah wasting time. Let's get going. Quinn, do you have any ideas?" Her stress allowed her Boston accent to slip out.

"What exactly would happen if we tried to tow it with the Spacevan?" Quinn asked.

"The X20 would break apart, and their bodies would be exposed to the vacuum of space," Kanara replied. "The air in them would cause them to expand like a balloon. It would be very painful and lead to a quick death."

"I guess that's off the table." Mary sighed. "Any other options?"

For the next half an hour, they ran through a myriad of ideas. The nanoboards were quickly filled with calculations, drawings, and ideas, but none of them seemed to work.

"Argh!" Mary collapsed into her chair. She stared at the ceiling as if it might hold all the answers to the universe, but it didn't, so she looked over at Quinn. He was contributing to the conversation more than when they'd first met, but he also appeared more anxious than she'd ever seen him. He was afraid of Harper, to be sure, but that didn't mean he'd ever want the man to die.

"So, we only have an hour and a half left to come up with a solution?" he asked.

"Only one hour and seventeen minutes now," Sarara corrected. "Remember, you will have to implement your solution before their vessel is crushed against its surface. Do not forget that you must also transport them over two hundred thousand miles back to Earth before their air supply is depleted."

Quinn gulped. "Thanks for reminding me."

"You are the two best human students I've had. With both of your combined genius, I am certain you will succeed."

"And what if we don't? Do you know what it was like to be Harper's second in command? Half of the guys expect me to fix all of his mistakes, and the other half take their frustrations out on me."

Mary was startled by his words, not by the urgency in them, but by their similarity to what her brother had said to her all those months ago. She hadn't thought of her younger brother Craig much since she'd joined the army, though she'd been writing letters home to her parents. Thinking back to him and the morning of her departure, an idea sparked in her mind.

She stood up. "I'm going to need some eggs."

A short while later, Mary returned from the mess hall with a bowl of eggs and other materials. Every one of the eggs had a hole at each end. Kanara picked one up to examine it.

"These shells are hollow. How did you accomplish this?"

Mary set the bowl on the desk. "It's called blowing an egg. You prick a hole in each end of a raw egg and blow in it to remove the insides. I used to do it with my brother when I was younger; I only just thought of it.

"I need to visualize the problem, and these are fragile enough to be a decent model of our ship. Now, all we have to do is figure out how to move these shells really fast without breaking them."

The other three looked at her, waiting for a clue.

"The obvious answer would be to hook them up with a towline, but as Kanara said earlier, it wouldn't work."

She trailed off as she picked up one of the hollow eggs and carefully threaded a string through the center of it with a toothpick. She tied it off and spun the egg over her head by the string, but it cracked almost immediately.

Mary sighed. "Just as I thought."

Quinn took an egg from the bowl. "These eggshells have enough fragility to replicate the ship's cracked hull?"

"No, but it's close enough to form a theory. The rest is just math, and that's simple enough with the Zalma computers."

"I see what you're getting at," Quinn said. "What if we stabilize the shell before moving it? Like putting a net around it?"

Mary nodded. Seeing no other object that might work, she removed one of her nylons and offered it to Quinn, who turned bright red but accepted it. He put an eggshell inside and began spinning it above his head. He started slowly, and the nylon stretched. Soon, he was spinning it as fast as Mary had. It seemed to work at first, but then the eggshell imploded from the pressure. Quinn sighed.

Mary took her nylon back. It was full of minuscule pieces of shell. "Good try. It might have worked, but the eggshell is still too fragile. Distributing pressure like that makes it last longer, but I doubt it will hold long enough to get them back to Earth in time. The ship would just crack, and they'd die out in space, net or no net," she tried to encourage Quinn.

His shoulders sagged.

"I was thinking that if we strengthened the shell with some kind of coating, it might be able to hold." She dipped the shell into a syrupy liquid, then removed it and allowed the coating to harden. However, this time when she tried to thread the shell, it broke. The coating had crushed the shell when drying.

They made several more attempts, each ending in failure. When the last shell was gone, Quinn threw himself into one of the chairs, head in his hands. He'd given up. "We just wasted a whole lot of precious time on *eggsperiments* and have nothing to show for it!"

Mary groaned. "If we don't do something soon, they're goners. This is impossible."

They could see the ship still hurtling toward the moon on the screens next to them. Another screen flashed red, fifty-three minutes and they'd be flattened on the moon's surface.

Despair was clouding the air of the tent, but then Sarara placed a hand on Mary's shoulder. "I am still new to the concept of faith, but I know I have it in you. You will solve this. The moon's gravity will not win," she said.

Mary jumped up. "Gravity? Gravity! I can't believe I missed this!"

"I beg your pardon? Missed what?" Sarara stared at her in surprise, taken aback by the sudden enthusiasm.

Quinn frowned, but Mary could see the gears turning in his head. "Are you thinking—?"

"The gravity gun!"

He looked up at her. There was confusion swirling in his eyes, but also hope. "But how?"

"By increasing the gravity on the metal—not on the ship as a whole, but on the hull itself. The force should be just enough to pull the ship together and mend the cracks. The men inside are organic, so it wouldn't affect them."

The engineer remained doubtful. "How will we know the exact amount of force we need so Harper and Holden aren't crushed? We don't have the time to spare."

"Now that we have a solution, we can use the computer to run simulations," Mary explained.

"Wait," Quinn said. "We could've had the computer run these simulations the whole time? Why not start with that? Why were we using *eggs*, of all things?"

"We couldn't start running the simulations without an understanding of the problem, and as I said before, I work better having something physical to see and touch." Mary turned to Sarara, whose renewed hope was expressed by the blooming of colors across her skin.

"I will begin running simulations right away. I knew you could do it." And in that moment, Sarara's smile was brighter than the sun.

*

"As you can see, this last prototype is a viable option. There is an eighty-six-point-eight percent chance of success," Kanara explained, pointing at the screen. They'd spent another twenty minutes running simulations and making corrections to their working gravity gun prototype. It wasn't perfect, but it should work.

Just then, Gen. Newman and the others returned. "Excuse me," he said, "we have twenty-one minutes and counting before impact. Do you have a plan or not?"

Mary jumped to attention. "Sir, yes, sir." Then she cringed. *Did I really say that? I'm hanging around these guys too much.*

"Well?" the general asked, sounding like he was trying his hardest to be patient but failing.

"We think we can use our gravity gun to save the ship. This gravity gun will.... How do I put this into layman's terms? It will magnetize the hull to temporarily seal the cracks so we can move it."

"Will it be strong enough to get them home?"

Sarara pointed to the screen. "As you can see, this last simulation shows there is an eighty-six-point-eight percent chance of success."

"I'm not going to lie; the technology is new and untested, but I don't see another choice," Mary said. "The same device should allow us to tow them back to Earth."

Newman nodded. "Dow, inform Harper and Holden that Kanara and Dr. Goss have a plan to bring them home. The two of them will fly up to meet them."

"Me, sir? You want me to go into space?" By all accounts, it didn't make sense. She wasn't an engineer or a pilot. Why would *she* be the one to go into space? She'd already done her part, and she felt she should step back and let others do theirs.

Newman didn't seem to agree with that sentiment. "I want them to see the one responsible for rescuing them," he said.

"Then why not Quinn?" Mary argued. "He helped just as much; I wouldn't have been able to put the gravity gun together if it weren't for him."

Quinn shook his head. He stepped forward and took Mary's hands into his own, meeting her eyes. "It was your idea to make the gravity gun in the first place, and it was your idea to use it on the ship like this. Any engineer could've helped with that, but without you, none of this would be possible. Go. You deserve it."

The Spacevan windshield changed from blue sky to black space, and the moon grew until it filled the window in seconds. Then the X20 came into view.

Kanara turned the spotlight on. Mary looked out and saw Harper and Holden through the window. Holden looked relieved. Harper locked eyes with Mary for a fraction of a second. His face flushed red, and he looked away.

Kanara touched his communicator. "Do not worry. We will have you home in no time."

Kanara activated the beam while Mary watched the monitor. The X20 hull strength reading moved from yellow to green.

"The hull is stable," she said.

Then the power fluctuated, and both ships jerked violently. Mary looked out the window. Harper floated and hit the control panel with his head. A sharp edge on the panel split his skin.

The four of them froze, hoping the ship didn't break apart. The X20 hull strength reading fluctuated but stopped in the green.

Kanara checked the readings on the computer. "Everything is OK. There is no further damage, and the hull is holding."

Mary fell into her seat, heart hammering. "It worked!" The Spacevan turned around and slowly increased speed with the powerless ship in tow.

As they reached the edge of the Earth's atmosphere, she turned to Kanara. "Will they be alright on re-entry? I know that this ship has deflectors to prevent it from burning up, but their systems are still down. Won't they be in trouble when they break the atmosphere?"

"They are in our wake, so it should not be a problem. I also extended our deflectors around them to ward off the heat."

Mary relaxed. "Good. I wouldn't want to have spent all that time on rescuing them, only to boil them in their own ship."

The Spacevan hovered as it lowered the X20 with the gravity beam, and Harper and Holden exited the ship as soon as they were safely on the ground. Then the gravity gun disengaged and the X20 crumbled to pieces.

Harper turned white as a ghost, and fidgeted in much the same way Quinn used to do compulsively. He refused to look at anyone.

The Spacevan landed, and Mary exited with Kanara.

"Ten-Hut!" Dow called, and it was not the usual call. There was fire in his voice, a fire that she had not heard before. Mary stiffened and saluted, something she hadn't done since the first time in the general's office. But, this time she knew how, she had seen it done several times a day for months. She stood straight and held her breath, noticing out of the corner of her eye that the other scientists were doing the same.

Gen. Newman strutted forward with purpose, and then when standing front and center, he returned the salute.

Everyone dropped their hand but maintained their stiff posture.

"Mr. Harper, is it true that you and the other engineers deliberately missed the lessons you were instructed to attend?" Newman asked.

Harper ducked his head. "Yes, sir. Sorry, sir."

"I can't hear you!" Newman shouted.

"Yes, sir. Sorry, sir."

"You *should* be sorry!" the general snapped. "Because of your foolishness, you and Lieutenant Holden both nearly died. Why on Earth did you disobey direct orders? Do you realize what an incredibly idiotic thing you did? If you weren't civilians I would court-martial every single one of you!"

"I didn't think we needed to, sir." It was a lame excuse, and it certainly sounded that way coming out of Harper's mouth.

Mary couldn't hold her breath any longer. *How does Malcolm do it? Oh right, he does breathe.* She let the air out as quietly as she could, and then took a deep breath. She heard some of the other scientists doing the same, obviously not as quietly.

Newman paused for a moment, suddenly looking amused. He laughed. "You didn't think you needed to?" he asked. Then, his whole demeanor shifted and he was shouting again. "You were informed of the mandatory nature of those lessons! I need to hear the real reason immediately! What do you have to say for yourselves!?"

Newman's glare extended to the rest of the engineers and scientists as well, who were hanging their heads in shame.

Finally, Harper looked up. "The ladies were talking nonsense."

"Do you still think they're talking nonsense?"

Harper replied quietly, "No."

"No what!?"

"No, sir!"

The general did not let up. "I made you the chief engineer because of your experience. But, you not only refused to learn from your assigned instructors, you blatantly disregarded the advice given to you and shunned a vital member of your team. Why?"

"Goss is just a girl, sir. What could she know?"

"So! You admit to being rescued by..." The general made an uncharacteristic nasal sound as he crouched into a childlike position. "...just a girl..." Resuming his military posture, he got in Harper's face. "...then? How embarrassing!"

Under normal circumstances, Mary would have broken out laughing, but this was no laughing matter, and everyone knew it.

Harper's face flushed even deeper red, but he said nothing.

The general was far from finished. "Now, what do you have to say to the 'girl' who saved your life?"

Harper lifted his head and turned to look at Mary. "Thank you," he said evenly.

"Like you mean it!"

"Thank you for saving my life!"

"Who are you talking to?" Newman snapped.

The muscles in Harper's jaw twitched. "Thank you for saving my life, Miss Goss!"

"*Doctor* Goss!"

"Thank you for saving my life, Doctor Goss!"

It was too hard to watch. Mary held eye contact for Harper's sake; otherwise, she'd have looked away.

Right in front of her was her worst nightmare, and she wouldn't wish it upon her worst enemy. *Harper already failed. He's already paid for his actions, hasn't he?* Why did Newman insist on this public humiliation? Dow didn't seem surprised, so she guessed that was just how it was done in the army.

"I think that it's time for new leadership, don't you?" Gen. Newman's voice was harsh, and Mary couldn't be more thankful that he wasn't speaking to *her* that way. She even spared a wince for Harper, despite her dislike for him.

"Yes, sir," Harper mumbled.

"Yes, *what*?"

Harper spoke up. "Yes, we need new leadership, sir!"

"Who do you think should replace you as the chief engineer, Mr. Harper?"

Harper's eyes shifted back and forth between Newman and Mary.

"I'm waiting."

"Randy Quinn should be the new chief engineer," Harper said.

"And who should lead this department?"

"Doc…Doctor Goss." Again, his answer was mumbled.

"Speak up!"

"Doctor Goss should lead this department, sir!" Harper shouted.

Satisfied, Newman turned to Quinn. "Mr. Quinn, do you agree with his assessment?"

Quinn nodded. "Yes, sir."

Mary's eyes popped. It was the first time Quinn didn't stutter.

"Very well." The general turned to Mary. "Dr. Goss, you are now in charge of this department. Quinn is your second as chief engineer. I want regular status updates. It looks like you both have made much more progress than I was led to believe."

"Yes, sir," she said. Her heart was racing, and she couldn't decide how she felt. Was she disgusted by his humiliating treatment of Harper or elated by her promotion? "Thank you, sir."

"Dismissed!"

The general left. Mary glanced at Quinn, who nodded back at her. One of the other scientists caught her eye and smiled just slightly, buoying her spirits. Soon, the rest of the crowd dispersed, leaving only Mary and Dow behind. In a moment of spontaneity, she launched herself at Dow and hugged him tightly. She pulled away just as quickly and stepped back. Dow stared back at her, similarly alarmed. It was tense for a moment, but then, simultaneously, they both burst into laughter.

[The day Harper's spaceship launched to the moon, I was at school doing arithmetic while history was being made. It's funny how the most important moments can happen when you're somewhere completely ordinary, doing something completely normal. By the time I learned what had happened, Dr. Goss had already saved two lives and proven that genius isn't about being right all the time—it's about solving problems when everything goes wrong.]

CHAPTER FIFTY-TWO

WHAT LOVE IS

Sergeant Malcolm Dow

EARTH–ZALMA BASECAMP, ARIZONA

Dow knew that Mary was his soul mate and wanted to ask her out on a date, but he didn't know if that was allowed. So, in his next meeting with Gen. Newman, he asked. "Are there any rules against dating a civilian consultant?"

Newman grinned. "No, there is no rule against you dating Doctor Goss."

Dow raised his eyebrows. "Doctor Goss?"

"Were you talking about someone else?"

"No, but how did you know?"

Newman chuckled. "The way you look at each other. Maybe you two are the last ones to figure it out."

"I just miss her when I'm away, or she's too busy to talk."

"So, have you talked to her about it?"

"No, I wanted to make sure that we were not breaking any rules first."

Newman nodded. "A wise choice."

"How do know it's love, sir?"

"I don't think I'm the right person to ask, but I think I can tell you what love isn't."

"OK." He silently waited for the general to continue.

Newman's eyes popped. "I was only joking, but let me see...." He formed a triangle with his fingers. "It's not love when she expects you to buy you a ring when you're not ready. It's not love to go out with someone because you are lonely, because she looks pretty, or because people say you'd make a great couple."

Dow chuckled and nodded. "I hear you." He paused. "It's just I feel good about myself when I'm around her."

Newman laughed. "By that definition, you could say I love everyone on the base."

Dow didn't know what to say.

Newman leaned forward quickly. "What I mean by that, is since I've taken command of this base, I feel different. I enjoy being with everyone here. I can't explain it."

"Was it like that in your previous command?"

Newman shook his head. "No."

"So, what changed?"

"I think it was General Jones. He believed in me when I didn't believe in myself."

Dow nodded. "Same here. It's like he's my grandpa or something."

Newman nodded. "Yes, he feels like the dad I wish I had. I guess that's a type of love. Not the type you feel for Dr. Goss, but...I want to do better, be better, because Jones trusts me, you know."

Dow nodded. "Yes, I know."

"And I want to help others, instead of being only concerned about myself."

"Yes, it shows. Everyone on the base respects you because of it."

Newman's eyes popped again.

"Thanks for the talk," Dow said. "I just wanted to be prepared, in case something happens."

CHAPTER FIFTY-THREE

INTERVIEWING A GENIUS

Charlotte "Charlie" Baker

EARTH–ZALMA BASECAMP, ARIZONA

It had been weeks since my last interview, so I was raring to go. Miss Dianne told me about it as soon as I showed up: I would be talking to their new scientist, who was a lady. Even more exciting, I was going there to interview them instead of them coming to the office. I could learn so much about them just by looking at their workspace.

That fact only made me more excited to meet her. She was just like me—people probably told her all the time that she couldn't do the job she wanted, but like me she ignored them and pushed through. She proved herself—and I would too.

Kanara flew me to the base. "Welcome to Area 21."

"Have they really moved the whole base twenty-one times?" I asked.

"Yes. They must move about once every week, and we must take everything with us." He escorted me to the classroom tent.

Sarara was already there, standing with a human lady with strawberry blond hair. *She must be the scientist!* I thought. She looked like she was Sgt. Dow's age. The two ladies looked at me.

"You must be Charlie," she said with a bright smile. "I'm Mary. It's so nice to meet you!" She kneeled down. "And this is?"

Sandy went up to her, wagging her tail, and Mary gave her a rub.

I wheeled forward. "That's Sandy. It's nice to meet you. Miss Dianne told me so much about you. You're so smart!" I glanced at Sarara. "Am I interviewing both of you today?"

"Whatever you like," Mary replied as she returned to Sarara. "I think it would be fun."

I pulled out my communicator, ready to get it set up. "*Wats...*"

Sarara held up her hand to stop me. "There is no need for another communicator. You are surrounded by them." She gestured to the tables and boards all around the room.

She was right. The distinctive silver metal was everywhere. "You're telling me that all of these are communicators? Even the chalkboards?"

Mary giggled. "Yes. It's a little much to get used to, isn't it? I'm so much more comfortable writing in a regular old notebook, but I've had to get used to using these instead because of all the secrecy."

I stared at the boards and tables all around me in amazement. Everything was floating, like they'd been suspended from the ceiling on invisible strings (I was pretty sure I saw that trick at a magic show my dad took me to). A thought suddenly occurred to me as I recalled something Miss Dianne had once said. "Watson, can you put up all my notes on the chalkboards?"

Immediately, my notes and videos appeared. I wheeled up to the screen that had Gen. Jones's image and touched it. It expanded to take up the full board and played the video with sound. *So cool!* As I watched it, someone came up behind me.

"Is that General Jones?"

I turned to see Mary looking curiously at the screen. "Yes, haven't you met him?"

"No, I only arrived a few months ago. They tell me he left just before I showed up, so we must've just missed each other."

I nodded. "Yes, it sounded like he was leaving right after we recorded this."

"*Communicator, stop, clear,*" Sarara said. "Shall we begin?"

I sat across from the two ladies. "*Communicators, record.*" I heard a beep of acknowledgment, then wondered who to interview first. I knew Sarara better since she was my friends' mom, so I turned to her first. "Please state your name and role."

"I am Sarara of Zalma. My husband and I are here to teach your people our technology."

I turned to Mary.

"I'm Doctor Mary Goss. Sarara is teaching me their science."

Excitement swelled in my chest. "Doctor?"

"Not a medical doctor, if that's what you are thinking. I have a doctorate in astrophysics."

"Astro-what?" I asked.

"Astrophysics. I study how things in the universe work. It was all theoretical until I met Sarara. We didn't have any way to test the ideas we had until the Zalmen brought us their technology."

"Ah.... You're good at explaining things," I said. "How far away is Zalma?" I looked back and forth at the two ladies, wondering who would answer.

Sarara did. "Approximately twelve light-years from here."

"And how long did it take you to get here?"

"Five months."

"Wow!"

"You are not surprised that our ships travel faster than light?" Sarara asked. She was staring at me, her colors fluctuating like Janara's did when she was confused.

I shook my head. "No, why?"

Mary giggled. "Every human who asked them those questions, have asked that next."

"Why?"

"Because Einstein's theory of relativity states that it's impossible," Mary said.

"Einstein? We learned about him in school. Isn't he the guy who invented the atomic bomb?" I asked.

"He theorized it, but he didn't build it, and he was deeply shaken when he learned what they did with his work," Mary explained. She herself looked deeply shaken.

Is she worried they'll use her work to make bad things like bombs too? Have they done it already? I shook my head again, this time to myself. *No, Janara and Takar's parents wouldn't let that happen.*

"He must've been very sad," I said. I decided to change the subject so Mary wouldn't be sad anymore. "So, what makes you different and how does that help you in your job?"

Mary chuckled. "Sarara has all this wonderful technology."

"Yes, but we lack imagination, and Mary has plenty of that."

"No imagination?" I asked.

Mary snickered. "Sarara is creative with her words and a great teacher."

"But I lack the ability to combine or change our technology the way Mary can."

"It sounds like you two make a pretty good team."

Mary nodded. "We do."

"What are you working on now?"

"Modifying gravity," she replied, in the kind of voice that told me she was about to talk about it a lot more. My friend Johnny used that voice when he was about to tell me all about his newest action figure.

"It's one of our basic skills," Sarara added.

I figured for the sake of the interview I should limit the science talk, and luckily Mary caught my hints, as she stayed fairly on topic. She told me all about Mr. Quinn and the gravity gun they were working on. It sounded so cool!

Then she told me about the experimental plane Mr. Harper launched to the moon! I couldn't believe it; we sent the spaceship to the moon, and I missed it! After all Takar, Janara and I did to see it, too. But then Mary told me that she and Mr. Harper would be working on a new spaceship and that I might be able to see it sometime. The fresh excitement completely dissolved my disappointment. I wanted to tell my mom and dad right away. How was I going to keep this a secret? *It's just for now,* I kept telling myself. *Eventually, I'll be able to tell them and everyone else about all this.*

As we finished up, I asked Mary if she wanted to come play with me, Janara, and Takar. She did, and Sarara also joined us for a few rounds of marbles—all of which I knew Takar would win. He was the best at the game.

When Mary and Sarara left, I turned to Janara and Takar. "Trip to the moon?"

They both turned white.

"We are sorry," Janara said.

"We tried to call you, but our communicators wouldn't work," Takar said.

I sighed. "The general must have ordered radio silence."

Janara chuckled. "Besides, there wasn't much to see. The plane went up and was gone for a few hours."

Then Takar laughed out loud. "But then Mary and Dad left in the Spacevan and towed it back home."

My heart seemed to jump into my throat. "What! What happened?"

"We don't know. No one would tell us, not even our mom and dad."

I was so thrilled by meeting Mary that I completely forgot about my "side project" for the rest of the week.

[Meeting Dr. Goss was like meeting a real-life superhero. She was proof that being different wasn't something to hide—it was exactly what made you special. I left that interview knowing I wanted to be like her when I grew up: brave enough to be smart, strong enough to be kind, and clever enough to save the day when it mattered most.]

CHAPTER FIFTY-FOUR

INTER-SHIP RELATIONS

Ambassador Ryan Wilcox
THE YMIT, SPACE

As Wilcox walked back to his quarters from training, he thought about the way Lt. Cameron and Joanua seemed to dance around each other. *Could they be more than friends?* They'd been working very closely on the Human–Zalman communication technology, and they also often ate together. But that was just so they could keep talking about work, right?

Wilcox hadn't dated many girls before. He knew he definitely wasn't the person to go to for relationship advice, but he liked to think he knew what love looked like. He'd seen it between his parents often enough—the understanding that passed between them, the light touches, the commitment in their eyes. But how did it feel?

He remembered the fluttering feeling in his belly when he'd taken Nellie to prom, but he'd been an awkward teenaged boy then. Now he was a man (*technically,* Donna would tease) and he was in the middle of a diplomatic mission. He didn't have time to worry about finding someone to settle down with.

But then his mind drifted to Edugra again, and he blushed. He quickly entered his room and shut the door. His main dealings had been with her father, Geogram, who had stayed on Earth. Now that they were heading to Zalma—an alien planet!—Wilcox found himself spending more and more time with Edugra. She and Donna were friends, but even Donna was branching out and spending more time with the others aboard the ship. Wilcox, despite being an ambassador by profession and a champion at negotiation, had never had luck making new friends.

Edugra had solved that for him.

It all started the first night they'd been on the ship when she'd joined him and Donna for dinner. Wilcox was planning to live on Zalma for as long as his ambassador role required, so he was intent on being as knowledgeable in their culture and way of life as possible. He'd even switched to a mostly vegetarian diet, with Donna's help. He'd started immersing himself even before they left, but being in space suddenly made it all feel real. They were really going to a different planet!

Edugra was by far more patient than her father. She listened to his questions with grace—even the stupid ones—and even seemed happy to answer. In return, he told her she could ask whatever she wanted about Earth.

"Really," he'd insisted between bites of his chickpea and rice bowl. "Anything you want to know."

Donna stood up. "I think I'll leave you two. I've got...something to take care of."

Wilcox watched her go, confused, but turned back to Edugra, who looked just as confused as him. They stared at each other for two brief seconds, before together they burst out laughing.

"I know much about Earth from your broadcasts, but as long as I live, I will never fully understand human interaction. Everything you say means so much!" she told him, still giggling.

"To be honest, I don't think a lot of *humans* understand what's going on half the time either." He reached forward gingerly to take her hand, and she met his eyes. Her whole head had gone pinkish, like before when she was embarrassed—but a little darker, which made him smile. It was a pretty color on her.

"Then how do you get anything done?" she asked. "If you do not change color, and you say things you don't mean…."

"It's not easy," he admitted. "That's why we always strive to do better. I've learned a lot about human interaction as the son of an ambassador. Earth has so many nations and cultures and languages…. It's a challenge to keep them all straight, but it's also such a treasure to be able to get to experience that whole other world—literally, in your case." He flashed her a grin.

She smiled back at him. "It is a treasure to be able to share it with you."

Even after weeks on the spaceship, his mind kept pinballing back to that conversation. What could she have meant? Was he just looking too deeply into it? She'd been lamenting the fact that conversations between humans always had hidden meanings—perhaps what she said was all on the surface.

But then Joanua had just turned that color too—that purplish color that wasn't red enough to be embarrassment but also not blue enough to be family related. *What does it mean?*

He had immersed himself in their culture for several months, and he felt as comfortable with them as with humans. But there would always be mysteries that he couldn't crack. He and Edugra worked well together, along with Donna, and maybe that's all it was—work.

He plunked himself down on his desk chair. "How would a relationship even work?" he asked aloud. "*Who would I even talk to about this?*" He remembered General Jones saying his door was always open.

"Perhaps I can be of assistance?"

Wilcox looked around. "*Who said that?*"

"Your communicator."

Wilcox looked down and saw he was touching it. He remembered that the two ways to activate it were to either call its name or by touch. He sighed. "*I wasn't asking you.*" He paused. "*But since you are here….*" He tried to think of how to phrase his question. "*I think I have feelings for Edugra, but…are humans and Zalmen…*" That just didn't sound right. "*…the people of Zalma compatible in that way?*"

The device was silent for a moment, then said, "*From my extensive research, I can deduce that your species are intellectually and emotionally compatible. Thus, romantic interaction is possible.*"

Wilcox felt his cheeks heat up again. He couldn't believe he was talking to a computer about such a personal problem. "*Do you think she likes me?*"

"*What color does she become when she sees you?*"

Wilcox recalled the subtle changes in Edugra's color. She was naturally purple, like her father, but she darkened so she was almost violet or indigo whenever she was around him.

"Um…*darker purple, more blueish.*"

"*That would indicate that she does have a romantic interest in you.*"

Wilcox went to Gen. Jones's quarters. The door was open, so he walked in. "Sir, can we talk?"

"What's on your mind, Ambassador?"

"In many states, interracial couples are still illegal. What's your opinion?"

Jones grinned and closed the door. "I think you and Edugra make a great couple."

Wilcox raised his eyebrows. "Edugra?"

Jones chuckled. "You are an ambassador, and isn't there a thing called diplomatic marriages?"

Wilcox grimaced. "That's usually for kings, and other rulers, and of the same species. How did you know it was *her*?"

Jones sat back. "The amount of time you two spend together."

"I just noticed Cameron's awkward movement around Joanua, and it made me wonder," Wilcox said.

Jones nodded. "I noticed it myself. I don't think they know either."

Wilcox chuckled. "Anyway, we spend so much time together because it's my job to learn their culture, but how do I know it's love?"

Jones put on his best poker face. "If you are asking, that probably means that it is. When you think of her, who's needs are you thinking about?"

Wilcox felt flush. "What do you mean?"

"Are you thinking about your needs, and what she can do for you?"

"No, of course not. I want to make her happy, do what's best for her."

"So, you are trying to impress her, make her fall in love with you?"

"No, it's not like that." Wilcox could barely breathe. "Oh, I can't explain it, never mind." He stood to leave.

Jones held up his hand and gestured to sit. "Sorry, I was testing you. What you're saying does sound like love." He paused. "Did you know my wife is from France?"

Wilcox looked Jones in the eye.

"Yes, it might not be the same, but there were cultural barriers on both sides that we still have to deal with."

"I suppose so, but…."

Jones held up his hand. "Cross culture is still cross culture. Sure, you might have the extra hassle of having external groups hating you, but dealing with a lady and her family is still the same."

"Are you serious? Edugra is from another planet! I am sure most people envy you when they see you together. Very few on either side will accept us."

Jones cocked his head. "It's true that American men adore French women, but her French parents were not so fond of losing their daughter, nor was she wanting to leave her country."

Wilcox nodded. "I supposed that may be the same," Wilcox said, then paused. "Thank you for your time, sir." He shook hands, and left.

CHAPTER FIFTY-FIVE

KIDNAPPED

Charlotte "Charlie" Baker

ROSWELL, NEW MEXICO

It was a regular hot evening, and I was heading home from the Roswell office when Sandy growled and ran ahead. All the way from the other end of the street I could see there was an army jeep parked outside my house. It wouldn't be General Newman or Sergeants Dow or Rabinowitz because they would have let me know by communicator first. I went as fast as I could, pushing my wheels to their limits. My heart was pounding in my chest.

It was that man! The blond soldier! He came marching out the front door, pulling my dad and forcing him into the vehicle while Mom cried out. Sandy barked wildly. She darted around the soldier's feet, snapping at his heels, but he kicked out at her. She jumped back, narrowly avoiding his boot, and I yelled. I'd almost reached them, but the jeep sped off with a puff of exhaust. I coughed and sputtered.

"Charlotte!" Mom yelled. She came racing down the walkway. She was a complete mess of worry. "Are you alright?"

I took a deep breath. "Where's he taking him? What are we going to do?"

"I don't know, sweetie." She brushed her hands over my face and shoulders, as if checking that I was OK. I waved her away; *Dad* was the one in trouble.

Then I looked at Sandy, but she just dropped to her belly on the sidewalk and covered her face with her paws and whined. "You're no help," I said to her.

Mom took my cheeks into her hands again, and this time, I let her. She brought my face to meet hers. "I'm sure you'll think of something, sweetie. You're my clever girl. Just put that detective hat of yours on, and you can solve anything. If the army took him, could your boss do something about it? What was his name again? General Jones?"

I shook my head. "General Jones went on a super-secret mission, so he can't help. It must have been that bad general who came around asking questions a few months ago. They must think he knows something."

"But why would they take him away? And, *where*?" Mom's worry lines showed up, so I reached out to smooth them down.

Where would an army person go when he didn't want to be found? The old warehouse! I need to get there fast.

"Don't worry, Mom. I'll find him. We just need to call the base." I needed a diversion. I slipped my hand into my pocket and touched Watson as I said, "Oh! Is that the phone I hear? That must be them now!" Sure enough, our home phone rang.

I hated lying to my mom, but it had to be done. As soon as she disappeared through the front door of the house, Sandy and I took off.

I sent a message to Miss Dianne before turning at the end of the street.

Sergeant Malcolm Dow

Dow was already running when he called out the command. *"Communicator, send an emergency message to General Newman, Sergeant Gilmore, and Kanara: Meet me at the Spacevan!"*

Kanara was at the controls as he arrived, ready to go. "Set course for the old warehouse," Dow said. He glanced out the door, looking for the others.

A few seconds later, the other two men arrived, and the door closed.

"What's the emergency?" Gen. Newman asked.

"Miss Dianne reported that Sergeant Lawless has Mr. Baker and we think he is going to the old warehouse. Lawless must think Baker knows something about the Zalmen." Dow looked out the windshield and was surprised to see that they were already there. An army jeep was parked in front of the building.

Newman turned to Kanara. "How fast were we going?"

"I would assume that it was faster than any human has ever traveled."

"Faster than the speed of sound?" Dow asked.

"Approximately one hundred times faster," Kanara replied.

The three sets of human eyes popped.

"General, what's the plan?" Sgt. Gilmore asked.

Newman started to talk, but remembered that he was part of a team. "Recommendations?"

"Lawless is clearly acting without official orders. He's just kidnapped a civilian and is holding him hostage! I suggest we go in there and tranquilize the both of them with the Zalmen short-term memory erasure darts. That way, we can safely return Mr. Baker to his home and detain Lawless for his breach," Gilmore said.

"For all we know, he could be acting on General Scornson's orders, and we all know how tricky Scornson can be." Newman said. "And how would we detain Lawless for an extended period without him finding out about our operation? Keeping him with us would just mean more work when moving bases."

"Then don't detain him. Just zap his memories and—"

"Gentlemen," Kanara interrupted.

Dow felt a rush of tingles down his spine, followed by a sense of peace and calm. He looked around for what caused it. The windshield screen zoomed in on Charlotte and Sandy, who were coming up the road toward them.

"Sir, should we intercept the girl?" Gilmore asked.

Newman opened his mouth, but no words came out. Dow recognized this as it had happened to him many times before, when his hunches wouldn't let him speak. Dow felt the tingles and the unusually calm feeling again. "Sir, if I may.... I think we should give Charlie a chance and let this play out."

"I agree," Newman said, then he looked around, like he was wondering who said it. His face went red. "I mean, I don't know why, but something is telling me we should let her try."

Gilmore opened his mouth, but nothing came out.

Dow smiled a knowing smile.

"We can't let our emotions impede our prime directive, to not be seen or give anyone reason to suspect our level of technology," Newman said.

Charlotte "Charlie" Baker

As I came around the corner, I could see the jeep outside. "Yep, they're in there.... Stay, Sandy." I wheeled up to the building and found the door was still open. I guessed he wasn't expecting anyone, so I leaned forward and peeked in.

Yes, it was definitely that young blond soldier that was with General Scornson. Dad was sitting in front of him in a metal foldout chair, looking frazzled but otherwise unharmed as the soldier yelled questions at him. I thought he would have tied my dad up, but I guess he knew he could outrun him if he tried to escape.

"Where are they?" the soldier yelled in Dad's face.

"I don't *know,*" Dad said in his exasperated voice. "Why would I know?"

"Mr. Baker, you know more than you're letting on. How else would you have written these?" Making a big show of it, he withdrew some crumpled papers from his pocket and held them in front of Dad's face.

I gasped. *My notes! I threw them out. That's what he was doing in our garbage! He must have thought that my dad wrote them.* I saw Dad's eyes widen. He would definitely recognize my handwriting. Then he put on a poker face.

"Where did you get this?" Dad asked.

"From your garbage," the soldier replied, sounding proud of his reconnaissance mission, despite the fact that he'd been rooting through our kitchen leftovers.

"I didn't write these," Dad said.

"Then who did?"

"I don't know. Someone must've put them in our trash."

The soldier scowled and got in Dad's face. "Tell me who wrote it!"

When Dad didn't answer, the soldier gave him a backhanded slap. Dad's face whipped to the side, but he looked back defiantly. He spat something red and wet to the concrete, but still said nothing. The soldier raised his hand again.

I couldn't take it anymore. "Stop!" I screamed. "I wrote it."

Dad stared at me, wide-eyed and pale-faced. "Charlotte? What are you doing? Get out of here!"

The soldier spun around. "Where did you come from?" he demanded.

He ran toward me, grabbed my wheelchair, and pushed me to my dad. Dad eyed the soldier with a glare. I knew my dad wouldn't let the soldier hurt me. I hugged him tight.

"What do you mean you wrote it?" the soldier asked me.

"Just what I said. I wrote it. Notes—for my children's book."

He sneered. "Children's book? And where did you get all this information?"

"I have my sources."

A rabid glint appeared in his eyes as he stared down at me. "Your *sources*? Who are your sources? Tell me now!"

Real fear clawed at my chest, but I swallowed it down and raised my chin. "A good reporter never reveals her sources," I told him.

"You're working for *them*, aren't you?"

I played dumb. "For who? If I was working for *them*, don't you think *they* would be here by now?" I made a show of looking around. "I don't see anyone."

Suddenly, Sandy whined and barked twice, exactly what I was expecting. They got my message and were letting me know that they were here.

The soldier didn't seem to notice. He shook the crumpled papers in one hand. "But you wrote *General J*. That's Jones! It has to be! Where did you get his name? You described him perfectly."

"From the diner," I said, "a couple of months ago. I was heading back to the Ashcroft ranch when I saw the tire tracks leading here. I figured that they must have brought the debris here, so I came. The guards wouldn't let me in, but I saw the green army car. When I went to town, I saw it again. The man entered the diner, and I followed him, but he wouldn't tell me anything other than his name. I'm sure *you* know all about it though, being in the army. What were they hiding here?"

"None of your business," he snapped.

"Is it yours?" I raised my eyebrow, mimicking an expression I'd seen on Gen. Jones's face.

"Charlotte...," Dad warned under his breath, but I squeezed his hand to keep him quiet.

"My what?" the soldier replied.

"Your business. I assume that if it was, you wouldn't have to ask *us* anything."

The soldier's face went red. "Don't get smart with me, young lady."

"Or what, you're going to hit a girl?"

The soldier's face went darker red. He stood up and paced back and forth. Then he turned back to me. "How about I beat up your old man?"

I looked at his uniform. There were no chevrons on his sleeves, nor a name tag. "How 'bout we call up your base and tell them what you're up to, *Private*!"

"That's Sergeant! Sergeant L—" He cut himself off and paled. "Argh!" He dashed out of the building.

Sergeant Malcolm Dow

Newman chuckled. "It looks like you're right, Gilmore; he's gone rogue. That was a clever trick Miss Baker did to make him nearly reveal his name."

Dow couldn't agree more. "Yep. His ego is so fragile, he couldn't stand being considered a lower rank."

The Jeep revved. Gravel spit out from under the tires and hit the building as it sped off.

"What now?" Dow asked, his eyes trailing after the Jeep as it disappeared around the bend. "Do we follow Lawless, or do we pick up Charlie and her dad?"

"Miss Dianne is about four minutes away," Kanara offered.

"Dow, you know Lawless the best. What do you think his motivation was?" Newman asked.

"I would assume that he is acting on his own, trying to impress his grandfather, General Scornson, by gaining intel."

Newman nodded. "Then there is no point following."

"We could report that he is offbase to his CO," Gilmore suggested.

"But then that would raise questions about how we knew," Dow replied.

"Let's return to base and make plans to prevent this from happening again, and strategies to deal with them when they do," Newman said. "We won't always have a twelve-year-old to save us."

Charlotte "Charlie" Baker

Dad was staring at me in amazement. "Honey, how did you...?"

"I'm a reporter, Dad. It's my business to know everything. He's obviously gone rogue since his uniform was blank. I'm guessing he grabbed a spare one to disguise himself. That's why I tried to trick his name out of him."

"But we didn't get his name."

"That's better, or he wouldn't want to leave any witnesses. I was gambling that he was dumb enough to reveal his rank, but not stupid enough to give his name."

Dad's eyes were wide. "That's a big risk." He smiled. "But it paid off."

I smiled back at him. "And, I just realized that he's been spying on *you*, not *us*, for weeks; I was wondering when he'd finally make a move. I'm just glad you're not hurt. I should've said something sooner." I tried to ignore the guilt swirling in my stomach.

"Oh, honey, it's not your fault! I didn't believe you when you told me. But look! You took care of him all by yourself. Now," he got up and winced, "it looks like we have a long walk home."

"My dear *Watson*, I'm sure we will find a ride," I said.

Dad chuckled and ruffled my hair. "You read too much."

"Is that a problem?"

He thought about it. "No, I'm beginning to see that you're all grown up. But I miss the little girl I once knew."

"Oh, Dad."

We went outside, finding Sandy right where I left her. She danced in circles, wagging her tail relentlessly until Dad scratched her behind the ears. Once Sandy calmed down, we began to make our way home. At the end of the driveway, we saw a car driving up. Dad was immediately defensive and stood in front of me.

As it got closer, the window rolled down. It was Miss Dianne. "What are *you* doing out here? Do you need a ride?"

Dad recognized her too. "I got kidnapped. And this one came to rescue me. What are you doing out here?" He turned toward me. "Did you somehow let her know where we'd be?"

I shook my head as Miss Dianne's eyes popped. "Kidnapped? By whom?" She played dumb really well.

Dad shrugged. "Some soldier. A sergeant, L-something, but we don't know who. Right now, we could use a ride into town."

She put the car into park and helped Dad lift me into the backseat then deposited my wheelchair in the trunk. Sandy hopped in beside me. Dad then got into the front passenger seat and Miss Dianne climbed in behind the wheel.

As we drove down the road, she glanced at my dad. "Do you want me to file a report?"

Dad chuckled. "I'm guessing you will, regardless of what I say."

Miss Dianne laughed with him. "True."

She drove us all the way back to our house. When we arrived, the sheriff was there. Dad thanked her and went to talk to the sheriff, leaving me, Sandy, and Miss Dianne by the car.

"You know you didn't have to do this. We were preparing to rescue him," she said after helping me get settled in my wheelchair.

"I know. But then you would have exposed yourself, right?"

Miss Dianne chuckled. "You gave quite a performance. We have communicators all over the warehouse. Kanara flew them out there as soon as I relayed your message. I have to say that General

Newman, Sergeant Dow, and I are all very proud of you."

"Were you watching?"

"Not me. The general asked me to stand by when they saw you approaching. But I heard you while I was driving. You were very brave."

All at once, the fear I held back in the warehouse came to the surface. I burst into tears and hugged Miss Dianne tightly. "I was so scared, but it felt like I was watching someone else talking through my body."

"It sounds like you had an out-of-body experience."

"A what?"

"It's a relatively new term. It used to be called astral projection or spirit walking. Some people believe that a guardian angel takes control of your body while your spirit watches."

"That sounds like what happened. I was watching, and thinking, like 'Hey, I'm doing really good.' Could that be the Zalmen?"

"Not that we are aware of. This kind of thing has happened long before the Zalmen came to Earth."

I pulled out my communicator. *"Watson, was that you?"*

"No, that was not me. However, I did sense another presence to confirm Miss Dianne's theory."

"What kind of presence?" I asked.

"I am sorry. I cannot elaborate any further."

"That's not much help." I cried some more, then perked up. "Maybe it was my guardian angel? Anyway, I couldn't let him hurt my dad, especially when it was my fault."

"It wasn't your fault," Miss Dianne said.

"But that sergeant found my notes. He got them from our trash."

"Yes, that's why you should only write on communicator paper, like I told you."

"But I had to write something! I couldn't keep it to myself, and they wouldn't let me share the truth. And I really was writing a children's book, a really watered-down version of everything that's happened. I wasn't going to give it to anyone. I just had to get it out somehow."

Miss Dianne smiled down at me. "I think it's a great idea. I'll try to sell it to the general, and we'll talk about it later. Just make sure to use your communicator paper."

"I will. Thanks, Miss Dianne. And...call me Charlotte. I don't need to be anyone but myself."

[That night changed everything for me. I'd gone from playing reporter to actually being one—asking the hard questions, protecting my sources, and standing up to bullies. But more than that, I'd learned that sometimes the most important stories are the ones you can't tell yet. Sometimes protecting the truth means keeping it secret until the world is ready to hear it.]

CHAPTER FIFTY-SIX

HUMBLE PIE

Dr. Mary Goss

EARTH–ZALMA BASECAMP, ARIZONA

Mary, Quinn, Kanara, and Sarara entered the classroom wearing their new uniforms. Harper, for a change, sat quietly at the back and didn't look at anyone. The others were sitting in what used to be the middle rows. However, the front table was moved to the front of the classroom where the four teachers stood.

Mary stepped forward. "As you can see, the four of us are now wearing our uniforms to represent that we are part of this team. If you feel like you are a member of the team, you should too."

Harper didn't react, but several of the engineers mumbled and nodded.

"From now on Mr. Quinn will be teaching you, because he understands the lessons, and he also understands how you learn."

Mary, Sarara, and Kanara sat, while Quinn tapped the tablet he was holding, and the nanoboards lit up with the Moad ship design.

"Welcome everyone. Today's lesson is about what we know about the Moad technology. You can see the Ferris wheel they use to create artificial gravity…."

After that day, everyone but Harper wore the uniforms, and productivity skyrocketed. In the evenings, she and Quinn would work on the gravity-related devices.

Harper, unsurprisingly, took the longest time warming up to her, and Mary suspected that it was equally her fault and the general's. Even a week after the spaceship mishap, he was still sending her cold glares, but he hadn't said anything to her. In fact, he hadn't spoken a single word to her at all, but she wasn't complaining. She was glad about it, actually. He followed the orders laid out by her and Quinn, and that was all she needed from him. Soon enough, his glares stopped too.

Mary was sitting at her desk when there was a knock(ish) on the side of the tent.

"Dr. Goss. May I come in?"

It took Mary a second to recognize his voice. "Harper?"

"Yes," came the solemn reply.

Mary didn't know how to answer. She was curious why he was there, but did she want her mortal enemy in her tent? "Come in?"

Harper pushed aside the tent flap, leaving it open, and walked in wearing the new uniform. He didn't carry himself the same way she remembered. When she'd first arrived, he was tall and proud, but now he seemed humble.

Mary's eyes popped. "You're wearing your uniform."

"You said that when we feel like being a part of the team, we should wear it."

Mary smiled.

"I have been doing some thinking these past couple of weeks—some real, hard thinking."

Mary nodded, inviting him to sit and go on. He took the empty chair across from her desk, the one usually reserved for Quinn.

He took a deep breath. "I see now that I've been a real jerk to you. There, I said it."

Mary waited to see if there would be an actual apology.

"All this really puts things in perspective for me, and I see now that I didn't treat you the way I should have. I just saw you as a young upstart who thought you knew better than me, and I've always been the best in everything I do."

Mary could relate.

Harper sighed. "You challenged my way of thinking, and I guess I was just afraid that I was wrong, and I've never been wrong before. But I *was* wrong, and it almost cost me everything. I'm sorry."

Mary let the words stew in the air, taking them in and turning them over in her head. Finally, she nodded. "I can relate to that," she replied honestly. "I accept your apology, and I want to return it. I, too, have thought of how things have changed. How *I've* changed."

Harper seemed surprised at her words.

"Back when Sergeant Dow first recruited me, I thought if I worked hard enough, I would earn respect, but that was a misguided notion. I burned bridges with any man who I believed wasn't supporting me. I thought the whole world was against me—my professors, my classmates, even my peers—but I was really just working against myself."

They looked at each other for a moment.

"I have since learned that if I want respect, I have to give respect." She let out a bitter laugh. "It took two men almost blowing themselves up for me to realize all of this. How stupid is that?"

"I don't think it's stupid at all," Harper countered. "You saved my life after everything I did to make yours a nightmare." His eyes met hers, purpose shining in them as if he could will her to agree with him. "Now, moving on to the other reason why I came to see you...."

"What is it?" Mary asked, intrigued.

"I had a few ideas for a new ship design. I was hoping you would help me with it."

She smiled. "I would be happy to. Despite what happened, your

X20 design showed real promise."

Harper rolled out the blueprints he was carrying.

Mary looked it over. "I'm impressed. You've incorporated human, Zalma, and what we know of Moad technology. Would you mind showing it to the class tomorrow, so we can all discuss it?"

Harper smiled and nodded.

[Watching Harper learn to be humble was like watching someone discover they had arms and legs they'd never used before. All that talent and knowledge he'd always had became ten times more powerful when he finally learned to share it with others.]

One day, Mary was sitting in the mess hall, when Malcolm sat next to her.

"I heard you've been working with Harper on a new ship," was the first thing he said. "How's that been going?"

"Great, actually. Yeah—" she said as she saw his raised eyebrows, "I'm kind of surprised myself. He came to me the other day to apologize. We really cleared the air, then he asked for my help with the new ship design, and here we are."

Malcolm nodded and took a bite of his mashed potatoes. "And here we ar…" He was suddenly cut off by a shrieking wail and Mary nearly jumped out of her seat. It was coming from her pocket—more specifically, from her communicator. Around the room, every other communicator was going off in the same way, sounding like a cacophony of bells, sirens, and whistles.

"What's going on?" Mary asked Malcolm, who shrugged as he pulled out Benjamin. He looked lost, then turned his communicator to her. It read, "The Zalma deflectors have failed! Invasion imminent!"

[I was doing homework when those alarms went off, completely unaware that our friends on Zalma were under attack. It's strange how the universe works—just when people start figuring out how to get along, something happens to remind you that not everyone wants peace. But that's exactly when teams become families, and families fight hardest.]

PART 5:
FRANK'S WOUNDLESS WAR

CHAPTER FIFTY-SEVEN

THE MOAD ATTACK ZALMA

General Frank Jones

THE YMIT, SPACE

"Everyone to the conference room." It was Edugra's voice, but she had never used the ship-wide intercom like that before, and her voice was stressed.

When Jones entered the conference room, he saw what he assumed was a live video feed from Zalma.

Captain Agugua stood beside the screen. "The deflectors are failing again. We all knew it would happen, but we thought we would get there in time. We are still two months away."

"How long do they have?" Jones asked.

"The Zalma scientists calculate a seventy-three percent chance that they will survive this round, but only an eleven percent chance that they will survive the next."

"The next?" Mr. Howard asked.

Agugua turned to Howard. "Moad is six of your light-years from Zalma. It takes the Moadites several years to travel at sub-light speed. But they have several ships constantly rotating between planets. About every twenty-six days, a ship arrives, attacks, firing everything that they have, and then returns home."

"How long are their attacks?" Sergeant Abbott inquired.

"Only a few days," Agugua replied.

"When the alliance was signed, Zalma was under attack, and the deflectors were failing. We talked your scientists through modulating the deflector frequency to be more effective against the Moadites' new weapons. Will that work again?" Jones asked.

"They have tried that as well, and it has not helped," Joanua replied.

"What about the evacuation?" Jones inquired.

"Only about half the population has been evacuated, and the other half is refusing to leave," Agugua said.

Jones sighed. "Are we going as fast as we can?"

"We are, sir."

"Is there anything we can do to move faster? Can we jettison cargo to make the ship lighter?" Lt. McKenzie asked.

Joanua shook her head. "No, our gravity drive doesn't work that way. Our weight doesn't affect our speed." Suddenly, her eyes lit up. "You mentioned last time that Dr. Goss strengthened the hull with a gravity beam. I think you called it *magnetizing the hull.*"

Jones nodded.

"I think that we can use that to strengthen our hull and double our speed."

"Great!" Jones looked around at the others. "Any other thoughts on how to help Zalma right now?"

Ambassador Wilcox raised his hand. "I could try to offer the Moadites a gift, a sample of the proposed technology."

"Do we know that they have received and understood our messages?" Jones asked.

"Yes, we sent the messages on their channel un-encrypted. Then, we heard them discussing our offer on their encrypted channel, but their opinion seems to be: Why trade what they can take?"

"Then a gift will not help. Anything else?" Jones looked around.

Howard raised his hand. "Could we send the Zalmen instructions to build weapons?"

Edugra sighed. "And who is going to fire them? Remember, my people are pacifists."

Wilcox leaned forward. "A computer?"

Joanua hummed. "Maybe…."

"This would be all well and good," Jones interrupted, "but secure communications or not, I don't feel comfortable transmitting technology. Someone could intercept it, and no matter how encrypted you make it, it's only a matter of time before someone decodes it."

The room was silent for about a minute.

Joanua's eyes lit up. "Sarara said that her new student theorized using an Einstein–Rosen bridge as a new way to communicate."

Jones nodded. "Dr. Goss. What did she come up with?"

"The theory is that two black holes might create a strong enough gravitational field to connect the two points on a quantum level, so that travel between the two points is instantaneous."

Jones raised an eyebrow. "Are you saying that we could instantly appear on Zalma?"

"Unfortunately not." Joanua sighed. "The connection is so small that only a signal can get through."

Lt. Cameron gulped. "So we need to find a black hole?"

Joanua giggled. "No, we need to create a gravitational field as strong as a black hole."

"That sounds dangerous," Wilcox said, his eyes wide.

Joanua nodded. "Yes, we would have to create a gravitational force stronger than a sun, and contain it so that it doesn't crush us."

"I agree with Ryan. That sounds too dangerous," Donna said. "I don't think it's worth the risk."

"I admit that there is a significant risk, but with our gravity technology, it is possible. To run the tests, I suggest we use probes and launch them a safe distance away."

Captain Agugua turned green. "And what would you call a safe distance?"

Joanua's skin fluttered through multiple shades of green, teal, and purple. "Out of any solar systems. For us, we could run a probe on a parallel course, about a billion miles away."

Jones frowned. "Are we benefiting anything from doing all that? What's the point of this if we have to broadcast over a billion miles?"

Joanua turned red. "Sorry sir, the distance is just for the tests. If we create a black hole, but do not contain it, we could destroy a solar system, but out here, we only have to worry about us."

Jones felt heat rush to his face. "Oh."

Joanua chuckled. "Luckily, it would destroy the probe and disappear, so it should be safe to test as long as nothing is close enough to be sucked in during that short time. Once we know we can contain it, we can move it closer."

"How much closer?" Howard asked.

"That depends on the test results. If the gravitational forces are one hundred percent contained, we could attach it to the ship."

Donna frowned. "That sounds like a lot of dangerous work. Is it worth it?"

"I believe so, if we want totally secure communications."

Jones held his hand up. "So, you're saying that you could send a signal that no one else would be able to intercept?"

"In theory, yes."

"How sure are you that we can do this?"

"Right now, I would say it could go either way. I would have to do some calculations, tests. Under normal circumstances, I would say it would take a year to design and implement."

Jones stood proudly and, with his commanding voice, said, "We can't wait that long. I want every scientist and engineer at our disposal working on this. Everyone here who can help with the design, everyone on Earth and on Zalma. I want you to contact them directly, so there are no delays. I want a feasibility study in twenty-four hours. Use the best encryption available.

Heck, use every encryption available, and add an extra layer that will only be used for this project, and then destroy the codes. Understood?"

Everyone in the room replied in unison, "Yes, sir!"

"Great, Mr. Howard, contact Dr. Goss. Joanua, contact the Zalma scientists. Captain Agugua, contact the Zalma Council and inform them of the change in the command structure. Ambassador Wilcox, inform the president. I will contact General Newman. If you are not involved, try to support those who are. Make sure that they eat, and no unnecessary distractions. Dismissed."

Did I just order the creation of a black hole? A force more powerful than the sun? Never in my wildest dreams....

It was only days later that things took a turn for the worse.

"General Newman, there has been a new development. There is a seventy-three percent chance that the Moad will break through the Zalma shield in the next few days."

"How far are you away?"

"Two months."

"Oh...." Newman arched his eyebrows, thought for a moment, then straightened his uniform. *"Well, I am sure you will be glad to hear that our team is finally working well together with Dr. Goss as the new leader."*

"Glad to hear it. What else have they been working on?"

"An Electromagnetic Pulse, or EMP, shorts out any electrical systems in range, without damaging anything else. It might disable the Moad ships, and it has no effect on Zalma technology."

"Good to know. Hmm, I wonder...." Jones paced around his room. "A weapon that disables ships and doesn't hurt the occupants. I wonder if the Zalmen would consider using it?"

"It's worth a shot."

"I'll take it to Captain Agugua. *Jones out.*"

*

Captain Agugua was still talking to the Zalma council when Jones returned to him.

"I'll call you back," Agugua said.

"What did they say?" Jones asked.

"As I suspected, they are not fond of having weapons on our planet. They are concerned that they might hurt the Moad."

"Did you tell them that they will either kill you or take you as slaves?"

"They have forbidden me from mentioning it."

"What about if you were to disable the Moad ships, not hurt them?" Jones asked.

"What do you mean?"

"Have you heard of an Electromagnetic Pulse? It can disable their ship without hurting anyone."

"If we were to disable them, what then?" Agugua asked.

"What do you mean?"

"If we disable them, will they just die in space?"

"Yes."

"We cannot directly or indirectly cause harm to another living creature."

"But they will *kill you*!"

"We will have to take our chances."

Jones entered the conference room. "Report!"

Joanua turned multiple colors. "We have built a gravity generator and put it on a probe we launched over an hour ago. We also launched several other probes to monitor the first."

"So, what's this going to tell us?"

Mr. Howard cleared his throat. "This'll tell us if we can create the gravity of a black hole and contain it. This'll not tell us if we can build the bridge."

"Hmm. What are the expected results?"

"Either the test will succeed, or it will not create sufficient gravity," Howard said, "or the gravity will implode the probe and possibly suck us in with it."

"And the chances of that are?" Jones asked.

"Slim, but there is still a chance."

"Do we have any other options?"

The room was quiet.

"Very well," Jones said. "Proceed with the test."

Joanua turned to her screens. "Powering up the gravity generator...."

A minute passed. Lt. Cameron stayed at Joanua's side; his presence seemed to calm her as she continued the test.

"We are registering the equivalent gravity of Earth inside the probe. The gravity shielding is working, and there is no change in gravity readings outside the probe. Increasing power."

No one even dared speak as they all watched the screens.

"We are registering the gravity of the sun inside the probe. Still no change outside the probe."

Everyone in the room breathed a sigh of relief.

"Increasing power." Again, the room was silent. "We are approaching the gravity of a black hole. There are some unusual readings inside the probe."

"What kind of readings?" Jones asked.

"I don't know. The sensors are being overloaded."

"Is it the gravity?"

"I don't see how."

"The gravity outside the probe is increasing at an exponential rate. The containment is failing!"

"Shut it down!" Jones commanded.

"Too late! The probe imploded. The other probes are being sucked in! Brace for the shockwave!"

The wave hit, and people were thrown out of their seats. Cups and papers flew everywhere. The ship shook violently for about a minute.

As Jones was one of the heavier men and wasn't as affected, he looked around to see if anyone needed help. Wilcox and Edugra crawled toward each other. Joanua, who had excellent balance, gripped Cameron to steady him. Donna was thrown past him in the shockwave. When she hit the floor, she grabbed the closest solid thing nearby—Abbott—who wrapped his muscled arms around her.

Jones looked around as the ship's stabilizers came back online and the trembling stopped. "Is everyone alright?"

"We're good!" Wilcox called out. He held Edugra, running his hands soothingly up and down her arms as her colors fluctuated.

Several other confirmations came from around the room. The worst injury was a bruised elbow, about which Howard complained loudly, drawing a peel of laughter from the crew.

"What happened?" Jones asked.

Joanua went to her station. "We were pulled half a billion miles toward the temporary black hole!"

Jones looked at Howard to translate.

The scientist looked forlorn. "We failed!"

CHAPTER FIFTY-EIGHT

NO WAY FORWARD

General Frank Jones

THE YMIT, SPACE

Shortly after the crew dispersed, Jones opened a video call to Gen. Newman to inform him of the results. "We're not sure when another test can be done, or if it would be worth repeating," he finished.

Newman's expression was solemn. "Yes. We were watching a relay of the test from here. No one was injured in the aftermath, I trust?"

"No."

"Good. What's the next step, then, sir?"

"I've yet to decide. We just received more bad news. The deflectors on Zalma are expected to fail in the next hour or two."

Newman's face fell. "Oh, so we really have failed."

"I am afraid so," Jones replied. "The Zalma council is still hopeful that the Moadites won't hurt them."

Newman grunted. "There is not much of a chance of that, is there?"

Jones shook his head. "Why don't you give your people the night off? They earned it. I'll do the same here."

Newman just nodded.

"And...why don't you head to your permanent base?"

"We have a permanent base?! Sir?!"

"Yes. It's probably not finished yet, but my sources tell me that Scornson's men haven't requested long range training flights in a while. Hopefully, they have given up on finding you. I'll enable you to access the rest of the route. *Jones out.*"

The call ended, and Jones turned away. He hung his head, a sigh of defeat ghosting from his lips. In front of his soldiers he had to keep up a strong front; only when he was alone could he let his burdens show.

What are we going to do now?

Jones opened his door.

Lt. Cameron entered. "Sir, during your departure speech you said you were available if we needed to talk?"

Jones nodded. "What can I do for you, Lieutenant?"

"During the shockwave, something strange happened."

"With Joanua?"

"Yes, how did you know?"

Jones closed the door. "We have been in space for several months. It's natural to want someone to talk to, or is it more than that?"

Cameron's eyes widened. "No! I mean, it just happened. I thought we were going to die, and somehow we ended up together. I don't even remember how. Is that love?"

Jones chuckled. "Maybe, maybe not. I think it's too early to tell, but that doesn't mean you can't be friends until you figure it out." Jones sighed; his heart sank. "Just be careful to keep it as friends until you both know. It's hard when one's in love, and the other isn't."

He paused. "I've seen many good people destroyed when their affections aren't returned and they settle for sex, it's an addiction. Like alcohol, they seemed happy for a short time, but then they seemed even lonelier, emptier, even obsessed with trying to make it work, but you can't make someone love you."

Cameron's eyes widened, then he stood up and shook Jones's hand. "Thank you, sir."

CHAPTER FIFTY-NINE

AREA 51

Sergeant Malcolm Dow

GROOM LAKE, NEVADA

Since Mary and Mr. Quinn had perfected their vehicle gravity engines, the base moves had become simple for Dow. All they'd had to do was attach the small invention to the undersides of the trucks and the general's limo, and bam! They could fly from place to place without leaving any tracks.

They'd been through thirty-nine areas prior. So as he drove the general's limo through the desert, the last thing Dow expected to see was a fence, a gate, and guards stationed outside. "Umm...sir. What do we do?" *Are those guards with us? They shouldn't see the flying cars!*

"It's OK, Sergeant," Gen. Newman called out from the back of the limo. "This is our final destination. Welcome to Area 51."

Dow nearly jumped out of his seat. His hands tightened around the wheel. "What?! You knew, and you didn't tell me until now?"

A chuckle rose from the backseat. "I didn't know myself until last night when General Jones enabled access to the route. It seems we're skipping right past the forties!"

As they pulled up to the gate, Dow recognized the guards. *I was wondering where they went after I approved them.* He tried to see further into the base, wondering when Gen. Jones had initiated construction. Jones always had multiple plans going at once.

The guards saluted. "General Newman, sir!"

Newman returned the salute, and the guards opened the gate.

The base butted right up to a tall mountain, and Dow could see rows of barracks and offices, five separate hangers (two in process of being built), and a wide-open space with at least one airstrip.

"Park near the barracks," Newman instructed.

Dow nodded and turned the limo toward them. The trucks behind him followed, each driver pausing only briefly to show their credentials at the gate. They parked in a line outside the low barracks buildings, and the troops assembled in front of Dow and the general. Mary and the other scientists stood to the side; she caught Dow's eye and flashed him a bright smile.

Newman spread his arms wide. "Welcome to our new home. Area 51," he announced.

The soldiers cheered.

"We were not scheduled to arrive here until the anniversary of the Roswell incident next July, but as we have an urgent situation in space, we needed a permanent base now. The place is still a bit of a work in progress, so be careful. Military personnel, you'll find barracks marked appropriately behind us. Science and engineering, meet me in hangar three."

Once the general had dismissed the soldiers, Dow walked over to Mary. Together, they and the scientists followed Newman to the arched metal building labeled with a massive silver '3'.

"The building's exteriors are coated with the communicator alloy. This will let them camouflage if needed."

They followed him inside to an office. For some reason, there was no desk. The walls were blank. Dow guessed they hadn't gotten around to furnishing it yet.

"Everyone in," he encouraged, so the entire group crowded into the room. "Alright, now that everyone's here.... *Communicator, take us to level one.*"

When the floor began to lower, Mary and Dow grabbed each other. A shadow fell over them and he looked up to see that a new floor was sliding in place above their heads from the walls on either side.

"Fascinating," Mary whispered beside him.

The floor under their feet came to a stop in a much larger room and melded seamlessly with the rest of the floor. Dow looked around to see Ambassador Geogram, Kanara, Sarara, and an army major waiting for them. Charlie was there too, holding her communicator up to record them. The walls glowed, and the table and chairs floated. It was a Zalma-style meeting room if he had to guess.

I'll never not be amazed by what they can do.

Charlotte Baker

Area 51 was amazing!

I grinned to myself, knowing I was there before even Sgt. Dow—yesterday, Sarara had invited me to come along with her and her family first thing in the morning, so I asked my parents if I could stay for a sleepover with my friends. Dad wouldn't agree because he had not met them before. I was disappointed, but that just meant that I had to get up early.

Kanara and Sarara gave Janara, Takar, and me the grand tour right when we got there, and I recorded everything I could with Watson, but I had to wait until Gen. Newman arrived before I learned anything important.

It was so interesting to watch Newman, Mary, Dow, and Rabinowitz, as well as many others, come down from the ceiling. As soon as they spread around the room, Newman began speaking.

"The president and General Jones initiated the construction of Area 51 as soon as the Alliance was signed. It was of the utmost secrecy. Not even I knew about it until last night. Now, Ambassador

Geogram and Major Thomas have been the ones in charge of the base, so I will turn it over to them."

The important-looking guy that I didn't recognize stepped forward. He was obviously Major Thomas.

"Thank you, General Newman," he said. "I would also like to thank Kanara, who was our engineer consultant, without whom building Area 51 would not have been possible."

Kanara nodded.

"This base is the most secure place on the planet. There are several entrance points. Authorized personnel must be recognized both by their face and their voice through our communicator security system. We are self-contained and can withstand any amount of bombardment. There are several levels below, containing more meeting rooms, science labs, hydroponic gardens, and living quarters, so you could live here indefinitely."

"Do we have to live down here, or can we live in the barracks with natural sunlight?" asked Mr. Harper. At least he looked a lot calmer than when I saw him yelling at the other men working on his spaceship.

"You can live in the above-ground barracks if you choose. You will find one of the barracks labeled 'Engineers'," the major said, then continued without waiting for a response. "The hangars above are for vehicles and traditional aircraft, all except hangar three, which is reserved for the Spacevan. All spacecraft will be developed and kept in a hangar built into the mountain. Your communicators have the floor plan and can answer any questions. Dismissed."

The crowd of engineers dispersed, and I stopped recording and dropped Watson into my lap. I waved at Dow and Dr. Mary, and they walked over.

"You seem to have beat us here," Mary said.

I grinned. "Yup! Special privileges for your press liaison!"

Dow reached down to ruffle my hair. I swatted him away, and he continued in a smooth motion to pat Sandy. We all laughed.

"How are things with your dad?"

"Good," I said. "Dad's treating me more like a junior reporter since the kidnapping."

I offered Mary and Dow a tour, which they readily accepted, though it was cut short the moment I showed Dr. Mary her new workspace. She was lost to us the moment we stepped inside.

Dow and I looked at each other with a shrug, but just then, Sarara ran into the lab with the brightest grin on her face. "I have just had the most wonderful news! The Zalma deflectors lasted long enough to stop the invasion. We have another month to prepare."

[Area 51 felt like graduating to the big leagues. This wasn't a temporary camp in the desert—this was a real base, built into a mountain, designed to last. It was our fortress, our sanctuary, and our launching pad for defending two worlds. For the first time since this all started, I felt like we were really, truly ready for whatever came next.]

CHAPTER SIXTY

A SECOND CHANCE

Miss Donna Warren

THE YMIT, SPACE

"Everyone to the conference room!"

Donna looked up in confusion. That was Edugra's voice over the loudspeaker, and she sounded happy. She glanced at Ambassador Wilcox, who looked just as confused.

"I wonder what that could be about," he said. His voice was despondent, just like his posture. What could Edugra be happy about? Her home planet and all her people were about to be destroyed.

Donna had to drag Wilcox along with her, luring him with the notion that maybe Edugra had gone hysterical with grief and he would need to be there to cheer her up. She didn't *really* believe that had happened, but Wilcox was being unreasonable.

When they got to the conference room, everyone else was already there. Captain Agugua was standing beside the screen at the front of the room—the one that showed them live footage of the ongoing battle on Zalma. This time, though, no explosions rocked the world. Donna gasped in delight.

The Moad ship seemed to have taken a run at the planet's deflectors, but it had bounced off. It was slowly spiraling away into space.

Agugua's smile was blinding. "The Moadites' attack stopped as our deflectors failed," he announced. "We think that they ran out of ammunition, because they flew their ship directly into the deflectors. As you can see here, that break provided enough time for the deflectors to regenerate and stop them."

Everyone breathed a sigh of relief. Donna glanced across to where Edugra was standing; the pink lady was nearly jumping for joy, unable to contain herself. Without warning, she launched across the room and wrapped Wilcox in her arms, swinging him around with surprising strength. Donna laughed. Luckily, they were ignored by the rest of the room's occupants.

"Does this mean we have another month before they return?" Lt. Cameron asked.

Agugua nodded. "We believe so."

"Great, so now all we have to do is to make this ship fly twice as fast, and then come up with a plan," Mr. Howard said.

Edugra let go of Wilcox, her whole body bright pink like she was embarrassed, but also with touches of violet. She jumped, lifting her arm and read a message on her clothing. "There is an incoming message from Zalma," she said, "One of the scientists has compared the readings from the probe to the nearest black hole, and found that they matched."

"Are you saying what I think you are saying?" Wilcox asked, looking at her. Donna noticed that his face had also gone entirely red.

"Yes," Joanua cut in, also reading her arm. "Before the probe broke up, it established a bridge to the black hole."

"So, our test was a success after all?" Jones asked.

"I still have to review the data, and there is lots of work to be done, but...." Joanua looked at Cameron, who nodded and placed a hand on her shoulder. She looked back at Jones. "Yes, we believe it will work."

"How do unions work on Earth?" Edugra asked.

"Unions? As in marriage?" Donna asked.

Edugra blushed. "I wasn't thinking that far. How do you know if a man is interested in you?"

Donna chuckled. "Well…there's two types of men, the ones who will make themselves look big and strong…"

"Like Mister Abbott?" Edugra asked.

Donna blushed. "That's *Sergeant* Bruno Abbott."

"I have not heard his first name before. Your people have so many titles; how do you keep them straight?"

Donna blushed again. "We just do…. Anyway, yes, Bruno is a perfect example. He makes himself look like the perfect protector and provider. But, you have to be careful with this type; they can also be demeaning, demanding, and controlling."

"Demeaning?" Edugra asked.

"Condescending. Some of them like to put you down to make themselves look bigger."

"Is *Bruno* like that?"

Donna chuckled. "No, but some of my previous boyfriends were. They weren't really interested in me; they wanted to show me off like a trophy."

"What's the other type like?"

"Other type…? Oh right, one type is the strong type, the other is the sensitive type."

"Like Ryan Wilcox."

"Nnnooo…. Yes, I guess he is." Donna chuckled. "You know, just a few weeks ago, I was jealous of you two."

"Jealous? Why?"

"I always thought we were high school sweethearts, but Ryan saw us more as brother and sister."

"And then what changed?"

"I don't know. I guess I'm wondering about Bruno."

"Wondering?"

"Yes, I never really thought of him before the shockwave."

"But you felt sorry for him when Joanua played the video of his attack."

Donna blushed. "Did I? I don't remember." She paused. "Anyway, the thing you need to know about the sensitive type is that they don't know if they like you for your looks or if they love you."

"So, how do you find out?"

"Either they spend most of their time looking at you, or wanting to get to know you."

"Well...Ryan is always talking about me and my culture."

"True, but that's his job."

"Oh."

"That doesn't mean that he's not interested in you; it's just harder to tell. How does love work on Zalma?"

"Love is a journey of self-discovery. You can't really love someone else until you first love yourself. So, a potential mate would encourage self-discovery, and they could learn about each other together."

Donna's eyes popped. "Oh. That's an interesting way of looking at it. Have you learned about yourself?"

"Yes. But, also in our culture, most unions have one logical and one emotional. Either can be male or female. I know one man who takes care of the children while his wife works as a doctor. In any case, it is the job of the emotional to get emotions from the logical."

"So, if you are the emotional, and he is the logical, it is your job to make him emotional?"

Edugra blushed. "Yes."

"This should be interesting. I can't wait."

CHAPTER FIFTY-SIX

COMMUNICATION

General Frank Jones

THE YMIT, SPACE

"Do you understand any of this scientific terminology?" Jones asked Gen. Newman on his communicator.

Newman sat back and steepled his fingers. *"I understand the basics, but not much more."*

"Our ship has been sending out probes for a week, and we try to make contact with the probe from Earth or Zalma, and then it implodes." Jones threw up his hands.

"Yes, but it rarely links to a black hole anymore, and before it implodes, it usually links to one of the planet's probes. Also, it takes much longer for it to implode, meaning they are getting close to stabilizing it." Newman smiled.

"I hope you're right," Jones said. "At least they've installed safeties, so the implosion isn't pulling us off course anymore."

"Yes, as I understand it, they feel safe enough to bring the probe into our solar system, and hope that they can bring it into Earth's orbit soon," Newman said.

"After the experience we had with the implosion, I wouldn't be in too much of a rush. I like Earth and don't want to lose it. The Zalmen said that there's no sign of intelligent life or technology in our system, other than Earth, so I think we can continue to transmit encrypted messages at short range," Jones said.

Newman's face went pale. *"Short range? You mean to Pluto?"*

Jones chuckled. "Wow! Everything is relative, isn't it? It didn't even cross my mind that I used to consider that an unachievable distance."

[The day they got the Einstein–Rosen bridge working was the day the universe got smaller.]

After a week's worth of hard work and long hours, the day finally came.

"We did it!" Lt. Cameron proudly announced. "We formed a bridge to both Earth and Zalma!"

Jones smiled. "Good news indeed!"

"We have started to receive the Earth's team's theories and schematics." Joanua turned red. "When I saw that data on magnetizing the hull, I remembered we were going to try to make our ship faster."

"Yes, we were distracted by the black hole." Jones paused, then smirked. "It sucked all our thoughts and energy, didn't it?"

Joanua stared at him silently, turned a dark green as she digested his play on words. He saw the exact moment understanding dawned on her, as she turned red, and laughed.

Jones raised an eyebrow. "Do you think it will work? Will we be able to get there before the next attack?"

"I don't know, sir. I will have to run some tests."

The very next day, Joanua brought him even more good news. "It worked. We are traveling three times faster. We should make it in time," she said.

"Well done," Jones replied.

Captain Agugua approached Jones. "General, with all the new weapons you are creating, the Zalma council is worried about the safety of the Moad."

Jones choked. "Did you say the safety of the Moad? Our enemy? You are worried about their safety?"

"Yes. As you know, our technology has safeties to prevent you from deliberately killing them, but what if you damage their ship beyond repair? Or one of these cannonballs you are making accidentally hits and kills someone on the ship?"

Oh boy. How do I handle this? "Captain, you know that I share your desire not to deliberately hurt anyone, but this is war. We can only do so much to stop them from attacking you without hurting them. Accidents happen, even outside of war."

Agugua changed colors many times. "Yes, but can we do anything to help them if such injuries do occur?"

"What are you proposing?"

"The council would like to send our medical people to treat their injuries, and our engineers to repair their ship," Agugua said.

Jones's heart felt like it stopped for a second or two. "If you did, the Moad would either take them hostage or kill them. I'm sorry, I can't allow that." *I have to give them some assurance, but what?* "However, I'mmmm...sure our engineers will be able to come up with a safe way to deliver medical supplies and equipment, as well as remotely repair their ship."

Jones reached out to shake Gen. Newman's hand, and stumbled forward when his hand went right through. "Wow, these three-dimensional glasses work pretty well," he said, then chuckled. "And they're not those red and blue lenses like our movies use."

Newman moved to sit down, but the chair wasn't there and he fell. Jones instinctively reached out to catch him, but his hands grasped at nothing.

Both men coughed, embarrassed.

"This is too realistic," Jones said. "We need a way to know what's really here, and what's not."

"I'm adjusting the transparency to fifty percent," Joanua said. In front of Jones, Newman's form faded, and Jones was able to see the wall through his head and torso.

The transparent Newman's eyes widened. *"General Jones, you look like a ghost."* He laughed. *"That's much better. At least we can tell the difference now."*

"Amazing, isn't it?" Jones took off the glasses, and Newman disappeared. He put them back on, and Newman's ghost was back in front of him. "Anyway, let's get down to business. The magnetized hull is working, and we expect to make it on time before the next ship arrives."

"The scientists are working well together, between your ship, Zalma, and Earth. They have refined the gravity gun, and it has the capability to push, pull, or hold an object in place," Newman replied.

"Yes, and I hear it also has the ability to crush an object, although they tell me that the Zalmen have installed safeties so that it will not crush a living creature, or an object with one inside of it," Jones said.

"Wow! They're serious about not hurting the people who are attacking them," Newman said.

"Yes. We've had to make plans for sending the Moadites medical supplies and to remotely repair enemy ships," Jones said.

"Unbelievable. The Zalmen never cease to amaze me," Newman said.

The ship's crew and Jones's team were in the conference room with no table. Gen. Newman, Sgt. Dow, Dr. Goss, Mr. Quinn and others appeared as holograms. Everyone was wearing glasses. In the middle a hologram of the Z3 space fighter floated.

"The Z3 started with Mr. Harper's X20 design, but has gone through several revisions," Dr. Goss said. *"It's equipped with conventional Earth weaponry, such as machine guns and cannon balls...."*

"But the gunpowder doesn't ignite without oxygen," Mr. Howard added.

"Yes. We tried compressed air in with the gunpowder, but then discovered that compressed air was sufficient to push the projectile," Quinn said.

"To let the Moad know that we mean them no harm, we have installed supplies that the Moad might need for their return home into the cannon balls. The nuclear torpedo is basically a small nuclear engine that explodes on impact or is manually detonated," Dr. Goss added. *"Likewise, the plasma torpedo has a nuclear engine and a plasma torch attached to the front. It should burn a hole through anything."*

Jones raised his hand.

Quinn anticipated and answered his question. *"But it's only enabled when permission is granted, like the EMP."*

Jones nodded.

"It was easy to create the Electromagnetic Pulse. The hard part was to focus it to only disable one target at a time. But we learned from focusing the black hole to communicate." Quinn took a breath and continued. *"As General Jones reminded me, we don't want the enemy to know about these technologies unless they already have them and use them against us, or as a last resort."*

He scanned the room to see if anyone had questions before continuing. *"The deflectors and lasers are installed and become active when the ship is damaged, conventional weapons run out of ammunition, or the ship has a human occupant and is about to receive fatal damage."*

"Very good. Where are we with the repair robots?" Jones asked.

"We have built repair robots to fix any ship too damaged to fly home," Howard answered. "These repair robots will also install a sample of the technology we wish to trade. The deflectors and anti-gravity will only kick in when they set their engines to ninety percent or more, and will allow them to fly about twice as fast.

The deflectors, of course, will also activate if an object is about to collide. We hope it will give them the incentive to trade."

"It will be interesting to see how they react," Ambassador Wilcox said.

"Yes it will," Jones said. "Remember everyone, we don't want them to know about our advanced technology or they will want to negotiate or steal it."

"We have only two pilots. Sergeant Abbott and I will each fly a fighter; the rest will be remotely controlled from Earth. Just like our 3D glasses, it will look like there is a pilot in them," Lt. McKenzie said.

"Also, we want the Moad to know that we are helping the pacifist Zalmen, but not who we are or where we are from. We don't want them coming to Earth any time soon. These pointy Z3's are a far cry from the Zalma box shaped ships," Jones said. "So, Captain Agugua lined us up so we appear to be coming from an empty solar system for our approach, and turned our invisibility off."

"A good precaution, sir," Newman said.

"It will be interesting to see if they take the bait," Wilcox said.

With that said, the meeting was dismissed, and everyone took off their glasses.

"We are a few days from Zalma, and are matching the first Moad ship's distance from the planet. We were surprised to discover four other Moad ships rapidly decelerating in hopes of joining the first invasion. The furthest ship appears to be enduring five times their normal gravity to make it on time," Jones said.

"Wow! Do you think they will survive?" Gen. Newman asked.

"They tell me that as long as they are in a bed or chair, our computer simulations show that they should be unharmed, depending on their physiology, of course. If they're reptilian, they should be able to handle more than we do," Jones said.

Newman raised his eyebrows, impressed.

"Our people have done their jobs. Our ships and warriors are ready for battle, so I'm ordering everyone to take some well-deserved rest. I suggest having a party sooner, so your people can recover before the battle," Jones said.

Newman chuckled. *"Yes, sir."* He signed off.

Jones opened his door.

Heavy footsteps came up the hallway. They faded again, then came back. Jones looked up. It was Sgt. Abbott, and from the sounds of it, he was agitated. "Sergeant!" Jones called.

Abbott entered quickly and saluted sharply. "Sir!"

Jones closed the door and returned the salute. Abbott lowered his hand, but he didn't look any less tense.

"What can I do for you, Sergeant?"

"You're the one who called me in, sir. What can I do for you?"

Jones kept his military stance. "You've been pacing the hallways for days. I know you're too independent to go to anyone for advice, but I really think you need some peace of mind. We have been in space for a long time, and I'm sure you're starting to feel lonely." Jones gave the sergeant a knowing look.

Abbott's eyes popped, and then he nodded.

"The black hole test was unlike anything anyone has ever experienced before. Some of us felt things we never experienced before."

Abbott grunted but reluctantly agreed.

"Now, I'm sure you know that there's no regulations against you dating a civilian. So, you must be concerned that being such a strong man, that you might hurt such a frail lady as Miss Warren."

Abbott looked at Jones with empty, almost watery eyes.

"The fact that you are concerned means you are not going to hurt her when you are in your right mind, so limit your alcohol. No matter how bad your day gets, or how much you want to celebrate, if you hit her when you're drunk, you will cause permanent injury or death and the party's over. Do you understand?"

"Yes, sir."

"And I'll put this in terms you'll understand. While love will make you strong, sex will tear you down mentally and physically. I've seen many good men doubt themselves and their worth. The next thing I know, they're taking suicide missions and not coming back."

Abbott dropped his head. "Yes, sir."

"The ones who found love would occasionally take difficult missions, but despite all odds, they came back. Make sure you know which one you're getting into. You're a good soldier, and I would hate to lose you."

Abbott's lips straightened.

That's probably as close to a smile as I'm going to get.

"Until then, there is no problem with getting to know her better. Is there anything else?"

"No, sir. Thank you, sir."

"Dismissed."

CHAPTER SIXTY-TWO

THE YMIT

General Frank Jones
THE YMIT, SPACE

[I wasn't there for the battle—I was in the underground meeting room at Area 51, watching displays with the other Earth team members.]

Approaching Zalma.

Jones stood at the front of the Ymit's bridge.

"Ship-wide and Einstein–Rosen Bridge communications, please. I would like to talk to everyone."

Edugra tapped her touchscreen, sounding a whistle throughout the ship. The Earthlings were used to hearing this sound on battleships and requested it be added.

"This is General Jones. We are about to make interstellar history. Two planets uniting against an aggressor. As far as we know, we have the upper hand with better technology, but we don't want the Moad to know how much better our technology is, or they will be scared and try to negotiate or steal it. They know that the Zalmen have deflectors, and that's all. They don't know about us humans, and this will be our introduction. When we engage them, remember to reserve our advanced technology unless necessary. Our goals are to:

"One, stop this attack.

"Two, give them honor and pride.

"Three, establish our superior technology. Remember, as much as we would like to end this war, it's unlikely to happen today. So, let's show them, *The Galaxy's Peacekeepers*! Is everyone ready?"

Jones heard several people say, *"Yes sir"* and *"Ready"* over the radio.

"Good luck, everyone." Jones nodded at the screen. "Earth Squad, you are clear to launch!"

"Roger that."

The nineteen remote-controlled Z3's detached. They had been built by the nanites, essentially grown on the outside of the Ymit. Lieutenant McKenzie and Sergeant Abbott's ships launched from the ship's hangar. They took flanking positions.

"Zalma colony ship. Are you ready?"

The ship was unarmed; it was built to move Zalma's population to New Zalma but it hadn't had a chance to leave. That's not why it was there. Its size was the perfect intimidation tool. With its deflectors, it would seem virtually indestructible.

"Ready," came the reply.

"Remember, no invisibility. We don't want them to know we have that. And you don't have to do anything but look big."

"Understood, General. After all these years, it will be a pleasure to see the attacks come to an end."

"It's a pleasure to be here. We'll call you if we need you." Jones gave Edugra the signal to close the channel.

The first Moad ship slowed as they saw the Ymit. The other four ships were approaching fast at different speeds and reversed, with the main engines on full to stop.

As they neared the first ship, the engines ceased, and the vessels turned forward, ready for battle.

"Open the Moad frequency and turn on the translator."

Edugra nodded.

"Moad ships. You have entered Zalma's space and are ordered to turn around." Jones listened for a minute, but there was no reply. He repeated the message with the same result. "Moad ships. You have entered Zalma's space. If you attack, we will return fire. Do you understand?"

"Plan Eight," was the response from one of the Moad captains.

"That was encrypted," Edugra confirmed.

"Yes, they don't know we can decrypt their messages, but we don't know what 'Plan Eight' is either."

The five Moad ships changed course and headed for the Ymit, and they were not stopping.

Jones's previous simulations had indicated that if a Moad ship rammed the Ymit at low speed, the ship would bounce off the deflector. At high speed, the Moad ship would be destroyed, but the Ymit would not be damaged. But he never anticipated five Moad ships. He wondered if they would survive.

"Fighters pull back. It looks like we are in for a game of chicken. Do not fire until fired upon." Jones turned around. "Captain Agugua, what is our distance?"

"500 miles and closing," the captain announced. "400 miles.... 300.... 200.... 100.... They are veering off."

Several flashes illuminated the screen as the Moad bombs detonated.

"Status report!" Jones barked out.

"All five ships released bombs as they veered. They detonated against our deflectors with no damage. The bombs do not appear to have propulsion. The fighters were not targeted and are not damaged," Mr. Howard reported.

"Lieutenant McKenzie, break off and engage," Jones ordered.

"Machine guns. Fire," was the response over the radio.

Jones was thankful McKenzie and Abbott were the only two pilots in space. The Earth pilots had about a tenth-of-a-second delay in their movements. Since Abbott was new to flying, he could use voice commands for things like takeoff and landing.

"Captain, bring us about."

A single fighter detached from each of the Moad main ships. McKenzie's squadron engaged them.

The Moad fighters, as well as their main ship gun turrets, fired.

"I'm hit. Minor damage. Disabling affected systems," one of the remote pilots said.

When McKenzie's group finished their pass, Jones noticed the primary ships were damaged and losing air. Then he noticed that the enemy fighters were not following their fighters. One of the main Moad ships fired at them.

"Torpedo! Evasive maneuvers!" McKenzie called.

There was a flash of bright light between the fighters as a nuclear explosive detonated.

Two of the fighters were destroyed, and the others were spinning out of control in different directions.

"Lieutenant McKenzie, damage report!" Jones called out, but there was silence. "Sergeant Abbott, damage report!" The silence continued. "Come in, Lieutenant McKenzie! Sergeant Abbott?"

The tense silence continued for about a minute before McKenzie's voice replied. *"I'm OK. The blast damaged our traditional systems and weapons. Switching to Zalma backups."*

"I'm OK too," Abbott said.

The fighters stopped spinning and once again focused on the enemy ships.

"Torpedo launched! Deflectors to maximum! Evasive maneuvers!"

Once again, there was another flash of light as a torpedo detonated, but this time the fighters had no problem evading it.

"The deflectors worked. No damage. I'm out of bullets. Switching to lasers."

McKenzie flew through enemy fighters as he dodged bullets and lasers. One of the Z3's exploded.

He got close to one of the Moad main ships, launching cannonballs, causing air to vent as they passed through and some small fires that extinguished quickly.

McKenzie damaged a Moad fighter, main ship gun turret, and torpedo tube. The damaged enemy fighter limped back to its main ship.

They lost another three Z3's.

From the bridge, Jones saw the occasional arcs of light as weapons and projectiles bounced off the Z3's deflectors.

They made several more passes and lost another eight Z3's, but the Moad main ship weapons were disabled.

One Moad fighter remained and was chasing Abbott. *"McKenzie, where are you?"*

"I'm on my way."

The three ships zigzagged across space.

"He's too close. I can't get a shot without hitting you," McKenzie said.

Abbott turned his fighter and headed directly for one of the Moad main ships.

"Abbott! Pull up!" Ambassador Wilcox shouted.

"Not yet," Abbott replied.

Donna was holding Wilcox's arm tight. Abbott's ship was on a collision course with the Moad main ship.

"Pull up!" Wilcox shouted.

"Not yet," Abbott replied.

Just before Abbott's fighter hit, he did an incredibly sharp turn.

"Wahoo! This thing can really fly!" Abbott announced through the radio.

Donna let out a sigh of relief. "Where did he learn that?"

Howard chuckled. "That was one of the maneuvers we programmed into his flight computer."

"Sorry to scare you," Cameron added.

Donna's face was white, and she quickly strode off the bridge.

The Moad fighter couldn't match the angle of the Z3, and scratched the surface before continuing pursuit.

"McKenzie, what's taking you so long? Get this guy off my butt," Abbott grumbled.

McKenzie was shooting, but couldn't get a hit. *"This pilot is good. Are you sure we can't just destroy this guy?"* he asked.

"Negative," Jones replied.

"Permission to use EMP?"

"Permission granted."

The Moad fighter suddenly lost power and was floating. McKenzie had to react fast to avoid a collision.

McKenzie's voice came over the radio. *"Mission accomplished. All enemy ship weapons disabled."*

The Moad main ship's engines lit up, and they tilted toward the planet. They each dropped a massive number of bombs, aiming toward the planet.

"Zalma colony ship, it looks like they are going to try breaking through. Be prepared to intercept the enemy ships and push them back into space." Jones was right, the deflectors failed, and the Moad ships made a run at the openings.

The giant ship lifted off from the planet, intercepting, and using its deflector, it pushed the enemy ships back into orbit, before dipping below the deflectors as they regenerated. Jones could not comprehend the size of the colony vessel. It was at least one hundred times larger than the Ymit, maybe even one thousand times.

The Zalma colony ship blocked their view of the planet.

The Moad ships remained motionless, except for their artificial gravity Ferris wheels, and it looked like the venting air holes were being patched. They had no weapons, and their transparent shields were badly damaged.

"Moad frequency and translation, please." Jones looked at Edugra, who nodded. "Moad ships. You are outnumbered and outgunned. Surrender!"

Edugra closed the channel.

They could hear the Moad captains arguing with each other.

"Repair your ships. Prepare for another bombing run. Spread out."

"My ship is too damaged. We must retreat."

"Yes, retreat."

"Stay and fight, you coward!"

"Fight!"

Jones shook his head. "All fighters. Re-engage."

As soon as the fighters turned to the Moad ships, one of their engines lit up and broke orbit.

After the fighters fired a few shots, the second Moad ship also broke orbit.

"Cowards! Get back here!" a Moad captain yelled.

The three remaining Moad ships took heavy damage, and another one left, and soon another.

The last Moad ship managed to get some weapons working, and returned fire, but was soon disabled again. Its engine lit up briefly but failed several times.

"The last ship has sustained too much damage," Joanua said.

"Shall we help them out?" Jones asked.

"Activating repair robots."

The repair robots detached from the Ymit and flew toward the damaged Moad ship. Some carried the gift engines and deflectors.

Jones watched what looked like little torpedoes and chuckled. "The Moad probably think we are going to finish them off. Won't they be surprised?"

After about half an hour, the air venting from the damaged ship stopped, and Joanua reported that they were successfully pumping in new air. *That should let the Moad captain know that he's not in any danger.*

About another half an hour later, Joanua announced that the sample deflector and artificial gravity had been installed. The nuclear engine was the hardest to fix and took another hour. As soon as Joanua announced that it was fixed, the engine lit up.

The repair bots returned to the Ymit with the fighters. The two pilots landed in the hangar, while the other fighters attached to the outside.

The Moad ship broke orbit.

"Moad frequency, please," Jones ordered.

Edugra nodded.

"We wish you a safe trip home. You may have noticed that the bombshells contain food and medical supplies." Jones waited for a reply, but the Moad were silent.

"What, nothing to say?" Jones signaled to Edugra again.

"Channel closed."

A voice came through the Moad channel and was translated. *"Hey, what about me?"*

"Who said that?" Jones asked.

"The damaged fighter. They are leaving without him," Edugra said.

"Captain Agugua, can you pick it up?" Jones asked.

"Yes."

"Sergeant Abbott." Jones paused while Edugra connected to him. After Jones heard his voice repeated, he said, "Prepare to receive a guest in the hangar."

"It's about time."

Agugua maneuvered the Ymit in front of the Moad fighter and matched its speed. As the Ymit slowed down, they could see on the screen the Moad fighter enter the hangar and landed with a thud. Agugua closed the outside doors and pressurized the room. Abbott entered and swung a baseball bat over his shoulder.

The Moad fighter's cabin opened, and a Jurassic bird-like being exited the ship.

The two warriors stared at each other for a minute, then circled. Abbott stopped, then ran toward the bird with the bat. The bird extended a spiked wing and easily threw Abbott against the wall. When he shook himself off, he noticed blood dripping from his forehead and grinned.

"He likes a challenge," Jones explained to Agugua.

Abbott ran again but ducked before the wing hit him. He swung the bat at the bird's chest, and the bird brought in its wings.

Jones couldn't see Abbott, but judging by the way the bird was twitching, Abbott was putting up a good fight. Then the wings opened wide, and Jones saw the blue light of Abbott's plasma dagger.

The bird waved a wing toward Abbott's legs but quickly retreated when he moved the dagger to intercept.

Abbott held the dagger up, and the bird backed toward the wall and sat down.

On the bridge, Wilcox was watching on the screen, and he nodded to Edugra to open a channel. "Your people have left you. You have no place to go," he said.

The bird looked around, wondering where the voice was coming from. A video feed from the bridge appeared on the wall.

Jones wondered if the translators worked. After about a minute the bird replied in squawks. It was a different sound than the reptilian language the Moad used. The squawks repeated and repeated, then the bird made the reptilian clicks which the computer translated. *"They are not my people. I don't have people."*

"I see that. You don't look like the reptiles we saw in the video from the original probe."

Again the bird squawked, then clicked. *"No, I have not seen anyone like myself since I was young."*

"Not since you were young?"

The bird squawked, and the computer immediately translated. *"No."*

"That must be sad."

The bird squawked, then clicked. *"Yes, sad."*

"Were you a prisoner?"

"They treated me well, as long as I did what they said. When I didn't, they hurt me."

"Well, as long as you don't hurt us, we won't hurt you. OK?"

Abbott looked up at the video feed and grunted.

"OK," the bird replied.

Abbott begrudgingly put his plasma dagger away and left the hangar.

Jones looked at Edugra.

"Our audio is turned off," she told him.

"Is he secure in there?" Jones asked.

"Yes, he has no place to go, and he can't damage anything," Agugua replied.

The Jurassic would squawk, then click in the reptilian language, then the computer would translate a word.

Wilcox's eyes popped. "It's training our translator with its language."

Jones turned to Wilcox. "Impressive." Then he turned to Agugua. "It can't access any of our personal or military information, can it?"

Agugua turned to Joanua. "Please make sure its access is restricted."

"Thank you," Jones said. He addressed the people on the bridge. "Our mission is complete!"

A cheer broke out.

"Captain, please take us home," Jones said.

"To Earth?" Agugua asked, looking at him with a crinkled forehead.

"No, sorry. Your home."

Agugua nodded. "Yes, sir!"

CHAPTER SIXTY-THREE

ZALMA

General Frank Jones
THE PLANET ZALMA

As the Ymit touched down, millions of cheering Zalmen crowded around the landing pad. The door opened, and the Zalmen crew went out first to greet the council. Then they all turned to the ship.

"Introducing our Earth heroes. First: General Frank Jones."

The crowd cheered as the general exited and greeted the council with a bow. They introduced the others in order of rank.

Jones addressed the crowd. "Thank you. We are glad to be of service. However, I fear that the war is not yet over. The Moad ships were designed for bombardment, not for defense. We caught them off guard. We may have won this battle, however, they are likely to return and in greater numbers, but we will be ready!"

[General Jones had no idea how right he was. We'd won our first space battle, but we'd also announced to the galaxy that Earth was a player now. We weren't just a backwater planet anymore—we were allies of Zalma, defenders of the innocent, and builders of impossible technologies. The universe was about to get a lot more interesting.]

THE ADVENTURE CONTINUES...

DID YOU ENJOY THIS BOOK?

Your feedback helps me provide the best quality books and helps other readers like you discover them.

It would mean the world to me if you took two minutes to share your thoughts about this book. You can leave a review with the retailer of your choice and/or send an email to *tony@tonybrichard.com* with your honest feedback.

Thank you, I really appreciate it.

ACKNOWLEDGMENTS

A big thank you to my wife Lydia, without whom I would not have started writing, and for helping me with my female characters. Thank you to my mom and dad for their love and financial support, and the rest of the family: Betty, Ruth, Susan, Peter, Melissa, and Sheila.

Thank you to our wonderful realtors, Caprice and Kylene, who went above and beyond to help us move while we were in the final edits of this book. We couldn't have moved without them.

Thank you to my editor, Carolin Petersen at Tigerpetal Press, who took my story and made it sound so much better.

Thank you to the many artists who have contributed work: Alex Perkins, Ahsan Zafar, germancreative, Sandra Drawz, Sunil Kumar, and Tunmbi Olaleye

Thank you to my military consultants: Charles Moffat, Dave Laxton, Nathan Lansky, and Richard Odey. Since I have no practical experience, they helped get the terms and character interactions just right.

Thank you to my critique group: Bette Kosmolak, Cheryl Rostek, Caryn Stroh, Helen Rowlett, Kirk McDougall, Laurie Mueller, Mike Harding, Reppy Andrews, Sam Stevenson, and Teri Arbuckle Harwood.

A final thank you to my beta readers: Donna Lynne Morgan, George Jones, Kelsea Reeves, Nadene D, Richard Penner, Sarah Tozer, Sasha Pinto-Jayawardena, Shelly Carriere, smkay70,

And everyone else who helped along the way.

ABOUT THE AUTHOR

Tony B. Richard lives in Lillooet, British Columbia. He is a computer programmer (coder) and instructor. This grand adventure has been in his head for decades, and during the Covid-19 pandemic, he thought it was finally time to put it down on paper.

"Differences are something to be celebrated, not feared."

—TONY B. RICHARD

YOU CAN CONTACT HIM WITH QUESTIONS OR COMMENTS AT:

Website: *www.tonybrichard.com*
Email: *tony@tonybrichard.com*
Facebook: *EarthsSecretAlliance*
X: *@TonyBRichard1*
Instagram: *tony_b_richard*
Goodreads: *Tony B. Richard*

www.ingramcontent.com/pod-product-compliance
Lightning Source LLC
LaVergne TN
LVHW041053080826
845145LV00007B/1557